OXFORD WORLD'S CLASSICS

THE BRIGHT SIDE OF LIFE

ÉMILE ZOLA was born in Paris in 1840, the son of a Venetian engineer and his French wife. He grew up in Aix-en-Provence, where he made friends with Paul Cézanne. After an undistinguished school career and a brief period of dire poverty in Paris, Zola joined the newly founded publishing firm of Hachette, which he left in 1866 to live by his pen. He had already published a novel and his first collection of short stories. Other novels and stories followed, until in 1871 Zola published the first volume of his Rougon-Macquart series, with the subtitle *Histoire naturelle et sociale d'une famille sous le Second Empire*, in which he sets out to illustrate the influence of heredity and environment on a wide range of characters and milieus. However, it was not until 1877 that his novel *L'Assommoir*, a study of alcoholism in the working classes, brought him wealth and fame. The last of the Rougon-Macquart series appeared in 1893 and his subsequent writing was far less successful, although he achieved fame of a different sort in his vigorous and influential intervention in the Dreyfus case. His marriage in 1870 had remained childless, but his extremely happy liaison in later life with Jeanne Rozerot, initially one of his domestic servants, gave him a son and a daughter. He died in 1902.

ANDREW ROTHWELL is Professor of French and Translation Studies at Swansea University. He has published widely on French literature from the nineteenth to the twenty-first centuries, with particular research interests in contemporary poetry and the visual arts, as well as translation technologies. His translations from the French include poetry by Bernard Noël, Jean-Michel Maulpoix, and Jacques Dupin; novels by Bruno Dumont; and essays by Jacques Derrida and Francis Jacques. He has previously translated for Oxford World's Classics Émile Zola's early novel, *Thérèse Raquin*.

OXFORD WORLD'S CLASSICS

For over 100 years Oxford World's Classics have brought
readers closer to the world's great literature. Now with over 700
titles—from the 4,000-year-old myths of Mesopotamia to the
twentieth century's greatest novels—the series makes available
lesser-known as well as celebrated writing.

The pocket-sized hardbacks of the early years contained
introductions by Virginia Woolf, T. S. Eliot, Graham Greene,
and other literary figures which enriched the experience of reading.
Today the series is recognized for its fine scholarship and
reliability in texts that span world literature, drama and poetry,
religion, philosophy and politics. Each edition includes perceptive
commentary and essential background information to meet the
changing needs of readers.

OXFORD WORLD'S CLASSICS

ÉMILE ZOLA

The Bright Side of Life

Translated with an Introduction and Notes by
ANDREW ROTHWELL

OXFORD
UNIVERSITY PRESS

OXFORD
UNIVERSITY PRESS

Great Clarendon Street, Oxford, ox2 6DP,
United Kingdom

Oxford University Press is a department of the University of Oxford.
It furthers the University's objective of excellence in research, scholarship,
and education by publishing worldwide. Oxford is a registered trade mark of
Oxford University Press in the UK and in certain other countries

First published as an Oxford World's Classics paperback 2018

Impression: 7

Published in the United States of America by Oxford University Press
198 Madison Avenue, New York, NY 10016, United States of America

British Library Cataloguing in Publication Data

Data available

Library of Congress Control Number: 2018941161

ISBN 978-0-19-875361-2

Printed in Great Britain by
Clays Ltd, Elcograf S.p.A.

CONTENTS

INTRODUCTION

*Readers who are unfamiliar with the plot may prefer to read
the Introduction as an Afterword.*

WHEN *The Bright Side of Life* (*La Joie de vivre*) came out in book
form in mid-February 1884, after serialization in the popular daily
Le Gil Blas over the preceding three months, Émile Zola was 44 years
old. On the face of it, he was already a literary success in France: the
notoriety of *L'Assommoir* (1877), a story of poverty and alcoholism in
working-class Paris, had brought him significant wealth, with which
he had bought his country residence on the banks of the Seine at
Médan. He was the acknowledged leader of the group of Naturalist
writers, including younger disciples Guy de Maupassant, Joris-Karl
Huysmans, and Henry Céard, which met there in the course of his
famous soirées. Since *L'Assommoir*, he had produced, with apparent
regularity, four more novels in his Rougon-Macquart saga about
a family in Second Empire France: *A Love Story* (*Une page d'amour*,
1878) on the amorous mores of the petite bourgeoisie; *Nana* (1880),
the scandalous story of a high-class prostitute; *Pot Luck* (*Pot-Bouille*,
1882) set in a modern apartment building; and *The Ladies' Paradise*
(*Au Bonheur des dames*, 1883), about department store retailing.
Yet *The Bright Side of Life*, which would turn out to be the twelfth
of the planned twenty Rougon-Macquart volumes, had been delayed.
Zola had begun work on it in 1880, buoyed by his recent completion
of *Nana*, but from the start he had struggled to establish the novel's
plot and setting. A succession of blows in his private life, including
marital difficulties and the death of his beloved mother, Émilie, then
led to a midlife crisis, culminating in a mental breakdown in October
1882 which left him unable to go on with what he had planned would
be an uncharacteristically private book—so he turned his attention
instead to *Pot Luck*, then *The Ladies' Paradise*. It was not until he had
completed the latter novel, on 25 January 1883, that he felt able to
return to *La Joie de vivre*, making its genesis, in the words of Henri
Mitterand, editor of the definitive edition of the Rougon-Macquart

cycle, 'more tormented, in the end, than that of any of the previous novels'.[1]

The Bright Side of Life is something of a neglected masterpiece, with a reputation in France for being one of the finest love stories of the nineteenth century, but not really fitting in with the large-scale canvas of the other Rougon-Macquart books; it sold only slowly, though it was critically well received. Mitterand stresses its significance for our understanding of Zola himself: 'Far from being a minor novel, *The Bright Side of Life* stands out as the work most deeply anchored in Zola's temperament and his private life.'[2]

Unlike the rest of the cycle, the novel is set neither in the Paris region, nor in Plassans (Aix-en-Provence), the family's fictional place of origin, but on the Normandy coast, and Pauline, the young orphaned heroine, is the only substantive connection with the family line. Born in 1852, she is the daughter of Parisian *charcutiers* (pork butchers) Lisa Macquart and Quenu, central characters in *The Belly of Paris* (1873). When the story begins, in 1863, Pauline's parents have died and she is taken to live with relatives on her father's side, her aunt and uncle Chanteau (Mme Chanteau is a daughter of the de la Vignière family, minor nobility fallen on hard times) and her cousin Lazare, in the fictional seaside village of Bonneville. In an interview in April 1880 with the journalist Fernand Xau, Zola described his planned future work, as yet without a title, as 'an intimate novel, with few characters, written with great simplicity of style, [. . .] a reaction against my previous works'.[3] A note in one of the preliminary sketches confirms that, after *Nana*, he wanted to compose something on a more domestic scale:

This is the novel I want to write. Good, honest people placed in a drama that will develop the ideas of goodness and pain. Then, it will all be down to how it is written. Not my usual symphony. A simple, straightforward story. Environment still playing its necessary role, but less to the fore; descriptions

---

[1] Émile Zola, *Les Rougon-Macquart*, ed. Henri Mitterand, iii ('Bibliothèque de la Pléiade'; Paris: Gallimard, 1964), 1757. All translations from the French are mine, unless otherwise stated.

[2] Zola, *Les Rougon-Macquart*, ed. Mitterand, iii 1762.

[3] Quoted by Nils-Olof Franzén, *Zola et La Joie de vivre: La Genèse du roman, les personnages, les idées* (Stockholm: Almqvist & Wiksell, 1958), 30. The present Introduction is heavily indebted to this seminal work on the novel's genesis; in particular, quotations from Zola's preparatory dossier are drawn from this source.

reduced to a minimum. The style direct, correct, forceful, without romantic flourishes. The kind of classical language I dream of writing. In a word, honesty in everything, *nothing dressed up*.[4]

While he largely keeps to these early prescriptions, we may already note that description, particularly of the sea and its various moods, plays a much more vital role in *The Bright Side of Life* than he originally planned. The early dichotomy of goodness and pain was certainly destined to remain the thematic axis on which the book turned. At times, the emphasis would seem to shift towards pain: 'for this to be a great book, the idea of pain would need to be dominant'; but then a renewed assertion of the role of goodness would come in to compensate: '*The book must be bathed in affection*. I want it to be a page from life, but a life that is simple and good, *smiling*.'

Since *The Belly of Paris*, Zola had set about the composition of all his novels in the same manner, starting by writing an extensive 'preparatory dossier' divided into four main parts: an outline Sketch (*Ébauche*) of the setting, plot, and main characters; then a section on 'Characters' containing a detailed portrait of each (including, in *The Bright Side of Life*, the dog Mathieu, based on Zola's own dog, Bertrand, and the cat Minouche), with their main biographical, physical, and psychological attributes; next, a section called 'Plans', containing a first plan in which narrative and descriptive elements were provisionally allocated to chapters, then a definitive plan for each, often completed only shortly before the actual writing of the chapter; and finally a 'Notes' section containing the fieldwork jottings and other documentation he had gathered to ensure the accuracy and realism of the background information. Chantal Pierre-Gnassounou comments that this highly rational approach, of which Zola made no secret, was intended as 'an exemplary illustration of the naturalist method':

The planning notes [preparatory dossier] seem to illustrate to perfection the two great principles of naturalist fiction enunciated in *Le Roman expérimental*: observation (as in the Notes) and experimentation (as in the Outline [Sketch], in which the story is invented).[5]

---

[4] Zola, quoted by Franzén, *La Genèse du roman*, 22. In this and other quotations from Zola, the emphasis is the author's own unless otherwise stated.

[5] Chantal Pierre-Gnassounou, 'Zola and the Art of Fiction', in Brian Nelson (ed.), *The Cambridge Companion to Émile Zola* (Cambridge: Cambridge University Press, 2007), 86–104, at 86. *Le Roman expérimental* (*The Experimental Novel*) was an important

In the earliest phase of work on the book, probably (though critics are divided on this point) around Easter 1880, Zola made no fewer than four different sketches, which show him groping for a structure and a narrative thread, often in directions quite divergent from the final story. Fundamental from the first, even before he had decided on the setting (a 'small town' in the provinces was as far as he had got at the stage), was to be the contrast between his new heroine and Nana:

Now I have my heroine, who is Pauline Quenu, born in 1852, making her the same age as Nana. In 1869, she is around 18. [...] If I take Pauline as my central figure, she can be the radical opposite of Nana, for in my distribution of temperaments she is her converse. Thus, where Nana gave herself to all, Pauline will give herself to just one, perhaps not even one; where Nana was unleashed on the world with no moral compass, no social or religious inhibitions, she will create duties for herself and have values, religion, respectability, etc.; but above all, she will produce virtue, as Nana produced vice.

Zola would later differentiate Pauline's type of goodness (*bonté*) from the straightforward honest virtue of Denise Baudu in *The Ladies' Paradise*, allowing her to show hereditary fits of temper and adding a heroic element to her struggle against jealousy and the temptation to infidelity (the first plan of Chapter 6 indicates: 'Pauline, violent and jealous, struggling for happiness against her heredity and the environment around her'). As he acknowledged in the same note, however, his main problem would be to build a narrative around Pauline. It took him a long time to construct the plot, with numerous false starts but using elements which, in different permutations, would eventually gel into the novel we now read. Among other divergent scenarios, he toyed with the idea of Pauline living with a herbalist tortured by his terrible invalid wife, perhaps marrying the son of the household, who has studied law, with the essential drama created by an epidemic, and maybe a manslaughter by *crime passionnel* to start things off.

In a letter of 6 March 1889 to a Dutch critic and admirer of his work, Jacques van Santen-Kolff, Zola revealed that he had long been thinking of writing a prose poem on the subject of 'la Douleur' (meaning both physical pain and moral-psychological anguish), an idea that had left its mark on Lazare's 'Symphony of Suffering' in

collection of essays that Zola published in 1880 (Paris: Charpentier), constituting his manifesto of Naturalism, a literature for the scientific age.

The Bright Side of Life.[6] This was to be the novel's overarching theme, and the opening of the second sketch brought Zola closer to the final mix of characters and plot:

Perhaps something much simpler would be better—Suffering can be represented by an invalid father horribly tormented by ??????? ??????? ??? ???, and a young man afflicted by a moral sickness, an impossible love; then set up in the middle, over and above them, a figure of health and heroic goodness, Pauline, a strong, delicate temperament, thinking of everything, soothing all physical and moral ills.

The invalid father eventually becomes Pauline's gout-ridden uncle, Monsieur Chanteau, while the young man, originally to have been called Albert and to have married Pauline, afflicted by 'constant thoughts of death which ruin his life, paralyse his actions, and turn everything into desolation', becomes Lazare. The great epidemic is forgotten: the drama and intensity of the book will have to be built up from the small, everyday sufferings of the characters. In the third sketch, Albert changes into Gérard and takes on more of the complex, contradictory characteristics of the future Lazare: 'Cowardly and brave, hard-working and lazy, lying and truthful, sincere and play-acting. The modern, contemporary *ego*.' Gérard would marry Pauline, then be unfaithful to her, and Zola was unsure whether to end the novel with the failure of the marriage or the birth of their child. The main difficulty would be how to reconcile what he intended to be the novel's lofty philosophical perspective with the banal, everyday realities of provincial life:

Overall, by way of philosophy I don't want to paint the small miseries and treacheries of (provincial) existence; on the contrary, I aim to paint a broad current of life, *suffering and goodness*; and—here lies the difficulty—not with my usual poetic means, but through a continual analysis of day-to-day events.

Throughout the later twists and turns of the plot development (in the fourth sketch, for instance, Gérard is a musician and acquires a mother who dies in Pauline's arms), Zola remained preoccupied with the need to harmonize his grand, universal themes of 'suffering and goodness' with the smaller-scale actions of his characters.

Despite a strong constitution that allowed him to sustain his punishing work rate, by 1880 Zola was becoming more and more afflicted

---

[6] Émile Zola, *Correspondance*, ed. B. H. Bakker, 10 vols. (Montreal: Presses de l'Université de Montréal; Paris: CNRS, 1978–95), vi. 377.

with hypochondria and psychosomatic disorders, fearing that he would not live to complete the planned twenty volumes of the Rougon-Macquart cycle. The theme of death was also taking on increasing prominence in his novels (in chapter 12 of *Nana*, for instance, Nana and Muffat are haunted by a fear of dying). His morbid anxieties were exacerbated by the unexpected loss, in quick succession, of two of his most admired friends and literary role-models, Louis Édmond Duranty (b. 1833), founder of the Realist movement, on 9 April, and his great mentor Gustave Flaubert (b. 1821), on 8 May. Then, on 17 October 1880, came the hammer blow of the death of his mother. Looking back on that time in a letter of 15 December 1883 to fellow author and friendly rival Édmond de Goncourt, Zola wrote that he stopped working on *The Bright Side of Life* 'because I wanted to put into the work a lot of myself and those dearest to me, and after the recent shock of losing my mother, I no longer had the courage to write it'.[7] The manner of her death was distressing and it left Zola completely disorientated, as his son-in-law, Maurice le Blond, relates in terms closely foreshadowing events in Chapter 6 of the novel:

Émile Zola's grief was a pitiable sight, his excessive nerves forced him to flee the sight of his dying mother, locked in her final struggle for life. He would wander around the countryside, or stay shivering in some room in the house. His wife Alexandrine looked after the patient with admirable devotion, particularly as the dying woman had developed a terror of her daughter-in-law, making dreadful scenes and accusing her of trying to poison her each time she gave her her medicine to take.[8]

When, in February 1883, Zola finally got back to work on the book, he started adding increasingly autobiographical elements to the plot, making Lazare more like himself, as he revealed in an article (published in English) with the title 'In the Days of my Youth', in the December 1901 issue of the American *Bookman* review: 'You will find some of my early foibles, some of my early restlessness, ascribed to Lazare Chanteau in *La Joie de vivre*.'

In early 1882, Goncourt noted in his diary confidences from Zola about his necrophobia, and how he and Alexandrine would lie awake in bed at night, as Lazare would do, thinking about death. Lazare's

---

[7] Zola, *Correspondance*, ed. Bakker, iv. 442–3.
[8] Quoted by Franzén, *Zola et* La Joie de vivre, 32.

obsessive-compulsive behaviours in Chapter 7 are also Zola's own, and had started to develop from around the age of 30, as he later confessed to Dr Toulouse, of the Sainte-Anne mental hospital in Paris, when interviewed for the introductory volume of the latter's medico-psychological case studies on the links between genius and neurosis. He reported suffering from arithmomania, an obsession with counting (street lamps, cabs, the stairs at home, the objects on his desk, drawers that he had to open a set number of times before going to bed), and he shared with Lazare the night-time superstition of 'opening his eyes seven times to prove to himself that he was not going to die'.[9] Little wonder, in these circumstances, that the nervous pressure on Zola should have led to a breakdown, or that he should have been unable to continue with *The Bright Side of Life* until he had grieved for his mother. Indeed, Hemmings suggests that he finally wrote the novel as a form of therapy: 'The book represented, for its author, an attempt to rid himself of his neuroses by projecting them into a story.'[10]

The Sea

The second phase of work started with three further outline sketches, before Zola began to write the definitive opening chapter on 25 April 1883. It is in the first of these sketches, which builds on the plot outline of the fourth of the old series, that he shifts the novel's setting from 'the countryside around Paris' to the Normandy coast. Like many well-off Parisians, Zola and his wife made a number of visits to Normandy, the first to Saint-Aubin in 1875, when he was 35 and had already published ten novels. Sea-bathing had become fashionable and many affluent Parisians travelled to the coast by train during the summer months, to take the waters and flee the stifling heat of the capital. The famous Normandy resorts of Trouville, Fécamp, and Étretat were already becoming the playground of the aristocracy, but they were too expensive for middle-class holidaymakers, who had to be content with more modest places such as Saint-Aubin or Arromanches-les-Bains, still largely unspoilt but with minimal facilities

[9] Édouard Toulouse, *Enquête medico-psychologique sur les rapports de la supériorité intellectuelle à la névropathie*, i. *Introduction générale—Émile Zola* (Paris: Société d'éditions scientifiques, 1896), 251–2.

[10] F. W. J. Hemmings, *Émile Zola* (2nd edn., Oxford: Oxford University Press, 1966). 180.

for visitors. Zola's initial impressions of the area were quite mixed: shortly after his arrival in Saint-Aubin, where he had taken Alexandrine in the hope that sea-bathing would improve her health, he wrote to Édmond de Goncourt: 'The country round here is horrid but the sea is fine, and there's a sweet-smelling breeze.'[11] A few days later, in a letter to his publisher, Charpentier, he restated his distaste for the coastline in what, for a novelist, is an extraordinary literary metaphor:

No, you can't imagine anything uglier. It's flatter than the pavement of a town in ruins, and deserted, grey, immense! A great bourgeois thing, stretching as far as the eye can see, mile after mile of prose.[12]

In contrast, however, he soon came to appreciate the grandeur and romantic potential of the seascape:

The view is superb—the sea, always the sea! It's blowing a gale, driving the waves up to within a few metres of our door. Nothing could be more grandiose, particularly at night. It's quite different from the Mediterranean, at once very ugly and very grand.[13]

He was particularly struck, as he wrote to Paul Alexis on 13 August, by the rapidity with which the weather and the sea's mood could change, effects which are well captured in the marine descriptions in *The Bright Side of Life*:

We have superb weather here, storms, hot sunny days, Neapolitan nights, phosphorescent seas, suddenly switching from one to the other. I've never known such varied changes of scenery. When the weather is dull and grey, the sea is grandiose in its immensity. I'm beginning to understand this part of the world, which at first I saw as abominably ugly.[14]

He had, he said, begun jotting down his impressions of the sea, 'for a grand descriptive episode of twenty pages or so that I dream of slipping into one of my novels'. The result, some eight years later, would be not just an episode, but the full-scale novel we have before us, in

[11] Letter of 9 August 1875, in *Correspondance*, ed. Bakker, ii. 407.

[12] Letter of 14 August 1875, in *Correspondance*, ed. Bakker, ii. 410. Zola continued: 'I don't know what old romantic residue is left in me, but I dream of cliffs with steps cut into the rock, storm-lashed reefs, and lightning-shattered trees trailing their hair in the sea.'

[13] Letter of 5 August 1875 to Maurice Roux, in *Correspondance*, ed. Bakker, ii. 405.

[14] *Correspondance*, ed. Bakker, ii. 408–9.

which the ever-changing sea forms a continuous descriptive and symbolic backdrop to the narrative.

In a reply of 7 July 1887 to an enquiry from van Santen Kolff about his compositional methods, Zola revealed the inspiration for the location of his novel:

Bonneville is none other than Vierville (between Port-en-Bessin and Grandcamp), a modified Vierville. I generally create the little village that I need in this way, keeping the neighbouring towns as they are in reality. That gives me greater freedom with my characters.[15]

Zola spent the summer of 1881 at Grandcamp, in the Calvados, and visited Vierville on his way between Grandcamp and Port-en-Bessin. A note in the preparatory dossier situates Bonneville '10 km from Arromanches and 12 km from Port-en-Bessin', which, as Pierre Cogny points out, is impossible because Arromanches is itself only about 10 km from Port-en-Bessin.[16] The real Vierville, a bathing resort with a long, straight beach of golden sand, backed by a small road and holiday villas, is indeed accessed by a road perpendicular to the sea descending a valley between the cliffs, but these are relatively low and the beach has no shingle bank or rocky pools. Zola presumably relocated Bonneville nearer to Arromanches, a stretch of coast with higher, eroding clay cliffs with a constantly changing foreshore of collapsed and unstable rocks, to add drama to the precarious situation of the houses in the hamlet, as well as to make the descent into the village more dramatic.[17] Cogny suggests that Bonneville may also owe something to Bernières-sur-Mer, which lies some 15 km east of Arromanches, because timber beach defences of the kind designed by Lazare were successfully implemented there in the 1850s, and the area also has suitably large amounts of seaweed.

As always with Zola, however, the novel's setting is not just a realistic decor, but a symbolic reflection of the characters' states of mind and their struggles, the milieu that, in conjunction with their heredity,

---

[15] *Correspondance*, ed. Bakker, ii. 156. The ironically named Bonneville ('Goodtown') obeys the naming convention prevalent in that part of Normandy, where even hamlets tend to end in '-ville'.

[16] Pierre Cogny, 'Émile Zola et la côte normande', *Paris-Normandie* (3 October 1955).

[17] Writing to Alexis on 17 September, Zola mentions a day trip by hired coach to Arromanches: 'Fine cliffs at Arromanches, a much more romantic coastline than our bare, flat beach' (*Correspondance*, ed. Bakker, ii. 419).

determines and reflects their action. Little Pauline is closely identified with the sea before her arrival in the Chanteaus' household:

Since leaving Paris, she had been constantly obsessed by the idea of the sea. She was dreaming about it, asking her aunt endless questions in the train and wondering aloud, every time she saw a small rise in the landscape, whether the sea lay beyond those mountains. At last, on the beach at Arromanches, she had stood there speechless and wide-eyed, her heart swelling with a deep sigh; then, from Arromanches to Bonneville, she had kept poking her head out of the cabriolet, despite the wind, to look at the sea which accompanied them along their way. And now here was the sea again, it would always be there, like something that belonged to her. Slowly, with a sweeping gaze, she seemed to be making it her own. (p. 11)

The sea, 'now so clear and gentle in the bright July sunshine' (p. 34), forms a benevolent backdrop to her developing relationship with Lazare, during their expeditions along the coast when they bathe and play innocently on the beach, an idyllic earthly paradise. But it is also the unpredictable and implacable enemy from which Lazare tries to wrest both industrial profit and safety from destruction for the Bonneville fishermen and their families:

It was one of the September flood tides, rushing in with shattering force; no alert had been issued, but the gale, which had been blowing from the north since the previous day, had swollen the sea so monstrously that mountains of water were rearing up on the horizon and sweeping in, before crashing onto the rocks. In the distance, the sea was black beneath the shadow of the clouds as they galloped across the livid sky. (p. 168)

As Olivier Got remarks in an article on Zola's Normandy, 'the novel takes its rhythm from these tides, the alternation of calm seas and destructive storms'.[18] As with the eponymous bar in *L'Assommoir*, or the mine in *Germinal*, the sea in *The Bright Side of Life* becomes virtually a character in its own right, interacting with people and mirroring the moral and material choices that confront them. On the swim out to the Picochets rocks, the sea is still Pauline's 'great friend':

She loved its salty breath and its chill, chaste waters, and she surrendered herself to it, happy to feel its immense liquid embrace on her skin, tasting the joy of this violent exercise that set her heart racing. (p. 62)

[18] Olivier Got, 'La Normandie de Zola', in Jean-Marc Bailbé (ed.), *Le Paysage normand dans la littérature et dans l'art* (Paris: Presses universitaires de France, 1980), 197.

Later, however, it seems to amplify her tormented self-doubt, when, unable to sleep, she gets up and looks out of her bedroom window, listening to its wailing voice:

she would lean there for hours, gazing out across the immense blackness, high above the sea whose lament rose to her ears, unable to sleep while the breeze fanned her burning bosom. (p. 203)

The ebb and flow of the tide is both metaphorical and literal when, in Chapter 9, it signifies the renewal of her relationship with Lazare:

A tide of memories came flooding back, with all the sweetness of long-dormant affections newly awakened. What was there in it to alarm them? They made no attempt to resist, languidly lulled by the sea and its endless, monotonous voice. (p. 243)

Perhaps most significantly of all, it is 'the rising tide of puberty' (p. 45) and desire, symbolized and materialized in the ebb and flow of her menstrual cycle, that turns Pauline into the life force and moral authority of the novel.

Lazare: Plumbing the Depths

Since the inspiration for *The Bright Side of Life* was largely personal, Zola only did background research at the stage of refining the second detailed plan, and it went on in parallel with the actual writing of the novel, from late April to late November 1883. The 'Notes' section of the preparatory dossier preserves evidence of the delving he did into domains and topics as diverse as medicine (female puberty, gout, heart disease, taken from Pierre Larousse's monumental encyclopedia the *Great Universal Dictionary of the Nineteenth Century*), chemistry (iodine, bromide, soda), types of seaweed, sea defences, tides, and procedures of adoption and inheritance. Franzén demonstrates that, to flesh out his material on the central theme, Zola made notes on an article by Charles Richet in the *Revue philosophique* of 1877 entitled 'Pain: A Study in Psychological Physiology' ('La Douleur: Étude de psychologie physiologique'), from which the novel uses several adapted quotations. The same volume contained a long review of the recently-published second edition of Francisque Bouillier's *On Pleasure and Pain*,[19] which seems to have led Zola to read the book

---

[19] *Du plaisir et de la douleur* (Paris: Hachette, 1877).

itself, for again he made extensive notes on the text and reused some of them more or less verbatim in the novel. Just before he began writing the first chapter, he received a letter dated 19 April 1883 from well-known naturalist Édmond Perrier on the chemical treatment of seaweed, of which he again used parts almost unedited in Chapter 3, putting the technical information in the mouth of Lazare. A few days afterwards, Gabriel Thyébaut, who had been his legal adviser for _Pot Luck_, wrote to him with extensive details on the legalities of guardianship which were incorporated into Chapter 1, and some time later, a second letter on emancipation from guardianship which was used in Chapter 3. Zola asked Céard for information about sea defences, and in reply received details about their construction taken from two encyclopedias. He then enquired of Céard, who had studied medicine, what books a medical student would need to read in his first and second years, and used his answer to constitute the list of Lazare's textbooks, including 'Bouillaud' on heart disease, whom Lazare reads obsessively at night in Chapter 6.[20] Finally, for his great tour-de-force childbirth scene in Chapter 10, which can be compared to the labour of Gervaise in _L'Assommoir_, Adèle in _Pot Luck_, and, later, Lise in _Earth_ (_La Terre_), he made extensive use of Lucien Pénard's _Practical Guide for the Obstetrician and Midwife_[21] (including the detail of the infant's protruding hand).

A particularly important research topic for Zola was German philosopher Arthur Schopenhauer (1788–1860), very fashionable in Parisian intellectual circles from the late 1870s onwards, about whose pessimistic school of thought he made no fewer than twenty-six pages of notes. Schopenhauer, best known for his 1818 book _The World as Will and Representation_, saw reality as the product of a blind and insatiable metaphysical will; the absolute absurdity of existence in such a world without God could lead only to resignation, abstinence, and absolute scepticism about progress. Zola, Céard, Maupassant, and

[20] Jean Bouillaud, _Traité clinique des maladies du cœur_ (_Clinical Treatise on Heart Disease_) (Paris: Librairie J.-B. Baillière, 1835), and Ernest Auburtin, _Recherches cliniques sur les maladies du cœur, d'après les leçons de M. le prof. Bouillaud_ (_Clinical Research into Heart Disease, after the Lectures of Professor Bouillaud_) (Paris: J. Viat, 1856).

[21] _Guide pratique de de l'accoucheur et de la sage-femme_ (Paris: J. B. Baillière et Fils, 1862; 5th edn., 1879). Interestingly, the title page states that Pénard, like Dr Cazenove, was a retired naval surgeon, though unlike Zola's fictitious medic, he had extensive experience of childbirth, being also a former professor of obstetrics at the Rochefort School of Medicine.

Huysmans, who discussed these ideas at length, saw them as the origin of a new *mal du siècle*, a neurotic condition summed up in late 1882 by fellow novelist Paul Bourget in *La Nouvelle Revue*:

We live in an age of religious and metaphysical collapse, in which all doctrines lie in ruins on the ground [ ] An anarchy of a unique order has become established among thinking people, [ ] a scepticism without compare in the history of ideas [...] The sickness of doubting even one's own doubt carries with it a cortege of infirmities, a wavering of the will, sophistical compromises of conscience, dilettantism, [...] weaknesses which make our admiration for those who have not lost the great virtues of the past all the greater.[22]

Bourget continued his diatribe with a dig at 'the distinguished spleen of the young generation of intellectuals', exemplified in *The Bright Side of Life* by Lazare. In his biography of Zola, Phillip Walker highlights the continuity of character between Lazare and an earlier generation of Romantic literary heroes:

Lazare is a naturalistic version of Goethe's Werther, Chateaubriand's René, and Flaubert's Frédéric Moreau rolled into one: an intelligent, sensitive, but extremely neurotic, pessimistic, bored, proud, selfish, unstable and ineffectual young man.[23]

Zola himself, in a note from his preparatory dossier, contrasted the earlier fashionable melancholy of Romanticism with the profound, Schopenhauerian scepticism that he saw as being generated by Naturalism:

No faith—A variety of Werther and René—Romanticism created the despairing, melancholy doubter—Naturalism is creating the sceptic who believes in the nothingness of the world, who denies progress. At bottom, terror in the face of death.

Schopenhauer disciples from Zola's circle, chief among them Huysmans and Céard, objected that Lazare's attitude was just a simplification and a caricature of the great man's thought, but Zola responded that this was exactly his point: the pessimism that had become fashionable in France, and that his book was opposing, was only an 'ill-digested'

---

[22] Note of 12 December 1882; cited by Mitterand in his edn. of Zola, *Les Rougon-Macquart*, iii. 1753–4.

[23] Philip Walker, *Zola* (London: Routledge and Kegan Paul, 1985), 160.

simplification, which was why its influence on the younger generation was so pernicious. But as Huysmans and others persisted in their pessimist faith, it marked the start of the amicable dissolution of the Naturalist group of writers whom Zola had gathered around him in the late 1870s.

Of course, this sceptic is not just Lazare, but also Zola himself, battling against his own tendency to nihilism and despair in the wake of his mental crisis of the early 1880s. He probably did not read any original work by Schopenhauer, but in May–June 1883, in preparation for Chapter 3 of the novel, he made extensive notes on the preface to J. Bourdeau's 1880 French translation of a selection of the philosopher's *Thoughts, Maxims and Fragments*,[24] as well as Théodule Ribot's earlier *Philosophy of Schopenhauer*.[25] In these notes, he identified no fewer than nine possible titles for his new novel, including the one he eventually chose. Of the others, three are direct quotations from Bourdeau: *La Vallée de larmes* (The Vale of Tears), *L'Espoir du néant* (Hope in Nothingness), *Le Vieux Cynique* (The Old Cynic); two come from Ribot's translation: *La Misère du monde* (The World's Misery), *Le Repos sacré du néant* (The Sacred Repose of Nothingness); and the final three are *La Sombre mort* (Grim Death), *Le Tourment de l'existence* (The Torment of Existence), and *Le Triste Monde* (World of Sadness). It is striking that *La Joie de vivre* (literally, *The Joy of Living*) is the only one of the nine that is not bleakly pessimistic, though it is surely to a greater or lesser degree ironic—an irony reflected in the title adopted for the present English translation, with its echo of the bitter-sweet crucifixion scene at the end of Monty Python's film *Life of Brian* (1979). In his 1889 letter to van Santen Kolff already quoted, Zola said he did not remember exactly how he came upon the title, but conceded its irony: 'I only know that I wanted at first a direct title such as *Le Mal de vivre* [Life's Unhappiness], but I came to prefer *La Joie de vivre* for its irony.'[26] The exact degree of irony he intended is, however, still debated by critics, and on that question turns our ultimate interpretation of the novel.

To Zola's dismay, *The Bright Side of Life* was received by his contemporaries as essentially a *roman à these* promoting the pessimistic

---

[24] Schopenhauer, Arthur, *Pensées, maximes et fragments... Traduit, annoté et précédé d'une vie de Schopenhauer par J. Bourdeau* (Paris: Germer Baillière, 1880).

[25] Théodule Ribot, *Philosophie de Schopenhauer* (Paris: Germer Baillière, 1874).

[26] See Franzén, *Zola et* La Joie de vivre, 77.

ideas of Schopenhauer. His English translator and biographer Ernest Alfred Vizetelly, who knew Zola well, was certainly in no doubt that the book was governed by almost unrelieved pessimism, writing in the preface to his revised (1901) translation *The Joy of Life*, originally published in 1886 under the sardonic title *How Jolly Life Is!*;

The title selected by him for this book is to be taken in an ironical or sarcastic sense. There is no joy at all in the lives of the characters whom he portrays in it. [...] Monsieur Zola is not usually a pessimist. One finds many of his darkest pictures relieved by a touch of hopefulness; but there is extremely little in the pages of 'La Joie de Vivre', which is essentially an analysis of human suffering and misery.[27]

According to Mitterand,[28] most contemporary reviewers, 'contrary to the author's true intentions', also read the title as 'poignantly ironic'. This position is echoed nearer our own time by Got, who calls it 'such a bitter book, with its dreadfully ironic title',[29] or Graham King, for whom it is 'bitterly and ironically titled';[30] while for Susan Harrow, the whole novel represents a 'modernist dystopia'.[31] Some contemporary critics saw the negativity as symptomatic of the age, 'the anxiety of [Zola's] whole generation'; Édouard Drumont, for instance, who would become an outspoken opponent of Zola's during the Dreyfus Affair, wrote in *La Liberté* of 18 February 1884:

This strange book, which offends against all delicacy and shocks all received ideas in art, is, despite everything, a singularly powerful work [...] It is fair to say, this is the first time we have seen Zola really being himself [...] He has held out a mirror in which modern man can see himself reflected.

On 27 April of the same year, in an article in *Le Gaulois* entitled 'The Girl' ('La Jeune Fille'), Guy de Maupassant gave the novel a very supportive review in which he tried, not entirely successfully, to stress the compassion behind Zola's bleak vision:

[27] (London: Chatto & Windus, 1901), 1.
[28] The unattributed quotations that follow are drawn from Mitterand's account of the novel's reception in his edn. of Zola, *Les Rougon-Macquart*, iii. 1771–2.
[29] Got, 'La Normandie de Zola', 185.
[30] Graham King, *Garden of Zola: Émile Zola and His Novels for English Readers* (London: Barrie and Jenkins, 1978), 259.
[31] Susan Harrow, *Zola, The Body Modern: Pressures and Prospects of Representation* (London: Legenda, 2010), 37 n. 24.

Émile Zola has introduced into the bitter irony of *La Joie de vivre* a prodigious sum of humanity. It is among his most remarkable novels, and he has written few others with the grandeur of this story of a simple bourgeois family, whose mediocre but terrible dramas play out against the superb backdrop of the sea, fierce as life and equally unforgiving, as it slowly, indefatigably, eats away at a poor fishing hamlet built in a fold in the cliffs. And over the whole book there hovers a black bird, its wings outstretched: the bird of death.

The novelist himself, in his second sketch of 1883, had highlighted the ambiguous significance of Bonneville, symbolizing Schopenhauer's futile 'will to life', but in a hopeless situation: 'The little village eaten up by the sea is an image of humanity under the crushing weight of the world, and it wants to live.'[32] In view of his own ambivalence about the book's message, it is perhaps scarcely surprising that critics should have failed to read it as the clear refutation of pessimism that Zola originally intended it to be.

Pauline, Joy, and Positivism

There is indeed a strong counter-current running against pessimism in *The Bright Side of Life*, a faith in scientific progress and human goodness, personified by the heroine, Pauline. If she is able, in the novel as finally written, to carry off this role with the strength and conviction that she does, it is only, in the view of Henri Mitterand, because Zola underwent a 'moral and philosophical convalescence'[33] over the preceding three years, thanks to the process of writing *Pot Luck* and, especially, *The Ladies' Paradise*. The latter novel of energetic, striving commercialism was written deliberately to counteract the fashionable climate of pessimism. In chapter 3, the book's principal character, self-made store magnate Octave Mouret, lambasts his vapid former schoolfriend, Paul Vallagnosc, a prototype for Lazare, as he sprawls on a sofa, languidly preaching the gospel of pessimist inactivity:

All the joy of action, all the gaiety of existence resounded in his words. He repeated that he was a man of his own time. Really, people would have to be deformed, they must have something wrong with their brains and limbs to

---

[32] Again, in the outline plan of Chapter 8 (7 in the final book): 'The village under threat from the sea is an image of humanity threatened by death and pain; and it wants to live.'

[33] Zola, *Les Rougon-Macquart*, ed. Mitterand, iii. 1754.

refuse to work in an age which offered so many possibilities, when the whole century was pressing forward into the future. And he laughed at the hopeless, the disillusioned, the pessimists, all those made sick by our fledgling sciences, who assumed the tearful air of poets or the superior expression of sceptics, amidst the immense activity of the present day.[34]

The phrase 'those made sick by our fledgling sciences' is repeated with reference to Lazare, in Zola's third sketch of 1883 for *The Bright Side of Life*:

The key thing, the very basis of Lazare, is to make him a pessimist, made sick by our fledgling sciences.

This may sound paradoxical, especially as physiology and medicine, in the hands of great pioneers such as Claude Bernard (1813–78), were areas in which some of the greatest scientific strides were being made at the time. Zola's point, however, is that the young generation had unrealistic expectations of what the scientific method was currently able to deliver, as Dr Cazenove exasperatedly points out to Lazare in Chapter 6, while attending Madame Chanteau in her illness:

'Listen to me, young man, I think I'm less of a fool than some, but this is not the first time an illness has caught me unawares and left me looking stupid… You're infuriating, you expect us to know everything, when it's already an achievement to understand even the basics of such a complicated machine as the human body.' (p. 146)

The answer, for Zola, was not to turn away in disgust and run into the arms of the Romantics or the pessimists, but to persevere, as he himself had done in his 1880 volume of collected essays on the novelist's craft, *The Experimental Novel* (*Le Roman experimental*), in seeking new applications of the rational, positivist method of enquiry championed by the great scientists.

His positivist faith in the future power of empirical science had been founded in the mid-1860s when, as a junior clerk in the advertising department of the Parisian publisher Hachette, he had struck up a friendship with one of the authors who called in regularly, the great critic and historian Hippolyte Taine (1828–93). A proponent of sociological positivism, Taine became a major theoretical influence on

---

[34] *The Ladies' Paradise*, trans. Brian Nelson (Oxford: Oxford World's Classics, 1995), 67 (adapted: Nelson translates 'our budding sciences', but a metaphor more suggestive of weakness and vulnerability is perhaps appropriate here).

Naturalism as Zola went on to develop it, and in a review of the new
edition of Taine's *Critical and Historial Essays* (*Essais de critique et
d'histoire*) which he published in *L'Événement* of 25 July 1866, Zola
had declared himself the 'humble disciple' of this theorist of inheritance, milieu, and moment as a complete explanation of human behaviour, who had declared in the introduction to his *History of English
Literature*:

Whether the facts are physical or moral ones is immaterial, they always have
a cause; there are causes for ambition, courage, truthfulness, as there are for
digestion, the movement of muscles, or animal heat. Vice and virtue are products just like vitriol and sugar, and every complex phenomenon is caused by
the combination of simpler phenomena on which it depends. Let us therefore
seek the simple origins of moral qualities, as we do of physical ones.[35]

In the midst of the controversy surrounding his new literary movement, Zola published in *Le Figaro* of 17 January 1881 a declaration of
faith which seemed to make science synonymous with naturalism (as
in the 'natural sciences'):

My credo is that naturalism, I mean the return to nature, the scientific
spirit extended into all our realms of knowledge, is the very agent of the
nineteenth century.[36]

Five months later, in the same newspaper, he publicly restated his
faith in science as the vehicle of modernity and progress:

I believe in my century, with all my modern sensibility. [...] I believe in
science, because it is the tool of the century, because it is bringing us the
only solid formula [...] Only science can save humanity.[37]

This redemptive function, initiated in Zola's view by the experimental methods of Taine and Bernard, is personified in *The Bright Side
of Life* by Dr Cazenove, a man without illusions or metaphysical
baggage, only too aware of his limitations as he battles to patch up
the mechanism of what he refers to as the human machine.[38] Zola

---

[35] *Histoire de la littérature anglaise* (Paris: Hachette, 1864); quoted in Hemmings,
Émile Zola, 55.
[36] Quoted by Walker, *Zola*, 153 (his translation).
[37] Quoted by Walker, *Zola*, 154 (his translation).
[38] During Pauline's illness in Chapter 4, Lazare asks Cazenove in angry frustration:
'So medicine's no use, then?' He replies: 'No use at all when the whole machine goes
wrong...' (p. 108).

describes Madame Chanteau's illness, in Chapter 6, as 'the breakdown of her mechanism, [...] like a clockwork running down' (p. 160); and when, in the following chapter, Lazare, concerned about growing old, 'listened to the clockwork ticking inside him, [...] he felt sure that the mechanism was winding down' (p. 235). Pauline herself reflects, in Chapter 9, on the deep understanding of the 'mechanism of life' (p. 60) that her reading of Lazare's anatomy and physiology textbooks has given her. But the most sustained medico-scientific analysis in the novel is provided by the gradual decline into gout-ridden paralysis of Pauline's unfortunate uncle:

Chanteau is a purely bodily phenomenon, he is a *man-machine* whose reactions the author observes with the impassibility of a doctor or a chemist examining a test tube.[39]

Virtually deprived of interiority, acting, and speaking almost exclusively by reflex, Chanteau is, for Zola, little more than a case study in positivist physiology.

If a strongly asserted faith in positivism is one plank of Zola's rampart against pessimism at this point in his life, the personality and attitude of the novel's heroine are perhaps even more crucial. Vizetelly, in the preface to his 1901 translation, concedes that Pauline, in contrast to the author's otherwise bleak irony, stands out as 'a beautiful, touching, almost consolatory creature [...], the embodiment of human abnegation and devotion'.[40] In the second 1883 sketch, as Zola is looking for the detail of his plot, he notes: 'Pauline is health, balance, honesty; she calms and consoles'; and again, in the preliminary plan for Chapter 2: 'Pauline is the bright side of life, she brings happiness. Always cheerful, a cheerful goodness.' The phrase 'the bright side of life', in a positive sense entirely devoid of irony, then recurs in a more detailed characterization of Pauline in the second detailed plan:

She is devoted to others. The bright side of life, through all the disasters, she picks herself up, and other people. Cheerful goodness, always cheerful, happy in her daily routine, hopeful for the morrow.

[39] Franzén, *Zola et La Joie de vivre*, 146 (emphasis original).
[40] *Joy of Life*, trans. Vizetelly, 1. In his later biography of Zola, written for both American and English audiences, Vizetelly remarks, rather negatively: 'So gray a work, which only the devotion and self-sacrifice of Pauline, the heroine, occasionally brightens, could not attract the mass of the reading public' (*Émile Zola, Novelist and Reformer: An Account of His Life and Work* (London: John Lane, The Bodley Head, 1904), 218).

This compensating, consoling role is confirmed in a sentence from the book's closing scene which Zola removed at proof stage from the *Gil Blas* serialization, no doubt because he felt it to be too explicit:

But if the world was all pain, she who brought charity stubbornly persisted in loving life, saying she was too healthy to be sad.[41]

With her robust health, equable temperament, and constantly positive activity, Pauline is thus clearly set up from the start to counterbalance Lazare's dilettantism and constitutional pessimism. Yet her role in the novel extends well beyond the psychological, for Zola also makes her the philosophical antidote to Lazare, giving her a fully equal voice on an intellectual level and allowing her to demonstrate, through her actions, the ethical superiority of joy over despair. Thus, a note in the third 1883 sketch referring to Lazare as a 'highly intelligent failure' and repeating again the leitmotif 'made sick by our fledgling sciences', establishes Pauline as the 'cure' for his pessimism:

Without dogmatism, Pauline must be the answer to those made sick by our fledgling sciences, through her abnegation, cheerfulness etc.

In Chapter 7, Cazenove joins the opposition to Lazare's lassitude and despair, supporting Pauline's vitalism with an Aristotelian injunction:

'Why can't you just live? Isn't it enough to be alive? Joy comes from action.' And Cazenove suddenly turned to Pauline, who was listening with a smile on her face.
   'Come now!' he said, 'tell him how you always manage to stay so cheerful!' (p. 178)

Then, as Zola was looking for an ending for *The Bright Side of Life*, the preliminary plan for the final chapter suggests an optimistic view of the future represented by little Paul, Lazare's son, who 'will perhaps not suffer from his father's moral sickness, the sickness of our fledgling sciences, the sickness of our era'.

   Perhaps more significant even than her psychological and philosophical role in the novel, however, is the reforming and modern view of women that Pauline represents. Franzén notes that Schopenhauer's pessimism was directly challenged by the ideas of the founder of Positivism, Auguste Comte (1798–1857), whose key moral principle,

---

[41] Quoted by Franzén, *Zola et* La Joie de vivre, 111.

'live for others', Pauline exemplifies. He quotes a statement by Jean Lacroix on the key regenerative function allotted to women in Comte's sociology:

But in Comte's eyes, the reign of the heart can only be ensured by giving a preponderant role to women. Hence his *Positivist Catechism*, which is addressed first to the woman to regenerate humanity, because, being naturally more altruistic, she is better able to understand, even intellectually, Positivism.[42]

Through the character of Pauline, Zola's exemplary female positivist, *The Bright Side of Life* presents a remarkably progressive manifesto for the education of women. In Chapter 2, the heroine develops a passionate interest in medical science through reading her cousin's textbooks, with their explicit anatomical engravings, hoping to achieve her 'dream of learning everything, in order to cure everything' (p. 47). In Chapter 3, she acts at first as a laboratory assistant for Lazare's experiments with seaweed, but rapidly becomes no less expert in the subject than he. In both cases, Zola shows her striving against the odds to become a self-trained scientist, in opposition to the bland diet of edulcorated mythology, piano playing, and deportment, combined with a veneer of religious observance ('a well-brought-up young lady had an obligation to set a good example and show respect for the curé', p. 40), that her aunt considers suitable for her. Zola is no less damning of Madame Chanteau's motives for teaching Pauline at home, than he is of the conventional alternative:

At boarding school, little girls heard all sorts of dreadful things; she wanted to be able to vouch for her pupil's perfect innocence. (p. 40)

A note in the character sheet for Louise contrasts Pauline's accurate, self-empowering knowledge of the facts of life, with the salacious tittle-tattle of other girls in the school which is all that a traditional middle-class education provides:

Moreover, [Louise] is a boarder in Caen: the young girl brought up in a boarding school, knowing everything and concealing the fact, as opposed to the young girl brought up in freedom, knowing everything and deriving from it health, and honour.

[42] Jean Lacroix, *La Sociologie d'Auguste Comte* (Paris, Presses universitaires de France, 1956), 62–3; quoted in Franzén, *Zola et La Joie de vivre*, 138.

This key idea of an upbringing based on intellectual freedom recurs in Chapter 4, when Pauline sympathetically explains to Louise the depravity of one of the disadvantaged village urchins:

Louise averted her gaze in disgust as Pauline, without the least embarrassment, told her the boy's story. The freedom of her upbringing allowed her to face human vice with the steadfast calm of charity, to know and speak about anything with innocence and frankness. Louise, on the other hand, made worldly-wise by ten years of boarding school, blushed at the ideas that Pauline's words awoke in her mind, warped by dormitory dreams. These were things one thought about, but never mentioned. (p. 89)

Zola's ideas on female education were influenced by the groundbreaking *Education: Intellectual, Moral and Physical* of 1861 by English philosopher, scientist, and political theorist Herbert Spencer (1820–1903),[43] a French translation of which had been published in 1878. Much admired also by Flaubert, this book was probably read by Zola, and he certainly read an article of 1877 summing up Spencer's ideas on the duties of 'parents, especially mothers', in educating their daughters about life (as a Victorian, Spencer could not mention the word 'sex').[44] He also read *Hygiene of the Young Girl* by a certain Dr A. Coriveaud, published in 1882, which asks its female readers:

Should a mother, a mother such as yourself, inform her daughter about what soon awaits her, and explain the causes of the troubles that are disturbing her?[45]

The good doctor's emphatic 'yes, certainly' would be echoed by Zola, and indeed Franzén hypothesizes that it was reading this book that led him to include in *The Bright Side of Life* the topics of puberty, menstruation, and sex education, absent from the early sketches. Despite her very believable jealousy, and the avarice and occasional violent outbursts caused by the family's inherited instability, Franzén concludes that Pauline represents Zola's ideal woman, a view supported by Dr Toulouse in his case study on the novelist, who states that 'the three things he finds most beautiful are youth, health, and goodness'.[46]

[43] (New York, D. Appleton and Company, 1861). Translated as *De l'éducation intellectuelle, morale et physique* (Paris: Baillière, 1878).

[44] G. Compayré, 'Les Principes de l'éducation', *Revue philosophique* (May–June 1877); quoted in Franzén, *Zola et* La Joie de vivre, 140.

[45] *Hygiène de la jeune fille* (Paris: J.-B. Baillière et fils, 1882).

[46] *Enquête medico-psychologique*, 259; quoted in Franzén, *Zola et* La Joie de vivre, 140.

Despite the undeniable irony of the book's title, therefore, it seems appropriate to conclude that the powerful thematic presence of pessimism and negativity in *The Bright Side of Life* is at least counterbalanced, in the powerfully drawn and complex character of Pauline, by a more optimistic philosophy. For Henri Mitterand, the novel exemplified the 'double current' flowing through the whole Rougon-Macquart cycle, exaltation of the life force ('la joie de vivre') on the one hand, and death and annihilation ('le mal de vivre') on the other:

It is not unreasonable to interpret the interaction of Pauline and Lazare as a juxtaposition of the two Zolas, the one trying to exorcise the other's familiar demons.[47]

Franzén takes a similar line, but his evaluation of the book's message seems to come down in the end on the positive, life-affirming side:

From the beginning, *The Bright Side of Life* is essentially just a vast antithesis. Zola opposes suffering, pain, and the forces of destruction, with goodness, compassion, and the indestructible forces of life.[48]

For Graham King, however, the novel rather plays out an evenly balanced debate between pessimism and joy, a philosophical experiment which Zola was undertaking on himself, without ultimately arriving at any clear conclusion:

Throughout the novel we witness the lives and beliefs of the two protagonists, the debaters, and with the novelist's summing up we are invited to make our own judgement at the end.[49]

We might instinctively wish for the victory of light over darkness, but the novelist's skill keeps the debate evenly balanced, and it is this ambivalent outcome, at once frustrating and intriguing for the reader, that gives the book, which Hemmings calls 'a true novel of ideas, of a kind Zola had not attempted up to then',[50] its lasting place in the Rougon-Macquart cycle.

[47] Zola, *Les Rougon-Macquart*, ed. Mitterand, iii. 1742. Franzén concurs, seeing the novel as 'a great dialogue, a drama between two opposite characters who are the mouthpieces of the novelist in the battle he fought with himself to overcome his vital problems' (*Zola et* La Joie de vivre, 34).

[48] Franzén, *Zola et* La Joie de vivre, 186.

[49] King, *Garden of Zola*, 264.

[50] Hemmings, *Émile Zola*, 183.

The expression *joie de vivre* itself has also had a long legacy in France's cultural life, though almost exclusively in its straightforwardly positive sense, and quickly passed into English usage as well. Zola was not the first to coin the phrase (though Maupassant credited him with its invention), but its use exploded after the novel's publication and the concept became interwoven with the changing social and philosophical value-systems of the late nineteenth and early twentieth centuries. As Alison Finch has shown, it became associated with everything from new forms of secular religion to a 'soft' form of Darwinism, a more palatable version of Schopenhauer's Will to Life, and later, Bergson's *élan vital*: 'within a few decades of Zola's novel, the phrase itself had become a given in French cultural consciousness', and even 'a convenient cliché'.[51] Nor was its influence limited to literature: virtually every movement in European modernist painting produced its own life-affirming interpretation of the theme. This trend began with Van Gogh, who paid direct tribute to Zola's novel in two pictures depicting the physical book, the first of which, *Still Life with Bible* (1885), juxtaposes an imposing illuminated Bible open at Isaiah 53 ('He is despised and rejected of men; a man of sorrows, and acquainted with grief') with a small yellow-bound copy of *La Joie de vivre*, to imply the artist's support for Zola's positivist philosophy and anticlericalism. The phrase itself occurs in the titles of other paintings, including Van Gogh's second canvas, *Oleanders and Zola's* Joie de vivre' (1888), Paul Signac's pointillist idyll *In the Time of Harmony: The Joy of Life—Sunday by the Sea* (1895–6), Henri Matisse's *Bonheur de vivre* (known in English as *The Joy of Life*) of 1906, Robert Delaunay's 1930 abstract *Rythme, joie de vivre*, and Pablo Picasso's *Joie de vivre (Antipolis)* of 1946. Kees van Dongen's more realistic 1922 canvas *Deauville, Joie de vivre* captures the fashionable summer social scene at a party at the resort, while Max Ernst's surrealist *Joie de vivre* of 1936, with its toothed stick-insects camouflaged in a luxuriant jungle of vines, stands out as the only thoroughly dystopian treatment. Perhaps truest to the philosophical and emotional ambiguity of Zola's novel is the 1937 painting *La Joie de vivre* by Belgian surrealist Paul Delvaux, the only version to depict directly the awkward triangular

---

[51] Alison Finch, '*Joie de vivre*: The Afterlife of a Phrase', in S. Harrow and T. Unwin (eds.), Joie de vivre *in French Literature and Culture: Essays in Honour of Michael Freeman* (Amsterdam and New York: Rodopi, 2009), 299–311, at 305.

love-conflict at its heart. The dominance, in both artistic and linguistic usage, of straightforwardly life-affirming interpretations of the phrase to which Zola gave such wide cultural currency is perhaps not surprising. It may also, however, be an additional factor in the relative neglect into which his story has fallen, with readers in search of drama and psychological tension not realizing that, behind the apparently naïve 'joy' of the title, such attributes are present in complex abundance.

TRANSLATOR'S NOTE

LA JOIE DE VIVRE was first translated into English by Ernest Alfred Vizetelly (1853–1922) under the title *How Jolly Life Is!: A Realistic Novel* (London: Vizetelly & Co., 1886); a revised edition was issued by the same publisher in 1889. The title became *The Joy of Life* when Vizetelly's translation was again revised for republication some twelve years later (London: Chatto & Windus, 1901). This final text remains the only other English version currently available, reissued multiple times, including as a Kindle eBook in 2016. The title was changed to *Zest for Life* in Jean Stewart's excellent mid-century translation (London: Elek Books, 1955), long out of print, and the two titles are combined in the more recent English edition, *The Joy of Life: Zest for Life* by Stephen R. Pastore (Grand Mal Press, 2013), which, however, is not readily obtainable and was not consulted during the preparation of the present edition.

While never exactly a bestseller in France, *La Joie de vivre* has always enjoyed the reputation of being a well-crafted, if somewhat uncharacteristic, example of Zola's writing. English-speaking readers, however, have generally found it dull and colourless, particularly as far as the characterization of Pauline is concerned. One blogger on the Rougon-Macquart cycle, for instance, describes her as 'a poor, saintly orphan', remarking that her 'passive martyrdom' reminds him of 'Dickens in his worst sentimental moments'.[1] This radical difference in appreciation is largely explained by the fact that the reception of Zola's novel in English has been almost entirely conditioned, up to the present day, by Ernest Vizetelly's heavily self-censored version of 1901, written in what Graham King calls, a little harshly, 'a cataleptic style which has the vivacity of concrete'.[2] The London-based publishing house of Vizetelly & Co., founded by Ernest's father Henry (1820–94), specialized in foreign literature, and in 1884 had secured the rights to publish English translations of all Zola's novels from *L'Assommoir* onwards. Ernest had already brought out English versions of *The 'Assommoir'*

---

[1] https://swiftlytiltingplanet.wordpress.com/2009/06/14/the-joy-of-life-by-emile-zola/ (accessed 30 October 2017).

[2] Graham King, *Garden of Zola: Émile Zola and His Novels for English Readers* (London: Barrie and Jenkins, 1978), 372.

and *Nana*, taking the precaution of cutting and modifying passages that might offend a prudish late-Victorian readership and draw the attention of the authorities to the activities of the publishing house. In 1886, he issued a first, no less cautious, translation of *La Joie de vivre*, to which he gave the ironic title *How Jolly Life is!*.

Zola's realism, and his unflinching focus on the physical side of life, had gained him an unsavoury reputation outside France, and especially in Victorian Britain, as a quasi-pornographer, so that taking on his novels was a genuine risk for publishers and their translators. His books even figured prominently in a House of Commons debate in 1888 on the subject of the corrupting influence of 'pernicious literature', exemplified by what Alfred, Lord Tennyson referred to as the 'troughs of Zolaism'.[3] As Anthony Cummins has shown, it was not so much that Zola's books were regarded as inherently obscene, even if many regarded them as disgusting or titillating: the better-educated sons of the bourgeoisie and aristocracy who could read him in French were assumed to have enough taste and discernment to avoid moral corruption.[4] The problem was that Vizetelly & Co. were making them available in English in two-shilling editions (a 'cheap dress') that could be afforded by almost anyone. Since the introduction of compulsory literacy by the Education Act of 1870, reactionary organizations such as the National Vigilance Association (NVA) had regarded Zola in English as a threat to the morals of the lower orders, Board School pupils, and shopgirls into whose hands his 'disgusting' literature might fall. As one newspaper put it: 'We have now to face an agent of moral corruption, no longer confined to persons willing and ready to be corrupted, but obtruding itself on everybody.'[5]

In October 1888, in a prosecution sponsored by the NVA, Henry Vizetelly was put on trial at the Old Bailey in London for a translation he had commissioned of *Earth*; he was convicted of obscene libel, and fined £100.[6] In order for Vizetelly & Co. to continue selling

---

[3] Tennyson, *Locksley Hall, Sixty Years After* (1886). See Anthony Cummins, 'Émile Zola's Cheap English Dress: The Vizetelly Translations, Late-Victorian Print Culture, and the Crisis of Literary Value', *Review of English Studies*, NS 60/243 (2008), 108–32, at 111 n. 9.

[4] See Cummins, 'Émile Zola's Cheap English Dress', 108–32.

[5] 'A Censorship of Morals', *St James's Gazette* (1 November 1888), 3; quoted in Cummins. 'Emile Zola's Cheap English Dress', 111.

[6] See E. A. Vizetelly, *Émile Zola, Novelist and Reformer: An Account of His Life and Work* (London: John Lane, The Bodley Head, 1904), 262–7; King, *Garden of Zola*, 238–40.

its other Zola titles, Ernest was required to 're-expurgate' them for reissue, although his efforts were limited, for reasons of economy, to deletion and rewriting on the existing stereotype printing plates, and they quickly proved insufficient. Henry was indicted again in 1889, this time for a total of twelve translations (eight of novels by Zola, and Flaubert's *Madame Bovary* among the others), and committed for trial in relation to seven, including the re-expurgated 1889 version of *How Jolly Life Is!*.[7] The ineptitude of his defence team having left him with no other course than to plead guilty, Henry was sentenced to three months in Holloway jail and forced to liquidate his publishing house. Zola's works were now too incendiary for anything other than private publication, and it was only from late 1892, when *The Debacle* was issued by Chatto and Windus, that it became possible once more to publish popular editions in Britain, and then only with extreme caution. So when, almost a decade later, Ernest came to revise yet again, for publication with Chatto and Windus, most of Vizetelly & Co.'s Zola translations, he was mindful of the fanatical prudery that had destroyed both his father's business and his health, and his 1901 version, now titled *The Joy of Life*, contained further cuts and revisions. It is that bowdlerized translation that still has wide currency today.

Zola himself was clearly aware of the difficulties faced by his publishers abroad, and seemed happy to sanction whatever 'adaptation' was necessary to get the works into print. While he was still writing *La Joie de vivre*, for instance, he was contacted about the translation rights for the book by a Swedish publisher, Albert Bonnier, apparently raising concerns and asking to see the manuscript. On 25 September 1883, Zola replied in the negative, but offered the following reassurance:

Tell your correspondent that the work, from a moral point of view, will offer no danger. It is the most praiseworthy tale of a young girl who devotes herself to those close to her, and gives them everything, her money and her heart. In any case, should a few passages displease, the translator could cut them.[8]

While Zola may have referred lightly to the prospect of cuts being made to *La Joie de vivre*, he probably did not anticipate the extent of

[7] Vizetelly, *Émile Zola, Novelist and Reformer*, 285–6; King, *Garden of Zola*, 245–6.

[8] Zola, *Correspondance*, ed. B. H. Bakker, 10 vols. (Montreal: Presses de l'Université de Montréal; Paris: CNRS, 1978–95), iv. 414. The following day, he wrote in similar terms to an unnamed recipient: 'If you find one or two passages a little lively, you could tone them down. In fact, it is a very moral work, entirely suited to an English audience' (*Correspondance*, iv. 415).

Ernest Vizetelly's zeal. His self-censorship, edulcorating or completely suppressing large and small chunks of Zola's material, is fascinating because it presents a fine-grained picture of Victorian neuroses about sex and the body, social proprieties and 'improper' relations, and the perceived threat to Christian values posed by positivist science, especially physiology. Suppressed or sanitized elements include references to sexual desire, reproduction (including Minouche the cat's amours), Pauline's self-instruction about anatomy from the engravings in Lazare's medical books, nudity and bodily functions (especially puberty and menstruation), undressing and female undergarments, physical proximity between unmarried man and woman, references to the human body as a machine, and the sexual transgressions of the inhabitants of Bonneville. As a result, key episodes such as Pauline's sexual jealousy and contemplation of her own naked body in Chapter 8, or Lazare's erotic satiation and disappointment in Chapter 9, are deprived of most of their force, and in some places barely make sense.

Most remarkable among Vizetelly's bowdlerizations, however, is his butchery of Zola's extraordinary tour de force description of the breech birth in Chapter 10. First, his squeamishness is such as to prevent him from writing the English words 'pregnant' or 'midwife' at all: bizarrely, he uses French *enceinte* and *accoucheuse* instead—the educated reader would doubtless understand, while the 'uneducated' would just have to work it out. He also refers euphemistically, both here and earlier, when Pauline experiences her first period, to the woman's 'state of health'. In the original French, the childbirth scene extends over many pages, and Zola presents a harrowingly physical account of the pain and danger of the process, for both mother and child. Vizetelly's chapter is less than half the length of Zola's, and of around 280 sentences which describe the fraught delivery, the first hundred or so are simply omitted, while all the rest are substituted by just four English sentences of bland cliché:

It was one of those dread hours when life and death wrestle together, when human science and skill battle together to overcome and correct the errors of Nature. More than once did the Doctor pause, fearing a fatal issue. The patient's agony was terrible, but at last science triumphed, and a child was born. It was a boy.

The 1889 text had been even more succinct: 'However, after a long and agonizing period of suspense, a baby boy was born, and it was alive.'

The way Zola actually wrote this climactic moment, after a prolonged
and tense build-up, is both more realistic and more moving:

And there were several dreadful minutes, with the unfortunate woman
screaming louder than ever, as the head emerged, pushing back the flesh
into a broad whiteish ring. Down below, between the two distended, gaping
cavities the delicate skin bulged horribly, stretched so thin that it threatened to split. There was a spurt of excrement, and with a final spasm the
child slid out, in a shower of blood and foul waters.

 'At last!' said Cazenove. (p. 276)

In view of the strong plea for female education and intellectual emancipation that Zola makes in *The Bright Side of Life*, and his condem-
nation of the respectable practice of keeping girls in ignorance of the
'facts of life', it is perhaps as ironic as it is regrettable that Vizetelly's
prudish version, suppressing almost all mention of 'relations between
men and women which English books never mention' in order to ensure
it remained suitable for 'family perusal'[9] in the long-gone Victorian
era, should have remained the only widely available witness to his
novel in English to the present day. Particularly so in the disservice it
has done to readers' appreciation of the subtlety and complexity of
the character of Pauline, of her physical and psychological experiences as a woman, and her moral agency throughout the book, which,
in the words of Franzén, 'raise her far above the noble heroines of the
conventional novel of the day'.[10]

In addition to restoring Vizetelly's cuts, the present translation
provides the reader with a version of the novel in more contemporary
English. In making his proof corrections, Zola consistently pruned
superfluous elements to tighten up the style, so in contrast to the more
expansive discourse expected by Vizetelly's Victorian readership, the
maximum concision of expression consistent with fluency has been
sought throughout. In order to retain a flavour of the setting in rural
Normandy, French titles (Maman, Mademoiselle, Monsieur le Curé,
Abbé Horteur) have been retained and proper names (Mathieu the dog,
Minouche the cat) have not been anglicized, while French administrative and legal terms ('Department', 'prefect', 'placed under seal')

    [9] 'La Griffe Rose', *The Spectator* (13 September 1862), 1029–30; quoted in Cummins,
'Émile Zola's Cheap English Dress', 113.
    [10] Nils-Olof Franzén, *Zola et La* Joie de vivre: *La Genèse du roman, les personnages, les
idées* (Stockholm: Almqvist & Wiksell, 1958), 60.

have also been explained in notes rather than paraphrased into approximate English equivalents. Some sense of historical distance is conveyed by the retention of specific names for archaic realia (types of carriage, the small 'sou' coin, the 'league' as a measure of distance), explained in notes as necessary, and no attempt has been made to undate Zola's pre-Freudian psychological vocabulary of nervous lesions and neuroses. Finally, the gap between the 'correct' speech of the middle-class characters and that of Véronique and the village children is approximately replicated by the use of non-standard patterns of spoken English.

I am most grateful to Judith Luna, who originally commissioned the present project, for her detailed and authoritative scrutiny of the manuscript as it progressed. The translation gained many of its more creative and fluent touches, and lost some significant errors, thanks to her perceptive intervention.

SELECT BIBLIOGRAPHY

The Bright Side of Life (*La Joie de vivre*) was initially serialized in sixty-six episodes in *Le Gil Blas* between 29 November 1883 and 3 February 1884, before being issued in book form by the Librairie Charpentier in Paris in February 1884. It is included in volume iii of Henri Mitterand's definitive scholarly edition of *Les Rougon-Macquart* in the 'Bibliothèque de la Pléiade' (Paris: Gallimard, 1964; 2nd edn. 1981). Paperback editions exist in the following popular collections: Folio, ed. Henri Mitterand, preface by Jean Borie (Paris: Gallimard, 1985); GF-Flammarion, ed. Colette Becker (Paris: Flammarion, 1990); Livre de Poche, ed. Philippe Hamon, preface by Yves Berger (Paris: Librairie Générale Française, 1985); Omnibus, ed. Julia Hung (Paris: Omnibus, 2013); Pocket Classiques, ed. Gérard Gengembre (Paris: Presses-Pocket, 1999). The novel was adapted into a critically acclaimed French television film (directed by Jean-Pierre Améris and starring Anaïs Demoustier as Pauline and Swann Arlaud as Lazare), broadcast on France 2 on 5 October 2011.

Studies on Zola, Naturalism, and The Bright Side of Life *in English*

Baguley, David (ed.), *Critical Essays on Émile Zola* (Boston: G. K. Hall, 1986).

Baguley, David, *Naturalist Fiction: The Entropic Vision* (Cambridge: Cambridge University Press, 1990).

Brown, Frederick, *Zola: A Life* (Baltimore and London: Johns Hopkins University Press, 1996).

Cummins, Anthony, 'Émile Zola's Cheap English Dress: The Vizetelly Translations, Late-Victorian Print Culture, and the Crisis of Literary Value', *Review of English Studies*, NS 60/243 (2008), 108–32.

Finch, Alison, '*Joie de vivre*: The Afterlife of a Phrase', in S. Harrow and T. Unwin (eds.), Joie de vivre *in French Literature and Culture: Essays in Honour of Michael Freeman* (Amsterdam and New York: Rodopi, 2009), 299–311.

Harrow, Susan, *Zola, The Body Modern: Pressures and Prospects of Representation* (London: Legenda, 2010).

Harrow, Susan, 'Zola: Colorist, Abstractionist', *Romanic Review* 102/3–4 (2011), 465–84.

Hemmings, F. W. J., *Émile Zola* (2nd edn., Oxford: Oxford University Press, 1966).

Jones, Derek (ed.), *Censorship: A World Encyclopedia* (London: Fitzroy Dearborn, 2001).

King, Graham, *Garden of Zola: Émile Zola and His Novels for English Readers* (London: Barrie and Jenkins, 1978).

Lethbridge, Robert, 'Zola and Contemporary Painting', in Nelson (ed.), *Cambridge Companion to Zola*, 67–85.

Lethbridge, Robert, and Terry Keefe (eds.), *Zola and the Craft of Fiction* (Leicester: Leicester University Press, 1990).

Nelson, Brian (ed.), *The Cambridge Companion to Émile Zola* (Cambridge: Cambridge University Press, 2007).

Pierre-Gnassounou, Chantal, 'Zola and the Art of Fiction', trans. Mark McCann and Brian Nelson, in Nelson (ed.), *Cambridge Companion to Zola*, 86–104.

Richardson, Joanne, *Zola* (London: Weidenfeld & Nicolson 1978)

Schom, Alan, *Émile Zola: A Bourgeois Rebel* (London: MacDonald, 1987).

Schor, Naomi, 'Mother's Day: Zola's Women', in Baguley (ed.), *Critical Essays on Zola*, 130–42.

Vizetelly, E. A, 'Some Recollections of Émile Zola', *Pall Mall Magazine*, 29 (1903), 63.

Vizetelly, E. A., *Émile Zola, Novelist and Reformer: An Account of His Life and Work* (London: John Lane, the Bodley Head, 1904).

Walker, Phillip, *Zola* (London: Routledge and Kegan Paul, 1985).

Wilson, Angus, *Émile Zola* (New York: William Morrow, 1952).

A CHRONOLOGY OF ÉMILE ZOLA

1840   (2 April) Born in Paris, the only child of Francesco Zola (b. 1795), an Italian engineer, and Émilie, née Aubert (b. 1819), the daughter of a glazier. The naturalist novelist was later proud that 'zolla' in Italian means 'clod of earth'

1843   Family moves to Aix-en-Provence

1847   (27 March) Death of father from pneumonia following a chill caught while supervising work on his scheme to supply Aix-en-Provence with drinking water

1852–8 Boarder at the Collège Bourbon at Aix. Friendship with Baptistin Baille and Paul Cézanne. Zola, not Cézanne, wins the school prize for drawing

1858   (February) Leaves Aix to settle in Paris with his mother (who had preceded him in December). Offered a place and bursary at the Lycée Saint-Louis. (November) Falls ill with 'brain fever' (typhoid) and convalescence is slow

1859   Fails his *baccalauréat* twice

1860   (Spring) Is found employment as a copy-clerk but abandons it after two months, preferring to eke out an existence as an impecunious writer in the Latin Quarter of Paris

1861   Cézanne follows Zola to Paris, where he meets Camille Pissarro, fails the entrance examination to the École des Beaux-Arts, and returns to Aix in September

1862   (February) Taken on by Hachette, the well-known publishing house, at first in the dispatch office and subsequently as head of the publicity department. (31 October) Naturalized as a French citizen. Cézanne returns to Paris and stays with Zola

1863   (31 January) First literary article published. (1 May) Manet's *Déjeuner sur l'herbe* exhibited at the Salon des Refusés, which Zola visits with Cézanne

1864   (October) *Tales for Ninon*

1865   *Claude's Confession*. A *succès de scandale* thanks to its bedroom scenes. Meets future wife Alexandrine-Gabrielle Meley (b. 1839), the illegitimate daughter of teenage parents who soon separated; Alexandrine's mother died in September 1849

1866   Resigns his position at Hachette (salary: 200 francs a month) and
       becomes a literary critic on the recently launched daily *L'Événement*
       (salary: 500 francs a month). Self-styled 'humble disciple' of Hippolyte
       Taine. Writes a series of provocative articles condemning the official
       Salon Selection Committee, expressing reservations about Courbet,
       and praising Manet and Monet. Begins to frequent the Café Guerbois
       in the Batignolles quarter of Paris, the meeting-place of the future
       Impressionists. Antoine Guillemet takes Zola to meet Manet.
       Summer months spent with Cézanne at Bennecourt on the Seine.
       (15 November) *L'Événement* suppressed by the authorities

1867   (November) *Thérèse Raquin*

1868   (April) Preface to second edition of *Thérèse Raquin*. (May) Manet's
       portrait of Zola exhibited at the Salon. (December) *Madeleine Férat*.
       Begins to plan for the Rougon-Macquart series of novels

1868–70 Working as journalist for a number of different newspapers

1870   (31 May) Marries Alexandrine in a registry office. (September)
       Moves temporarily to Marseilles because of the Franco-Prussian War

1871   Political reporter for *La Cloche* (in Paris) and *Le Sémaphore de
       Marseille*. (March) Returns to Paris. (October) Publishes *The Fortune
       of the Rougons*, the first of the twenty novels making up the Rougon-
       Macquart series

1872   *The Kill*

1873   (April) *The Belly of Paris*

1874   (May) *The Conquest of Plassans*. First independent Impressionist
       exhibition. (November) *Further Tales for Ninon*

1875   Begins to contribute articles to the Russian newspaper *Vestnik Evropy*
       (*European Herald*). (April) *The Sin of Abbé Mouret*

1876   (February) *His Excellency Eugène Rougon*. Second Impressionist
       exhibition

1877   (February) *L'Assommoir*

1878   Buys a house at Médan on the Seine, 40 kilometres west of Paris.
       (June) *A Page of Love*

1880   (March) *Nana*. (May) *Les Soirées de Médan* (an anthology of short
       stories by Zola and some of his naturalist 'disciples', including Mau-
       passant). (8 May) Death of Flaubert. (September) First of a series of
       articles for *Le Figaro*. (17 October) Death of his mother. (December)
       The Experimental Novel

1882   (April) *Pot Luck* (*Pot-Bouille*). (3 September) Death of Turgenev

1883 (13 February) Death of Wagner. (March) *The Ladies' Paradise* (*Au Bonheur des Dames*). (30 April) Death of Manet

1884 (March) *The Bright Side of Life* (*La joie de vivre*). Preface to catalogue of Manet exhibition

1885 (March) *Germinal.* (12 May) Begins writing *The Masterpiece* (*L'Œuvre*). (22 May) Death of Victor Hugo. (23 December) First instalment of *The Masterpiece* appears in *Le Gil Blas*

1886 (27 March) Final instalment of *The Masterpiece*, which is published in book form in April

1887 (18 August) Denounced as an onanistic pornographer in the *Manifesto of the Five* in *Le Figaro*. (November) *Earth*

1888 (October) *The Dream*. Jeanne Rozerot becomes his mistress

1889 (20 September) Birth of Denise, daughter of Zola and Jeanne

1890 (March) *The Beast in Man*

1891 (March) *Money*. (April) Elected President of the Société des Gens de Lettres. (25 September) Birth of Jacques, son of Zola and Jeanne

1892 (June) *La Débâcle*

1893 (July) *Doctor Pascal*, the last of the Rougon-Macquart novels. Fêted on visit to London

1894 (August) *Lourdes*, the first novel of the trilogy *Three Cities*. (22 December) Dreyfus found guilty by a court martial

1896 (May) *Rome*

1898 (13 January) 'J'accuse', his article in defence of Dreyfus, published in *L'Aurore*. (21 February) Found guilty of libelling the Minister of War and given the maximum sentence of one year's imprisonment and a fine of 3,000 francs. Appeal for retrial granted on a technicality. (March) *Paris*. (23 May) Retrial delayed. (18 July) Leaves for England instead of attending court

1899 (4 June) Returns to France. (October) *Fecundity*, the first of his *Four Gospels*

1901 (May) *Toil*, the second 'Gospel'

1902 (29 September) Dies of fumes from his bedroom fire, the chimney having been capped either by accident or anti-Dreyfusard design. Wife survives. (5 October) Public funeral

1903 (March) *Truth*, the third 'Gospel', published posthumously. *Justice* was to be the fourth

1908 (4 June) Remains transferred to the Panthéon

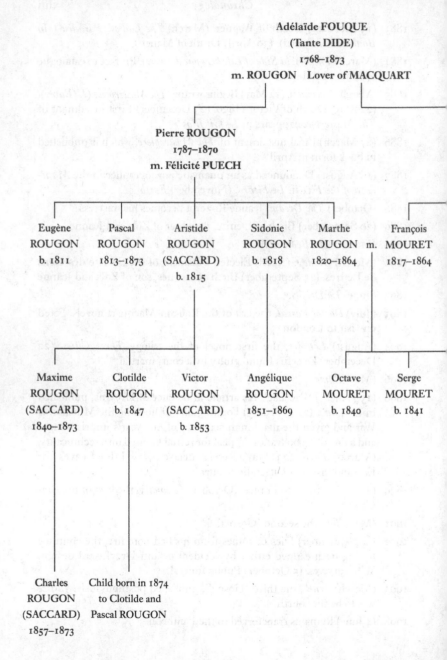

Adélaïde FOUQUE
(Tante DIDE)
1768–1873
m. ROUGON   Lover of MACQUART

Pierre ROUGON
1787–1870
m. Félicité PUECH

| Eugène ROUGON b. 1811 | Pascal ROUGON 1813–1873 | Aristide ROUGON (SACCARD) b. 1815 | Sidonie ROUGON b. 1818 | Marthe ROUGON 1820–1864 m. | François MOURET 1817–1864 |

| Maxime ROUGON (SACCARD) 1840–1873 | Clotilde ROUGON b. 1847 | Victor ROUGON (SACCARD) b. 1853 | Angélique ROUGON 1851–1869 | Octave MOURET b. 1840 | Serge MOURET b. 1841 |

Charles ROUGON (SACCARD) 1857–1873

Child born in 1874 to Clotilde and Pascal ROUGON

FAMILY TREE OF THE ROUGON-MACQUART

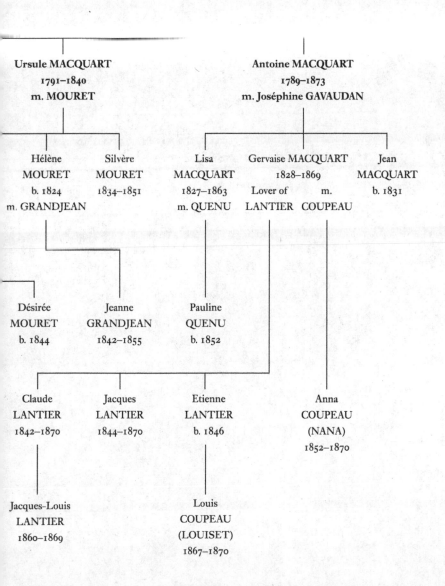

Ursule MACQUART
1791–1840
m. MOURET

Antoine MACQUART
1789–1873
m. Joséphine GAVAUDAN

Hélène
MOURET
b. 1824
m. GRANDJEAN

Silvère
MOURET
1834–1851

Lisa
MACQUART
1827–1863
m. QUENU

Gervaise MACQUART
1828–1869
Lover of   m.
LANTIER COUPEAU

Jean
MACQUART
b. 1831

Désirée
MOURET
b. 1844

Jeanne
GRANDJEAN
1842–1855

Pauline
QUENU
b. 1852

Claude
LANTIER
1842–1870

Jacques
LANTIER
1844–1870

Etienne
LANTIER
b. 1846

Anna
COUPEAU
(NANA)
1852–1870

Jacques-Louis
LANTIER
1860–1869

Louis
COUPEAU
(LOUISET)
1867–1870

THE BRIGHT SIDE OF LIFE

CHAPTER 1

WHEN the cuckoo clock in the dining room struck six, Chanteau gave up all hope. He lowered himself painfully out of the armchair where he had been warming his gouty legs in front of the coke fire. For the past two hours, he had been waiting for Madame Chanteau who, after a five-week absence, was bringing home from Paris that very day their little cousin Pauline Quenu, a ten-year-old orphan to whom they had agreed to act as guardians.

'I can't understand it, Véronique,' he said as he opened the door to the kitchen, 'Something must have happened to them.'

The maid, a tall woman of thirty-five with a man's hands and the face of a gendarme, was busy removing from the fire a leg of mutton which was in danger of being overdone. She uttered no words of reproach, but the rough skin of her cheeks blanched with annoyance.

'Madame will have stayed on in Paris,' she said curtly. 'What with all this endless carry-on, that's been upsetting the whole household!'

'No, no,' explained Chanteau, 'yesterday evening's telegram said that the little girl's affairs had all been sorted out... Madame was going to arrive in Caen* this morning and call on Davoine. At one o'clock she'd be getting back on the train, at two she'd have got off in Bayeux,* at three, old Malivoire's berline* would have dropped her at Arromanches,* and even if Malivoire had taken his time getting it hitched up, Madame should have been here by four, four-thirty at the latest... It's not above ten kilometres from Arromanches to Bonneville.'*

With her gaze fixed on the joint, the cook listened to all these calculations and nodded. After a moment's hesitation, Chanteau added:

'You'd better walk as far as the bend and take a look, Véronique.'

She looked at him, even paler with pent-up anger.

'Me? Why on earth?... Since Monsieur Lazare is already splashing around out there looking for them, there's no point me getting all muddy too.'

'It's just', Chanteau murmured softly, 'that I'm starting to worry about my son... There's no sign of him either. What can he have been doing out on the road for the last hour?'

So, without saying another word, Véronique grabbed her old black woollen shawl off its nail and wrapped it round her head and shoulders.

Then, seeing that her master was following her into the hall, she snapped at him:

'For goodness' sake go back to your fire, if you don't want to be bawling all day tomorrow with your aches and pains.'

Slamming the front door behind her, she stood at the top of the steps, slipped into her clogs and shouted out into the gale:

'God help us, all this bother for a snotty-nosed brat!'

Chanteau was unmoved. He was used to the maid's violent outbursts; she had entered his service at fifteen, in the very year of his marriage. Once he could no longer hear the clumping of her clogs, he slipped away like a schoolboy on holiday, to post himself at the far end of the passage, in front of a glazed door which looked out over the sea. There he stood, short and paunchy, rather red in the face, staring dreamily out at the sky through big blue eyes which bulged beneath the snowy skullcap of his close-cropped hair. He was barely fifty-six, but the attacks of gout that afflicted him had made him old before his time. Distracted from his worries, his gaze lost in the distance, he mused that little Pauline would win Véronique over in the end.

Anyway, was it his fault? When that Parisian notary had written to inform him that his cousin Quenu* had died, just six months after his wife, and had entrusted him in his will with the guardianship of his daughter, he had not felt able to refuse. It was true they hadn't seen much of each other, as the family was scattered. Years before, Chanteau's father had set up a business in Caen dealing in wood from the Nord,* after leaving the south of France and criss-crossing the country working as a carpenter's labourer; while the young Quenu, on the death of his mother, had gone up to Paris, where another of his uncles had later made over to him a substantial *charcuterie** in the heart of Les Halles.* They had only met on two or three subsequent occasions, when the pain of his gout had forced Chanteau to abandon his own business and travel to Paris to consult the top specialists. However, the two respected each other, and the dying man had perhaps imagined for his daughter a life in the healthy sea air. In any event, since she had inherited the *charcuterie*, she would be far from a financial burden. Madame Chanteau's agreement had in the end been so enthusiastic that she had wanted to spare her husband the dangerous fatigue of a journey to Paris, and so she had gone off alone, traipsing around tirelessly and busying herself with all the arrangements. Chanteau's only concern was that his wife should be happy.

But what could be keeping the two of them? His fears returned as he stared at the leaden sky across which the west wind was driving great black clouds, like sooty rags trailing their tatters in the distant sea. It was one of those March storms which furiously batter the coast with huge spring tides. The sea was just starting to come in, still only showing as a thin white band of spume against the distant horizon; and the beach, so expansively exposed that day, a barren league of dark seaweed and rocks, pocked with mournful pools, wore an awful air of melancholy in the gathering gloom that descended from the clouds in their fearful flight.

'Perhaps the wind has blown them over into a ditch?' murmured Chanteau.

He was overcome by the urge to see for himself. He opened the glass door and ventured out in his slippers onto the gravelled terrace, which looked down over the village. A few drops of wind-lashed rain stung his face, and a violent gust tugged at his blue jacket of coarse woollen cloth. But he battled on, bareheaded, hunched up against the wind, until he could lean on the balustrade and look down onto the road below. This road plunged into a cleft between two cliffs, looking as if the rock had been split by a giant axe-blow, and down this rift had washed the few square metres of soil on which the twenty-five to thirty hovels of Bonneville were perched. Each tide seemed bound to wash them from their narrow bed of pebbles and smash them against the cliff face. To the left lay a small beaching harbour, a sandbank onto which men were hauling up a dozen boats, with rhythmic shouts. There, fewer than two hundred souls eked out a desperately poor living from the sea, clinging to their rock with the stupid obstinacy of molluscs. Above the miserable roofs which the waves stove in every winter, part-way up the cliff, there could be seen only the church to the right and the Chanteaus' house to the left, separated by the ravine of the road. That was the entirety of Bonneville.

'Dreadful weather, eh?' a voice called out.

Looking up, Chanteau recognized the curé, Abbé Horteur, a thickset man with a peasant's neck, whose five decades had yet to streak his red hair with grey. In front of the church, within the cemetery, the priest had set aside a vegetable patch for himself, and he was standing there looking at his early lettuces, squeezing his cassock between his knees to stop the gale from blowing it over his head. Chanteau, unable to make himself heard above the wind, had to be content with a wave of his hand.

'I think they're not wrong to be getting the boats out,' shouted the priest at the top of his voice. 'Come ten o'clock, they'd be dancing a merry dance.'

Then, as a violent gust did finally make his cassock into a hat, he fled behind the church.

Chanteau had turned away, bracing his shoulders against the blast. With streaming eyes, he glanced at his salt-scorched garden and the brick wall of his two-storey house with its double row of five windows, the shutters in danger of being ripped from their fastenings. Once the gust had passed, he leaned out to look up the road again, but Véronique was already coming back, gesticulating.

'Monsieur, whatever are you doing outside? Will you go back indoors at once!'

She caught up with him in the passage and scolded him like a naughty child. When he was in agony again tomorrow, she was the one who'd have to look after him, wasn't she?

'Didn't you see them?' he asked meekly.

'Of course not... Madame will obviously be taking shelter somewhere.'

He did not dare tell her she should have gone further. Now he was most anxious about his absent son.

'What I did see', continued the maid, 'is that the whole place is in a terrible state. People are scared it will be the death of them this time... Only last September, the Cuches' house was cracked from top to bottom, and just now, on his way up to ring the Angelus,* Prouane told me it would surely be down by the morning.'

Just at that moment a tall young man of nineteen came bounding up the three front steps. He was broad-browed, with very clear eyes and wisps of brown beard framing his long face.

'Ah! very good, here's Lazare!' said Chanteau with relief. 'You're drenched, my poor lad!'

The young man was hanging up his sailor's jacket, soaked by the deluge, in the hall.

'Well?' his father asked again.

'Well, there was no sign of them!' replied Lazare. 'I went as far as Verchemont* and took shelter in the shed at the inn, keeping an eye on the road, which is a complete sea of mud. Nobody! Then I was afraid you'd be worrying, so I came back.'

He had left the *lycée* in Caen that August after taking his baccalaureat exams, and for the last eight months had been roaming the cliffs, unable to settle on a profession, passionate only about music, much to the despair of his mother. She had set off annoyed with him for refusing to accompany her to Paris, where she dreamt of finding him a position. The whole household was going to the dogs, in an atmosphere of unintentional rancour, such as is to often the case together at close quarters.

'Now that I've put you in the picture,' the young man continued, 'I've a good mind to push on to Arromanches.'

'No, no, it's getting dark,' exclaimed Chanteau. 'Surely your mother won't leave us without news! She's bound to send a telegram... Listen! Isn't that a carriage?'

Véronique had opened the door again.

'It's Doctor Cazenove's cabriolet,'* she announced. 'Were you expecting him, Monsieur? Goodness gracious! It's Madame!'

All three rushed down the steps. A huge mountain dog, a Newfoundland cross, which had been sleeping in a corner of the hall, shot out as well, barking furiously. The noise also brought into the doorway a small white cat of delicate demeanour, but at the sight of the muddy courtyard, she flicked her tail in disgust and sat down primly at the top of the steps, to observe.

Meanwhile, a lady of around fifty had jumped down from the carriage with the agility of a young girl. She was small and thin, with hair that was still jet black and a face that would have been pleasant, were it not for the large nose, eloquent of an ambitious nature. The dog bounded up and put its great paws on her shoulders to lick her face, which annoyed her.

'Down, Mathieu, down, that's quite enough! Will you get down, you great lump!'

Lazare followed the dog across the yard, calling out as he went:

'Is everything all right, Maman?'

'Yes, yes,' replied Madame Chanteau.

'Goodness gracious, we were worried sick,' said the father, who had followed his son out, despite the wind. 'Whatever happened?'

'Oh, we had problems the whole way,' she replied. 'First, the roads are in such a dreadful state, it took us nearly two hours to get from Bayeux. Then at Arromanches one of Malivoire's horses went lame and he didn't have another one, so I could see us having to spend the night at his house... In the end, the doctor was kind enough to lend us his cab, and brave Martin here has driven us...'

The coachman was an old man with a wooden leg, an ex-sailor whose amputation had been performed by Cazenove when he was a naval surgeon, and had subsequently remained in his service. He was busy tethering the horse. Madame Chanteau interrupted herself to say to him:

'Martin, do please help the little girl down.'

Nobody had yet given any thought to the child. As the cabriolet's hood came down very low, all that could be seen of her was her mourning dress and little black-gloved hands. In any event, without waiting for the driver's help, she jumped lightly down in her turn. A gust of wind made her clothes flap and sent curls of her light brown hair flying up from beneath her crêpe-trimmed hat. She was big for a ten-year-old, and had full lips and a broad white face, the pale look common to all Parisian girls who are brought up living behind the shop. They all stared at her. Véronique, who had been hastening across to greet her mistress, stopped short and stood to one side, with an icy, jealousy expression on her face. But Mathieu showed no such reserve, launching himself into the child's arms and licking her face.

'Don't be afraid!' called out Madame Chanteau, 'he won't hurt you.'

'Oh! I'm not afraid,' replied Pauline softly, 'I like dogs.'

And indeed, she remained quite calm despite Mathieu's boisterous greeting. Her serious little face, framed in mourning black, broke into a smile and she smacked a kiss on the Newfoundland's great muzzle.

'What about the people, aren't you going to kiss them too?' continued Madame Chanteau. 'Here, this is your uncle, since you call me Auntie... And this tall rascal's your cousin, he's not nearly so well behaved as you.'

The child was not in the least bit bashful. She pecked everyone on the cheek, finding a few words for each, with the grace of a young Parisienne already well schooled in manners.

'I am most grateful to you, Uncle, for having me to live with you... Cousin, I'm sure we will get along very well...'

'What a sweet child!' exclaimed Chanteau in delight.

Lazare looked at her in surprise, for he had imagined her as more of a timid, awkward little girl.

'Oh yes, sweet indeed,' replied the older lady, 'and brave too, you've no idea!... In the carriage, we had the wind full in our faces, blinding us with spray. The hood was flapping like a sail, and time and again I thought it was going to be ripped off. Well, young Pauline here thought it was all great fun... But why are we all standing around like this? There's no point in getting even wetter, here comes the rain again.'

She looked round for Véronique. Seeing her standing aloof with a sour expression on her face, she said in ironic tones:

'Good evening, my girl, and how are we today? If you're not going to ask after me, perhaps you could go down to the cellar and fetch up a bottle for Martin? We had to leave our trunks, but Malivoire will bring them along first thing in the morning...'

She suddenly stopped and rushed over to the cabriolet in alarm.

'Where's my bag? Oh, thank goodness, I was scared it might have fallen out on the road.'

It was a large black leather bag, grey with wear at the corners, which she refused to entrust to her son. At last they were on their way indoors when a fresh blast of wind made them halt, fighting for breath, just before the entrance. The cat, sitting there with a quizzical air, looked on as they battled against the gale, and Madame Chanteau enquired whether Minouche had behaved herself in her absence. The name Minouche brought another smile to Pauline's serious little face. She bent down to stroke the cat, which immediately rubbed itself up against her skirts, with its tail up. Seeing the family finally climbing the steps and reaching the shelter of the hall, Mathieu had resumed his loud barking, in solemn celebration of their return.

'Oh, it's so nice to be home,' said Madame Chanteau. 'I was beginning to think we would never get here... Yes, Mathieu, you are a good doggy, but do shut up. Please stop him barking, Lazare, he's deafening me!'

However, the dog would not desist, and the Chanteaus' entry into their dining room was accompanied by his joyous serenade. They ushered Pauline, the new daughter of the house, along in front of them, followed by Mathieu, still barking, with Minouche tagging along behind, her sensitive fur bristling at the din.

In the kitchen, Martin had already downed two glasses of wine, and he now left, his wooden leg tapping across the tiled floor, calling out goodnight to all. Véronique had just put her mutton joint back on the fire, as it had gone cold. She looked round the door and asked:

'Will you be taking dinner now?'

'Indeed, we will,' said Chanteau, 'it's seven o'clock. Just be a good girl and wait until Madame and the little one have got changed.'

'But I haven't got Pauline's trunk,' Madame Chanteau pointed out. 'It was fortunate we didn't get soaked through to the skin... Take off your coat and hat, my sweet. There, take her things, Véronique... And help her off with her boots, won't you? I've got slippers for her.'

The maid had to kneel before the child, who had sat down. Meanwhile, Madame Chanteau had taken from her bag a pair of little felt slippers which she put on the girl's feet herself. Then she held out her own boots for Véronique to remove, dived once more into the bag and pulled out her slippers.

'Shall I serve?' asked Véronique again.

'Just a minute... Pauline, come into the kitchen and wash your hands and splash your face... We're starving, we can have a proper clean-up later.'

Pauline was the first to reappear, leaving her aunt bending over a basin of water. Chanteau had resumed his position in front of the fire, sunk in his great yellow-velvet armchair, and was rubbing his legs mechanically for fear of an imminent attack of gout, while Lazare stood cutting bread at the table, where four places had been set for the past hour and more. The two men smiled rather awkwardly at the child, unable to find anything to say. She was calmly inspecting the room and its walnut furniture, her gaze moving from the sideboard and half-dozen chairs to the hanging lamp of polished brass, and dwelling particularly on five framed lithographs, the *Four Seasons* and a *View of Mount Vesuvius*, which stood out against the brown wall-paper. No doubt the faux oak panelling, with its plaster showing through where the paint had flaked off, the parquet floor covered in ancient greasy stains, and the general untidiness of this shared family room, made her homesick for the marbled *charcuterie* she had left behind the previous day, for her eyes grew sad and she seemed for a moment to sense the bad blood lurking behind the jovial facade of this unfamiliar environment. Finally, after lingering for a while on a very old barometer in a gilded wooden case, her gaze settled on a strange construction which took up the whole mantelpiece, lying in a glass case with thin strips of blue paper glued along its edges. It looked like a toy, a miniature wooden bridge, but one of extraordinarily complex design.

'That was built by your great-uncle,' explained Chanteau, pleased to have found a topic of conversation. 'Yes, my father started out in life as a carpenter... I've always kept his masterpiece.'

He was not ashamed of his origins, and Madame Chanteau put up with the bridge on the fireplace, despite the irritation of this cumbersome curiosity reminding her that she had married the son of a manual worker. But already the little girl was not listening to her uncle: through the window, its muslin curtains tied back with cotton loops, she had glimpsed the vast horizon, and she strode briskly across the room and stood there looking out. Since leaving Paris, she had been constantly obsessed by the idea of the sea. She was dreaming about it, asking her aunt endless questions in the train and wondering aloud, every time she saw a small rise in the landscape, whether the sea lay beyond those mountains. At last, on the beach at Arromanches, she had stood there speechless and wide-eyed, her heart swelling with a deep sigh; then, from Arromanches to Bonneville, she had kept poking her head out of the cabriolet, despite the wind, to look at the sea which accompanied them along their way. And now here was the sea again, it would always be there, like something that belonged to her. Slowly, with a sweeping gaze, she seemed to be making it her own.

Darkness was falling from the leaden sky, the galloping clouds whipped along by gusting squalls. Nothing could be made out now amid the chaos of the gathering gloom except the pale margin of the rising tide. It was an ever-widening band of white foam, an endless succession of sheets of water sweeping across the expanses of seaweed and submerging the rocky slabs in its gently gliding approach, like a caressing hand. But in the distance the roar of the waves was swelling, enormous breakers were rearing up, and at the foot of the cliffs a deathly gloom weighed on deserted Bonneville, its inhabitants taking refuge indoors while their boats, abandoned above the shingle, lay like the washed-up carcases of giant fish. The rain blanketed the village in a blurring mist, and only the church still stood out clearly against a pale patch of sky between the clouds.

Pauline stood in silence. Her little heart swelled once more and, choking with emotion, she let out a long sigh which seemed to expel all the breath from her body.

'It's a bit wider than the Seine, isn't it?' said Lazare, coming to stand behind her.

The little girl was a continual surprise to him, and since her arrival he had felt shy like an awkward schoolboy.

'Oh yes!' she murmured quietly, without turning her head.

He was about to call her *tu*,* but checked himself. 'Doesn't it make you afraid?'

She looked at him in astonishment.

'No, why?... The waves won't ever come up as far as this, will they?'

'Well, you never can tell,' he said, yielding to an urge to tease her. 'Sometimes they break right over the church!'

But she burst out laughing. Her serious little person was overcome by loud, healthy merriment, the joy of a rational being amused by nonsense. And she called him *tu* first, as she playfully took hold of his hand: 'Oh, Cousin, you must think me very silly! Would you still be here if the sea really came up over the church?'

Lazare laughed in his turn and clasped the child's hands; they were now firm allies. At that very moment, in the middle of their laughter, Madame Chanteau returned. She seemed very pleased and said, as she dried her hands:

'I see you have made friends... I was sure you would get on.'

'Shall I dish up now, Madame?' interrupted Véronique from the kitchen doorway.

'Yes, all right my girl... But first you'd better light the lamp,* we can't see a thing in here.'

Night was indeed falling so quickly that the dining room was now dark except for the red glow of the fire. This made for further delay. Finally, the maid lowered the lamp and the laid table appeared in the bright pool of light. Everyone was sitting down, Pauline between her uncle and cousin and opposite her aunt, when Madame Chanteau jumped up again with the alacrity of a skinny old woman unable to keep still.

'Where's my bag?... Just a moment, my sweet, I'll get you your beaker... Take the glass away Véronique, the child is used to her beaker.'

She took out a slightly battered silver beaker* which she wiped with her napkin, and set it down in front of Pauline. Then she put her bag away on a chair behind her. The maid ladled out the vermicelli soup, sullenly warning them that it was very overcooked. Nobody dared complain, they were all too hungry, slurping it up from their spoons. Next came the boiled beef. Chanteau, glutton that he was, barely touched it, holding himself in reserve for the leg of mutton. But when this appeared on the table, there was general consternation. It was as dry as leather; nobody could eat that.

'No need to tell me,' said Véronique calmly, 'you should've got a move on!'

Pauline was cheerfully sawing her meat up into small pieces and eating it anyway. As for Lazare, he was never aware of what was on his plate, and would have devoured slices of bread as if they had been chicken breasts. Chanteau, however, stared balefully at the roast.

'And to go with it, Véronique, what have you got?'

'Sautéed potatoes, Monsieur.'

With a demoralising gesture, he slumped back in his armchair. The maid went on:

'If Monsieur wishes me to bring back the beef?'

But he declined with a gloomy shake of the head. Might as well eat bread as boiled beef! Good Lord, what a dinner! And the weather, too, was against him, for it meant there was not even any fish! Madame Chanteau, a very small eater, looked pityingly at him.

'My poor man,' she said suddenly, 'I really feel for you... I've a present that was meant to be for tomorrow, but since we're on starvation rations this evening...'

She had reopened her bag and was taking out a terrine of foie gras. Chanteau's eyes lit up. Foie gras was forbidden fruit, a delicacy he adored, but absolutely prohibited by his doctor.

'I'm only letting you have enough for one piece of bread, you know,' continued his wife. 'Be reasonable, or next time you won't get any at all.'

He had grabbed the terrine and started helping himself with trembling fingers. He was often riven with terrible conflicts between his dread of a fresh attack of gout and his fierce gluttony, and it was gluttony that almost always won the day. Food was just too nice, and if it left him writhing in pain afterwards, so be it!

After watching him chop himself a big hunk of bread, Véronique went back to her kitchen, muttering:

'Hah, we'll see how Monsieur bawls tomorrow!'

This word always came naturally to her lips and was accepted by her employers because she said it in such a matter-of-fact way. Monsieur did indeed bawl whenever he had an attack, and the expression was so appropriate, it never occurred to them to remind her of her place.

The dinner ended with much good humour. As a joke, Lazare snatched the terrine from his father's grasp. But when the cheese came round, a Pont-l'Évêque* with biscuits, the greatest amusement was caused by Mathieu's sudden reappearance. Until then he had been asleep somewhere under the table. He had been roused by the arrival of the biscuits, which he seemed to smell in his sleep, and every evening, at that exact point in proceedings, he would shake himself and do his rounds, gazing soulfully up at each diner in turn. Lazare was usually the first to give in to his dumb entreaties, but this evening, on his second round of the table, Mathieu fixed his gentle, human eyes on Pauline and, detecting in her a great friend of people and animals, rested his enormous head on her little knee, gazing up at her in tender supplication.

'Oh, look at him begging!' said Madame Chanteau. 'Gently, Mathieu, don't snatch at it like that!'

The dog had wolfed down the piece of biscuit that Pauline was offering him and, with his head on her knee again, was begging for more, still gazing up at his new-found friend. She laughed and kissed him, highly amused by his laid-back ears and the black patch round his left eye, the only mark on his long, white curly coat. But then an incident occurred: jealous Minouche jumped lightly up onto the edge of the table and, purring, her back arched, with all the grace of a young kid, started butting the child's chin with her head. It was her way of getting you to stroke her; you would feel the cold touch of her nose and the grazing of her sharp teeth, while she pushed with one front paw, then the other, like a baker boy kneading dough. Pauline sat there in raptures between the two creatures, the cat to her left, the dog to the right, monopolized and shamelessly exploited by them both, until she had shared out all her dessert between them.

'Just push them away,' said her aunt, 'or they won't leave you a crumb.'

'What does that matter?' she replied with simplicity, only too happy to let herself be exploited.

They had finished. Véronique cleared the table. The two animals, seeing there was nothing left, sloped off without any thanks, giving their lips a last lick.

Pauline got up and went over to the window, trying to peer out. Since the soup course she had been watching the window darken, gradually turning black as ink. Now it was an impenetrable wall, a mass of gloom that had swallowed everything, sky, water, village, even the church itself. Without being scared by her cousin's jokes, she strained to make out the sea, devoured by curiosity to know how far up the tide was going to come. All she could hear was the rising tumult, a groaning, monstrous voice growing more menacing by the minute amid the shrieking wind and lashing rain. Not a glimmer, not even a pale fleck of foam, could be seen in the chaotic darkness, there was just the noise of the galloping waves whipped along amid the void by the storm.

'Gracious!' said Chanteau, 'it really is coming up... And still two hours to go till high tide!'

'If the wind was directly from the north,' explained Lazare, 'I think it would be the end of Donneville. Fortunately, it's coming at us from the side.'

The small girl had turned round to listen to them, her big eyes filled with concern and compassion.

'Ha!' continued Madame Chanteau, 'we're warm and dry, others will just have to look after themselves. We all have our troubles... Pauline, my darling, would you like a nice hot cup of tea? After that, we'll go up to bed.'

Véronique had spread out across the cleared table an old red tablecloth patterned with large flowers, around which the family generally sat of an evening. They all went back to their places. Lazare, who had briefly left the room, returned with an inkpot and pen, and a bundle of papers; settling himself in the light of the lamp, he began copying out music. Madame Chanteau, who had been gazing affectionately at her son ever since her return, suddenly said to him in a very sharp tone:

'At your music again, are you? Can't you spare a single evening for us, even on the day when I come home?'

'But Maman, I'm not going anywhere, I'm staying here with you... You know this doesn't keep me from chatting. Go on, say something, and I'll reply.'

And he carried on copying, spreading his papers over half the table. Chanteau had stretched himself out luxuriously in his armchair, hands dangling limply. In front of the fire Mathieu was dozing off, while Minouche, who had leapt straight up onto the tablecloth, was giving herself a thorough clean, holding one leg up in the air and carefully licking the fur on her belly. The brass ceiling-lamp seemed to radiate a cosy intimacy, and soon Pauline, who was smiling at her new family through half-closed eyes, exhausted and nodding in the warmth, was unable to keep awake any longer. Her head slipped into the crook of her folded arm, and she dozed off in the peaceful lamplight. Her delicate eyelids were like silken veils drawn across her gaze, and small regular breaths issued from her pure lips.

'She must be dead on her feet,' said Madame Chanteau, lowering her voice. 'We'll wake her so she can drink her tea, then put her to bed.'

Then silence descended. Against the rumbling background of the storm, the only sound to be heard was the scratching of Lazare's pen. A profound peace reigned, a drowsiness born of familiar habits and life ruminated on every evening in the same place. For a long time, the father and the mother looked at each other without a word. Finally, Chanteau asked hesitantly:

'And in Caen, are Davoine's accounts looking healthy?'

She shrugged her shoulders in annoyance.

'Hardly! Didn't I warn you that you were getting into deep water?'

Now that the little girl was asleep, they could talk. They spoke in low tones, at first only intending to exchange information rapidly with each other; but their feelings soon got the better of them, and bit by bit all the problems of the household came out.

On the death of his father, the former carpenter, who had run his timber business with the reckless daring of an adventurer, Chanteau had found the firm in deep trouble. Being sedentary and routinely cautious by nature, he had been content simply to rescue the business by putting its affairs in order, and to make a modest but respectable living from the guaranteed returns. The sole element of romance in his life was his marriage to a primary school teacher whom he had met at a friend's house. Eugénie de la Vignière, the orphan child of ruined minor gentry from the Cotentin,* was intending to instil in him her own sense of ambition. But he, incompletely educated since he had only been packed off belatedly to boarding school, shrank from any major undertaking, and frustrated his wife's domineering will by his own native inertia. When they were blessed with a son, she transferred onto the child all her hopes of a great fortune, sent him to the *lycée* and gave him extra work every evening. However, a final disaster was to upset all her calculations: Chanteau, who had suffered from gout since the age of forty, ended up having such painful attacks that he talked of selling the business. This would mean a much-reduced lifestyle, gradually using up their small savings, with the child later cast out into the world without being able to rely on the first twenty thousand francs* that she had dreamed he would have.

So Madame Chanteau had insisted on at least taking charge of the sale. The business was producing some ten thousand francs of income a year, on which they lived rather expensively, because she was fond of entertaining. It was she who had discovered a certain Davoine, and hatched the following scheme: Davoine would buy the timber business for one hundred thousand francs, but would pay them only fifty thousand; by surrendering the other fifty thousand to him, the Chanteaus would remain his partners and share in the profits. This Davoine seemed a man of keen intelligence, and even if he did not succeed in making the business more profitable, it meant five thousand francs they could depend on, which, added to the three thousand in interest produced by the fifty thousand, made a yearly income of eight. They could get by on that until their son had made his way in the world, when he would lift them out of their penurious existence.

And so it was arranged. As it happened, two years earlier Chanteau had bought a house by the sea, in Bonneville, picked up at a bargain price from a customer who had gone bankrupt. Instead of selling it on, which had at one point been her intention, Madame Chanteau decided that they would retire there, at least until the start of Lazare's triumphant rise. Giving up her receptions and burying herself in a hole in the middle of nowhere was a form of suicide for her; but as the original house was going to Davoine along with the business, she would have had to rent somewhere else in any case. So she plucked up the courage to reduce their expenditure, with the firm intention of making a triumphant return to Caen once her son was in some important post there. Chanteau went along with everything. As for his gout, it would just have to put up with the seaside location, and moreover, of the three doctors he consulted, two had been obliging enough to declare that the sea breezes would be a grand tonic for his general health. So one May morning, the Chanteaus set off to settle permanently in Bonneville, leaving fourteen-year-old Lazare behind at the *lycée*.

Five years had gone by since that heroic uprooting, and the family's fortunes were now going from bad to worse. As Davoine went in for big speculative investments, he was constantly demanding fresh advances and risking the profits in new ventures, so the balance sheet was practically always in the red. In Bonneville, they were reduced to living on the three thousand francs of interest, in such reduced circumstances that they had had to sell the horse, while Véronique cultivated vegetables in the garden.

'But look here, Eugénie,' ventured Chanteau, 'if I got into deep water, it was partly your fault.'

But she would not accept any responsibility, preferring to forget that their association with Davoine had been her doing.

'What do you mean, my fault?' she replied tartly. 'Am I the sick one?... If you hadn't been ill, we might have been millionaires by now!'

Whenever his wife's bitter feelings spilled over like this, he would hang his head in shame and embarrassment that his bones should harbour the family's enemy.

'We must be patient,' he murmured. 'Davoine seems sure his next deal will come off. If the price of pine goes up, we'll make a fortune!'

'Anyway, what's the problem?' interrupted Lazare, still copying out his music. 'We still have enough to eat... You really shouldn't worry so. Personally, I couldn't care less about money!'

Madame Chanteau shrugged a second time.

'You'd do well to care a bit more about it, and stop wasting your time on that nonsense.'

To think, it was she who had taught him to play the piano! Nowadays the very sight of a piece of music exasperated her. Her last hope was crumbling: the son she had aspired to see become a prefect,* or an important judge, talked of writing operas, and she could see him in later life trudging through the muddy streets to give private lessons, as she had done.

'Anyway,' she went on, 'here's the summary for the last three months that Davoine gave me... If things carry on like this, we'll be the ones owing him money, come July.'

She had put her bag on the table and taken out a folded sheet of paper, which she held out to Chanteau. He took it reluctantly, turned it over and finally put it down in front of him without opening it. At that moment Véronique brought in the tea. A long silence descended, and the cups remained empty. Close to the sugar bowl, Minouche, her paws tucked underneath her, had closed her eyes in deep contentment, while Mathieu, lying in front of the fire, was snoring like a man. And the voice of the sea continued to strengthen outside, a formidable bass rumble to accompany the peaceful little sounds of this drowsy interior.

'Perhaps you should wake her up, Maman?' said Lazare. 'She can't be comfortable, sleeping like that.'

'Yes, yes,' muttered Madame Chanteau absently, staring at Pauline.

They all three looked at the slumbering child. Her breathing had become even quieter, her pale cheeks and rosy lips had the still softness of a bouquet of flowers in the lamplight. Only her long brown hair, tousled by the wind, cast a shadow on her delicate forehead. Madame Chanteau's thoughts turned back to Paris, and all the difficulties she had just encountered; she was astonished by her own enthusiasm for taking on this guardianship, but moved by an instinctive regard for a wealthy ward, in strictest honour, and with no ulterior motive concerning the fortune which she would hold in trust.

'When I first went into the shop,' she slowly began to explain, 'she was wearing her black frock, and she came up to kiss me on the cheek, sobbing her little heart out... A very fine shop too, a *charcuterie*, marble and mirrors everywhere, just across from Les Halles... And there I found a servant girl, knee-high to a grasshopper, fresh and pink, who had informed the notary, had had everything placed under seal,* and was calmly carrying on selling black pudding and sausages... This Adèle told me how our poor cousin Quenu had died. Ever since he had lost his wife Lisa, six months before, he had been feeling his blood was congested; he kept putting his hand up to his throat as if he were undoing his tie; until one evening they found him face down in a bowl of dripping, looking quite purple... His uncle Gradelle went the same way.'

She stopped speaking and a new silence fell. A dreamy smile passed fleetingly over Pauline's sleeping face. 'And my mandate, did that work out all right?' asked Chanteau.

'Yes, that was fine... But your lawyer was quite right to leave the name of the proxy blank, for as it turns out, I couldn't have acted on your behalf, women aren't allowed to do that... As I said in my letter, as soon as I arrived I went to sort things out with the Parisian notary who sent you the extract from the will appointing you as guardian. He immediately filled in the mandate in his head clerk's name, which he told me is what they often do. And so we concluded our business... At the magistrate's office, I got them to appoint to the family council three relatives on Lisa's side, two young cousins, Octave Mouret* and Claude Lantier,* and one cousin by marriage, a Monsieur Rambaud, who lives in Marseilles; then, on our side, Quenu's that is, I went for three nephews, Naudet, Liardin, and Delorme. As you can see, it's a most suitable family council, one that will let us do as we think fit in the child's best interests... And at their first meeting they appointed the surrogate guardian, who I had to choose of course from Lisa's side of the family, Monsieur Saccard...'*

'Ssh, she's waking up!' Lazare interrupted.

And indeed, Pauline had just opened her eyes wide. Without moving, she gazed in wonder at these people speaking around her, then with a sleepy smile her eyelids closed again in exhaustion, and her motionless face took on once more the milky transparency of a camellia petal.

'Saccard, isn't he the speculator?' queried Chanteau.

'Yes,' replied his wife, 'I met him and we had a talk. A charming man... He's got fingers in so many pies, he warned me not to expect too much help... But that'll be fine, we don't need anyone else. Now that we've taken on the child, we've taken her on, haven't we? I don't like other people meddling in my affairs... After that, the rest was sorted out in no time; fortunately, your mandate gave us all the necessary powers. The seals were removed and an inventory of the estate was made, then the shop was sold at auction. A stroke of luck, two bidders in hot competition, and we got ninety thousand francs cash, on the nail! The notary had already discovered sixty thousand in securities, in a drawer. I asked him to buy more of them so now we have one hundred and fifty thousand francs invested in solid stocks and shares, which I was only too pleased to bring back home with me, after handing the chief clerk the letter discharging him of his mandate, along with the receipt for the money which I had asked you to send me by return of post... And look, here it all is!'

She thrust her hand back into her bag and pulled out a bulging packet containing the share certificates, tied up between the two cardboard covers of one of the *charcuterie*'s old ledgers from which the pages had been torn out. The green marbling of the cover was specked with grease. Father and son both stared at this huge fortune laid out on their worn-out tablecloth.

'The tea's getting cold, Maman,' said Lazare, finally putting down his pen. 'Shall I pour?'

He stood up and began filling the cups. His mother did not answer but continued to gaze at the certificates.

'Of course,' she went on in a slow voice, 'at the final meeting of the family council that I called, I asked for my travel expenses to be reimbursed, and the annual allowance for the child's board and lodging here with us was set at eight hundred francs. We're less well off than she is, we can't afford to give her charity. We are none of us out to make money from the child, but we really can't be dipping into our own pockets. We'll reinvest the interest on her fortune, we'll virtually double her capital by the time she comes of age... Lord knows, we're only doing our duty! We must respect the wishes of the departed. And if we do put in something of our own, perhaps that will bring us luck—we certainly do need it... The poor little thing was so upset, and she sobbed and so bitter tears when she said goodbye to her nurse! I so want her to be happy here with us.'

Both men were distinctly moved.

'Well, I certainly won't be unkind to her,' said Chanteau.

'She's such a darling,' added Lazare, 'I'm already growing very fond of her.'

At that point Mathieu, scenting the tea in his sleep, gave himself a shake and returned to place his great head on the edge of the table. Minouche also stretched, arching her back with a yawn. There was a general stirring, and the cat eventually reached out her neck to sniff the packet of certificates between the greasy cardboard covers. As the Chanteaus turned towards Pauline, they saw her staring, wide-eyed, at the papers in the tatty ledger, which she recognized.

'Oh, she knows well enough what's in there,' continued Madame Chanteau. 'Don't you, my sweet? I showed you in Paris... That's what your poor father and your poor mother have left you.'

Tears rolled down the little girl's cheeks. Her grief still tended to well up like this, with all the suddenness of a spring shower. But already she was smiling through her tears, amused by Minouche who, after giving the certificates a long sniff, and no doubt attracted by the smell, started kneading and purring once more, butting her head against the corners of the ledger.

'Minouche, leave it alone!' cried Madame Chanteau. 'Money isn't for playing with!'

Chanteau laughed, and Lazare too. By the edge of the table a very excited Mathieu barked at the cat, his burning gaze devouring the certificates which he seemed to think were some tasty snack. And the whole family relaxed in boisterous amusement. Delighted with the game, Pauline seized Minouche in her arms, stroking and rocking her like a doll.

Fearing that the child might fall asleep again, Madame Chanteau got her to drink her tea straight away. Then she called Véronique.

'Bring the candles... If we sit here nattering, we'll never get to bed. I can't believe it's ten o'clock! I was already nodding off over dinner!'

But a man's voice was heard, coming from the kitchen, so she questioned the maid when she brought in the four lighted candlesticks.

'Who's that you've been talking to?'

'It's Prouane, Madame... He's come to inform Monsieur that things are very bad down in the village. It seems the tide is smashing everything to bits.'

Chanteau had reluctantly agreed to become mayor of Bonneville, and Prouane, a drunkard who acted as beadle* for Abbé Horteur, also held the post of town clerk; he had been a naval petty officer, and wrote with a schoolmaster's hand. Hearing calls for him to come in, he appeared with woollen hat in hand and jacket and boots dripping wet.

'So what's all the fuss about, Prouane?'

'Well, Monsieur, it's the Cuches' house, been swept away good and proper this time, it has... And if it carries on like that, the Gonins are for it next... All of us were there, Tourmal, Houtelard, me, the others. But what can you do? You can't fight the bitch, it just swallows up another slice of our land every year, regular.'

Silence. The four candles were burning with tall flames, and the sea, that he referred to as the bitch, could be heard crashing against the cliffs. The tide was now at its peak, and the house shuddered with every breaking wave. They were like giant artillery detonations, deep, regular explosions amid the continual rattling of stones on the rocks, like the crackle of small-arms fire. And to this din was added the roaring moan of the wind, while the rain beat down with redoubled force, seeming at times to spatter the walls with a hail of bullets.

'It's the end of the world,' muttered Madame Chanteau. 'What about the Cuches, where will they find shelter?'

'Someone will have to put them up,' replied Prouane. 'For the moment, they're at the Gonins'. You should've seen it! The little one, just three, drenched to the skin! And the mother in her petticoat showing everything she's got, if you'll pardon the expression! And the father, with his head split open by a falling beam, struggling to save their bits of stuff!'

Pauline had got up from the table. Going back over to the window, she listened with all the gravity of a grown-up. Her face bore an expression of distraught compassion, her full lips trembled with urgent sympathy.

'Oh, Auntie,' she said, 'those poor people!'

She stared out of the window, into the black abyss where the shadows had become even denser. The swollen, churning sea seemed to have galloped up as far as the road, but nothing could be seen, as if it had blotted out the little village, the rocky coastline, and the whole horizon, in a flood of inky blackness. This came as a painful surprise to the child: the water had seemed to her so beautiful, and now it was attacking people!

'I'll come down with you, Prouane,' exclaimed Lazare. 'Perhaps there's something we can do to help.'

'Oh yes, Cousin!' murmured Pauline with shining eyes.

But Prouane shook his head.

'No point troubling yourself, Monsieur Lazare. You wouldn't be able to do any better than the rest of us. We can only stand there and watch it demolish whatever it likes, and when it's had enough, well, all we can do is say thank you kindly... I just came up to inform Monsieur le Maire.'

At this, Chanteau grew angry, annoyed at this drama that would ruin his night's sleep and make work for him in the morning.

'And anyway,' he exclaimed, 'what a stupid place to build a village! It's obvious, you've stuck yourselves right in the path of the sea! No wonder it's swallowing up your houses one after the other... So why do you stay in such a hole? Just get out!'

'But where to?' asked Prouane, listening in astonishment. 'We are here, Monsieur, and here we will stay... Everyone has to live somewhere.'

'That's true enough,' opined Madame Chanteau. 'And, you know, here or somewhere else, there'll always be problems... We were just going to bed. Goodnight. It'll be clear in the morning.'

Prouane left with a respectful bow, and Véronique could be heard bolting the door behind him. Each holding their candlesticks, they gave Mathieu and Minouche, who both slept in the kitchen, a last stroke. Lazare had collected up his music, while Madame Chanteau clutched the certificates in the old ledger under her arm. She also picked up Davoine's statement of accounts from the table where her husband had left it. It was a document that broke her heart, and there was no point leaving it lying around.

'We're going up, Véronique,' she called. 'Don't be prowling around too long now.'

As only a grunt came back from the kitchen, she continued in a lowered voice:

'What's the matter with her? It's not as if I'd brought her a babe in arms to look after.'

'Leave her be,' said Chanteau. 'You know how moody she gets... Well, here we all are. So, goodnight everyone.'

Chanteau slept on the ground floor, on the far side of the corridor, in the old living room converted for his use into a bedroom. This meant that when he was having an attack, he could be pushed up to the table or out onto the terrace in his invalid chair.* He opened his door and hesitated a moment longer, feeling his legs heavy with an incipient attack of gout, which a stiffness in his joints had given him cause to fear since the previous day. It had definitely been a big mistake to eat that foie gras; this knowledge now filled him with despair.

'Goodnight,' he repeated in long-suffering tones. 'You always sleep so soundly... Good night, my little sweetie. Have a lovely rest, you can expect to, at your age!'

'Good night, Uncle,' Pauline replied, giving him a kiss.

The door closed. Madame Chanteau guided the little girl upstairs ahead of her. Lazare followed them.

'I won't be needing any lullabies to get to sleep tonight, and that's a fact,' declared the older lady. 'And actually, I find the racket outside quite soothing, I don't mind it at all... In Paris, I missed that feeling of being shaken about in my bed.'

The three of them arrived upstairs. Pauline, carefully holding her candle upright, enjoyed this single-file climb up the stairs, each carrying a light that cast dancing shadows on the walls. As she hesitated on the landing, not knowing where her aunt was leading her, she was given a gentle push.

'Go on, straight ahead... This is a spare room, and here opposite is mine... Come on in a moment, I want to show you something...'

The bedroom was hung with yellow cretonne with a green foliage pattern, and very simply furnished in mahogany, with a bed, a wardrobe, and a secretaire.* A small round table stood on a red rug in the middle. Once she had shone the candle into every corner of the room, Madame Chanteau went over to the secretaire and pulled down the lid.

'Come and look,' she continued.

She opened one of the little drawers and, with a sigh, placed in it Davoine's disastrous accounts. Then she emptied another drawer above it, took it out and shook out some dust, and as she prepared to deposit the certificates in it, said to the watching child:

'You see, this is where I'll keep them, they'll be there all on their own… Would you like to put them away yourself?'

Pauline felt embarrassed, for reasons that she could not explain. She blushed.

'Oh, Auntie, it doesn't matter.'

But already the old ledger was in her hand and she had to place it at the back of the drawer, while Lazare held out his candle to light up the inside of the secretaire.

'There,' continued Madame Chanteau, 'now you know where they are. And don't worry, we'd rather starve than… Remember, first drawer on the left. They'll stay there until you are a big enough girl to look after them yourself… Minouche won't be able to nibble them in there, will she?'

At the idea of Minouche opening up the secretaire to nibble the papers, the child burst out laughing. Her momentary awkwardness had disappeared and she was playing with Lazare who, to amuse her, was purring like the cat while pretending to attack the drawer. He too was laughing out loud. But his mother solemnly closed the lid and double-locked it with an energetic twist of her wrist.

'So that's that,' she said. 'Come on Lazare, stop larking about… Now I'm going up to check she's got everything she needs.'

The three of them filed back out onto the stairs. Up on the second floor, Pauline, hesitating once more, opened the left-hand door, but her aunt called out:

'No, not that side! That's your cousin's room. Yours is across the way.'

Pauline had stopped short, marvelling at the size of the room, a great attic cluttered with objects, a piano, a divan, a vast table, books and pictures. Finally, she opened the other door and was filled with delight, although her room seemed tiny in comparison. The wallpaper was light brown, with blue roses. There was a cast-iron bedstead with muslin drapes, a dressing table, a commode, and three chairs.

'You should have everything you need,' murmured Madame Chanteau, 'water, sugar,* towels, a bar of soap… Sleep well. Véronique will be in the little room next door, so if you are scared in the night, just knock on the wall.'

'And then, I'm always here too,' declared Lazare. 'If a ghost appears, I'll come running, with my great sword.'

The doors of the two facing rooms stood open, and Pauline's gaze went from one to the other.

'There's no such thing as ghosts,' she said with a laugh. 'You'll have to keep your sword for robbers. Goodnight, Auntie. Goodnight, Cousin.'

'Goodnight, my dear. Can you get ready for bed on your own?'

'Yes, of course... I'm not a little girl any more, in Paris I did everything for myself.'

They both kissed her goodnight, and as she went away, Madame Chanteau told her that she could lock the bedroom door. But the child had already rushed to the window, eager to find out whether it looked out on the sea. The rain was streaming down the glass so hard that she did not dare open it. Outside, everything was pitch-dark but the sound of the waves crashing below made her feel happy. Then, despite being so exhausted she could barely keep her eyes open, she went round the room and looked at the furniture. The idea that she now had a room to herself, separate from the others, where she would be allowed to spend time on her own like a grown-up, filled her with pride. But just as she was about to turn the key in the lock, having taken off her dress and standing there in her petticoat, she hesitated, suddenly feeling uneasy. Suppose someone came in the night, how would she escape? She shivered for a moment and opened the door. Across the way, still standing in the middle of his room, she saw Lazare, who looked at her.

'What's the matter?' he said, 'have you lost something?'

She blushed very red and thought about telling a lie, before her natural honesty asserted itself.

'No, nothing,' she replied. 'It's just that locked doors make me feel scared, so I'm not going to lock mine, and if I knock, I'd like you to come and see what's the matter... You, I mean, not the maid.'

He came towards her, charmed by her sweet and childish sincerity.

'Goodnight,' he repeated, holding his arms out towards her.

At which she flung her own thin arms around his neck, a little girl oblivious of her state of undress.

'Goodnight, Cousin.'

Five minutes later, she had courageously blown out her candle and was snuggling down in her muslin-curtained bed. For a long while, fatigue made her flit in and out of a dreamy sleep. First, she heard Véronique clumping upstairs without the slightest attempt to be quiet, then noisily dragging her furniture across the floor. Later there was just the din of the storm outside, grumbling thunder, rain lashing insistently down on the roof, wind rattling the windows and whistling in under the door. For a further hour the bombardment continued, and each crashing wave shook her with its deep, muffled thud. It seemed to her as if the house, in its heavy, deserted silence, were being swept out to sea like a ship. Now, snug in her warm blankets, her thoughts drifted, with pity and sympathy, down towards the poor souls whom the sea was driving from their own beds. Then came oblivion, and she slept with barely a breath.

CHAPTER 2

FROM the very first week, Pauline's presence brought joy into the house. Her glowing health, common sense, and calm smile soothed away the unspoken bitterness from the Chanteaus' lives. In her, the father had found a nurse, while the mother was happy that her son was spending more time at home; only Véronique continued to grouse. It was as if the hundred and fifty thousand francs locked up in the secrétaire made the family feel more prosperous, even though the money remained untouched. A new bond had been created, a new hope amid their ruin, even if they did not fully understand what it was.

The next day but one, in the night, Chanteau was laid low with the attack of gout he had been dreading. For the last week he had felt tinglings in his joints, shivers in his limbs, and an invincible aversion to exercise. Although he had gone to bed that evening in a more relaxed frame of mind, at three in the morning a pain erupted in the big toe of his left foot. Thence it leapt to the heel, before spreading to the whole ankle. From then until first light he moaned softly, sweating beneath the bedclothes, not wanting to disturb anyone. The whole family lived in fear of his attacks, so he waited to the last minute before calling for help, ashamed of falling ill again and despairing at the furious response his illness would provoke. And yet, as Véronique walked past his door around eight o'clock, he was unable to stifle a yelp at a particularly stabbing pain.

'Ha, here we go again,' groaned the maid. 'He'll soon be bawling.'

She entered the room, watching his head tossing from side to side while he groaned in pain, and her only comment by way of consolation was:

'What do you think Madame's going to say?'

And indeed, once Madame had been alerted, she came along in her turn, her shoulders slumped in a gesture of exasperation and despair. 'Not again!' she said. 'I've barely got home before it starts!'

She harboured a resentment against his gout that went back fifteen years. She loathed the illness like an enemy, cursing it as the destroyer of her existence, the ruin of her son, the death of her ambitions. But for the gout, would they have been exiled to this village in the middle of nowhere? And despite her good nature, she reacted to her husband's attacks with shuddering aversion, declaring herself unskilled and incapable of caring for him.

'Oh God, it hurts so much!' stammered the poor man. 'This attack will be worse than the last, I can feel it… Don't stand there watching if it upsets you, but do send for Doctor Cazenove at once.'

Then the household was thrown into turmoil. Lazare set off for Arromanches, even though the family no longer had much faith in doctors. Over the last fifteen years Chanteau had tried all sorts of drugs, but with every new treatment, the disease worsened. At first the attacks had been mild and infrequent, but they had soon increased in number and violence, and now both feet were affected, and even one knee was threatened. The patient had already experienced three changes of fashion in his medication, and his poor body had become a guinea pig in which a range of highly touted remedies fought it out. After having been copiously bled, he had been radically purged, and now they were stuffing him full of autumn crocus and lithium hydroxide.* And so, in the fatigue caused by his impoverished blood and debilitated organs, his gout was gradually turning from acute to chronic. Local treatments scarcely worked any better: leeches left him with rigid joints, opium prolonged his attacks, and blistering* gave him ulcers. Neither Wiesbaden nor Carlsbad had any effect, and a season in Vichy* had nearly killed him.

'Oh God, it's so painful!' repeated Chanteau, 'it feels like dogs gnawing at my foot.'

And, anxious and agitated, he kept twisting his leg first one way, then the other, in hope that the change of position would bring some relief. But the attack continued to worsen and every movement made him groan. Soon he let out one continuous howl, in the paroxysm of his pain. He was shivering and feverish, and consumed by a raging thirst.

But Pauline had just slipped into the room. Standing before the bed, she looked down at her uncle, with a serious expression on her face, but no tears. Madame Chanteau was at her wits' end, exasperated by his screams. Véronique had tried to rearrange the blanket because the patient found its weight unbearable, but when she came near him with her masculine hands, he howled even louder and forbade her to touch him. He was terrified of her, and accused her of lumping him around like a bag of washing.

'Well then, no point in sending for me, Monsieur!' she said as she walked out in high dudgeon. 'Them as rejects help will just have to help themselves.'

Slowly Pauline had gone up closer, and with the light dexterity of her child's fingers she lifted the blanket. He felt a momentary relief, and accepted her assistance.

'Thank you, my child... And there too, where it's folded over. It weighs half a ton... Oh, not so quick, you gave me a fright.'

In any case, the pain came back with even greater intensity. As his wife tried to busy herself about the room, opening the curtains, putting a cup back on the bedside table, he complained again.

'Please don't walk about like that, you make everything shake... Every step you take feels to me like a hammer blow.'

She did not even try to apologize, or do as he asked. This was always how it went; in the end, they left him to suffer on his own.

She simply said: 'Come along, Pauline. You can see that your uncle can't bear our company.'

But Pauline stayed. She trod so lightly that her little feet barely brushed the parquet. And from that moment, she took her place at the patient's side, and he would not allow anyone else in the room. As he said, he would have liked to be nursed by a breath of air. She had an instinctive understanding of his pain and how to ease it, anticipating his wishes, adjusting the light in the room or giving him cups of watery gruel that Véronique brought to the door. What soothed the poor man the most was to see her always near him, perched demurely on a chair and looking at him constantly with her big sympathetic eyes. He tried to find some distraction in telling her about his pains.

'Just now, you see, it's as if someone was prising the bones of my foot apart with a blunt knife, and at the same time, I'd swear they were pouring warm water onto my skin.'

Then the pain would change: his ankle was being tightly bound with wire, and his muscles were stretched to breaking point, like violin strings. Pauline listened obediently, seeming to understand everything and remaining untroubled by his howls of pain, concerned only with helping him to feel better. She was bright and cheery, and managed to make him laugh between the groans.

When Doctor Cazenove finally arrived, he was astonished, and he planted a great kiss on the little nurse's head. He was a wiry and vigorous man of fifty-four who, after thirty years of service in the Navy, had recently retired to Arromanches, where he had been left a house by a late uncle. He had been a friend of the family ever since he had cured Madame Chanteau of a worrying sprain.

'Well, well, and here we are again,' he said. 'I've rushed over here to wish you good day. But you know that I can't do any more for you than this child can. My dear fellow, when a man has hereditary gout and is past fifty, all he can do is put up with it. Added to which, you've done yourself a lot of no good with medicines of all kinds... You know the only remedy: patience and flannel!'

He liked to put on a show of scepticism. In the course of thirty years he had seen so many poor wretches at death's door, eaten away by diseases in all climates, that he had become modest in his ambitions and generally preferred to let nature take its course. Nevertheless, he examined the swollen toe, its skin dark red and shiny, moved up to the knee which was also becoming inflamed, and noted on the edge of the right ear the presence of a little hard white bead.

'But Doctor,' moaned the sick man, 'you can't just leave me suffering like this!'

Cazenove's manner had become serious. The bead of tophic matter* intrigued him, and faced with this new symptom, his faith in medicine returned.

'Good heavens!' he murmured, 'I'm prepared to try alkalines and salts... It's evidently turning chronic.'

Then he lost his temper.

'But it's your own fault for not sticking to the diet I prescribe... Never any exercise, always lounging in your armchair. And wine, I'll wager, and meat too, am I right? Admit it: you've been eating rich food.'

'Oh, just a morsel of foie gras,' Chanteau confessed feebly.

The doctor threw up his arms, calling on the elements to bear witness. Nevertheless, he drew some phials from his heavy overcoat and started to prepare a draught. As a topical treatment,* he simply wrapped the foot and knee in cotton wool, held in place with oilcloth. When he left, it was to Pauline that he repeated his instructions: one spoonful of the draught every two hours, as much gruel water as the patient would drink, and above all, strict fasting.

'If you think we can stop him from eating!' said Madame Chanteau as she was showing the doctor out.

'No, Auntie, he will be good, you'll see,' ventured Pauline. 'I'll make sure he is.'

Cazenove looked at her, amused by her thoughtful expression. He kissed her once more, on both cheeks.

'Now there's a young lady who's born to help others,' he declared with the same penetrating look in his eye as when he was making a diagnosis.

Chanteau bawled for a week. Just when the attack seemed to be over, his right foot had become affected and the pain had flared up with renewed violence. The whole household was on edge, Véronique took refuge in her kitchen to avoid having to listen, and even Madame Chanteau and Lazare sometimes fled the house, it made them so nervy and upset. Pauline alone remained in the sickroom, where she also had to contend with the patient's whims: insisting on eating a pork chop, shouting that he was starving, or calling Doctor Cazenove a donkey because he couldn't even cure him. At night especially, his pain would become even worse, and Pauline could barely get two or three hours' sleep. However, she was robust and cheerful, and no small girl ever grew up healthier. Madame Chanteau was relieved, and finally accepted this help from a child who was able to restore peace to the household. When at last Chanteau's convalescence began, Pauline regained her freedom, and a bond of camaraderie grew up between herself and Lazare.

In the early days, they would go up to his spacious quarters. He had had a partition knocked down, so that he now occupied half of the second floor. A little iron bedstead was hidden in a corner, behind an ancient, torn screen. Against one wall, a thousand books were stacked on shelves of unpainted pine, classics and odd volumes which he had discovered in an attic in Caen and brought to Bonneville. Near the window, a huge old Norman wardrobe* overflowed with an extraordinary jumble of objects, from mineral samples and broken tools, to children's toys with their stuffing hanging out. And there was also the piano, with a pair of fencing foils and a mask on top of it, to say nothing of the huge table in the middle of the room, which had been a drawing table, very high, and so cluttered with papers and pictures, tobacco pots and pipes, that it was difficult to find a hand's breadth of clear space to write in.

Once Pauline was given the run of this chaotic space, she was in raptures. She spent a whole month exploring the room, making fresh discoveries every day: a *Robinson Crusoe* with engraved illustrations that she found in the bookshelves, or a Pulcinella* doll rescued from under the wardrobe. As soon as she got up in the morning, she would run across from her room to her cousin's and install herself, then go back again in the afternoon, practically living there. From the first day, Lazare had accepted her like a boy, a little brother nine years his junior, but so happy and funny, with her wide intelligent eyes, that he felt completely comfortable in her presence, smoking his pipe, sprawling in a chair with his legs in the air and a book in his hand, or writing long letters into which he would slip flowers. But on occasion, this companion of his could become terribly disruptive. Suddenly she would climb on the table, or jump in a single bound through the hole in the screen. One morning, when he turned round, not having heard her for a while, he saw her wearing the fencing mask with a foil in her hand, bowing to an imaginary opponent. And although at first he shouted at her to calm down, then threatened to throw her out, it usually ended up in an alarming chase in which they turned the room upside down, the pair of them leaping about with the agility of goats. Then she would fling herself round his neck and he, becoming a small boy once again, would spin her round like a top with her skirts flying in the air, as they both collapsed in childish laughter.

Then the piano captured their attention. It was an old Érard instrument* of 1810 on which, long ago, for fifteen years, Mademoiselle Eugénie de la Vignière had given lessons. The mahogany case had lost its polish, and the strings within sighed distantly, making sweet but subdued sounds. Unable to persuade his mother to buy him a new piano, Lazare pounded this one with all his might, without managing to extract from it the Romantic sonorities which swarmed in his brain, and it became his habit to augment them with his voice to achieve the desired effect. His musical passion soon led him to take advantage of Pauline's indulgence: he had a captive audience, and he would trot out his repertoire for whole afternoons at a time. It was the most complicated kind of music, particularly the still-unrecognized works of Berlioz and Wagner.* And he would hum and groan along, in the end making as much noise with his throat as his fingers. The child found such days very boring, but she nevertheless sat there quietly listening, for fear of offending her cousin.

Sometimes, dusk would fall while they were thus absorbed. Then Lazare, intoxicated with rhythm, would recount his great dreams. He too would become a musician of genius, whatever his mother said, whatever anyone said. At the *lycée* in Caen he had had a violin teacher who was impressed by his musical talents and predicted a glorious future for him. He had taken composition lessons in secret, and now he was working by himself, already with a vague idea in mind, a symphony on the theme of the Earthly Paradise; he had even composed one piece, about Adam and Eve driven out by the Angels, a march of solemn and gloomy character which one evening he agreed to play for Pauline. The child expressed her approval, saying it was very good; then she took him to task. She was sure that composing music must give him a lot of pleasure, but might he not have been wiser to obey the wishes of his parents, who wanted him to become a prefect or a judge? The whole household was distressed by this dispute between mother and son—he, talking of going to Paris to sit exams for the Conservatoire,* she giving him until next October to decide on a proper career. Pauline supported her aunt's plan and had announced to her, with calm conviction in her voice, that she would make it her business to persuade her cousin. They joked about it, but then Lazare angrily slammed the piano lid, calling her a 'horrid petite bourgeoise'.

For three days they were not on speaking terms, then they made up. In order to convert her to the joys of music, he took it into his head to teach her the piano. He positioned her fingers on the keys, and kept her for hours running up and down scales. But her lack of dedication really upset him. She was just looking for entertainment, and found it amusing to make Minouche walk up and down the keyboard, performing barbarous symphonies with her paws; she could swear the cat was playing his famous Exodus from the Earthly Paradise, which made the composer himself laugh. Then their wild chases would begin again, as she flung her arms about his neck and he whirled her round in the air, while Minouche, entering into the spirit of things, bounded from the tabletop onto the wardrobe. As for Mathieu, he was not allowed to join in because he was too boisterous.

'Just leave me alone, you petite bourgeoise, you!' exclaimed Lazare again one day in exasperation. 'Maman can teach you the piano if she wants.'

'Your music's useless,' said Pauline bluntly. 'If I were you, I'd become a doctor.'

Deeply offended, he stared at her. Doctor now, was it? Wherever did she get such ideas? He was fervent in his enthusiasms, and flung himself into his musical passion with an impetuosity that promised to sweep all before it.

'Listen,' he shouted, 'if they stop me from becoming a musician, I'll kill myself!'

Summer had completed Chanteau's convalescence, and Pauline was able to follow Lazare outdoors. The great upstairs room was left empty and the two companions galloped off on wild rambles. For a few days they were happy with the terrace, where a few clumps of wind-scorched tamarisk* grew; then they ventured out into the yard, breaking the chain on the well, scaring the dozen scrawny hens that fed on grasshoppers, and playing hide-and-seek in the empty stable and coach house, with plaster crumbling from its walls. Next, they went into the kitchen garden, an arid piece of ground where Véronique toiled like a peasant, with four beds growing gnarled vegetables, planted among pear trees whose stumps of branches were all bent in the same direction by the north-westerly gales; and it was from there that, opening a small gate, they found themselves on the cliffs, beneath the open sky, with the expanse of the sea before them. Pauline had not lost her passionate curiosity about this immense stretch of water, now so clear and gentle in the bright July sunshine. She would still look out at the sea from every room in the house; but she had not yet been able to get close to it, and a complete new life opened up when she found herself set free, in Lazare's company, to roam the living emptiness of the beaches.

What wonderful adventures they had! Madame Chanteau grumbled and tried to keep them at home, despite her trust in the little girl's common sense. So they never went out across the yard, where Véronique would have seen them, but slipped away through the kitchen garden, disappearing until the evening. They soon tired of walks around the church, the corners of the cemetery shaded by yew trees, and the curé's handful of lettuces, and within a week they had also exhausted what Bonneville had to offer, with its thirty houses backed up against the cliff and the shingle bank on which the fishermen beached their boats. Much more amusing was to wander far along the base of the cliffs at low tide: they walked on fine sand over which crabs scuttled, jumped from rock to rock among the seaweed, across rivulets of clear water teeming with shrimps; not to mention the things they caught, mussels eaten raw and without bread, strange creatures that they took home in the corner of a handkerchief, unexpected discoveries like a stranded flounder or a small lobster at the bottom of a hole. The sea would ~~somin limit up mud immations~~ catch them by surprise, so they would pretend to be stranded and take refuge on a reef while they waited for the tide to go down again. They revelled in it, and would come home dishevelled and soaked up to the shoulders, so accustomed to the salt air of the outdoors that they would complain the room was stuffy as they sat beneath the lamp in the evening.

But their greatest joy was bathing. The beach was too rocky to attract families from Caen or Bayeux: whereas each year the cliffs of Arromanches became more covered in chalets, no bathers ever turned up in Bonneville. A kilometre from the village, towards Port-en-Bessin,* the two of them had discovered a delightful spot, a little bay nestling between two ramparts of rock and covered in fine golden sand. They named it Treasure Bay, imagining twenty-franc gold coins tumbling about in its remote waters. It was their private place, and they undressed there without embarrassment. Continuing to talk, he would half turn away to button up his costume; she would momentarily hold the edge of her shift in her mouth, before appearing with a woollen garment wrapped tight around her hips, like a boy. In the course of a week, he taught her to swim: she picked it up much more quickly than the piano, and she was so daring that she often swallowed great mouthfuls of seawater. In this tingling cold, they laughed with all the joy of youth whenever a bigger wave sent them flying into each other. They emerged shining with salt and let their bare arms dry in the breeze, without any interruption to their boisterous games. It was even more fun than fishing.

The days went by, the beginning of August arrived, and still Lazare had not made up his mind. That October, Pauline was due to enter a boarding school in Bayeux. As they lay stretched out on the sand, after the sea had filled their limbs with a joyous fatigue, they talked about the future, in quite serious tones. She eventually awakened his interest in medicine by telling him that, had she been a man, she could think of no more thrilling career than making people better. As it happened, for the past week the Earthly Paradise had not been going so well, and he had begun to doubt his genius. Moreover, there

had been famous doctors: he recalled the great names, Hippocrates,*
Ambroise Paré,* and so many others. But one afternoon he whooped
with joy, for the idea for his real masterpiece had come to him: the
Paradise piece was stupid, he'd abandon that and embark on a Symphony of Suffering, in which he would score in sublime harmonies
Humanity's despairing lament as it wept beneath the heavens; he would
reuse his Adam and Eve March, and turn it straight into a March of
Death. For a week, his enthusiasm mounted from hour to hour, his
plan embraced the whole universe. A further week went by, then one
evening his little companion was astonished to hear him remark that
he actually wouldn't mind studying medicine in Paris after all. It had
occurred to him that this would bring him closer to the Conservatoire:
the important thing was being there, afterwards he would see. Madame
Chanteau was overjoyed. She would have preferred her son to be a civil
servant or a magistrate, but at least doctors were respectable men who
earned a lot of money.

'You must be the good fairy!' she said as she kissed Pauline. 'My
little darling, you are certainly rewarding us for having taken you in!'

Everything was settled. Lazare would leave on the first of October.
So, in September their expeditions resumed with renewed enthusiasm, as the two companions sought to bring their gloriously free
existence to a suitable conclusion. They would linger until nightfall
on the sands of Treasure Bay.

One evening as they lay there side by side, they watched the stars
come out like fiery beads in the darkening sky. She looked on gravely,
with the calm admiration of a healthy child. He blinked nervously,
full of agitation since he had begun preparing his departure, as his
attention flitted from one fresh ambition to the next.

'Aren't the stars lovely?' she said solemnly, after a long silence.

He allowed a new silence to settle. His gaiety of spirit no longer
rang so true, an inner anxiety troubled his wide-eyed gaze. In the sky,
the swarm of stars grew denser by the minute, like shovelfuls of
embers flung into the infinite.

'They didn't teach you that, did they?' he murmured at last. 'Each
star is a sun, around which spin objects like the earth, and there
are billions of them, with billions more beyond, and more, and still
more…'

He fell silent, then continued with a great shudder choking his
voice:

'I don't like looking at them… They scare me.'

The rising tide was sighing a distant lament, like a crowd desperately bewailing its misery. Against the immense horizon, quite dark now, twinkled the flying dust of the worlds; and amid this lamentation of the earth oppressed beneath the infinite quantity of stars, the child thought she could hear, close by, the sound of sobbing.

'What's the matter? Aren't you well?'

Giving no reply, he lay there in tears, his face hidden behind his violently clenched hands, as if to stop himself seeing. When he was able to speak, he stammered out:

'Oh, I want to die, just die!'

The memory of this astonishing scene stayed with Pauline. Lazare dragged himself to his feet and they returned home to Bonneville in the dark, the rising tide washing round their feet, unable to find anything to say to each other. She watched him walking in front of her, and he seemed diminished in stature as he leaned into the westerly wind.

That evening, a newcomer awaited them in the dining room, chatting to Chanteau. For the last week, the family had been expecting Louise, a girl of eleven and a half who came to spend a fortnight in Bonneville every year. Twice they had made fruitless trips to Arromanches to fetch her, then all of a sudden, she had turned up one evening when she was not expected. Louise's mother had died in Madame Chanteau's arms, commending her daughter into her care. The father, a banker from Caen called Monsieur Thibaudier, had remarried six months later, and already had three other children. Much occupied with his new family and with his mind filled with figures, he left the little girl at boarding school and was happy to be rid of her in the holidays, when he could send her to stay with friends. He seldom troubled to bring her himself, so Mademoiselle had been delivered by a servant, a week late—there were so many calls on Monsieur's time! And the servant had gone back at once, promising that Monsieur would do his very best to come and collect Mademoiselle.

'Hurry up, Lazare,' exclaimed Chanteau. 'She's here!'

Smiling broadly, Louise kissed the young man on both cheeks. Yet they hardly knew each other, for she was cloistered in her boarding school and he barely a year out of *lycée*. Their acquaintance scarcely went back beyond the last holidays, and even then he had treated her rather formally, already sensing coquettishness in her disdain for the noisy games of childhood.

'Now then, Pauline, aren't you going to kiss her?' asked Madame Chanteau as she came in. 'She's eighteen months older than you... I'd like the two of you to be friends.'

Pauline looked at Louise, slender and delicate, with irregular but most charming features and beautiful fair hair, curled and put up like a lady's. Seeing Louise embrace Lazare, she had turned pale. And when the new arrival cheerfully embraced her, she returned the kiss with trembling lips.

'Whatever's the matter?' asked her aunt. 'Are you cold?'

'Yes, a little, the wind is rather chill,' she replied, blushing at her lie.

At dinner, she ate nothing. Her eyes remained fixed on the others and a fierce black gleam sparked in them as soon as her cousin, her uncle, or even Véronique paid any attention to Louise. But she seemed particularly upset when Mathieu, doing his customary round of the table during dessert, went to rest his great head on the new girl's knee. She called him over in vain: he was not going to leave this kind person who plied him with sugar.

When they got up from the table, Pauline disappeared; then Véronique, who was clearing away, came back from the kitchen and said triumphantly:

'Well, now! Madame thinks her little Pauline is such a sweetie, but do come and see what she's up to in the yard!'

Everyone went to look. Behind the coach house, the child had backed Mathieu up against the wall and, quite beside herself with fury, was bashing him on the skull with all the strength of her little fists. Stunned and cowed, the dog made no effort to defend himself. They rushed out to her but she kept on hitting and had to be carried away, out of control, rigid with rage, so upset that she was put straight to bed, and her aunt had to spend part of the night by her side.

'Such a sweetie, such a sweetie,' repeated Véronique, delighted to have finally found a flaw in the pearl.

'I remember them telling me about her tempers, in Paris,' said Madame Chanteau. 'She's jealous, and that's not a nice quality... In the six months that she's been here, I had already noticed a few little things, but really, trying to knock the poor dog unconscious, that's going too far!'

The next day, when Pauline came upon Mathieu again she held him tight in her trembling arms, kissed him on the muzzle with such floods of tears that they feared a fresh outburst of hysterics. Yet she could not correct her behaviour, there was an inner compulsion which drove all the blood in her veins up to her brain. It seemed that these violent fits of jealousy came from the distant past, the heritage of some maternal ancestor* showing through the admirably balanced temperament of her father and mother, of whom she was the living image. As she was very sensible for a moment too, she explained that she was trying her best to overcome her tempers, but just could not manage it. They left her feeling saddened, like some shameful infirmity.

'I love you all so much, why must you love other people?' she replied, hiding her face on her aunt's shoulder, when the latter went up to her room to remonstrate with her.

And so, despite her best efforts, Pauline found the presence of Louise very hard to bear. Since her arrival had been announced, she had awaited her with anxious curiosity, and now she was impatiently counting the days until she would go away again. Still, she found Louise attractive: she dressed well, and carried herself like a refined young lady, with the winning charm of a girl who has known too little affection at home. But whenever Lazare was there, it was precisely this seductive womanly elegance, an awakening of the unknown, that disturbed and irritated Pauline. And yet the young man always treated her as his favourite and made fun of Louise, saying that he was bored of her airs and graces, and talking of leaving her to act the lady on her own, so they would be free to go off and amuse themselves together. But their rough and tumble games were suspended; they all looked at pictures in the bedroom instead, or strolled at a respectable pace on the beach. It was going to be a completely wasted fortnight.

One morning, Lazare announced that he would be leaving five days early. He wanted to get settled in Paris, where he was due to meet up with one of his former classmates from Caen. Pauline, who had been despondent for the last month at the thought of her cousin's departure, supported his new resolution and, plunging into joyful activity, helped her aunt pack his trunk. Then, once old Malivoire had taken Lazare away in his berline, she ran upstairs and locked herself in her room, where she wept long and bitterly. That evening she treated Louise very kindly, and their second week in Bonneville was most pleasant. When her father's servant came to collect Louise, explaining that Monsieur had been unable to leave his bank, the two little friends threw themselves into each other's arms and swore to love each other for ever.

Then, slowly, a year went by. Madame Chanteau had changed her mind: instead of sending Pauline away to boarding school, she would keep her at home, swayed above all by Chanteau's lamentations that he couldn't do without the child, though she did not admit this self-interested motive, but spoke of looking after Pauline's education herself, and felt quite rejuvenated at the idea of getting back into teaching. At boarding school, little girls heard all sorts of dreadful things; she wanted to be able to vouch for her pupil's perfect innocence. They dug out from Lazare's bookcase a Grammar, an Arithmetic Primer, a Treatise on History and even a condensed Mythology, and Madame Chanteau took up her ferule again to give a single lesson each day, which included dictation, arithmetic, and recitation. Lazare's big bedroom was turned into a study, Pauline had to resume her piano practice, as well as learn deportment, the principles of which her aunt inculcated with severity as a corrective to her tomboy manner. Since she was both docile and intelligent, she was a quick learner, even when she found the subject tedious. Only one book really bored her: the catechism. She could not understand why her aunt bothered to take her to Mass of a Sunday morning. What was the point? In Paris, she was never taken to Saint-Eustache,* even though it was just round the corner. She did not find it easy to grasp abstract ideas, so her aunt had to explain to her that in the country, a well-brought-up young lady had an obligation to set a good example and show respect for the curé. Madame Chanteau's own piety had only ever been one of convenience, part of a good education, in much the same way as deportment.

Meanwhile, the sea continued to pound Bonneville twice a day with its perpetual swell, and Pauline grew up with the spectacle of the immense horizon always before her. She no longer played, as she had nobody to play with. Once she had galloped round the terrace with Mathieu, or taken Minouche on her shoulder for a walk to the end of the kitchen garden, her only amusement was to gaze out at the sea, which was a constantly living thing, blue-grey in the December storms, a delicate shimmering green in the first sunshine of May. Moreover, the year was a happy one, and the good fortune that her presence seemed to have brought to the household manifested itself again when the Chanteaus received an unexpected payment of five thousand francs from Davoine, to forestall their threatened dissolution of the partnership. The aunt went off scrupulously to Caen every quarter to collect Pauline's dividends, deducting her expenses and the maintenance allowance set by the family council, then buying further securities with the rest, and each time she came home she insisted on the little girl going with her to her room, opened up the special drawer in the secretaire, and repeated:

'See, I'm putting this one on top of the others... The pile is growing bigger, isn't it? Have no fear, it will all be there for you, with not a centime* missing.'

One fine morning in August, Lazare turned up out of the blue with the news of his complete success in the end of year exams. He was not due home until a week later but had wanted to surprise his mother. They were all overjoyed. In his fortnightly letters, he had been displaying a growing passion for medicine. Now that he was back, he seemed to them completely changed, no longer talking about music, but going on ad nauseam with stories about his professors, and delivering scientific lectures on every subject under the sun, from the food being served, to the wind that was blowing that day. He was in the grip of a new fever, he had thrown himself body and soul into the idea of becoming a doctor of earth-shattering genius.

Pauline especially, after flinging her arms around his neck like a little girl unable to hide her affections, could not get over how different he seemed. She was almost upset that he no longer discussed music, even just a little, for amusement. Was it really possible to stop liking something that you used to love so much? The day she questioned him about his symphony, he started joking about it, saying all that nonsense was over and done with, which made her quite sad. Then she noticed him behaving awkwardly in her presence, laughing an ugly laugh and showing signs, in his eyes and his manner, of ten months of an existence that could not be divulged to young girls. He had unpacked his trunk himself in order to hide his books, novels and scientific tomes full of engravings. He no longer whirled her round like a top with her skirts flying, and was sometimes put out when she insisted on coming in and spending time in his room. Yet, she had barely grown at all, and she looked straight back at him with her gaze of pure innocence. After a week, their tomboy friendship picked up again. The rough sea breezes cleansed him of the taint of the Latin Quarter,* and he became a child once more in the company of this robust child with her happy laughter. Everything began again as before, their chases around the big table, races in the kitchen garden with Mathieu and Minouche, and expeditions to Treasure Bay, where they bathed innocently in the sunshine, laughing joyfully as their under-shirts slapped against their legs like flags. That particular year Louise, who had come to Bonneville in May, went to spend the summer holi-days near Rouen* with other friends. Two delightful months passed without a single quarrel to spoil their friendship.

In October, the day when Lazare repacked his trunk, Pauline watched him piling in the books that he had brought home with him and left locked in the wardrobe, without thinking of opening a single one.

'So, you're taking them with you?' she asked disappointedly.

'Yes, of course,' he replied. 'They're for my studies... Ah, by heaven, how I'm going to work! Nothing's going to hold me back.'

A deathly quiet descended on the little house in Bonneville, the days unfolded uniformly with their round of regular habits, against the backdrop of the sea and its eternal cycle. But that year there occurred in Pauline's life a noteworthy event. She made her first Communion in June, at the age of twelve and a half. Gradually, reli-gion had gained a hold over her, a serious religion more elevated than the mere responses to the catechism, which she still trotted out without understanding them. In her young rational mind, she had arrived at the idea of God as a most powerful, all-knowing master who directed everything so that earthly matters worked in accordance with justice, and this simplified notion sufficed to create common ground with Abbé Horteur. He, a son of peasant stock with a thick skull through which only the letter of religion had penetrated, was content with its external practices, with orderly and respectable manifestations of devotion. He took care of his personal salvation, but as for his parish-ioners, if they damned themselves, that was their own lookout! For fifteen years he had attempted, in vain, to scare them, so now he asked of them only to have the good manners to walk up to his church on important feast days. The whole of Bonneville did indeed go, out of lingering habit, despite the sinful degeneracy in which the villagers wallowed. His indifference to other people's salvation passed for tol-erance. Every Saturday he would come round to play draughts with Chanteau, even though the mayor, on the pretext of his gout, never set foot in church. Anyway, Madame Chanteau did the necessary, attending services regularly and taking Pauline along with her. It was the curé's great simplicity that gradually won the child over. In Paris, people spoke contemptuously in front of her about priests, such hypo-crites whose black robes concealed all manner of vices. But this one, living beside the sea, seemed to her a genuinely good man, with his heavy shoes and sunburnt neck, and the appearance and speech of a poor farmer. One observation in particular had impressed her: Abbé Horteur was a passionate smoker of his great meerschaum pipe, but since he felt guilty about it, he would secrete himself at the bottom of his garden to smoke in solitude among his lettuces, and the little girl was greatly touched, without knowing why, by the flustered way he concealed the pipe when anyone caught him at it. She took Communion with great seriousness, along with two other little girls and a lad from the village. That evening, as the priest was dining with the Chanteaus, he declared that in Bonneville he had never known a girl at her first Communion who had been so well behaved before the holy altar.

That year things went less well: the rise in the price of pine that Davoine had been predicting for so long failed to materialize; the news from Caen was bad, people saying that since he was forced to sell at a loss, the business was inevitably heading for disaster. The family led a frugal existence, the three thousand francs of interest just sufficient to cover the basic household necessities, with everything pared down to the minimum. Madame Chanteau was mainly worried about Lazare, who sent her letters that she kept to herself. He seemed to be leading a dissolute life, and pestered her with constant demands for money. In July, as she was going to collect Pauline's dividends, she paid an unannounced visit to Davoine. The previous two thousand francs he had handed over had already gone to Lazare, and now she managed to prise a further thousand out of him, which she sent at once to Paris. Lazare wrote back that he would not be able to come home if he did not pay off his debts.

They waited a week for him. Every morning a letter arrived putting off his departure to the next day. His mother and Pauline went to Verchemont to meet him. They embraced at the roadside and walked home together in the dust, followed by Lazare's carriage containing just his trunk. But this homecoming was less joyful than the previous year's triumphant surprise. He had failed his exams in July and was full of bitterness against his professors, sounding off about them all evening, a set of donkeys with whom he had had it up to here, as he put it. The following day, in front of Pauline, he flung his books down on a shelf in the wardrobe and declared that they could stay there and rot. His sudden disgust filled her with consternation, she listened to him jeering sarcastically about medicine and challenging it to cure even the common cold, then one day when she spoke up to defend science with all the verve and belief of her young years, he mocked her ignorant enthusiasm so severely that she turned scarlet. In any event, he was still resigned to becoming a doctor, that farce was as good as any other, and none of it would be any fun in the end. She was indignant about these new notions he had brought home with him. Where had he got them from? Bad books, no doubt, but she no longer dared argue with him, feeling powerless in her total ignorance, and embarrassed by her cousin's sneering laughter when he affected to know things he could not tell her. Thus, the holidays went by in a continual round of taunting. During their walks now he seemed bored, saying the sea was stupid and always the same; yet he had started writing poetry to kill time, carefully composed sonnets about the sea, full of rich rhymes. He refused to go swimming, having discovered that cold-water bathing was completely inimical to his temperament; for, despite his dismissal of medicine, he always expressed such views dogmatically, just as he would damn or save people with a single word. Towards the middle of September, when Louise was due to arrive, he suddenly spoke of returning to Paris on the pretext of preparing for his exams; those two little girls would bore him witless, he might as well go back to his Latin Quarter existence a month early. Pauline had become gentler, the more he hurt her feelings. When he was short with her or took pleasure in reducing her to despair, she just looked at him with the same mild, laughing eyes that would calm Chanteau whenever he was bawling in pain during an attack. In her mind, her cousin must be unwell, he was looking on life in the way old people do.

The day before his departure, Lazare seemed so pleased to be leaving Bonneville that Pauline wept.

'You don't love me anymore!'

'Silly little thing! I've got to make my way in life, haven't I?... Don't be such a crybaby!'

Already she was brave again, and she smiled.

'Work hard this year, so that you'll come home happy.'

'Oh, there's no sense in working all that hard. Their exams are so stupid! If I failed, it's because I couldn't be bothered to try... I'll do it this time because I don't have enough money to live the easy life, which is the only intelligent thing for a man to do.'

In the first days of October, once Louise had returned to Caen,

Pauline resumed lessons with her aunt. The third year of her course was due to focus on an expurgated history of France, and mythology for young ladies, a form of higher learning designed to help them understand the paintings in galleries. But the child, who had been so assiduous the previous year, now seemed slow on the uptake; she would sometimes fall asleep over her homework, and sudden flushes turned her cheeks pink. A wild tantrum against Véronique, who she said did not like her, put her in bed for two days. Then there were changes in her that she found upsetting, the gradual development of her body, budding curves which felt swollen and painful, dark shadows of wispy down on the most hidden and delicate parts of her skin. When she looked furtively at herself at bedtime, a feeling of unease and embarrassment came over her which made her quickly blow out the candle. Her voice was acquiring a deeper tone that she found ugly, she was unhappy with herself, spending days in a sort of nervous expectation, not knowing what she was hoping for, and not daring to speak of these things to anyone.

Finally, around Christmas, Pauline's state of health began to worry Madame Chanteau. She was complaining of stabbing pains in her lower back, she ached all over and had feverish episodes. Once Doctor Cazenove, who had become great friends with Pauline, had questioned her, he took her aunt to one side and advised her to explain matters to her niece. It was the rising tide of puberty, and he told her that he had known young girls become sick with terror when faced with that bloody and chaotic flood. At first the aunt resisted, she thought it an unnecessary precaution and was unwilling to go into such intimate details: her own system of education was based on complete ignorance, and the avoidance of uncomfortable facts until such time as they became self-evident. However, as the doctor insisted, she promised that she would say something, though did nothing about it that evening, then put it off from one day to the next. The child was not the timorous sort, and anyway, many girls had no warning before it happened. All in good time, she would explain that this was simply the way of it, without opening herself up in advance to unsuitable questions.

One morning, just as Madame Chanteau was leaving her bedroom, she heard shrieks from Pauline's room and went up in great anxiety to investigate. The young girl was sitting in the middle of the bed with the covers thrown back, white with terror and calling for her aunt in a continuous howl; her spread, naked legs were stained with blood and she was staring aghast at what had come out of her, with none of her usual bravery.

'Oh, Auntie, Auntie!'

Madame Chanteau had understood at first glance.

'It's nothing, my darling. Don't worry yourself about it.'

But Pauline, still examining herself and sitting up stiffly as if she were injured, did not even hear her.

'Oh, Auntie, I felt something wet, then look, just look, it's blood! It's the end for me, the sheets are full of it.'

Her voice died away, she thought that all the blood in her veins was gushing out in that red river. Her cousin's wail of despair, which at the time she had not understood, now came to her own lips in her terror of the infinite heavens:

'It's the end, I'm going to die.'

Her aunt, her head spinning, tried to find respectable words, a lie that would calm her down without revealing anything to her.

'Come now, don't worry your head about it; if you really were in any danger, I'd be more worried, wouldn't I? I give you my word, this is something that happens to all women. It's just like a nosebleed...'

'No, no, you're only saying that to keep me quiet... I'm going to die, I'm going to die.'

Now it was too late. When Doctor Cazenove arrived, he feared brain fever. Madame Chanteau had put Pauline back to bed, telling her she should be ashamed of her fears. Days passed and Pauline emerged from her crisis, astonished to find herself thinking about new and mysterious things, but always with the same obstinate question at the back of her mind, to which she kept searching for an answer.

It was the following week that she got back down to work, and appeared to develop a passionate interest in mythology. She now spent all her time in Lazare's great bedroom, which still served as her study; she had to be called for every meal, and she would come down in a state of distraction, stiff from sitting. But, at the top of the house, the Mythology lay unopened on the end of the table: what she spent entire days reading, her eyes dilated by the urge to learn, her forehead pressed into her two hands, chill from concentration, were the textbooks that had been left in the wardrobe. Lazare, in the heady days of his medical enthusiasm, had bought works which were of no immediate use to him, Longuet's *Treatise on Physiology*, the *Descriptive*

Anatomy of Cruveilhier,* and these were precisely the ones left behind when he had taken his working books with him. As soon as her aunt's back was turned, she would take them out, then calmly put them back at the slightest sound, acting not like a girl with a guilty curiosity, but a studious one whose family were standing in the way of her vocation. At first, she had not understood much, put off by technical terms that she had to look up in the dictionary. Then, realizing that she needed a method, she had first pored over the *Descriptive Anatomy*, before moving on to the *Treatise on Physiology*. And so this child of fourteen learnt, as if by homework from school, things generally concealed from virgins until their wedding night. She leafed through the plates in the *Anatomy*, superbly detailed and realistic engravings, dwelling on each organ in turn, delving into even the most secret, those which have been made into the shame of man and woman; yet she felt no shame, hers was a serious purpose, going from the organs that give life to those that regulate it, sustained and preserved from carnal ideas by her love of all that was healthy. The gradual discovery of this human machine filled her with admiration. She read all about it with a passion: neither her old fairy stories, nor *Robinson Crusoe*, had ever opened up her mind in this way. Then the *Treatise on Physiology* was like a commentary on the engravings, and now nothing remained hidden from her. She even found a *Manual of Pathology and Clinical Medicine*,* and went into the details of dreadful illnesses and the treatments for each. Many things were beyond her, but she gained the first inklings of the knowledge needed to bring relief to sufferers. Her heart ached with pity and she revived her earlier dream of learning everything, in order to cure everything.

And Pauline now knew why the bloody flow of her puberty had spurted forth as if from ripe grapes trodden at harvest time. This mystery explained filled her with gravity, as she felt the tide of life surging within her. She was puzzled and bitter at her aunt's silence, and the complete ignorance in which she was trying to keep her. Why leave her in such terror? It wasn't fair, there was nothing wrong with knowing.

In any event, no further signs appeared for two months. Madame Chanteau said one day:

'Another time, if you notice what you saw in December, do you remember? don't be alarmed, it's nothing to worry about.'

'Yes, I know,' the girl replied calmly.

Her aunt gave her an alarmed look.

'What do you know, exactly?'

Then Pauline blushed at the idea of having to lie to keep her reading secret. She could not bear lying, she preferred to confess all. When Madame Chanteau, opening the books on the table, came across the engravings, she stood there appalled. And she had been taking such trouble to find innocent explanations for Jupiter's dalliances! Really, Lazare ought to have kept such abominations under lock and key. And she interrogated the guilty girl at length, with all sorts of precautions and euphemisms. But Pauline's candour completed her embarrassment. What of it? That was just how we were made, there was nothing wrong. Her passion was a purely intellectual one, no gleam of surreptitious sensuality yet lit up the child's wide, clear eyes. On the same shelf, Pauline had found novels, but these had put her off from the very first pages, they were so dull and stuffed with expressions she did not understand. Her aunt, more and more disconcerted, yet also somewhat relieved, was content to lock the wardrobe and take away the key. A week later the key was left lying around again, and occasionally Pauline would allow herself, as a kind of recreation, to read the chapter on neuroses with her cousin in mind, or the one on treatments for gout, with the idea of relieving her uncle's suffering.

In any case, notwithstanding Madame Chanteau's strictures, nobody took particular care of their language in her presence. The household animals would also have instructed her, even if she had not read those books. She took a special interest in Minouche: the cat was a slattern who, four times a year, would go out on extravagant orgies. Such a delicate creature, constantly preening herself and never stepping outside without a shudder for fear of sullying her paws, she would suddenly disappear for two or three days at a time. She could be heard yowling and scrapping, and there in the darkness, burning like candles, were the eyes of all the tomcats of Bonneville. Then she would come home in a disgusting state, a bedraggled slut with her fur so scraggy and filthy that she would lick herself clean for a week. Afterwards she would resume her haughty and supercilious airs, rubbing up against people's faces without seeming to notice that her belly was swelling. One fine morning they would find her with kittens, which Véronique would carry off in a corner of her apron to drown. And Minouche, wretched mother that she was, would not even go looking for them; she was accustomed to being relieved of them in that way, and thought this was all there was to motherhood. She would carry on licking herself, purring and giving herself airs, until one evening she went off again, caterwauling and with claws at the ready, in search of another bellyful. Mathieu was a better father to these offspring who were not his own, because he always insisted on licking clean all the newborn creatures, then would go whimpering along behind Véronique's apron.

'Oh, Auntie, this time we must let her keep one!' said Pauline with every new litter, both shocked and fascinated by the cat's amorous behaviour.

But Véronique would have none of it.

'Certainly not! We don't want her dragging it around everywhere with her!... And anyway, she isn't the least bit bothered about them. She has all the pleasure, and none of the bother.'

Pauline's love of life, which became daily more potent, made her 'a mother to all creatures', as her aunt put it. Every living, suffering animal inspired in her an active affection which she poured out in care and caresses. Paris was forgotten, she felt as if she had roots here, in this rough ground swept by winds from the sea. In under a year, the barely formed child had turned into a strapping young girl with solid hips and a broad chest. Now the troubles of this period of growth—the discomfort of her body swelling with sap, the anxious embarrassment of her heavier bosom, the fine dark down on the dusky satin of her skin—were fading into the past. On the contrary, she now rejoiced at her own blossoming, the victorious sensation of growing and ripening in the sun. The rising tide of blood that burst forth in showers of red rain now filled her with pride. From morning till night the house rang with the deeper resonance of her singing voice, which now delighted her, and at bedtime, when she glanced down from the rounded bloom of her breasts to the inky smudge that shaded her pink belly, she would smile with happiness and momentarily breathe in the scent of her new womanhood, like a fresh bouquet. Her acceptance of life, her love of all its functions, without fear or loathing, was accompanied by the triumphant song of her own radiant health.

Lazare, that year, did not write home properly for six months. Only occasional notes arrived to reassure his family. Then he bombarded his mother with a succession of letters. Having failed his exams again in November and become increasingly disillusioned with his medical studies, which dealt with such unpleasant things, he had now thrown himself into yet another passion, this time for chemistry. By chance he had made the acquaintance of the illustrious Herbelin,* whose discoveries were revolutionizing science at that time, and had entered his laboratory as a technician, though without admitting that he was abandoning medicine. Soon, however, his letters were full of a new project, outlined tentatively at first, then with growing enthusiasm. It was a plan for the industrial exploitation of seaweed that would bring in millions, thanks to the new techniques and reagents discovered by Herbelin. Lazare listed his reasons for optimism: help from the great chemist, the ease of obtaining raw materials, the low cost of the facilities. Finally, he gave formal notice that he no longer wished to become a doctor, joking that he preferred selling medicines to sick people rather than killing them off himself. He ended each of his letters with the argument of a quick fortune, also dangling before his family the promise that he would never go away again, but would build the factory there, close to Bonneville.

Months went by, and Lazare still did not come home for the holidays. All through the winter he set out the details of his plan in closely written pages which Madame Chanteau would read out loud of an evening, after dinner. One evening in May a grand council was held, for he required a categorical answer. Véronique lurked in the background, removing the tablecloth and spreading the red cover in its place.

'He's the spitting image of his grandfather, disorganized but enterprising,' declared the mother with a glance at the former carpenter's masterpiece, the presence of which on the mantelpiece was a constant irritation to her.

'He certainly doesn't get it from me, I hate change,' muttered Chanteau between groans, lying in the armchair with his legs stretched out while his attack subsided. 'But you're not exactly the steady type either, my dear.'

She shrugged her shoulders as if to say that at least her activities were underpinned by logic. Then she went on, speaking slowly:

'Anyhow, there's nothing for it but to write and tell him to follow his inclinations… I wanted him to become a magistrate; a doctor was not so nice, but now he's going to be a pharmacist… As long as he comes home and makes a lot of money, that will at least be something.'

It was really the idea of the money that convinced her. In her devotion to her son, she had identified a new dream: she saw him as a very wealthy man with a big house in Caen, a member of the Departmental Council,* perhaps even a deputy.* Chanteau had no views, preferring to wallow in his illness and leave the higher responsibilities for the family's affairs to his wife. As for Pauline, despite her surprise and her tacit disapproval of her cousin's continual changes of direction, her opinion was that he should be allowed to come home and attempt his grand venture.

'At least we'll all be living together,' she said.

'And for all the good Monsieur Lazare will be doing himself in Paris!' Véronique ventured to add. 'He'd be better off here, with some proper home cooking.'

Madame Chanteau was nodding in agreement. She picked up the letter she had received that morning.

'Wait, he also goes into the financial side of the business.'

Then she read out what he had written, adding her own comments. It would take around sixty thousand francs to set up the small factory. In Paris, Lazare had run into one of his former classmates from Caen, 'Tubby' Boutigny, who had dropped out of the Latin stream in the third year and was now a wine salesman. Boutigny was very enthusiastic about the project and would put up thirty thousand; he would make an excellent partner, an administrator whose practical know-how would ensure it was a material success. That left thirty thousand to be borrowed, because Lazare wanted to keep a half-share of the assets in his own hands.

'As you've just heard,' continued Madame Chanteau, 'he's asking me to approach Thibaudier on his behalf. The idea is a good one. Thibaudier will lend him the money straight away... As it happens, Louise is a little under the weather and I'm planning to bring her over for a week, so I'll have an opportunity to speak to her father.'

A troubled look had come into Pauline's eyes and her lips tightened convulsively. On the other side of the table, Véronique stood wiping a teacup and watching her.

'I had actually thought of an alternative,' murmured the aunt, 'but since industry always involves some risk, I'd vowed not to mention it.'

Then, turning to the young girl:

'Yes, my sweet, it occurred to me that you might lend your cousin the thirty thousand francs yourself... You could never make a better investment, your money might well earn twenty-five per cent, because your cousin would give you a share of the profits, and it makes my heart

bleed to think of all that wealth going into someone else's pocket…
Only, I don't want you to put your money at risk. It's a sacred trust,
it's all upstairs, and I will return it to you untouched.'

Pauline listened, paler now and riven by an inner conflict. She had
inherited a streak of avarice from her parents, Quenu and Lisa; their
love of the hard cash that passed across their counter, and all her early
education in the *charcuterie*, had taught her respect for money and
fear of not having enough of it, and an unfamiliar feeling, a base,
shameful meanness, now stirred in the depths of her kind heart.
Moreover, her aunt had so often shown her the drawer in the secretaire where her inheritance lay dormant, that she found the thought
that she might see it melt away in her cousin's careless hands almost
infuriating. So she kept quiet, but was tormented as well by the image
of Louise bringing him a great bag of money.

'Even if you were willing, I'd refuse,' continued Madame Chanteau.
'It's a matter of conscience, isn't it, my dear?'

'Her money's her money,' replied Chanteau, crying out in pain as
he tried to raise his leg. 'If anything went wrong, we'd get the blame…
No, no! Thibaudier will be only too pleased to help.'

But with a sudden thrill of emotion, Pauline finally found her voice.

'Oh, don't do that, it would make me feel bad; I must be the one to
lend Lazare the money. Isn't he like a brother to me?… It would be so
mean of me to refuse, now that you've mentioned the idea to me…
Let him have the money, Auntie, let him have it all.'

The effort she had just made brought floods of tears to her eyes; and
she smiled, embarrassed at having hesitated, yet with a twinge of
regret that left her with a sinking feeling. She had to argue to persuade
her aunt and uncle, who persisted in stressing the riskier aspects of the
undertaking. On this occasion, they behaved with perfect integrity.

'So, come here and kiss me,' said the aunt finally, giving way to
tears. 'You're a good little girl… Lazare will take your money, because
you insist on it.'

'What about me, don't I get a kiss too?' asked the uncle.

There were tears and exchanges of kisses all round the table. Then,
while Véronique served tea and Pauline called Mathieu, who was barking out in the yard, Madame Chanteau added, as she wiped her eyes:

'It's a great comfort that she's so generous-minded.'

'Hah!' grumbled the maid, 'she'd give the shirt off her back to stop
the other one funding him.'

It was a week later, a Saturday, that Lazare came home to Bonneville. Doctor Cazenove, who was invited to dinner, was to bring the young man in his cabriolet. Abbé Horteur, who was also invited, arrived first and was playing draughts with Chanteau, who lay convalescing in his armchair. The attack had gone on for three months and never before had he been in so much pain, so now it felt like heaven, despite the terrible itching that tormented his feet: the dry skin was flaking off, and the oedema* was almost gone. Véronique was cooking roast pigeon, and as his incorrigible gluttony reasserted itself, his nose twitched every time the kitchen door opened, much to the curé's sage disapproval.

'You aren't concentrating on the game, Monsieur Chanteau... Believe me, you really should be careful at dinner this evening. Succulent food is no good for a man in your condition.'

Louise had arrived the previous day. When Pauline heard the doctor's carriage, they both rushed out into the courtyard. But Lazare seemed to have eyes only for his cousin, exclaiming in astonishment:

'Why, can this really be Pauline?'

'Yes, of course it's me.'

'My goodness, what have they been feeding you to make you grow up so fast?... You'll be getting married next!'

She blushed, laughing joyfully, her eyes gleaming with pleasure at his approving scrutiny. He had left behind a tomboy, a schoolgirl in a cotton smock, and now saw before him a tall young woman in a white spring dress with pink flowers, that prettily hugged her bosom and hips. But her expression became serious again as she looked at him in turn and found him older, standing less erect: his youthful laugh was gone, and a slight nervous twitch ran over his face.

'Well, well,' he continued, 'I'm going to have to take you seriously now... Greetings, partner.'

Pauline blushed redder at that word, which filled her with happiness. After he had kissed her, it was all right for him to kiss Louise: she was not jealous.

Dinner was a delight. Chanteau, cowed by the doctor's threats, ate reasonably. Madame Chanteau and the curé concocted marvellous plans for enlarging Bonneville, once the area had become rich from the seaweed scheme. Nobody went to bed until eleven. Upstairs, as Lazare and Pauline were going into their separate rooms, the young man asked jokingly:

'So, since we are all grown up, won't we be saying goodnight anymore?'

'Of course we will!' she exclaimed, flinging her arms round his neck and kissing him full on the mouth, with all her former childish impetuosity.

CHAPTER 3

TWO days later, a particularly low tide uncovered deep-lying rocks. In the surge of enthusiasm that always took hold of Lazare at the start of each new undertaking, he refused to wait any longer, but set off with bare legs and just a linen jacket over his bathing costume. Pauline joined in the expedition, also in her bathing costume and wearing the heavy shoes that she kept for shrimping.

When they were a kilometre out from the cliffs, surrounded by a field of seaweed still dripping from the falling tide, the young man's enthusiasm knew no bounds, as if he were discovering for the first time this immense marine harvest which they had walked across together a hundred times before.

'Look, just look!' he shouted, 'look at all that produce!... And nobody's doing anything with it, but it goes on like that out to a depth of a hundred metres!'

Then, with joyful pedantry, he named all the species for her: zostera,* like fine, pale-green hair, forming a succession of vast lawns that stretched away to infinity; ulva,* with its broad, thin, lettuce-like leaves, transparent but glaucous; serated wrack and bladderwrack, so abundant that their vegetation covered the rocks like tall moss; and, as they followed the tide down the beach, they encountered larger and stranger-looking species such as the laminaria,* especially Neptune's Belt, which looked like a strip of greenish leather with curly edges that had been cut to fit a giant's chest.

'What bounty going to waste, eh?' he continued. 'We're such fools!... In Scotland, at least they're smart enough to eat ulva. We only make zostera into vegetable fibre, and use the wracks for packing fish. The rest is just poor-quality fertilizer that we leave to the peasants along the coast... To think that science hasn't advanced beyond the primitive stage of burning a few cart-loads of seaweed to make soda!'

Pauline, up to her knees in water, was enjoying the cool, salty sensation; and her cousin's explanations interested her deeply.

'So,' she asked, 'you're going to distil all that?'

The word 'distil' greatly amused Lazare.

'Yes, distil, if you like. But it's all pretty complicated, you'll see, my dear... Never mind, just listen and Pilly. We conquered land vegetation, didn't we? Plants, trees, all the things we use, the things we eat... Well, perhaps the conquest of marine vegetation will make us even richer, the day someone makes up their mind to attempt it.'

The two of them, burning with enthusiasm, were collecting samples. They gathered armfuls of seaweed and forgot how far out they had gone, so that on the way back they had to wade through water up to their shoulders. And Lazare continued his explanations, repeating things his mentor Herbelin had said: the sea is a vast reservoir of chemical compounds, seaweed is always working to aid industry by condensing in its tissues the salts that are present in low concentrations in the waters where it lives. So the problem was, how to extract all these useful compounds economically from seaweed. He spoke of taking the ash, impure soda as already used commercially, and separating it out to obtain perfectly pure bromides and iodides of sodium and potassium, sodium sulphate, and other salts of iron and manganese, so that no residue would be left from the raw material. What filled him with enthusiasm was the hope of not wasting a single useful substance, thanks to the refrigeration method invented by the illustrious Herbelin. There was a great fortune to be made.

'Good heavens, what a state you're in!' exclaimed Madame Chanteau when they returned home.

'Don't be cross,' replied Lazare with a laugh, dumping his bundle of seaweed in the middle of the terrace. 'Look at that! We've brought you a fresh collection of five-franc pieces.'

The following day, a full cartload of seaweed was brought up by a farmer from Verchemont, and research began in the big bedroom on the second floor. Pauline was appointed laboratory assistant. For a month they worked furiously; the room rapidly filled up with dried specimens, jars with strands of weed floating in them, and strangely shaped instruments. A microscope occupied one corner of the table, the piano disappeared beneath boilers and retorts, the wardrobe itself bulged fit to bursting with specialized books and papers which were constantly consulted. And indeed, the small-scale experiments they carried out in this way, with meticulous care, gave encouraging results. Herbelin's refrigeration method was based on the discovery that certain substances crystallize at different low temperatures, so it was just a matter of creating and maintaining the correct temperature for each to be separated out from the others and successively deposited. Lazare burnt some seaweed in a pit, then washed the ash and cooled it with a refrigeration system based on the rapid evaporation of ammonia. But it would be necessary to carry out this operation on a large scale, to take it out of the laboratory and into industrial production, by installing equipment and running it economically.

The day when he separated as many as five distinct substances from the mother liquor,* the room rang with his cries of triumph. In particular, there was a remarkable proportion of potassium bromide. This was a fashionable remedy that would sell like hot cakes! Pauline danced around the table with all her girlish grace, then ran noisily down the stairs and straight into the dining room, where her uncle was reading his newspaper and her aunt was marking table napkins.

'Aha!' she cried, 'now you can be ill whenever you like, we'll have the bromide to make you better!'

Madame Chanteau, who had been suffering from nervous attacks for some time, had just been put on a bromide diet* by Doctor Cazenove. She smiled as she said:

'Will you have enough to cure everyone, because these days everyone's nerves are a mess?'

The young girl, strong of limb, her joyous face bursting with health, flung wide her arms as if to distribute her cure to the four corners of the earth.

'Yes, yes, we'll flood the world with it... That'll put an end to their great neurosis!'*

After inspecting the whole coast and discussing possible locations, Lazare decided to set up his factory in Treasure Bay. It combined all the right conditions: a vast expanse of beach virtually paved with flat rocks, which would make it easier to harvest the seaweed; direct transport via the Verchemont road; cheap land, raw materials close at hand, and located a sufficient but not excessive distance away. Pauline joked about the name they had given the bay in the old days, because of its fine golden sand: they hadn't known how true it would turn out to be, now they would be finding real 'treasure' in the sea. They made a splendid start, with the fortunate purchase of twenty thousand square

metres of deserted heathland, and building permission from the prefect obtained after a delay of just two months. At last, labourers set
about the construction work. Boutigny had turned up, a short, red-
faced man of about thirty, very vulgar and not at all to the Chanteaus'
taste. He had refused to live in Bonneville, claiming to have discovered
a very comfortable house in Verchemont, and the family's coolness
towards him increased with the discovery that he had just brought
a woman to live there, doubtless some tart he had picked up in a house
of ill repute in Paris. Lazare shrugged his shoulders, mortified by
their provincial narrow-mindedness; she was very nice, a blonde who
must be quite the devoted sort to accept being dumped in such a godforsaken place, though he did not press the point, for Pauline's sake.
All that was expected from Boutigny, in the end, was active supervi-
sion and intelligent organization of the work; and in that he turned
out to be a marvel, constantly on his feet, fired with a passion for
management. Under his orders, the walls rose rapidly.

Then, for the next four months while the buildings were going up
and the equipment being installed, the Treasure Factory, as they had
started to call it, became the destination of their daily walk. Madame
Chanteau did not always accompany the young people, so Lazare and
Pauline went rambling off together as they had in years gone by. Only
Mathieu would follow them, but he now tired quickly, dragging his
great paws along, and lay down when he got there with his tongue
lolling out, panting in short, rapid breaths, like a blacksmith's bel-
lows. He was also the only one who still went swimming, leaping into
the sea when they threw him a stick, which he was clever enough to
pick up in the trough of a wave, to avoid getting a mouthful of salt
water. On each visit, Lazare would put pressure on the builders, while
Pauline offered a few practical suggestions, some of them very much
to the point. He had ordered the equipment from Caen, to his own
designs, and workmen had arrived to assemble it. Boutigny was starting to show signs of anxiety at the constantly rising costs. Why had
they not been content to start with just the space and machines that
were strictly necessary? Why such complicated buildings and such
enormous apparatus designed for large-scale production, when it would
have been wiser to expand gradually, once they had a clear understanding of the manufacturing conditions and sales potential? Lazare
would lose his temper. His vision was an ambitious one, he would have
liked to give the factory a monumental facade overlooking the sea,

proclaiming to the limitless horizon the grandeur of his idea. Then the visit would conclude in a flurry of optimism: why penny-pinch, when they were on the brink of a fortune? They would return home in fine spirits, and Mathieu, who constantly lagged behind, was not left out of the good humour: Pauline and Lazare would suddenly hide behind a wall, then laugh like children as the dog, bemused to find himself all alone and thinking he was abandoned, bounded around in comic terror.

Every evening they were greeted at home with the same question.

'Well then, is everything going to plan, are you pleased?'

And the answer was always the same.

'Yes, yes... But they're taking for ever.'

These were months of close friendship between them. Lazare manifested a lively affection towards Pauline, partly out of gratitude for the money that she had put into his business. Gradually, he once again stopped thinking of her as a woman and lived alongside her as if in the company of another man, a younger brother whose qualities he valued more highly every day. She was so logical, so very brave, of such smiling goodness that she finally inspired in him an unspoken esteem, a tacit respect, against which he still tried to defend himself by teasing her. Calmly she told him about the books she had read, her aunt's horror at the sight of the anatomical plates, and for a moment he stood nonplussed and full of embarrassment before this girl, with her wide candid eyes, who already knew so much. This made their relationship even closer, and he grew accustomed to speaking freely about everything that arose in the course of their joint researches, when she was helping him, using the specific term in the straightforward manner of a scientist, as if no alternative existed. She herself would tackle any question, apparently for no other reason than the pleasure of learning and being helpful to him. But she often amused him, as her education had so many gaps and comprised an extraordinary jumble of conflicting notions: her aunt's schoolmistress ideas on the one hand, in which life was reduced to coy boarding-school norms, and on the other, the precise details that she had read in the medical textbooks, the physiological truths about man and woman which explained how life actually worked. Whenever she let slip a naïve remark, he would laugh so loudly that she lost her temper: instead of mocking, wouldn't he have done better to explain where she had gone wrong? Generally, such disputes would end in a lesson, with him filling a gap her education, like a young chemist above petty social conventions. She already knew too much to remain ignorant of the rest. In any case, a slow process of change was underway, as she kept on reading and gradually putting together all the things she heard and saw, while still showing respect for Madame Chanteau, and listening with a serious expression to her prudish nod. It was only with her cousin, in the large bedroom, that she became a masculine lab assistant, to whom he could shout:

'Hey, come and look at this Floridia... It's only got one sex.'

'So it has,' she replied, 'great bunches of male organs.'

Yet a vague uneasiness was stirring in her. Sometimes, when Lazare jostled her in a brotherly way, her heart would thump and she would feel breathless for a few seconds. The woman in her, ignored by them both, was reawakening in the very instincts of her flesh and her blood. One day, as he was turning round, he jabbed her with his elbow. She cried out and clutched her chest. What was the matter? Had he hurt her? But he'd hardly touched her! Instinctively he went to pull aside her shawl and see. She backed away and they stood there face to face, embarrassed and smiling awkwardly. On another day, in the course of an experiment, she refused to put her hands in cold water. He was astonished and angry: why not, what had got into her? If she wasn't going to help him, she might as well go back downstairs. Then, seeing her blush, he understood, and gawped at her open-mouthed. So, this tomboy, this younger brother, was actually a woman? You couldn't brush against her without her letting out a shriek, and you couldn't depend on her right through the month. Every new incident came as a surprise, like an unexpected discovery that embarrassed them both and disturbed their relationship of masculine camaraderie. Lazare seemed only to find it irritating; they weren't going to be able to work together, since she wasn't a man and the merest trifle could upset her. As for Pauline, she was left with a sense of malaise and anxiety which also had a delicious and charming aspect.

From that moment on, the young girl began to develop feelings of which she spoke to no one. She did not lie, she simply kept silent, from anxious pride but also from a sense of shame. Several times she thought she was ill, on the brink of some serious ailment, because she went to bed with a fever and tossed and turned in insomnia, completely overwhelmed by the turbulent new sensations swirling within her. Then, when daybreak came, she simply felt exhausted and did not even mention it to her aunt. She also had sudden hot flushes, a general nervous excitement, unexpected thoughts which later disgusted her, and above all, dreams from which she would awaken angry with herself. In spite of the books she had read, the anatomy and physiology that she had pored over with a passion, she remained physically such a virgin that with every new phenomenon, she fell back into her childish bewilderment. Then she calmed down as she thought more about it: she was not unique, she had to expect the mechanism of life, devised for everyone else, to work itself out in her as well. One evening after dinner, she spoke about the stupidity of dreams: wasn't it infuriating to be lying there on your back, defenceless and vulnerable to the strangest imaginings? What really exasperated her was the death of the will in sleep, the complete surrender of the self. Her cousin, with his pessimistic theories, also spoke against dreams, as disturbing the perfect happiness of oblivion, while his uncle made a distinction between pleasant dreams and the horrible nightmares caused by fever. But she was so insistent that a surprised Madame Chanteau questioned her about what was in these nighttime dreams of hers. Then she babbled that it was nothing, absurd nonsense, things too vague to remember. And that was all true, for in her dreams, which were played out in a kind of half-light, vague figures would brush up against her. Her feminine sexuality was awakening to the life of the flesh, without any clear image ever giving precise form to the sensation: she saw nobody, and could believe she had just been caressed by a summer sea breeze, coming in through the open window.

However, Pauline's great affection for Lazare seemed daily more ardent, and this was not due solely, in their seven-year fraternal friendship, to the instinctive awakening of her womanhood: she also felt a need to devote herself to him, for she had the illusion that he was more intelligent and stronger than herself. Slowly, her fraternal friendship was turning into love, with the exquisite hesitations of a dawning passion: shivers of overloud laughter, furtive and lingering touchings, the whole enchanted embarkation for the land of noble affections, driven by the reproductive instinct. Protected by his Latin Quarter excesses and with no curiosity left to satisfy, he continued to see her as just a sister, completely beyond the realm of his desire. She, on the contrary, a virgin living in an isolated situation where he was the only man, came gradually to adore him and devoted herself to him entirely. When they were together, from morning to night, she seemed to exist through his presence, her gaze seeking his, eager to serve him.

Around that time, Madame Chanteau was astonished by Pauline's piety. Twice she saw her go to confession. Then, all of a sudden, the young girl seemed to have fallen out with Abbé Horteur, even refusing to attend Mass three Sundays in succession, and only going back to avoid offending her aunt. She never offered any explanation, but she must have been hurt by the abbé's questions and comments, for his way of putting things was not subtle. It was then that, with the instinct of a devoted mother, Madame Chanteau guessed at Pauline's growing love. She kept her own counsel, however, not even mentioning it to her husband. This inevitable adventure had caught her unawares, because until then the possibility of affection, perhaps even marriage, had not come into her plans. Like Lazare, she had gone on treating her ward like a little girl; now she wanted to think things over, and she resolved to keep a close eye on them, though in reality she did nothing about it, for she was basically unconcerned with anything except her son's pleasure.

The hot days of August had arrived, and one evening the young man decided that they would go for a swim the following day on their way to the factory. Obsessed by her ideas of propriety, the mother accompanied them despite the fierce heat of the three o'clock sun. She sat down beside Mathieu on the burning pebbles beneath her parasol, and the dog also tried to edge his head into the shade.

'But where's she going?' asked Lazare at the sight of Pauline half-disappearing behind a rock.

'She's getting changed, for goodness' sake!' said Madame Chanteau. 'Turn away, you're embarrassing her, it's not decent.'

He stood there in complete astonishment and took another look in the direction of the rock, where a corner of white underskirt fluttered, then glanced again at his mother and resolved to turn his back. But he undressed quickly himself, without further comment.

'Are you ready yet?' he shouted at last. 'What a lot of fuss! Are you getting into your Sunday best?'

Pauline skipped nimbly out, with a forced laugh suggestive of mild embarrassment. Since her cousin's return they had not yet gone swimming together. She was wearing a proper one-piece swimming costume drawn in by a waistband and barely covering her hips, which emphasized her slimness, her supple back and high bosom, and gave her the appearance of a Florentine marble statue. Her bare arms and legs, and her little bare feet in sandals, were still as white as a child's.

'Well,' said Lazare, 'how about swimming out to the Picochets?'

'All right, the Picochets it is,' she replied.

Madame Chanteau called out:

'Don't go too far out… I'm always so frightened when you do!'

But they had already waded into the water. The Picochets, a group of rocks a few of which remained exposed at high tide, were about a kilometre distant. They swam towards them side by side, without hurrying, like two friends setting out for a stroll along a fine straight path. At first, Mathieu followed them; then, seeing that they were still heading out to sea, he returned to shake himself and spray Madame Chanteau with water. Futile exploits were an affront to his lazy nature.

'You're the sensible one,' said the older lady. 'How in heaven's name can they take such risks?'

She was now barely able to make out the heads of Lazare and Pauline, bobbing on the waves like small clumps of seaweed. There was quite a big swell, they were rocked gently by its rise and fall as they swam on, calmly chatting about the marine plants passing beneath them in the crystal-clear waters. Feeling tired, Pauline floated on her back, looking up at the sky, just a dot in the blue immensity. The sea that was rocking her was still her great friend. She loved its salty breath and its chill, chaste waters, and she surrendered herself to it, happy to feel its immense liquid embrace on her skin, tasting the joy of this violent exercise that set her heart racing.

But then she gave a little cry. Her cousin questioned her anxiously.

'What's the matter?'

'I think my strap has snapped… I straightened my left arm too quickly.'

And they both joked about it. She had started swimming gently again, laughing in an embarrassed way as she realized the extent of the disaster: the stitching of the shoulder strap had given way, exposing her whole shoulder and breast. Much amused, the young man suggested she hunt through her pockets in case she had some pins about her. When they arrived at the Picochets, he climbed out onto a rock, as they normally did, to get his breath back before setting off on the return journey. She continued swimming around the reef.

'Aren't you going to get out?'

'No, I'm quite happy in the water.'

He thought she was being silly, and grew cross with her. Was that a sensible thing to do? She might run out of energy on the way back if she didn't take a breather first. But she remained adamant and did not even answer, gliding quietly around with water up to her chin to conceal the white nakedness of her shoulder, which gleamed indistinctly like milky mother of pearl in a shell. Towards the open sea, the rocks were hollowed out into a sort of cave where, in days gone by, they had played at Robinson Crusoe, looking out over an empty horizon. In the other direction, back on the beach, Madame Chanteau was a black speck, no bigger than an insect.

'You're so pig-headed!' exclaimed Lazare finally as he plunged back into the water. 'If you want to drown, I'll leave you to it, I swear I will!'

Slowly they set off back. They were both sulky and in no mood to talk. Hearing that she was getting out of breath, he told her she should at least float on her back. She seemed not to hear. The rip was getting bigger, and the slightest movement to turn over would have meant her breast breaking the surface, like some flower from the deep. Then he must have understood; and seeing how tired she was, sensing that she would never make it to the beach, he went resolutely over to support her. She tried to fend him off and carry on alone, but in the end she was forced to give in. He held her tightly across his body, and that was how they got back to the shore.

In a state of shock, Madame Chanteau ran down to meet them while Mathieu, up to his belly in the waves, was howling.

'Oh my God, how rash you have been! Didn't I tell you it was too far?'

Pauline had fainted. Lazare carried her onto the sand like a child and she stayed pressed against his chest, half naked by now, both of them streaming with salty water. All at once she gave a sigh and opened her eyes. When she recognized the young man, she burst into deep sobs, smothering him in a nervous embrace and kissing his face all over. It was an almost unconscious reaction, an impulse of love welling up unchecked after her experience of mortal danger.

'Oh, you are so good! Oh! how I love you, Lazare!'

He stood there, stunned at the impetuosity of her kisses. While Madame Chanteau was getting her dressed, he turned away of his own accord. The walk back to Bonneville was slow and laborious; they both seemed completely shattered. Madame Chanteau walked between them, reflecting that the time had come for a decision.

There were other reasons for concern in the family. The factory at Treasure Bay was now complete and for the last week they had been trialling the equipment, but the results were very disappointing. Lazare was forced to admit that he had set up certain components incorrectly. He went off to Paris to consult his mentor, Herbelin, and came back in despair: everything would need to be done again from scratch, the great chemist had made improvements to his method which required major changes to the apparatus. Meanwhile, the sixty thousand francs had already been used up and Boutigny was refusing to put in another penny: from morning till night he talked bitterly of money squandered, with the insufferable insistence of a practical man who had been right all along. Lazare could have hit him. He might have given up there and then, were it not for his anguish at the thought of Pauline's thirty thousand francs going down the drain. His honesty and pride rebelled: this was unacceptable, he must find more money, they couldn't now abandon a business which in due course would bring in millions.

'Don't you worry,' his mother kept saying as she saw him sick with dithering. 'It's not as if we didn't know where to turn to raise a few thousand more.'

Madame Chanteau was hatching a plan. Initially coming to her as a total surprise, the idea of a marriage between Pauline and Lazare now struck her as being most suitable. After all, there was just a nine-year difference in age between them, nothing unusual these days. Wouldn't it be an elegant solution? Lazare would be working for his wife, he could stop tormenting himself about his debt, and even borrow the money he needed now from Pauline. Deep down in her heart, Madame Chanteau did feel vague scruples, the apprehension of an ultimate catastrophe that would ruin her ward. Only, she dismissed such an outcome as impossible: was Lazare not a man of genius? He would make Pauline rich, so it was she who had most to gain. It mattered little that her son had no money, he would be worth a fortune when she gave him away.

The marriage was decided very simply. One morning Madame Chanteau went into Pauline's room to question her, and with smiling composure the girl immediately poured out her heart. Then her aunt persuaded her to pretend to be fatigued, and that afternoon went alone with her son to the factory. On the way home, she explained her scheme to him at length, telling him how much his little cousin loved him, how suitable the marriage was, and the benefits it would bring for everyone. At first, he seemed amazed. The idea had never occurred to him; and how old was the child anyway? Then he was overcome with emotion; of course, he was very fond of her too, and would do as they wished.

As they came back into the house they found Pauline setting the table, to keep herself busy. Her uncle, having let his newspaper fall onto his knees, was watching Minouche as she fastidiously licked her belly.

'Well now, guess what?' said Lazare, hiding his emotion behind a show of jollity. 'We're to be married!'

Pauline just stood there holding a plate and went very red, unable to utter a word.

'Who is?' asked her uncle suddenly, as if he had just woken up.

His wife had mentioned it to him that morning, but the cat's delight in running her tongue over her fur had captured his full attention. However, he quickly recollected.

'Ah yes, of course!' he said.

Then he gave the young people a knowing look, while his mouth twisted in response to a sudden painful twinge in his right foot. Pauline had gently put the plate down, and, turning to Lazare, she said:

'If you'd like to, so would I.'

'So, that's settled then,' said Madame Chanteau, hanging up her straw hat. 'Now give each other a kiss!'

Pauline went up to Lazare, her hands outstretched. Still laughing, he clasped them in his own, and began to tease her.

'So, you've stopped playing with dolls, have you? That's why you hid yourself away and nobody could even see you wash your delicate fingers! And your chosen victim is to be poor old Lazare?'

'Oh Auntie, make him shut up or I'll run away!' murmured Pauline in embarrassment, trying to slip his grasp.

But gradually he drew her closer, playfully as in the days of their schoolroom friendship; then suddenly she gave him a smacking kiss on the cheek, which he returned by accident on her ear. Then some private thought seemed to cloud his mood, and he added sadly:

'You're not getting a very good deal here, you poor child! If you only knew how old I really am, inside! Still, since you're willing to put up with me...'

Dinner was an exuberant affair. Everyone talked at once, making all kinds of plans for the future, as though this was the first time they were all gathered together. Véronique, who had come in just as the engagement was being announced, stormed back to the kitchen and slammed the door without a word. Over dessert they began to discuss serious matters. Madame Chanteau explained that the wedding could not take place for another two years: she wanted to wait until Pauline came of age, to avoid any possible accusations that she and her son might have taken advantage of her youth. Pauline was dismayed at the two-year wait, but deeply touched by her aunt's honesty, and stood up to give her a kiss. A date was agreed; the young couple would have to be patient, but meanwhile they would earn the first instalments of their future millions. Thus, the money question was broached amid general enthusiasm.

'Take the money from the drawer, Auntie,' Pauline kept saying, 'and let him have as much as he wants. It's his as much as mine now.'

Madame Chanteau would not hear of it.

'No, no, I won't take out a penny more than is necessary... You know you can trust me, I'd rather have my hand cut off... You need ten thousand francs for the factory; well, I'll get the ten thousand out for you, but the rest stays under lock and key. It's my sacred duty.'

'With ten thousand francs, I'm certain of success,' said Lazare. 'All the major expenditure has already been made, it would be criminal to lose confidence now. You'll see, you'll see... And you, my darling, I want you to wear a gold dress, like a queen, on our wedding day.'

Their joy was further increased by the unexpected arrival of Doctor Cazenove. He had just been attending to a fisherman whose fingers had been crushed beneath a boat, and they pressed him to stay for a cup of tea. The great news did not seem to surprise him. However, when he heard the Chanteaus enthusiastically talking up the industrialization of seaweed, he looked anxiously at Pauline, and murmured:

'Well, it's certainly an ingenious idea, and worth a try. But stocks and shares are definitely safer. If I were you, I'd aim to be happy from the start, in a modest sort of a way...'

He stopped short as he saw a cloud come over the young girl's eyes, and the warm affection he felt for her led him to continue, against his own convictions:

'But, there's something to be said for making money, too, so you'd better make lots of it... And I'll come and dance at your wedding, you'll see. Yes, I shall dance the Caribbean Zambuco, I bet you don't

know how it goes... Watch this! you whirl both arms around like
a windmill and slap your thighs, dancing round the prisoner after he's
been cooked, and the women are chopping him up.'

The months resumed their placid course. Pauline had now regained
her smiling composure, since only uncertainty could upset her frank
nature. The confession of her love and the fixing of a wedding date
seemed to have quelled even the stirrings of her flesh, and she
accepted quite calmly the flowering of her being, the slow blossoming
of her body, and the crimson rush of her blood which for a while had
tormented her by day and assailed her by night. Was this not the universal law? Loving meant growing. In any case, her relations with
Lazare hardly changed: they carried on working together as before,
he constantly busy, and protected from passionate urges by his passing adventures in Paris, and she so simple and upright in the tranquil
assurance of her virginity and her learning that she was shielded as if
by a double armour. Sometimes, however, they would take each other
by the hand, in that big untidy room, and laugh together in tender
complicity. Perhaps, while leafing through some treatise on marine
botany, their heads would gently touch; or, as they examined a crimson flask of bromine or a purple specimen of iodine, they would lean
calmly against each other; or, bending over the instruments that cluttered the table and the piano, her face would come close to his; or she
would call him over to lift her up so that she could reach the top shelf
in the wardrobe. But those hourly contacts never went beyond the
legitimate, tender gestures that might be exchanged in the sight of
grandparents, an affectionate friendship between betrothed cousins,
spiced with the merest hint of joyful sensuality. As Madame Chanteau
put it, they were behaving in a most sensible manner. Whenever
Louise arrived, with her coquettish airs and graces, and interposed
herself between them, Pauline did not even seem jealous.

A whole year went by in this fashion. The factory was now in operation, and the problems it gave them may well have provided their
greatest protection. Once the difficult reinstallation of the apparatus
was finished, the first results seemed excellent. The yield was admittedly modest, but with improvements to the method and extra care
and energy, they were sure to reach enormous levels of production.
Boutigny had already found substantial outlets for their products;
more than they could supply, in fact. Their fortune seemed assured.
So, from now on, they pursued this hope stubbornly, ignoring warn-

ings of ruin, and the factory became a pit into which they flung money by the handful, always convinced that they would find it again in the form of a huge gold ingot, at the bottom. Each fresh sacrifice only made them more obstinate.

The first few times, Madame Chanteau would not take any money from the drawer in her secretaire without telling Pauline.

'There are some payments due on Saturday, my dear,' she would say, 'and you are three thousand francs short. Will you come upstairs with me so we can decide which securities to sell?'

'But you can choose on your own, Auntie,' Pauline would reply.

'Oh no, my dear, you know I never do anything without asking you. It's your money.'

Gradually, however, Madame Chanteau grew less scrupulous. One evening Lazare confessed to her a debt that he had concealed from Pauline, five thousand francs-worth of copper pipes which had not even been used. She had just come back from a visit to the secretaire with her niece, so seeing her son's despair, she went back upstairs on her own and took out the extra five thousand francs, vowing to replace it as soon as the first profits came in. But from that day on, the breach was opened, and she grew accustomed to helping herself without keeping count. In any case, she had started to find it humiliating, at her age, to be continually subject to the approval of a mere child, something for which she bore Pauline a grudge. She would get her money back all right, but even if it did belong to her, that was no reason why they should be unable to lift a finger without her permission. Once she had begun to raid the secretaire, she stopped insisting that the girl go along with her. This came as a relief to Pauline, for, despite her generous heart, she found these withdrawal visits distressing: her reason alerted her to impending disaster, and all her mother's economical prudence rebelled within her. At first, she was surprised by Madame Chanteau's silence, for she could tell that money was still going out, just without her being consulted. Soon, however, she came to prefer it that way. At least it spared her the trial of seeing the bundle of papers dwindle with each visit. From now on, between Pauline and her aunt there was only a quick exchange of looks at certain times: an anxious stare from Pauline, when she guessed at some new borrowing, followed by an evasive glance from Madame Chanteau, resentful at having to avert her gaze. Thus, the seeds of hatred were sown between them.

Unfortunately, that year Davoine was declared bankrupt. Though the disaster was not unexpected, it came as a terrible blow to the Chanteaus. They were left with their three thousand francs of interest to live off. Everything they were able to rescue from the collapse of the timber business, some twelve thousand francs, was also invested in their, bringing their total income up to three hundred a month. And so, after a fortnight Madame Chanteau was obliged to take fifty francs more of Pauline's money: the butcher from Verchemont was waiting with his bill, and she could not send him away unpaid. Then there was a hundred francs to buy a laundry boiler, and smaller amounts, ten francs for potatoes or fifty sous* for fish. She found herself supporting both Lazare and the factory on a daily basis with shamefully petty sums, then stooped even lower, taking out coppers for household expenses in a miserable attempt to fend off creditors. Especially towards the end of each month, she would often slip discreetly upstairs and return almost at once with her hand in her pocket, reluctantly extracting, one by one, the coins needed to pay some bill. Once she had got into the habit, she came to rely entirely upon the contents of the secretaire, giving in to temptation without further resistance. However, each time she succumbed to her obsession and opened the lid, it would let out a slight squeak which set her nerves on edge. What a piece of old junk! To think that she had never been able to afford a proper desk of her own! At first, when there had been a fortune stuffed inside, the venerable secretaire had seemed to lend the household an air of gaiety and prosperity, but now it preyed on her mind, like Pandora's poisonous box with all the evils of the world inside, oozing misfortune from every crack.

One evening, Pauline ran in from the yard, calling out:

'It's the baker!... We owe him for three days, two francs eighty-five.'

Madame Chanteau fumbled about her person.

'I shall have to go upstairs and look for my purse,' she murmured.

'Don't worry,' said Pauline without thinking, 'I'll get it. Where is it?'

'No, no... I'm not sure, you wouldn't find it.'

Madame Chanteau blustered on, then she and Pauline exchanged silent looks which made them both turn pale. After a painful pause, the aunt went upstairs, trembling with suppressed rage and sensing that her ward knew perfectly well where the two francs eighty-five would be coming from. And in any case, why had she so often shown her the money sitting in the drawer? She was frustrated at having been so open and scrupulous: the girl must now be imagining her every move, as she opened, rummaged, closed the lid. Back downstairs, she paid the baker, then her anger against Pauline exploded.

'Look at the state your dress is in, whatever have you been doing? Drawing water for the vegetables, I'll bet. Will you kindly leave Véronique to get on with her own jobs? I swear you get filthy on purpose, you seem to have no idea what it costs! Your allowance isn't all that great, I can't make ends meet anymore!'

And on and on she went. At first Pauline attempted to defend herself, but now she listened in silence, with a heavy heart. For some time, she had been aware that her aunt was feeling less and less affectionate towards her. When she found herself alone with Véronique, she burst into tears, and the maid busied herself noisily with her pots and pans, as if to avoid taking sides. She still grumbled about Pauline, but now, in her rough way, she was beginning to sense an injustice.

Winter came round, and Lazare lost heart. Once again, his passion had turned sour, and the factory now filled him with fear and loathing. In November, fresh money worries plunged him into a panic. He had dealt with earlier crises, but this one reduced him to trembling and hopeless despair, and he cursed science. His idea of exploiting seaweed was stupid! However much they perfected their methods, they would never succeed in wresting from nature something it did not want to yield. He even belittled his mentor, the great Herbelin, who, having been kind enough to go out of his way and visit the factory, had stood in embarrassment before the apparatus which, he said, was perhaps too large-scale to work with the same precision as his small laboratory version. In short, the result seemed clear: in these refrigeration reactions, no means had yet been found of maintaining the low temperatures necessary for the different substances to crystallize out. Lazare had certainly been able to extract from seaweed a certain quantity of potassium bromide, but since he could not adequately isolate and remove the four or five other impurities, the process was a failure. He was sick of the whole business, and he admitted defeat. One evening, when Madame Chanteau and Pauline pleaded with him to keep calm and make one final effort, there was a very painful scene, with angry recriminations, bitter tears, and doors slammed so violently that Chanteau jumped out his skin in his armchair.

'You'll be the death of me!' screamed Lazare as he rushed away to lock himself in his room, wallowing in childish despair.

The next morning, he came down to breakfast with a sheet of paper covered in figures. Out of Pauline's one hundred and eighty thousand francs,* almost a hundred thousand was already used up. Was there any sense in carrying on? Good money would go after bad; the same panic as the previous day had turned him white as a sheet. And his mother was now taking his side, who had never admired him, and loved him to the point of complicity in his failings. It was only Pauline who still tried to object. The figure of one hundred thousand francs had come as a complete shock to her. What had things come to? He had taken more than half her fortune, and those hundred thousand would be wasted if he did not carry on the fight! But her words were in vain, and while she spoke, Véronique was clearing the table. Then, to stop herself from launching into recriminations, Pauline went and locked herself in her room in despair.

She left an embarrassed silence behind her as the family sat round the table, not knowing what to say.

'Well, the child is certainly mean with her money,' said Madame Chanteau eventually, 'and that's a nasty flaw. I won't have Lazare worrying himself to death, with all this stress and vexation.'

Then Chanteau interjected timidly:

'Nobody told me anything about such a huge sum... A hundred thousand francs indeed! My goodness, that's dreadful!'

'A hundred thousand, what of it?' retorted Madame Chanteau sharply. 'We'll get it all back for her... If our son marries her, he is certainly man enough to earn a hundred thousand francs.'

Straight away, they set about winding up the business. It was Boutigny who had terrified Lazare by presenting him with a disastrous report of the situation. They were about twenty thousand francs in debt. Once Boutigny saw that his partner was proposing to withdraw, he initially announced his own intention of going to Algeria, where a splendid position awaited him. But later, he said he would be prepared to take on the factory by himself, although he seemed so very reluctant, and made the accounts look so complicated, that in the end he obtained the site, buildings, and equipment against just the repayment of the twenty-thousand-franc debt. When Lazare managed at the last minute to extract from him a promissory note for a further five thousand, payable in quarterly instalments, it felt like a victory. The next day, Boutigny started selling off the copper apparatus for scrap and adapting the buildings for the commercial manufacture of common soda, using an entirely conventional process which involved no scientific research at all.

Pauline, rather ashamed at her first reaction of thrift and caution, had regained her cheery and helpful demeanour, as if to make amends for something wrong that she had done. So when Lazare produced the note for the five thousand francs, Madame Chanteau was triumphant, and insisted on her niece going upstairs with her to see it put away in the drawer.

'There, at least we've got five thousand francs back... And it's all yours, my dear. My son has refused to take a penny in compensation for all his trouble.'

For some time now, Chanteau had been fretting as he sat in his armchair, nursing his gout. Although he never dared refuse his signature, he was greatly alarmed at the way his wife was administering their ward's fortune. That sum of a hundred thousand francs kept ringing in his ears. How could they possibly cover up such a deficit when the time came to submit their accounts? And the worst of it was that Saccard, the surrogate guardian, whose Parisian speculations were the talk of the town, had just recalled Pauline's existence, having apparently forgotten about her for almost eight years. He had written to ask after her, and was even talking of calling on them in Bonneville one morning, on his way to a business meeting in Cherbourg. What could they possibly say if he demanded a statement of their accounts, as he had every right to do? His sudden interest after such a long period of indifference was alarming.

When Chanteau finally broached the subject with his wife, her reaction was one of curiosity rather than anxiety. Her first intuition was close to the truth: she suspected that Saccard, entangled in his many millions of speculations, had run out of money and was considering taking control of Pauline's fortune, to make it multiply tenfold. Then she went wildly off track, wondering whether it might have been the girl herself who had written to her surrogate guardian, with revenge in mind. When her husband expressed his horror at such a suggestion, she invented a whole complicated story of anonymous letters sent by the Boutigny hussy, a creature they refused to have in the house, who was dragging their good name through the mud in all the shops of Verchemont and Arromanches.

'But I don't give a damn what they think!' she said. 'The girl may not be eighteen yet, but I only have to marry her off to Lazare and straight away, she will be legally emancipated.'

'Are you sure?' asked Chanteau.

'Of course I am! I was reading about it in the Code only this morning.'

For Madame Chanteau was indeed now studying the Civil Code.*
In the struggle against her lingering scruples, she looked to it for
excuses, and as her honesty crumbled, progressively destroyed by the
temptation of such a large and uncomplicated sum of money within her
reach, she had become interested in underhand ways of taking financial control.

However, she still hesitated to bring the marriage plan to a conclusion. After the financial disaster, Pauline would have preferred to speed
things up: why put it off for six more months, until she was eighteen?
It would be better to get it over and done with, without waiting until
Lazare had found a job. She ventured to say as much to her aunt, who,
caught off guard, invented a lie. Closing the door, she whispered that
Lazare was afflicted by a secret anxiety: he was extremely sensitive, and
hated the thought of marrying her before he could bring her a fortune, now that he had compromised hers. The girl listened in astonishment, quite unable to understand such far-fetched scruples: even
if he had been rich, she would have married him for love; and anyway,
how long would they have to wait? Perhaps for ever? Then Madame
Chanteau protested, saying she would do her best to overcome his
exaggerated sense of honour, provided they didn't rush things; and,
in conclusion, she made her niece swear not to say anything, as she
feared he might do something impulsive and suddenly leave home, if
he found out his secret had been guessed and talked about. Pauline,
filled with disquiet by her aunt's remarks, had to resign herself to waiting and keeping silent.

Meanwhile, whenever Chanteau's fear of Saccard got the better of
him, he would say to his wife:

'If it's the way to put things right, please get the two children married at once.'

'There's no rush,' she replied. 'The danger isn't imminent.'

'But since you want them to marry one day... You haven't changed
your mind, have you? It would be the death of them.'

'Death of them, indeed!... As long as a thing is not done, if it turns
out to be unwise, it need not be done at all. And anyway, they are free
to do as they like; we'll see later on if they're still so keen on the idea.'

Pauline and Lazare had resumed their former existence in common, while the unusually harsh winter weather kept them indoors.

During the first week, Pauline found Lazare so melancholy, ashamed of himself and embittered against everything, that she lavished attention on him and treated him like an invalid. She even felt pity for this tall young man, whose lack of perseverance and courage of a merely nervous type explained his failures, and she gradually began to assume a chiding, maternal authority over him. At first, he completely lost his temper, vowing to become a peasant and work the land, then hatching one wild plan after another for making an instant fortune: he was embarrassed to eat his family's bread, and would not remain a burden on them an hour longer. But as the days slipped by, he constantly put off implementing his ideas, merely coming up each morning with a new plan which would take him in a single bound to a pinnacle of wealth and honour. Then, scared by her aunt's false revelations, Pauline would remonstrate with him: nobody wanted him to worry himself like that; he could look for a position in the spring, and would find one straight away, but until then they would make sure he had a rest. By the end of the first month she seemed to have calmed him down, and he fell into a state of idle listlessness, with a mocking resignation in the face of what he termed 'life's burdens'.

Now Pauline detected in him a troubling change of personality, worsening by the day, which filled her with repugnance. His previous outbursts of temper, flaring up and dying down again like burning straw, seemed to her preferable to the way he now sneered at everything, delivering his bitter professions of nihilism in a monotone. Amid the winter peace of the forsaken hole that was Bonneville, it was as if his Parisian connections, his reading and discussions with fellow medical students, had all started coming back to him. It was the legacy of a half-digested pessimism, a few brilliant aphorisms and the great, dark poetry of Schopenhauer.* Pauline well understood that her cousin's railings against humanity sprang from anger at his own defeat, the disaster of the factory that had shattered his world. But she could not perceive the deeper reasons, and simply protested ardently when he reverted to his old arguments about the illusion of progress and the ultimate futility of science. Wasn't that idiot Boutigny on the way to making his fortune from commercial soda? So, what was the use of ruining himself to invent a better way and discover new laws, when mere empiricism had won out in the end? This was his constant point of departure, and he would always conclude by saying, with a tight-lipped sneer, that the only good that would ever come of science would

be if it discovered a way of blowing the whole universe to smithereens
by means of some colossal explosive shell. Then he would trot out
a string of chilling jokes about the devious tricks of the Will that ruled
the world, and the blind stupidity of our instinct for self-preserva-
tion. The whole of life, he said, was pain, and he came round to the
doctrine of the Indian fakirs, that annihilation was the ultimate release.
When Pauline heard him affecting a horror of action and predicting
the final suicide of nations, a mass stampede into the darkness of oblivion as they refused to beget new generations, once their intelligence
was sufficiently developed for them to realize the cruel, imbecilic role
an unknown power made them play, she grew angry and tried to find
arguments against him. But to no avail, for she was ignorant of such
things, and, as Lazare told her, had no head for metaphysics. But she
refused to admit defeat, and roundly condemned his Schopenhauer
when he tried to read some passages to her—a man who wrote such
vile slanders about women, whom she would gladly have strangled, were
it not for his fondness for animals!* In robust health, always confident
in her cheerful routine and hopeful for the morrow, in the end she
reduced her cousin to silence by her loud laughter, triumphant in all
the thrusting vigour of her puberty.

'Now look!' she would cry, 'you're talking nonsense. It will be time
to think about dying once we're old.'

The idea of death, which she spoke of so lightly, always made him
solemn, and he would look away. Generally, he changed the subject,
after murmuring:

'You can die at any age.'

Pauline eventually realized that Lazare was terrified of death. She
remembered his fear-stricken cry that night as they had gazed up at
the stars. She now saw him blanch on hearing certain words, and fall
silent as if to conceal some unmentionable affliction. It was a great
surprise to her to realize what dread of annihilation was felt by this
vehement pessimist, who talked of snuffing the stars out like candles
amid the universal massacre of living things. This illness of his went
back a long way, and she was far from suspecting how serious it now
was. As he advanced in years, Lazare had become haunted by death.
Until his twenties, he had felt only a slight chill of foreboding at
night, as he went to bed. But now he could not lay his head on his
pillow without his whole face turning to ice at the thought of his irremediable end. Gripped by insomnia, he could not resign himself to

the inevitable, which played itself out in lugubrious images before his mind. And once he finally fell asleep from sheer exhaustion, he would wake with a start and jerk bolt upright, his eyes staring with terror, clenching his hands together as he stammered into the darkness: 'Oh God! Oh God!' His chest felt as if it would burst and he thought he was dying; and it was not till he had struck a light and woken up fully that he would calm down a little. These panic attacks always left him ashamed at his idiotic appeal to a God whose existence he denied, at yielding to the hereditary weakness of humanity by emitting its cry for help as it was crushed beneath the burden of existence. But still the attacks returned every night like some evil, exhausting passion that his reason was powerless to resist. Even during the day, a casual word or an unguarded thought, coming from a scene glimpsed or something he had read, would bring this same dread flooding back. One evening, as Pauline was reading the newspaper to her uncle, Lazare rushed out of the room, profoundly depressed by the fanciful visions of some storyteller who pictured the sky in the twentieth century filled with fleets of balloons, conveying travellers from one continent to another. He would no longer be there, his eyes would never gaze upon those balloons which receded, far beyond the limits of his existence, into an abyss of future centuries that filled him with dread. In vain did his philosophers repeat that not a spark of life was ever lost, the Ego within him raged against the idea of its own end. This inner turmoil had already stripped him of any cheerfulness. Whenever Pauline, who did not fully understand his changes of mood, noticed him trying to hide his anguish out of shame and anxiety, her heart melted with compassion; she was moved to show him every kindness, and make him happy again.

They whiled away their days in the big room on the second floor, surrounded by seaweed specimens, jars, and instruments that Lazare had not found the energy to dispose of. The seaweed was dry and crumbling and the bottles discoloured, while the instruments had become unusable as they gathered dust. But they were warm and snug together, amid the disorder. Often, the slates were lashed from morning till night by the December rains, while the west wind roared like an organ between the cracks in the woodwork. Whole weeks went by without a ray of sunshine, and all they had to look at was the grey sea, an immense expanse of greyness into which the earth seemed to dissolve. Pauline filled the long, empty hours by classifying a collection

of Floridiae which they had gathered the previous spring. At first
Lazare, with a show of boredom, just watched her mounting the deli-
cately branching forms with their soft, watercolour tints of red and
blue; but soon, bored stiff and having forgotten his theoretical com-
mitment to inactivity, he cleared the piano of the dented apparatus and
unwashed flasks piled on top of it. Another week, and his old passion
for music was once again taking possession of him. This was the primary lesion in his character, the artist's cracked temperament which
had also shown itself in the now failed scientist and industrialist. One
morning, as he was playing through his Death March, the idea of the
great Symphony of Suffering which he had once aimed to compose
filled him with excitement once more. It all seemed worthless except
the March, the only part he would keep, but what a subject, what
a creative challenge, in which he would sum up his whole philosophy!
To open, there would be the creation of Life by the capricious Ego of
some higher power; then would come the illusion of happiness and
the duplicity of existence, portrayed in striking passages, a coupling
of lovers, a massacre of soldiers, and a god expiring upon a cross; and
throughout, the cry of evil would mount, the screams of humanity
would fill the heavens, until the final hymn of deliverance, whose
celestial sweetness would express the joy of universal annihilation. The
next day he set to work, hammering out chords on the piano and covering the music paper with black notes. As the instrument was on its last
legs and sounding ever feebler, he would also drone out the tune in his
own voice, like a tolling bell. Never before had he been so completely
absorbed in a task that he forgot his meals, and although the din
offended Pauline's ears, she supported him loyally, saying how good it
was, and neatly copying out the score for him. He was quite sure that
this time, he really did have his masterpiece.

Yet he eventually grew calmer. He had just the opening left to write,
but he could not find the inspiration. He'd have to leave it alone for
a while, and he sat there smoking cigarettes, with his score spread out
on the great table in front of him. Pauline in her turn played phrases
from it on the piano, making elementary mistakes. It was at that moment
that their intimacy began to be a danger to them. He no longer had
the worries of the factory to occupy his mind and tire his body, and
now that he found himself shut up in Pauline's company, with nothing to keep him busy, his blood tormented by idleness, he developed
a growing attraction to her. She was so light-hearted and kind, so

joyous and devoted! At first, he had believed he was just yielding to an impulse of gratitude, a redoubling of that fraternal affection she had inspired in him ever since childhood. But gradually his previously dormant desire burst back into life, and at last he began to recognize this younger brother, with whom he had rubbed shoulders for so long without noticing her different scent, as a woman. So he now blushed as much as she did whenever he brushed against her. He no longer dared come up behind her and lean over her shoulder to take a look at the music she was copying. If their hands happened to meet, they would each stammer out apologies, breathing quickly and with their cheeks on fire. From now on, whole afternoons were spent in palpable awkwardness, leaving them worn out and tormented by a vague craving for a happiness they could not have.

Sometimes, to relieve one of those embarrassing moments that caused them such exquisite anguish, Pauline would tease him with the frank boldness of a wise virgin.

'Did I ever tell you about a dream I had? Your friend Schopenhauer, in the other world, heard about our marriage, and his ghost came back in the night to tickle our feet.'

Lazare gave a forced laugh. He realized she was making fun of his constant contradictions, but his whole being was now filled with an infinite tenderness which quite disarmed his hatred of the life instinct.

'Don't be cruel,' he mumbled, 'you know how much I love you.'

She assumed a stern expression.

'Take care, or you will delay the day of deliverance!... You're wallowing in egotism and delusion once again.'

'Be quiet, you wicked tease!'

Then he would chase her round the room while she continued to taunt him with fragments of pessimistic philosophy, in the pontificating tones of a Doctor of the Sorbonne.* But when he caught her, he no longer dared to hold her in his arms and pinch her for punishment, as in days gone by.

One day, however, the pursuit was so frantic that he grabbed her violently round the hips. She guffawed with laughter, while he threw her back against the wardrobe, thrilled to feel her struggling.

'Ha! I've got you this time! Now what shall I do to you, eh?'

Their faces were touching and she was still laughing, but her laughter died away.

'No, no, let me go, I won't do it again.'

He smacked a rough kiss on her lips. Then the room started spinning and they felt as if a burning wind were whirling them into an abyss. She was falling backwards beneath him until, with a sudden effort, she broke free. For a moment, they stood there in consternation, their cheeks burning, not daring to look at each other. Then she ░░░ ░░░░░ ░░ ░░░░░░ ░░░ ░░░ ░░░ ░░░ ░░░░ ░░ ░░░░ ░░░░░░░░░░ ░░░ ░░░░░░░░░

'You hurt me, Lazare.'

From that day on, he avoided even the warmth of her breath or the brush of her dress. His sense of honour rebelled against the thought of any foolish lapse or squalid conquest. Despite the girl's instinctive resistance, he was sure she could be his, carried away by the heat of her blood in the first embrace, loving him so much that she would give herself entirely if he asked; but he determined to be wise for them both, conscious that he would be the guilty party in any adventure whose danger he alone had the experience to foresee. However, his love was only sharpened by this battle with himself. Everything had conspired to fan its flame: the idleness of the last few weeks, his show of indifference, his disgust with life which had spawned a new and passionate desire to live and love, and to fill the boredom of his empty hours with fresh suffering. And now his state of nervous exaltation was exacerbated by music, which bore them away together, on its ever-spreading wings of rhythm, to a land of dreams. He began to believe himself possessed by a mighty passion and vowed to cultivate his genius by its pursuit. There was no longer any doubt that he would be a famous musician, for he only needed to follow the promptings of his heart. Everything seemed purified, he felt moved to fall to his knees and adore his good angel, and it did not even occur to him to hasten their marriage.

'Look, come and read this letter I've just received,' said Chanteau one day in great alarm to his wife, who had just come up from Bonneville.

It was another letter from Saccard, a threatening one this time. Ever since November he had been writing to ask for a statement of Pauline's accounts, and since the Chanteaus had only come up with evasive answers, he finally announced that he meant to put their refusal before the family council. Though she would not admit it, Madame Chanteau was no less alarmed than her husband.

'The swine!' she murmured after reading the letter.

They gazed at each other in silence, white-faced. In the stuffy air of the little dining room they could already hear the clamour of a scandalous lawsuit.

'There's no time for delay,' continued Chanteau. 'Marry her off now, since that would make her legally independent.'

But the mother seemed to find this expedient more distasteful every day. She expressed her fears: who could tell whether the young pair were suited? Two good friends could make a dreadful married couple. Lately, she said, she had been struck by numerous unfortunate remarks.

'No, you see, it would be wrong to sacrifice them for our own peace of mind. Let's wait a while longer... And besides, why marry her now? She was eighteen last month, so we can apply for her legal emancipation.'

Her self-confidence was returning; she went upstairs to fetch her Code and they pored over it together. Article 478 they read with relief, but Article 480 perplexed them, for it stated that guardians must submit accounts of their ward's estate to a trustee appointed by the family council. It was true that she held all the members of the council in her sway and could make them appoint whoever she wanted, but who should she choose, where could she find someone suitable? The problem was how to replace Saccard, the surrogate guardian, with a more obliging trustee.

All at once, inspiration came to her.

'What about Doctor Cazenove?... He knows a bit about our situation, and he won't refuse.'

Chanteau nodded approvingly. But he gazed intently at his wife, preoccupied with one thought in particular.

'So,' he said at last, 'you'll hand over the money? What's left of it, I mean?'

Madame Chanteau did not answer straight away. She was looking down and leafing through the Code with nervous fingers.

Then with an effort she replied:

'Of course I will, it will be good riddance, you've seen the accusations that are already being made against us... Dear me, it's enough to make you doubt your own judgement! I'd give five francs to get it out of my secretaire tonight. And we'd always have had to return it in any case.'

The next day, when Doctor Cazenove made his usual Saturday round in Bonneville, Madame Chanteau spoke to him of the great favour they hoped to ask of his friendship. She confessed the whole situation and explained how the money had been swallowed up in the disaster of the seaweed factory, without the family council ever having been consulted. Then she went on at length about the planned marriage and the bonds of affection that united them all, which the scandal of a court case would destroy.

Before promising to help, the doctor insisted on a talk with Pauline. He had long realized that she was being exploited and her fortune was being frittered away; and, though he had held his tongue until then for fear of upsetting her, he felt that now they were trying to make him into an accessory, it was his duty to warn her. The matter was discussed in the girl's own room. Her aunt was present at the start of the interview; she had gone up with the doctor to inform him that the marriage now depended on Pauline's legal emancipation, for Lazare would never consent to marry his cousin while he might be accused of doing it just to avoid submitting his accounts. Then she left the room, protesting that she had no wish to influence the girl whom she already called her darling daughter. Pauline, overcome with emotion, immediately begged the doctor to do them the delicate favour whose necessity had just been explained to him in her presence. He tried in vain to enlighten her as to her situation: she would be despoiling herself and giving away all her rights, and he even expressed his fears for her future, one of complete ruin, ingratitude, and great suffering. At each new dark prediction, she protested indignantly, refused to listen, and showed a feverish eagerness to sacrifice herself.

'No! don't try to make me regret it. I have a mean streak in me, though it doesn't show, and it's hard enough for me to keep that under control... Let them take it all. They can have the rest of it, if only it will make them love me more.'

'So,' said the doctor, 'it's affection for your cousin that is prompting you to strip yourself of your fortune?'

She blushed without replying.

'But what if, after some time, your cousin stopped loving you?'

She stared at him in horror. Her eyes filled with great tears and a cry of indignant love burst from her heart.

'No, oh no!... How can you say such a hurtful thing?'

Then Doctor Cazenove gave in. He did not have the courage to excise the illusions of love from such a generous heart. Life's cruelty would come to her soon enough.

Madame Chanteau conducted the campaign with astonishing skill and intrigue. This battle made her feel young again. She set off once more for Paris, taking with her the necessary powers. She quickly won the members of the family council over to her point of view, and they had in any case never paid much attention to their responsibilities, which they treated with characteristic indifference. Those on Quenu's side of the family, cousins Naudet, Liardin, and Delorme, fell in with her wishes, and of the three on Lisa's side, only Octave Mouret took any persuading, while the other two, Claude Lantier and Rambaud, at that time in Marseilles, were content to forward their written approval. To them all, she poured out a moving but complicated story of the old Arromanches doctor's affection for Pauline, and his apparent intention to leave his money to her if he were allowed to look after her interests. As for Saccard, he also gave in after three visits from Madame Chanteau, who presented him with a brilliant scheme for cornering the Cotentin butter market, thanks to a new system of transport. So Pauline's emancipation was formally pronounced by the family council, and former naval surgeon Cazenove, on whom the magistrate had received most satisfactory reports, was named as trustee. A fortnight after Madame Chanteau's return to Bonneville, the inspection of the guardianship accounts took place in the simplest manner. The doctor had come round to lunch, and they had lingered a while at the table, discussing the latest news from Caen, where Lazare had just spent two days dealing with a threat of legal action from that scoundrel Boutigny.

'By the way,' said the young man, 'Louise is due to pay us a surprise visit next week... I hardly recognized her; she is living at her father's now, and has become quite the elegant young lady. Oh, we did laugh!'

Pauline looked at him, astonished at the warmth of feeling in his voice.

'Talking of Louise,' exclaimed Madame Chanteau, 'I travelled with a lady from Caen who knows the Thibaudiers. I was flabbergasted, it seems Thibaudier is giving his daughter a dowry of a hundred thousand francs. With the hundred thousand from her mother, the girl will have two hundred thousand altogether... Two hundred thousand francs, she'll be rich!'

'Huh,' said Lazare, 'she doesn't need all that, she's pretty as a picture... and such a tease!'

A gloomy look came into Pauline's eyes and her lips gave a slight nervous twitch. However, the doctor, who had not taken his eyes off her, raised his small, almost empty glass of rum.

'Now then, we haven't drunk your health yet... Here's to your happiness, my friends! Get married quickly, and have lots of children.'

Unsmilingly, Madame Chanteau slowly raised her glass, while her husband, who was not allowed spirits, simply nodded approvingly. But Lazare had just clasped Pauline's hand in such a charmingly spontaneous way that it brought all the blood rushing back to her cheeks. Wasn't she his kind angel, as he called her, the passionate wellspring of inspiration from which the lifeblood of his genius would always flow? She squeezed his hand in return. They all clinked glasses.

'To your hundredth birthdays!' continued the doctor, who had a theory that one hundred was the prime of life.

This time it was Lazare who turned pale. That casually mentioned number sent a shiver down his spine, alluding to a future when he would no longer exist, the eternal dread of which lurked deep within his flesh. A hundred years from now, what would be left of him? What stranger would be sitting drinking at this same table? He drained his little glass with shaking fingers, while Pauline had seized his other hand and was giving it a maternal squeeze, as though she could see the icy breath of the irremediable passing across his pallid face.

After a silence, Madame Chanteau said with gravitas:

'Now then, shall we conclude our business?'

She had decided that the signing would take place in her room, for greater solemnity. Since he had been taking salicylate,* Chanteau's mobility had improved. Holding on to the banister, he followed his wife upstairs. Lazare was talking of going out onto the terrace to smoke a cigar, but his mother called him back and insisted that he must be there, at least as a formality. The doctor and Pauline had already gone on ahead. Mathieu, perplexed by this procession, tagged along behind.

'What a nuisance that dog is, always following people around!' cried Madame Chanteau as she tried to shut the door. 'Well then, come on in, I don't want you scratching outside... Here we are, no one will come and disturb us... As you see, everything is ready.'

And indeed, pens and an inkpot were set out on the round table. The bedroom had the stuffy atmosphere and deathly silence of a room that is rarely used. Only Minouche would laze there for days on end, whenever she managed to sneak inside in the morning, and in fact she had been asleep in the eiderdown. She looked up in surprise at this invasion, staring at them with her green eyes.

'Do sit down! Sit down!' Chanteau kept saying.

Then matters were quickly settled. Madame Chanteau withdrew into the background, leaving her husband to play the part for which she had been coaching him since the previous day. Ten days earlier, to comply with the law, Chanteau had handed Pauline, in the presence of the doctor, a thick notebook containing the accounts of his guardianship, with income listed on one page and expenditure on the opposite one. All the outgoings had been deducted, not just Pauline's maintenance allowance, but also legal fees and the cost of journeys to Paris and Caen. So it was just a matter of approving the accounts by private deed.* But Cazenove, taking his responsibilities as trustee seriously, raised objections about the finances of the seaweed factory, and obliged Chanteau to go into details. Pauline threw the doctor a pleading glance: what was the point? She herself had helped draw up the accounts, which her aunt had copied out in her most elegant copperplate hand. Meanwhile, Minouche had sat up in the middle of the eiderdown, the better to view these curious goings-on. Mathieu, having meekly lain his great head on the edge of the rug, now rolled onto his back, enjoying the cosy warmth of the wool, wriggling and twisting with grunts of pleasure.

'Oh Lazare, do make him be quiet!' cried Madame Chanteau at last, with impatience. 'I can't hear myself think.'

The young man was standing in front of the window, gazing intently at a distant white sail in an attempt to conceal his embarrassment. He was overcome by shame as he listened to his father's detailed account of the money squandered in the disaster of the factory.

'Shut up, Mathieu!' he said, prodding the dog with his foot.

Mathieu thought he was going to have his belly scratched, which he adored, so only growled louder. Fortunately, all that remained to be done was to sign the documents. With a stroke of the pen, Pauline hurriedly agreed to everything. Then the doctor, as though reluctantly, scrawled his signature with a great flourish on the stamped sheet of paper.* A painful silence fell.

'The credit account', Madame Chanteau continued, 'is seventy-five thousand, two hundred and ten francs and thirty centimes... I will now hand that sum over to Pauline.'

She walked over to the secretaire and lowered the lid, which opened with the squeak that had so often alarmed her. But now she was in a solemn mood, and when she opened the drawer, they saw the old ledger cover inside. It still looked the same, with its green marbling and its grease spots, but thinner, and the reduced pile of securities no longer threatened to burst its parchment binding.

'ɴᴏᴛ ᴀᴛ ᴀʟʟ, ᴜɴᴄᴏᴍᴍᴏɴ ᴘᴀᴜʟɪɴᴇ, 'ʏᴏᴜ ᴋᴇᴇᴘ ɪᴛ, ᴀᴜɴᴛɪᴇ'

Madame Chanteau would not hear of it.

'We've handed in our accounts,' she said, 'and now we must hand over the money… It belongs to you. You remember what I told you when I put it there, eight years ago? We don't want to keep a penny of it.'

She took out the securities and insisted on Pauline counting them. There were seventy-five thousand francs' worth, along with a small packet of gold, wrapped in a piece of newspaper, which made up the balance.

'But where am I to keep it all?' asked Pauline, flushed at the thought of handling so much money.

'Lock it away in your chest of drawers,' her aunt replied. 'You're grown up enough to look after your own money. I don't want to set eyes on it again… Look, if you really don't want it, give it to Minouche, she's got her eye on you.'

The Chanteaus had paid up, and their cheerfulness was returning. Lazare, much relieved, played with the dog, making him chase his own tail, arching his back and spinning round and round like a top; while Doctor Cazenove, in the spirit of his role as trustee, was promising Pauline to collect her dividends and advise her on investments.

Downstairs, at that very moment, Véronique clattered her pots and pans together. She had crept upstairs, and, listening at the keyhole, had overheard some of the figures. During the last few weeks, her secretly growing affection for Pauline had dispelled any of her lingering prejudices.

'So, they've got through half her money, have they?' she growled in fury. 'Disgusting, I call it… Of course, she didn't have to come and live here, but is that any reason to steal the shirt off her back? Certainly not, and to be fair to the child, I could end up getting quite fond of her!'

CHAPTER 4

THAT Saturday, when Louise, who was coming to spend two months with the Chanteaus, stepped down onto their terrace, she found the whole family gathered there. The very hot August day, refreshed by a sea breeze, was drawing to a close. Abbé Horteur had already come round to play draughts with Chanteau, while Madame Chanteau sat close by, embroidering a handkerchief. A few yards away, Pauline stood before a stone bench on which she had lined up four of the village urchins, two girls and two boys.

'Well, well, so here you are already!' exclaimed Madame Chanteau. 'I was just going to fold up my work to come and meet you at the junction.'

Louise cheerfully explained that old Malivoire had driven her like the wind. She was very well, and didn't even want to change her dress; and while her godmother went in to see that the room was ready, she hung her hat on the catch of a shutter. She kissed them all and then, laughing and affectionate, threw her arms round Pauline's waist.

'Now just look at me!... Haven't we both grown up such a lot? I'm over nineteen now, you know, and quite the old maid...'

She broke off, before quickly adding:

'Congratulations, by the way! Now don't be shy, I hear it's all planned for next month.'

Pauline had returned her embrace with the affectionate seriousness of an elder sister, although she was actually the younger by eighteen months. A slight flush coloured her cheeks at this allusion to her marriage to Lazare.

'No, no, you've been misinformed, I assure you,' she replied. 'Nothing's been fixed yet, we're thinking of sometime in the autumn.'

Madame Chanteau, when pressed on the subject, had indeed mentioned the autumn, despite a reluctance to commit herself which the two young people had already started to notice. She had gone back to her original excuse for delay, saying that she would much rather her son found a position first.

'Oh, all right,' said Louise, 'keep it a secret if you want... But you will invite me, won't you? And where's Lazare? Isn't he here?'

Chanteau, who had just lost to the abbé, answered for her: 'So you didn't bump into him, Louisette? We were just saying you might perhaps arrive together. He's been in Bayeux making an application to the sub-prefect, but he'll be back by this evening, perhaps quite late.'

Then, returning to the draughtboard:

'My turn to begin, Abbé... You know, we will get those groynes built in the end, the Department really can't refuse us a grant.'

This was a new adventure into which Lazare had thrown himself with his usual enthusiasm. During the spring tides the previous March, the sea had swept away two more of Bonneville's houses. The village, perched on its narrow shingle beach, was being progressively eroded away, and would eventually be pushed right back under the cliff unless substantial defences were built to protect it. But it was of so little significance, with its thirty hovels, that Chanteau, as mayor, had tried in vain for the last ten years to draw the sub-prefect's attention to the desperate plight of the villagers.

In the end Lazare, spurred on by Pauline in her anxiety to push him into renewed activity, had come up with a grand scheme for a system of groynes and revetments* to hold the sea at bay. But it would cost money, twelve thousand francs at least.

'That one's mine, old friend,' said the priest, taking one of Chanteau's pieces.

Then he obligingly launched into an account of Bonneville as it used to be.

'According to the old folk, there used to be a farm in line with the church, a full kilometre out from the present shore. The sea has been nibbling away at their land for over five hundred years... It's extraordinary, it must be punishment for the sins of each generation, visited on the next.'

Pauline, meanwhile, had returned to the stone bench where the four dirty, ragged urchins were waiting with mouths agape.

'Whatever is that?' Louise asked her, not daring to venture too close.

' "That" is just some little friends of mine,' replied Pauline.

Her charitable works now extended across the whole area. She had an instinctive love for the wretched and was never repelled by their miserable condition, taking this empathy to the extreme of making little splints for hens with broken legs, and putting out bowls of leftovers at night for stray cats. She felt a constant concern for all suffering creatures, and relieving their distress was a necessity and a joy to her. So the poor flocked to her outstretched hands, like pilfering sparrows swarming round the open windows of a barn. The whole of Bonneville, that handful of fishermen afflicted by disasters and battered by spring tides, came up to see the young lady, as they called her. But she was particularly fond of the children, little boys in worn-out trousers with their pink flesh showing through, and pale, half-fed girls gazing ravenously at the buttered bread she brought out for them. The cunning parents played on Pauline's kind-heartedness and sent along the most sickly and ragged of their brats, to exploit her compassion to the maximum.

'As you can see,' she said with a laugh, 'I hold my salon, just like any lady, on Saturdays, when my friends come to visit. Look here, little Gonin, stop pinching that daft lump of a Houtelard lad. I shall get cross with you if you don't behave... Let's just try and do things properly.'

Then the handouts began. She chivvied them into line in a maternal way. The first she called forward was young Houtelard, a lad of ten, sallow of complexion, with a dull and timid expression. He showed her his leg: he had a long graze on the knee and his father had sent him to the young lady for something to put on it. It was Pauline who supplied arnica* and soothing liniment to everyone around. Her passion for healing had led her little by little to acquire a well-stocked medicine chest, her pride and joy. Once she had dressed the lad's knee, she whispered some details to Louise.

'These Houtelards are quite well off, they're the only rich fishing family in Bonneville. The big boat belongs to them, you know... Only, they are dreadfully mean with money, and live in the filthiest squalor imaginable. And the worst of it is that the father, after beating his wife to death, has married the maid, an appalling woman even rougher than him. Now, between the two of them, they're killing this poor child.'

Then, without noticing her friend's look of concern and disgust, she called another child over.

'Now, little one, did you take your quinine tonic properly?'

This was the daughter of Prouane, the verger. She looked like an infant Saint Teresa,* pockmarked with scrofula, flushed and skinny, with big bulging eyes already showing a hysterical gleam. She was eleven years old, but looked barely seven.

'Yes, Mam'selle,' she stammered, 'I drunk it all up.'

'Liar!' cried the priest, without looking up from the draughtboard. 'Your father stank of wine again last night.'

This made Pauline cross. The Prouanes had no boat, but made their living catching crabs and shrimps and gathering mussels. With the additional income from the verger's position, they might still have put bread on the table every day, were it not for their drinking. Both father and mother were often to be seen sprawled in the doorway, stupefied by Calvados, the fearsome cider brandy of Normandy, and the little girl would step over them to drain their glasses. When no Calvados was to be had, Prouane would drink his daughter's quinine tonic.

'And to think I go to such trouble to make it!' said Pauline. 'All right, I will keep the bottle here and you can come up and drink your medicine every evening, at five o'clock... And I'll give you a little raw mince, as prescribed by the doctor.'

Next it was the turn of a tall lad of twelve, the Cuche boy, an urchin lean and scraggy from precocious vice. To him she gave a loaf, some beef stew, and a five-franc piece. His was another dreadful story: after the destruction of their house, Cuche had left his wife and gone to live with a female cousin, while the wife had now taken refuge in a ruined customs post, where she would sleep with anyone, despite her repulsive ugliness. She was paid in kind, or would occasionally be given a few coppers. The boy, who witnessed it all, was close to starvation, but whenever anyone offered to rescue him from that den of iniquity, he would bound away like a wild goat.

Louise averted her gaze in disgust as Pauline, without the least embarrassment, told her the boy's story. The freedom of her upbringing allowed her to face human vice with the steadfast calm of charity, to know and speak about anything with innocence and frankness. Louise, on the other hand, made worldly-wise by ten years of boarding school, blushed at the ideas that Pauline's words awoke in her mind, warped by dormitory dreams. These were things one thought about, but never mentioned.

'And then', Pauline went on, 'there is this last little blonde girl, just nine, so sweet and rosy-cheeked, the daughter of the Gonins, the couple with whom that Cuche rascal has moved in... The Gonins were once well off, with a boat of their own, but the father went down with paralysis of the legs, a common complaint in the villages around here, and Cuche, who was then just an ordinary sailor, soon became master of the boat, and of the wife as well. Now the whole house belongs to him, and he beats the poor old invalid, a tall man who spends his days and nights lying in an old coal chest, while the sailor and his cousin have kept the bed for themselves, in the same room... So, I look after the child. Unfortunately, when blows are flying, she sometimes gets in the way, and in any case, she is far too intelligent and sees things she shouldn't...'

Here Pauline broke off to question the child.

'How is everything at home?'

The little girl had been watching carefully as Pauline told her story in an undertone. Her pretty but depraved face lit up with sly laughter as she guessed the details.

'They beat him again,' she said, still giggling. 'Last night, Ma got up and took a lump of firewood to him... Oh Mam'selle, it would be kind of you to give him a little wine, for they have just put him a jug of water by the coal chest and told him he can drop dead.'

Louise gestured in disgust. What appalling people! How could her friend take an interest in such horrors? How could it be that so close to a city like Caen, there existed these dreadful holes where people lived like complete savages? For surely only savages could offend like this against both divine and human laws.

'No, my dear,' she murmured as she went to sit down near Chanteau, 'I've had quite enough of your little friends. Let the sea sweep them away, they won't get any sympathy from me!'

The abbé had just crowned one of his pieces. He exclaimed:

'Sodom and Gomorrah! I have been warning them for twenty years... Now it's up to them!'

'I applied to have a school here,' said Chanteau, annoyed at seeing the game turn against him; 'but there aren't enough children, so they have to walk to Verchemont, and they either don't go at all, or play truant on the way.'

Pauline looked at them all in amazement. If the poor were clean, there would be no need to wash them. Evil and poverty went together, and she was never repelled by suffering, even when it seemed to be the consequence of vice. She simply expressed, with an expansive gesture of protest, her charitable tolerance. She was just promising the Gonin girl that she would visit her father, when Véronique appeared, pushing another little girl in front of her.

'Here, Mademoiselle, another one for you.'

The newcomer was very young, five at most and dressed all in rags, with a filthy face and matted hair. Instantly, with the extraordinary self-possession of a child prodigy in the art of roadside begging, she began to whine:

'Take pity on us... My poor dad what's broken his leg...'

'Isn't this the daughter of the Tourmals?' Pauline asked Véronique. But the priest interrupted angrily:

'The little hussy! Take no notice of her, the father sprained his ankle a good twenty-five years ago... They're a family of thieves who live entirely from stealing! The father's involved in smuggling, the mother pilfers from the fields around Verchemont, and the grandfather poaches oysters at night from the government beds at Roqueboise...* And one can see from their daughter's company that a little beggar, a thief they send into people's houses to make off with anything left lying about... Just look at her, sizing up my tobacco box!'

Indeed, the child's magpie eyes, after scanning every corner of the terrace, had lit up eagerly at the sight of the antique box. And she was not at all put off by the abbé's narrative, but repeated her plea as calmly as if he had not said a word:

'Broke his leg, he has... Please Mam'selle, spare us a little something.'

This time Louise started laughing, amused at this runtish five-year-old who was already as rascally as her parents. Pauline, however, kept her serious expression and took out a new five-franc piece from her purse.

'Now listen,' she said, 'I will give you the same amount every Saturday if I hear a good account of you during the week.'

'Lock up your silverware,' exclaimed Abbé Horteur, 'or she'll be off with the lot.'

Pauline gave no reply, but simply dismissed the children, who slunk away with many a 'Thank you kindly' and 'God bless you!' Meanwhile Madame Chanteau, who had just come back out of the house after checking Louise's room, was grumbling under her breath about Véronique. It was intolerable, now the servant too was admitting beggars! As if Mademoiselle didn't bring enough of them into the house as it was! Scum the lot of them, devouring Pauline's inheritance and then laughing in her face! Of course, it was her money and she could throw it away if she felt like it, but encouraging vice in this way was really too bad. Madame Chanteau had heard her promise to the little Tourmal girl of a hundred sous every Saturday. Another twenty francs a month going out! A king's ransom would scarcely cover it!

'To be clear,' she said to Pauline, 'I do not want to see that little thief here again. You may be mistress of your fortune now, but I cannot allow you to ruin yourself so stupidly. I'm morally responsible for you... Yes, my dear, I mean it: ruin yourself, and sooner than you think!'

Véronique, who had gone back into her kitchen fuming at Madame's reprimand, now reappeared and called out rudely:

'Butcher's here! Wants his bill paying, forty-six francs ten.'

Madame Chanteau was left speechless with embarrassment. Fumbling in her pockets, she gave a gesture of surprise, then muttered under her breath:

'Well, Pauline, have you got enough on you? I've no change and I'd have to go upstairs. We can settle up later.'

Pauline went out with the maid to pay the butcher. Since she had been keeping the money in her chest of drawers, the same charade had been acted out each time a bill was presented for payment. She was being regularly milked of small amounts in this natural-seeming way. Her aunt no longer even bothered to take out the money herself, she simply asked Pauline for it and let the girl rob herself with her own hands. At first, an account had been kept and ten francs here or fifteen francs there were repaid, but soon the figures got so complicated there was talk of sorting it all out later, after the wedding; which did not stop Pauline from paying for her board and lodging, now increased to ninety francs, punctually on the first of each month.

'There goes more good money of yours, after the bad!' grumbled Véronique in the passage. 'Me, I'd have packed her off to fetch her own change! Surely to God it's not right, them fleecing you like this!'

When Pauline came back with the receipt, which she handed to her aunt, the curé was loudly triumphant. Chanteau had been beaten hollow, he hadn't even taken a single piece. The sun was setting, its slanting rays turning the sea crimson, while the tide lapped gently in. Louise, gazing into the distance, was smiling at the immense and joyous horizon.

'Our dear Louise is off with the fairies,' said Madame Chanteau. 'Hello... Louisette, I've had your trunk taken upstairs... So, you and I are to be neighbours once again!'

Lazare did not come home until the following day. After his visit to the sub-prefect of Bayeux, he had decided to go on to Caen and see the prefect himself. And even if he had not actually come back with the grant in his pocket, he stated his conviction that the Departmental Council would award them at least twelve thousand francs. The prefect had shown him out with categorical assurances that Bonneville would not be left to its fate, the authorities were fully behind the zealous efforts of the villagers. Only, Lazare was despondent, for he foresaw all kinds of delays, and being forced to postpone the realization of any of his desires was becoming a torture to him.

'I swear', he exclaimed, 'that if I had twelve thousand, I'd rather put up the money myself... It wouldn't even take that much to do the preliminary experiments... And when they finally approve their grant, you'll see the problems it will bring us! We shall have all the engineers in the Department breathing down our necks. Whereas, if we made a start without them, they'd be obliged to acknowledge our results... I'm sure of my plan. When I outlined it to the prefect, he was impressed by its simplicity, and the value for money.'

He was now filled with excitement at the prospect of taming the sea. His feelings towards it were bitter, since he secretly blamed it for the financial disaster of the seaweed factory; and, though he did not levy any accusations openly, he harboured thoughts of one day taking his revenge. And what vengeance could be better than to put a stop to its blind destruction, to be able to call out in commanding tones: 'Not one inch more!' Beyond the grandeur of the struggle, this enterprise also had a philanthropic aspect that further increased his enthusiasm. When his mother saw him spending days on end whittling pieces of wood, his nose buried in treatises on mechanics, she shuddered at the memory of his grandfather, the enterprising but disorganized carpenter whose useless masterpiece slumbered in its glass case. Was the old man to be reborn in Lazare, to complete the family's ruin? Then, she allowed herself to be won over by this son whom she adored. If he succeeded, as of course he was going to, it would be a first step on the ladder, a noble and glorious deed that would redound widely to his credit, and he could easily go on to be whatever he liked, and rise as high as his ambition led him. From that day on, the whole family dreamt of nothing but humiliating the sea and chaining it up below the terrace like a cowed, submissive dog.

Lazare's scheme was in fact, as he said, extremely simple. He would drive great piles into the sand and cover them with planks, behind which the shingle, swept in by the tide, would accumulate to form an impregnable barrier, and against it the waves would break in vain, so that the sea itself would build the very fortification designed to keep it at bay. The system would be completed by groynes, long beams fixed to sturdy posts, acting as breakwaters and running out to sea in front of the shingle revetment. Finally, if there was money enough, they might build two or three great stockades, strong wooden frames covered in planks, whose solid mass would withstand the force of the very highest tides. Lazare had discovered the original concept in the *Complete Carpenter's Handbook*,* a small, crudely illustrated volume probably bought long ago by his grandfather; but he had improved on the idea, after considerable research into the theory of forces and the strength of different materials, and was particularly proud of a novel sloping arrangement of the groynes which, he claimed, made success a certainty.

Pauline once again showed keen interest in her cousin's research. Like him, she was always fascinated by experiments that led into unknown territory. Only, her more realistic nature left her with few illusions as to the risk of failure. When she saw the rising tide swelling and sweeping up the shore, she cast doubtful glances at the models Lazare had built, the rows of miniature piles, groynes, and revetments that now littered his big bedroom.

One night, Pauline lingered very late at her window. For the last two days, her cousin had been talking of burning the lot, and one evening, in an outburst over dinner, he had exclaimed that he was off to Australia, since there was no place for him in France. She stood there, preoccupied by such thoughts, while the flood tide battered Bonneville in the darkness. Each crashing wave made her tremble, and she seemed to hear, at regular intervals, the screams of poor creatures being swallowed up by the sea. Then the inner struggle between her love of money and her generous heart became unbearable, and she closed the window to shut out the sounds. But the distant crashes of the breakers still shook her as she lay in bed. Why should they not attempt the impossible? What did it matter if her money were flung into the sea, if there was just a chance of saving the village? And she fell asleep at dawn, imagining her cousin full of joy, released from his brooding melancholy, having perhaps found his true vocation at long last, and made happy by her, owing everything to her.

In the morning, before going downstairs, she called out to him. She was laughing.

'You know what? Last night I dreamt that I was lending you your twelve thousand francs.'

He grew angry and made a violent gesture of refusal.

'Do you want me to go away and never come back? No! the factory was the last straw. The shame of it is killing me, if truth be told.'

Two hours later he accepted, clasping her hands in passionate gratitude. It would simply be an advance; there would be no risk to her money, for there could be no doubt that the Departmental Council would award the grant, particularly once work had already started. And that very evening the Arromanches carpenter was sent for. The project was continued along the beach, with intense discussions over estimates. The whole household was swept up in the project.

Madame Chanteau, however, was furious when she heard of the twelve-thousand-franc loan. This astonished Lazare, and puzzled him. His mother bombarded him with curious arguments: it was certainly true that Pauline advanced them small sums from time to time, but she would now think herself even more indispensable, and they could perfectly well have asked Louise's father to put up the money. And Louise herself, with her dowry of two hundred thousand francs, made far less of a nuisance with her fortune. Madame Chanteau was forever alluding to this figure of two hundred thousand francs, and she seemed full of irritation and disdain at the remnants of that other fortune which, having dwindled away in the secretaire, was now doing the same in the chest of drawers.

Chanteau, egged on by his wife, also feigned annoyance. This hurt Pauline greatly: even while she was letting them use her money, she felt less loved than before; she sensed all around her a resentment that she could not understand, and which increased by the day. As for Doctor Cazenove, he also grumbled whenever she went, as a formality, to consult him; but he had been obliged to agree to all her loans, large and small. His trusteeship was a fiction, he was unable to stand up to these people who always received him as an old friend. On the day of the twelve-thousand-franc loan, he declined any further responsibility.

'My dear child,' he said, taking Pauline to one side, 'I no longer want to be your accomplice. Stop asking my advice, ruin yourself as you see fit... You know very well I can never resist when you plead with me, but afterwards I feel bad about it, and my conscience is anything but clear. I prefer not to know about things I can't approve of.'

Pauline looked at him, deeply touched. Then, after a pause, she replied:

'Thank you, dear Doctor... But isn't that the best way? What does it matter, so long as I'm happy?'

He took her hands and squeezed them in a sad, fatherly manner.

'Indeed, just so long as you're happy... After all, unhappiness can come at a high price too.'

Naturally, in the heat of his battle against the sea, Lazare had completely given up music. A fine coating of dust lay on the piano, and the score of his great symphony had been put away in a drawer thanks to Pauline, who had collected up the sheets of manuscript, including some from under the furniture. In any case, he was now dissatisfied with certain parts of it; for instance, the celestial pleasure of final annihilation, evoked rather banally in waltz rhythm, might be better expressed as a very slow march. One evening, he declared he would start again from scratch, when he had the time. His surge of desire and his unease at continuous contact with his young cousin seemed to have vanished, along with his musical inspiration. His masterpiece was postponed to a more suitable moment, just like his great passion, which he seemed able to hasten or put off at will. He started treating Pauline once more like an old friend, or a spouse who would give herself to him whenever he chose to embrace her. Since April, they had no longer been living in such enclosed proximity, and the wind had cooled their glowing cheeks. The great study was deserted as the two of them roamed the rocky beach in front of Bonneville, looking for the best locations for the piles and groynes. Often, they would walk back through the chill water, tired and pure of heart as in the far-off days of childhood. Whenever Pauline teased him by playing the famous March of Death, Lazare would exclaim:

'No, stop it! It's just a lot of nonsense!'

On the very evening of the carpenter's visit, Chanteau went down with another attack of gout. He was now suffering almost one a month, and the salicylate, which at first had given him some relief, seemed now to be increasing their violence. For a fortnight, Pauline remained tied to her uncle's bedside. Lazare, who was continuing his investigations on the beach, started to invite Louise along with him, to get her out of earshot of the invalid's screams, which scared her. Since she occupied the spare room above Chanteau's, she could only get to sleep by covering her ears and burying her head in the pillow. Once outdoors she became all smiles again, thoroughly enjoying the walk and forgetting about the poor man bawling indoors.

They had a delightful fortnight. At first, the young man was puzzled by his new companion. She was very different from Pauline, shrieking whenever a crab brushed against her boot, and so scared of the water that she was in fear of drowning whenever she had to jump across a pool. The pebbles hurt her little feet, she kept her parasol open the whole time and wore gloves up to her elbows for fear a patch of her delicate skin might be exposed to the sun. But after his initial astonishment, Lazare became gradually seduced by her timid grace and helplessness, constantly appealing to him for protection. She did not have Pauline's simple open-air freshness, but rather a warm heliotrope scent that went to his head; this was no longer a boy roaming along at his side, but a real woman, and an occasional glimpse of her stockinged legs in the wind sent the blood coursing through his veins. True, she was not as pretty as Pauline, she was older and already slightly faded, but she had a bewitching charm, her small, supple limbs moved with an easy motion, and her whole dainty figure seemed to offer the promise of bliss. Lazare felt as if he had only just discovered her, and he no longer recognized the skinny little girl he had known. Was it really possible that the long years of boarding school had turned her into such an alluring young creature, so aware of the male in him despite her virginity, with all the lies of her education lurking in the limpid pools of her gaze? Little by little he developed a peculiar attraction to her, a perverse passion which transformed his former childhood friendship into a refined sensuality.

Once Pauline was able to leave her uncle's room and go out again with Lazare, she immediately noticed a change between him and Louise, complicit glances and laughter from which she was excluded. She asked them what was so funny, but it never made her laugh. For the first few days she took a motherly attitude, treating them as foolish youngsters too easily amused. But this soon made her melancholy, and every outing became a trial. She never complained, merely alluding to stubborn migraines, until her cousin advised her to stay at home, at which she became cross and refused to leave him alone, even in the house. One night at about two o'clock, Lazare, who had stayed up to finish a plan, was astonished to hear footsteps outside his door and opened it to look. His amazement increased when he saw Pauline, wearing only her petticoat, leaning over the banister and listening for sounds from the rooms below. She told him she had heard someone crying out in pain. But this lie brought a blush to her cheek, and Lazare too turned pink as a suspicious thought crossed his mind. From that moment on, without anything more being said, a coldness fell between them. Lazare would turn away from her, thinking it ridiculous of her to sulk over such trivia, while Pauline, as her gloom deepened, refused to leave him alone with Louise for a minute, observing their every movement and suffering agonies in her room at night if she had caught them confiding together on the way back from the beach.

The construction work was now underway. After nailing stout planks across a row of piles to make the revetment, a gang of carpenters were putting the finishing touches to the first groyne. This was of course just a test, which they were rushing to complete before an expected spring tide; if the timbers held out, the rest of the defence system would be built. Unfortunately, the weather was dreadful. The rain poured down without respite and everyone in Bonneville was soaked as they went out to watch the pile-driver sinking the stakes into the sand. On the morning of the predicted spring tide, an ink-black sky hung over the sea and from eight o'clock the rain fell with redoubled violence, erasing the horizon with a glacial mist. This was a huge disappointment, for the whole family had planned to go and watch as the planks and piles triumphantly resisted the assault of the great waves.

Madame Chanteau decided to stay behind with her husband, who was still far from well. Great efforts were made to persuade Pauline to stay too, for she had been suffering from a sore throat all week: she was a little hoarse and ran a slight temperature every evening. But she rejected all advice to be careful and insisted on going down to the beach, since Lazare and Louise were going. Louise, though she always looked so fragile and on the verge of fainting, proved to have tremendous nervous strength in her pursuit of gratification.

And so they all three set off after lunch. A squall had swept away the clouds, an unexpected bonus that they greeted with triumphant laughter. The swathes of blue sky overhead were so broad, with just an occasional ragged black cloud drifting across, that the girls insisted on taking only their parasols. Lazare alone carried an umbrella. In any event, he would see that they came to no harm, and would find them shelter if the rain came down again.

Pauline and Louise walked on ahead. However, once they got to the steep slope leading down into Bonneville, Louise seemed to slip on the sodden earth and Lazare rushed to offer his support. Pauline was obliged to walk behind them. Her earlier high spirits had evaporated and she noticed with a suspicious eye that her cousin's arm kept brushing against Louise's waist in a caressing manner. Soon she was aware of nothing but this contact, everything else disappeared—the beach, where the local fishermen stood waiting with sceptical expressions, the rising tide, the groyne already white with foam. On the horizon, a black band of storm clouds was galloping towards them.

'Damn it!' muttered Lazare, turning round, 'we've got another drenching coming... But the rain should hold off long enough for us to see what happens, then we can take shelter with the Houtelards across the way.'

The tide, which had the wind against it, was coming in with frustrating slowness. The wind would doubtless also stop it getting as big as had been expected. However, nobody left the beach. The new groyne, by now half submerged, was working very well, parting the waves, which broke and seethed with foam right up to the feet of the onlookers. But the greatest triumph was the victorious resistance of the piles. As each wave dashed over them, sweeping shingle with it, the pebbles could be heard falling and piling up behind the planks with a noise like an upturned cartload of stones; the wall was gradually building itself, successfully forming the promised breakwater.

'I told you so!' shouted Lazare. 'Now you can tell the sea just where it gets off!'

Standing near him, Prouane, who had been drunk for the last three days, shook his head and stuttered:

'We'll see about that, when the wind blows the other way.'

The other fishermen kept silent. But, from the sardonic smiles of Cuche and Houtelard, it was plain they had precious little confidence in such contrivances. Besides, however much the sea might crush them, they didn't want to see it tamed by a bourgeois runt. They'd have a good laugh all right, the day the waves swept away his beams like so many bits of straw! The place might get smashed up, but the joke would still be on him!

Suddenly, the storm burst; great drops fell from the livid clouds which had moved in to fill three-quarters of the sky.

'It's nothing, let's stay a little longer!' cried Lazare in great excitement. 'Look, look! not a single pile has moved!'

He had opened his umbrella over Louise's head. She pressed closer to him, looking like a shivering turtle dove. Pauline, whom they had forgotten, looked on in impotent rage, feeling her face on fire from the warmth of their embrace. The rain was now pouring down, and suddenly Lazare turned round and shouted to her:

'What's the matter? Are you mad?... At least put your parasol up!'

She was standing there rigid in the downpour, which she seemed not to notice. She answered in a hoarse voice:

'Leave me alone, I'm quite all right.'

'Oh Lazare,' said Louise in distress, 'please make her come under here!... There's room for all three of us.'

But Pauline, in her stubborn anger, did not even deign to refuse. She was fine, why didn't they just leave her alone? After pleading with her in vain, Lazare continued:

'This is stupid, let's dash over to the Houtelards'!'

Pauline snapped back:

'You dash wherever you like... Since we came here to watch, that's what I'm going to do.'

The fishermen had fled. Pauline was standing motionless in the pouring rain, facing the timbers, which were now being completely submerged by the waves. The spectacle seemed to absorb her, despite the grey spray blowing off the rain-pocked sea and blotting out the view. Her streaming dress showed great dark patches of wet around the shoulders and arms, and she only consented to move from the spot once the west wind had blown the storm clouds away.

The three of them walked home in silence. Not a word was said to either Monsieur or Madame Chanteau about their adventure. Pauline hurried off to change into something dry, while Lazare described the complete success of the experiment. That evening, over dinner, Pauline had a high temperature again, but she insisted there was nothing wrong with her, despite her obvious difficulty in swallowing each mouthful. In the end, she was even rude to Louise, who was concerned and kept asking sympathetically how she felt.

'Really, the girl is becoming quite unbearable, with her tempers,' murmured Madame Chanteau behind her back. 'There's no point in trying to say anything to her.'

That night, about one o'clock, Lazare was woken up by a rasping cough which sounded so dry and painful that he sat up in bed to listen. At first, he thought it was his mother; then, as he listened harder, the floor shook with the sudden thud of a falling body, so he leapt out of bed and threw on his clothes. The noise seemed to have come from the other side of the wall: it could only be Pauline. He snapped several matches with his fumbling fingers, but once he had lit his candle and opened the door, he saw to his surprise that the one opposite was open. Lying on her side across the doorway was Pauline, in her nightgown, with bare arms and legs.

'What's the matter,' he exclaimed, 'did you trip?'

It occurred to him that she might have been prowling around and spying on him again. But she did not reply and just lay there with her eyes closed, as if unconscious. It seemed that she had been on her way to seek help when she had felt dizzy and collapsed on the floor.

'Pauline, answer me, I beg you... Where does it hurt?'

He bent down and shone the light on her face. She was extremely flushed and seemed in the grip of a high fever. His instinctive embarrassment at her virginal semi-nakedness made him hesitate to pick her up and carry her bodily over to the bed, but immediately gave way to brotherly concern. Without noticing her state of undress, he grasped her round the waist and thighs, unaware of the feeling of her womanly skin against his masculine chest. Once he had got her back on the bed, he began to question her once more, before even thinking of pulling up the covers.

'For goodness' sake speak to me! Have you hurt yourself?'

The jolt had made her open her eyes, but she still did not say anything and just stared up at him. Then, as his questions became more insistent, she finally put her hand up to her throat.

'It's your throat that's hurting, is it?'

At last, with a great effort, she replied in a sibilant whisper:

'Please don't make me speak... It hurts too much.'

And she was instantly seized with another fit of coughing, the same hoarse cough he had heard from his room. Her face had turned almost blue, and the pain was so great that her eyes filled with tears. She put both hands up to her poor head, throbbing with the hammer blows of a severe headache.

'You caught that today!' he stammered in a panic. 'It wasn't very sensible of you, when you already weren't feeling well!'

But he checked himself as his eyes met her imploring gaze. Her hand was fumbling for the bedclothes, so he pulled them up round her neck.

'Just open your mouth, will you, and let me look?'

It was all she could do to unclench her jaws. Bringing the candle close, Lazare was just able to see the back of her throat, which was bright red, dry, and shiny. It was obviously a throat infection, but her burning fever and terrible headache filled him with alarm about its exact nature. The poor girl's face wore such an agonized expression of suffocation that he was seized with a wild fear she might choke to death before his very eyes. She could no longer swallow, and every attempt shook her whole body. A fresh bout of coughing made her pass out again, and in a state of complete panic he ran out to beat on Véronique's door with his fists.

'Véronique! Véronique! Get up! Pauline's dying!'

When Véronique, half-dressed and seriously alarmed, entered Mademoiselle's room, she found Lazare standing there cursing and gesturing wildly.

'What a godforsaken hole, you could die here like a dog, with help over two leagues* away!'

He strode towards her.

'Try and find someone to send, get the doctor to come straight away!'

She went over to the bed and gazed down at the sick girl, startled to see her so flushed, and filled with fear in her growing affection for this child to whom, at first, she had taken such a dislike.

'I'll go myself,' she said simply. 'That will be quickest... Madame can light the fire downstairs if you need it.'

Then, half awake, she pulled on her heavy boots and wrapped a shawl round her, and after alerting Madame Chanteau on the way downstairs, strode off down the muddy road. The church clock struck two, and it was so dark that she kept stumbling over piles of stones.

'What's the matter?' asked Madame Chanteau, coming upstairs.

Lazare barely gave her an answer. He had been frantically hunting through the wardrobe for his old medical textbooks, and was now bending down in front of the chest of drawers, turning pages with trembling fingers while he tried to remember his old lectures. But everything was jumbled up in his head, and he kept going back to the table of contents, unable to find what he wanted.

'It's probably just a bad migraine,' said Madame Chanteau, who had sat down. 'It's best just to let her sleep.'

At which he exploded.

'A migraine! A migraine indeed!... Look, Maman, you're driving me mad just sitting there and doing nothing. Go down and heat up some water!'

'I don't suppose there's any need to disturb Louise, is there?' she asked.

'No, no, there's no point... I don't need any help. I'll shout if I do.'

Once he was alone again, he went over to Pauline and held her hand in order to take her pulse. It was a hundred and fifteen. And he ﬂ ﻻ ﻴﻟ ﻮ ﻬﻟ ﺍ ﻮ ﻬﻟ ﺍ ﻮ ﻬﻟ ﺍ ﻮ ﻬﻟ ﺍ ﻮ ﻬﻟ ﺍ ﻮ ﻬﻟ ﺍ ﻮ ﻬﻟ ﺍ ﻮ ﻬﻟ ﺍ ﻮ ﻬﻟ ﺍ ﻮ ﻬﻟ ﺍ ﻮ ﻬﻟ
eyelids remained closed, but with that pressure of her hand she was thanking and forgiving him. Though she could not smile, she still wanted him to know that she had heard, and was deeply touched that he was there alone with her, thinking of no other woman but her. Normally, he hated seeing anyone in pain, and would flee from a relative who was the least bit unwell, for he was a very poor nurse, he claimed, so bad at controlling his nerves that he feared bursting into tears. And so Pauline was both surprised and most grateful to see him devote himself to her in this way. He himself could not have explained the warmth of feeling that inspired him, or the necessity he felt of relying on himself alone to care for her. The ardent squeezing of her little hand overwhelmed him, and he tried to encourage her.

'It's nothing, my sweet. Cazenove will be here soon... Above all, don't be frightened.'

She kept her eyes closed as she murmured plaintively:

'Oh, I'm not frightened... I'm worried about the trouble I'm causing you.'

Then, in an even quieter whisper, she breathed:

'Please say you forgive me... I was horrid today.'

He bent down to kiss her on the forehead, as if she were his wife. Then he turned away, choking back the tears. It occurred to him at least to make her a sleeping draught while they waited for the doctor. He found Pauline's little medicine chest in a small cupboard. But he was afraid of making a mistake, so kept asking her about the different phials, until finally he poured a few drops of morphine into a glass of sugared water. Each time she swallowed a spoonful of it, her throat hurt so much that he hesitated to give her another. That was all, he felt there was really nothing more he could do. Waiting was becoming a torture. When he could no longer bear seeing her suffer and his legs ached from standing by her bed, he sat down and opened his books again in the hope of finally identifying the illness and its treatment. Could it be a kind of membranous tonsillitis? But he had not seen any pseudomembranes* on the arches of the soft palate. Stubbornly, he went on reading the description of that condition and its treatment, losing his way amid long sentences whose meaning escaped him, and getting bogged down in pointless details, like a child trying to memorize some obscure lesson. Then a sigh would bring him anxiously back to the bedside, his head buzzing with medical terms whose barbarous-sounding syllables only increased his anxiety.

'Well?' asked Madame Chanteau, who had come quietly back upstairs.

'No change,' Lazare replied.

Then, in frustration:

'It's dreadful, the time that doctor is taking... you could die twenty times over!'

As the doors had been left open, Mathieu, who slept under the kitchen table, had also come up, since he had a mania for following people into every room of the house. His great paws padded across the tiled floor like old felt slippers. He seemed delighted at the nighttime excitement, wanting to jump up to Pauline, and even started chasing his tail, with an animal's insensitivity to the woes of its masters. Infuriated by his untimely antics, Lazare gave him a kick.

'Get out or I'll strangle you!... Can't you see, you idiot?'

The dog, startled at being struck, sniffed the air as if with sudden understanding and went to lie down humbly under the bed. Madame Chanteau was indignant at Lazare's act of cruelty. Without waiting, she went back down to the kitchen, saying curtly:

'Whenever you're ready... The water's heating up.'

Lazare heard her, in the stairwell, grumbling that it was disgusting to kick a creature like that, and he'd probably end up beating her too if she stayed. Usually so devoted to his mother, he made an angry gesture of exasperation behind her back. He kept going over to see how Pauline was. Now completely in the grip of her fever, she seemed utterly prostrate, and her only sign of life amidst the glacial silence of the room was the harsh wheezing of her breath, which was starting to sound like a death rattle. Then Lazare was seized again by an absurd, irrational fear: she would surely suffocate if help did not arrive soon. He paced up and down the room, constantly glancing at the clock. It wasn't yet three, Véronique couldn't be at the doctor's yet. He followed her in his mind along the Arromanches road in the pitch darkness: she would have passed the oak wood and be arriving at the little bridge, she could save five minutes by running down the hill. Then a violent need to know what was happening made him open the window, though he could make out nothing in the inky blackness. There was only a single light gleaming at the far end of Bonneville, doubtless the lantern of some fisherman putting out to sea. It was all so lugubrious and melancholy, a dark chasm in which it seemed to him that all life was plunging to extinction. He closed the window, then opened it again, only to close it once more after a short while. He was beginning to lose all sense of time, and was astonished to hear the clock strike three. By now the doctor would have his horse harnessed and his cabriolet would be flying along the road, piercing the darkness with its yellow eye. Lazare grew so numbed with waiting, as the sick girl's breathing grew ever more laboured, that he woke with a start as, towards four o'clock, rapid footsteps were heard on the stairs.

'At last, you're here!' he exclaimed.

Doctor Cazenove immediately ordered a second candle to be lit so that he could examine Pauline. Lazare held one while Véronique, dishevelled by the wind and spattered with mud to the waist, stood by the head of the bed with the other. Madame Chanteau looked on. The patient, who was very drowsy, could not open her mouth without groaning. Once the doctor, who had been deeply worried when he arrived, had laid her gently back down, he went to the middle of the room with an expression of relief.

'Your Véronique gave me quite a fright!' he said in an undertone. 'From the extraordinary things she told me, I thought it must be a case of poisoning... As you can see, I've stuffed my pockets with drugs.'

'It's quinsy,* isn't it?' Lazare asked.

'Yes, just quinsy... There's no immediate danger.'

Madame Chanteau gave a gesture of triumph, as if to say she had known all along.

'No immediate danger,' repeated Lazare with fresh alarm, 'are you worried about complications?'

'No,' answered the doctor, after some hesitation, 'but with these wretched sore throats you can never be sure.'

He admitted that there was nothing to be done, and said he would prefer to wait till the next day before bleeding the patient. But as Lazare pleaded with him at least to do something to relieve her pain, he agreed to try mustard poultices. Véronique brought up a basin of hot water, and the doctor himself applied the wet plasters, sliding them along the girl's legs from knee to ankle. But they only added to her discomfort, the fever continued unabated and the headache was becoming unbearable. Soothing gargles were also prescribed, and Madame Chanteau prepared an infusion of bramble leaves, but they had to be abandoned after the first attempt, for pain prevented Pauline from swallowing. It was nearly six o'clock and dawn was breaking when the doctor finally took his leave.

'I'll come back around noon,' he said to Lazare in the passage. 'Don't be concerned... It's just a little pain.'

'And is pain such a little thing?' cried the young man, to whom the very idea of suffering was intolerable. 'People shouldn't have to endure pain.'

Cazenove stared at him and raised his hands to the heavens at such an extraordinary assertion.

When Lazare went back into Pauline's room, he sent his mother and Véronique away to lie down for a while. He himself could not have slept. And he saw the dawn come up in that untidy room, the mournful dawn that follows an agonizing night. With his brow pressed to the window, he was gazing out despairingly at the gloomy sky, when a sound made him look round. He thought it was Pauline getting out of bed, but it was Mathieu, forgotten by everyone, who had finally crept out of hiding to be near the girl. Her hand hung down outside the blankets, and the dog began licking it with such gentleness that Lazare, very touched, put his arm round his neck and said:

'Poor old fellow, your mistress is sick, you see... but it's nothing to worry about, and the three of us will soon be rambling around together again.'

Pauline had opened her eyes and, despite the pain that contorted her features, she was smiling.

There then began that anxious existence, that nightmare of long hours spent in a sickroom. Lazare, on an impulse of wild affection, shooed everyone away, barely allowing his mother and Louise in each morning to ask after Pauline; only Véronique, whose fondness for her he felt was genuine, was allowed to stay. To begin with, Madame Chanteau had tried to impress upon him the impropriety of a young man nursing a girl in this way; but he protested—was he not her husband? And anyway, didn't doctors look after women too? Between the young people themselves, there was indeed no self-conscious modesty. Suffering, and the possibility of imminent death, kept any sensual feelings at bay. He attended to all her needs, helping her sit up or lie down again like a compassionate brother who saw before him not a desirable body, but only the fever that made it shake. It was like an extension of their vigorous childhood, a return to the days when they first bathed together in chaste nudity, when he treated her like a little girl. The outside world vanished, nothing existed for them beyond the next medicine to be taken, the hours passing in vain hope of an improvement, the lowest details of bodily life suddenly taking on enormous importance, as on them depended the day's joy or sorrow. As the nights followed the days, Lazare's life seemed to hang suspended over a deep abyss, into whose dark void he feared to plunge at any moment.

Every morning, Doctor Cazenove came to see Pauline, and sometimes he even called again in the evening after dinner. Since his second visit, he had decided to bleed her freely. But the fever, after abating a little, had returned. Two days went by and he was clearly concerned, unable to account for the persistence of the attack. As the girl was finding it more and more difficult to open her mouth, he could not examine the back of her throat, which seemed to him swollen and livid red in colour. Finally, as Pauline was complaining of an increasing tightness which made her neck feel as if it were about to burst, the doctor told Lazare one morning:

'I suspect an abscess.'

The young man took him into his own room. The previous evening, while leafing through his old pathology manual, he had chanced on the section about retropharyngeal abscesses, which protrude into the oesophagus and can cause death from suffocation by compressing the trachea. He turned very pale and asked:

'So is this the end for her?'

'I do hope not,' the doctor answered. 'We must wait and see.'

But he himself could no longer conceal his anxiety. He had to admit that he was almost completely powerless in this case. How could he look for an abscess at the back of that contracted throat? And in any case, lancing it too soon could have serious consequences. It was best to let nature take its course, though it would be a very long and painful process.

'I'm not God Almighty,' he exclaimed, when Lazare reproached him with the uselessness of his learning.

The affection which Doctor Cazenove felt for Pauline expressed itself in an increasingly brusque and blustering manner. The tall old man, wizened like a briar, had been deeply moved. For more than thirty years he had knocked about the world, going from ship to ship and working in hospitals in every corner of the colonies; he had dealt with on-board epidemics and dreadful tropical diseases, elephantiasis in Cayenne and snake bites in India; he had killed men of every colour, studied the effects of poison on Chinese people, and risked the lives of negroes in delicate vivisection experiments. And now this little girl with a sore throat was upsetting him so much that he could not sleep; his iron hands shook, and his routine indifference to death deserted him, so fearful was he of a fatal outcome. So he strove to conceal such an unworthy emotion in a show of contempt for suffering. We were all born to suffer, so why make a fuss about it?

Each morning Lazare would say to him:

'Try and do something, Doctor, I beg you… It's dreadful, she can't even doze for a moment. She's been moaning all night.'

'But damn it all, it's not my fault!' the doctor finally snapped back in exasperation. 'You can't expect me to cut her throat to cure her!'

Then the young man grew angry in his turn.

'So medicine's no use, then?'

'No use at all when the whole machine goes wrong… Quinine brings a fever down, purgatives will move the bowels, and bleeding is the treatment for apoplexy… But everything else is down to luck. You must just put your trust in nature.'

This outburst was provoked by his anger at not knowing what to do. Normally he did not dare disavow medicine so directly, even though he had practised it too much not to be sceptical and humble about it. He would spend hours at a stretch sitting by the bedside observing the patient, then go off without even leaving a prescription, for his hands were tied and he could only look on as the abscess came to its full development, approaching ever closer to the fine line between life and death.

A whole week dragged by with Lazare in an anxious frenzy. From one minute to the next, he too feared that nature would give up the struggle, that Pauline's every painful gasp of breath might be her last. He saw the abscess clearly in his mind's eye as a huge obstruction in her windpipe, which only had to swell a little more to block the passage of air completely. His two years of ill-digested medical studies magnified his alarm. It was pain above all that drove him to distraction, sparking in him a nervous revolt, a wild protest against existence.

Why should such an abomination as pain exist? Was not all such bodily torture, such twisting and burning of the muscles, monstrously pointless, when it was a poor girl's body, so white and delicate, that the disease was attacking? Obsessed by this evil, he constantly returned to the bedside. He kept questioning her, even at the risk of tiring her out, was the pain any worse? Where was it now? Sometimes she would take his hand and lay it upon her neck; it was there, like an intolerable weight, a ball of molten lead, choking her as it throbbed. The migraine never left her, she could not find a comfortable position for her head, and she was tortured by insomnia: in the ten days that she had been prostrate with fever, she had not slept for two hours. One evening, to crown her misery, she developed terrible earache, and during these attacks she would pass out with the pain, feeling as if the bones in her jaws were being crushed. But with admirable courage, she did not let Lazare know the pain she was enduring, sensing that he was almost as ill as she was, his blood burning with her fever and his throat constricted by her own abscess. Indeed, she would often lie to him, forcing a smile in her moments of greatest pain, saying that it was calming down now and he should go and rest a little. The worst thing was that the back of her throat was now so inflamed she could not even swallow her own saliva without crying out in pain. Then Lazare would wake with a start: so was it all beginning again? Once more he questioned her, asking her where it hurt, but with her eyes closed and her face twisted in pain, she still fought to deceive him, mumbling that it was nothing, just a tickle, that was all.

'Go back to sleep and don't worry about me… I'm going to sleep too.'

Every evening she acted out this pretence of going to sleep, to persuade him to lie down. But he insisted on sitting up in an armchair to watch over her. The nights were so bad that he could never see the darkness fall without feeling a superstitious terror. Would the sun ever rise again?

One night, Lazare was sitting close by the bed, holding Pauline's hand in his own as he often did, to let her know he was still there and would not leave her. Doctor Cazenove had departed at ten o'clock, irritably declaring that he could take no further responsibility for the outcome. Until that moment, the young man could console himself with the belief that Pauline was unaware what danger she was in. In her hearing, mention was made of just an inflammation of the throat which, though very painful, would pass as simply as a head cold. She herself seemed quite calm, putting on a brave face and remaining cheerful despite the pain. She would smile as she heard them discussing plans for her convalescence. That particular night, she had just been listening to Lazare again planning a walk on the beach for her first outing. Then silence fell and she seemed to be sleeping, but a quarter of an hour or so later she murmured quite distinctly:

'My poor friend, I think you will be marrying another woman.'

He was shocked, and a chill ran down his spine.

'What do you mean?' he asked.

She had opened her eyes, and was looking at him with her look of brave resignation.

'Come on, I know what's the matter with me... and I'm glad I do, for I shall at least be able to kiss you all goodbye.'

At this, Lazare protested vehemently that she was mad to think such things, she'd be back on her feet within a week! But he let go of her hand and made an excuse for rushing to his own room, for he was choking back the tears. There in the darkness he threw himself down on his bed, in which he had not slept for so long, and sobbed uncontrollably. A chilling certainty had suddenly gripped his heart: Pauline was going to die, perhaps that very night. And the thought that she knew, that her silence until then had been out of womanly courage and consideration for the feelings of others, even in the face of death, completed his despair. She knew, she would anticipate her death agony, and he would be there, powerless to help! Already he could imagine their final farewells; the whole scene unfolded with harrowing detail in the darkness of his room. It was the end of everything, and grasping the pillow convulsively in his arms, he buried his head in it to smother the sound of his sobbing.

The night, however, ended without disaster. Two more days went by. And now a new bond had sprung up between them: the constant presence of death. Pauline made no further mention of the gravity of her condition, but found the strength to smile; Lazare, too, managed to appear quite calm and confident of her imminent recovery; yet both knew, whenever their eyes met in a long, caressing gaze, that they were saying a long goodbye. In the night especially, when Lazare kept watch beside her, they could almost hear each other's thoughts, as the threat of eternal separation filled even their silences with emotion.

Nothing could be more cruelly sweet, and never before had they felt such a fusion of their being.

One morning, at sunrise, Lazare was surprised how calm he felt at the idea of death. He tried to remember dates: since the day when Pauline had fallen ill, he had not once felt, running down his spine, that chill shudder at the thought of ceasing to be. If he dreaded losing his soulmate, it was a different kind of terror, in which the destruction of his own ego had no part. His heart bled within him, but he felt as if this battle he was waging against death put him on an equal footing with it and gave him the courage to look it in the face. Perhaps, too, his dazed exhaustion had simply numbed his fear. He closed his eyes to avoid seeing the sun coming up, and tried to reproduce the old thrill of horror by stoking his fear and telling himself that he, too, must die one day; but there was no reaction, he had become indifferent to all that, and everything had taken on a peculiar lightness. Even his pessimism melted away before that sickbed, and rather than plunging him deeper into hatred of the world, his revolt against pain became just a burning desire for health, a frustrated love of life. He no longer talked of blowing up the earth as if it were some uninhabitable ruin; the single image that obsessed him was of Pauline restored to health, walking arm in arm with him in the sunshine; and he felt only one need, to lead her once more, laughing and sure-footed, along the paths they had walked together.

That same day, Lazare became convinced the end had come. By eight o'clock Pauline was overcome with nausea, and each retching effort caused an alarming choking fit. Soon she began to shiver, shaking so violently they could hear her teeth chattering. Lazare, in a state of terror, shouted from the window for a boy to be sent to Arromanches at once, although the doctor was expected, as usual, around eleven. The house had been plunged in mournful, empty silence since Pauline was no longer able to enliven it with her vibrant activity. Chanteau spent his days downstairs in silence, staring at his legs in fear of another attack while there was no one to nurse him; Madame Chanteau forced Louise to go out, and the pair of them spent their time outdoors, having now become very close; only Véronique's constant heavy tread up and down disturbed the quiet of the staircase and the empty rooms. Three times Lazare had gone to lean over the banister in his impatience to know if the servant had managed to get someone to run the errand. He had just gone back in and was looking at the patient, who seemed a little calmer, when the door, which he had left ajar, gave a slight creak.

'What is it, Véronique?'

But it was his mother. That morning she was due to take Louise to visit friends somewhere near Verchemont.

'Little Cuche went off straight away,' she said. 'He's got good legs.' Then, after a silence, she asked:

'So, no improvement, then?'

With a helpless gesture, Lazare merely pointed to Pauline, lying as still as if she were dead, her face bathed in cold sweat.

'We shan't go to Verchemont, then,' she continued. 'Aren't they stubborn, these illnesses nobody understands?... The poor child is really having a terrible time of it.'

She had sat down, chattering on in the same subdued monotone.

'Just think, we had planned to start at seven o'clock, but luckily Louise has overslept... And all the callers I've had this morning, you'd think they were doing it on purpose! The grocer from Arromanches came round with his bill, and I had to pay him, and now the baker is downstairs... Another forty francs on bread last month! I really can't imagine where it's all going!'

Lazare was not paying attention, fully absorbed as he was by the fear Pauline's trembling might return. But this monotonous flow of chatter was irritating him, so he tried to get his mother out of the way.

'Will you give Véronique a couple of towels to bring up to me?'

'Of course, the baker will have to be paid,' Madame Chanteau continued, as though she had not heard. 'He has already spoken to me, so Véronique can't tell him I've gone out... Oh! I'm fed up with this house! It's getting me down, I can't manage it all... If only Pauline were not in such a bad way, she'd let me have the ninety francs for her board and lodging in advance. It's the twentieth today, so it would only be ten days early... The poor child does look very weak...'

Lazare rounded on her abruptly.

'What's that? What are you after?'

'You don't know where she keeps her money, do you?'

'No!'

'I dare say it's in her chest of drawers. Suppose you took a look?'

He refused with an exasperated gesture. His hands were shaking.

'Please Maman! For pity's sake, leave me alone.'

These remarks were exchanged in hurried whispers, at the far end of the room. A painful silence fell, then a quiet voice came from the bed:

'Lazare, take the key from under my pillow and give my aunt whatever she wants.'

They were both dumbfounded. Lazare protested, refusing to look in the chest of drawers; but he had to give in so as not to distress Pauline. Once he had handed his mother a hundred-franc note, he went to slip the key back under the pillow and found the patient shaking with another bout of the shivers, like a sapling on the point of snapping. And from her poor closed eyes, two great tears rolled down her cheeks.

Doctor Cazenove did not arrive until his usual time. He had seen no sign of young Cuche, who was probably larking about somewhere along the road. Once he had heard what Lazare had to say and taken a quick look at Pauline, he exclaimed:

'She is saved!'

Those bouts of nausea and dreadful shivers were simply signs that the abscess was bursting at last. There was no longer any risk of suffocation, and the problem would now sort itself out. Great was their joy! Lazare accompanied the doctor downstairs, and since Martin, the old sailor with the wooden leg who had stayed on in his service, was drinking a glass of wine in the kitchen, everyone else decided to drink a toast. Madame Chanteau and Louise took a little walnut liqueur.

'I never felt particularly alarmed,' said the first. 'I was certain it would turn out to be nothing serious.'

'All the same, the poor child has had a dreadful time!' exclaimed Véronique. 'To be sure, I couldn't be happier, not if I'd been given five francs!'

Just at that moment, Abbé Horteur appeared. He had come round for news, and accepted a drop of liqueur to keep everyone company. Every day he had called in like this, in a neighbourly fashion. When, on his first visit, Lazare had made it clear that he could not see the patient for fear of alarming her, the priest had calmly replied that he quite understood. He would content himself with saying his Masses for the poor young lady. Chanteau, as he clinked glasses with him, praised his tolerance.

'But as you can see, she's recovered without need of your prayers!'

'Each to his own salvation,' declared the curé sententiously, draining his glass.

Once the doctor had gone, Louise insisted on going upstairs to kiss Pauline. She was still in dreadful pain, but pain no longer seemed so important. Lazare joyfully called out to her to take heart, and, dropping all pretence, even exaggerated the danger she had faced, telling her that three times he had thought she was dead in his arms. She, however, made no great show of joy at being saved, though she was deeply conscious of the pleasure of being alive, after bravely facing the prospect of death. Her pain-filled face relaxed into a tender expression as she clasped her cousin's hand and murmured to him with a smile:

'So, my dearest, there's no escape, and I shall be your wife after all.'

At last her convalescence began, with long periods of rest. She slept peacefully for days at a time, breathing easily, in healing oblivion. Minouche, who had been banished from the room during the stressful hours of her illness, took advantage of this calm to slip back in again: she would jump lightly onto the bed and quickly curl up in a ball beside her mistress, spending whole days in the warmth of the sheets, or preening herself for hours and licking interminably at her fur with such delicacy that Pauline was not even aware of her presence. Meanwhile Mathieu, who had also been readmitted to the room, lay on the bedside rug, snoring like a man.

One of Pauline's first indulgences, the following Saturday, was to have her little friends from the village brought up to her room. She was now allowed the occasional boiled egg, after the starvation diet to which she had been subjected for three weeks. Though she was still very weak, she was able to receive the children sitting in a chair. Lazare had to rummage in the chest of drawers again to bring her some five-franc pieces. But after she had questioned the poor children and insisted on settling what she referred to as her arrears, she felt so exhausted that she had to be put back to bed in a faint. She also took an interest in the groynes and the revetments, asking every day whether they were still standing firm. Some of the timbers had already given way, and her cousin was not telling the truth when he said that only a couple of planks had come adrift. One morning when she was alone, she slipped out of bed, anxious to watch the high tide crashing against the distant defences; but once again her returning strength let her down, and she would have collapsed, had Véronique not entered the room in time to catch her in her arms.

'Take care, I'll tie you down in bed if you don't behave!' said Lazare jokingly.

He still insisted on sitting up with her at night, but was so exhausted he would fall asleep in his armchair. To start with, he had taken a keen delight in watching her drink her first bowls of broth. The health that was returning to this young body was an exquisite thing, a renewal of life which he also felt in himself. But later, once the pain had gone and he had grown used to her being well again, he ceased to rejoice at what had once seemed an unhoped-for blessing. All he felt, now the struggle was over, was a dazed release of nervous tension, a confused sense that the universal void had returned.

One night, Lazare had been sleeping deeply when Pauline heard him wake with a sigh of anguish. In the feeble glow of the night light she glimpsed his terror-stricken face, wide-eyed with horror, and his hands clasped together in supplication. He was stammering brokenly:

'God!... Oh God!'

Anxiously, she bent over him.

'What's the matter, Lazare?... Are you in pain?'

The sound of her voice made him tremble. Had she seen him? He sat there embarrassed and could only invent a clumsy lie.

'Nothing's the matter with me... It was you moaning just now.'

The fear of death had returned in his sleep—a fear without cause, as though spawned by nothingness itself, a fear whose icy breath had woken him with a great shiver. Oh God! One day he would have to die! This thought swelled in his mind and left him gasping for breath, while Pauline, who had lain her head back on her pillow, looked at him with her expression of motherly compassion.

CHAPTER 5

EVERY evening in the dining room, once Véronique had cleared the table, the same conversation would begin again between Madame Chanteau and Louise, while Chanteau, his head buried in a newspaper, offered only the briefest replies to his wife's occasional questions. During the fortnight when he had believed Pauline to be in danger, Lazare had never come down for meals; now he was dining downstairs again, but as soon as dessert was served he would go back up to sit with the invalid. And as soon as he started up the stairs, Madame Chanteau would pick up her complaining from the day before.

She always began with expressions of tender concern:

'Poor boy, he's wearing himself out... It really isn't reasonable for him to risk his health like this. He hasn't slept properly for the past three weeks... He's grown even paler since yesterday.'

And she would also express sympathy for Pauline: the dear child was in such pain, it was impossible to spend a minute in her room without feeling sorry for her. But then she gradually came round to the disruption that her illness was causing to the household: everything was at sixes and sevens, it was impossible to have anything hot to eat, it was getting to the point where life was hardly worth living. Then she broke off suddenly to ask her husband:

'I don't suppose Véronique remembered your marshmallow* water?'

'Yes, yes,' he replied over the top of his newspaper.

Then she lowered her voice to speak to Louise.

'It's a funny thing, but that unfortunate Pauline has never brought us any luck. And to think that some people still look on her as our good angel! Oh yes, I know the gossip that's doing the rounds... In Caen, they're saying—aren't they, Louisette?—that she has made us rich. Rich, indeed! You can tell me the truth, I take no heed of scandalmongers!'

'Well, yes,' murmured the girl, 'people do gossip about you, as they do about everyone else. Last month I had to correct a notary's wife who was discussing your situation without knowing the first thing about it... You can't stop people from talking.'

After that, Madame Chanteau gave vent to her true feelings. Yes indeed, they had become the victims of their own generosity. Hadn't they managed perfectly well without help from anyone, until Pauline arrived? And where would she be now, on what street-corner in Paris, if they hadn't had the heart to take her in? It was all very well for people to gossip about her money, but it had never given them personally anything but trouble—indeed, it seemed to have brought ruin on the household. Surely the facts spoke for themselves: her son would never have got involved with that idiotic seaweed business, or wasted his time trying to stop the sea from destroying Bonneville, if his head had not been turned by the unlucky Pauline. If she had lost some money in the process, well, that was her own lookout; the poor boy, on the other hand, had damaged both his health and his future prospects! Madame Chanteau poured out her bile against the hundred and fifty thousand francs, the smell of which still clung about her secretaire. It was the thought of the large sums swallowed up, and the small amounts still being taken every day and thus increasing the debt, that so infuriated her, as if she felt that this was the acid that had eaten away at her honesty. By now that process of corrosion was complete, and she loathed Pauline for all the money that she owed her.

'What's the good of talking to such an obstinate creature?' she went on. 'She's horribly mean-spirited, but she can also be shockingly extravagant. She'll toss twelve thousand francs into the sea for those Bonneville fishermen, who just laugh at us, and feed all the lousy brats in the neighbourhood, while I tremble, quite honestly, whenever I have to ask her for a couple of francs. Explain that if you can... Despite all her show of charity to others, she has a heart of stone.'

Often Véronique would enter the room, carrying crockery or bringing in the tea, and hang around to listen, sometimes even venturing a remark of her own:

'Mademoiselle Pauline, a heart of stone! Oh, how can Madame say such a thing?'

Madame Chanteau would reduce her to silence with a stern look. Then, resting her elbows on the table, she would embark on complicated calculations, talking as if to herself.

'Her money's no longer for me to look after, thank goodness, but I'd like to know how much of it there is left. Less than seventy thousand francs, I'll warrant... Now then, let's work it out: three thousand already wasted on trial beach defences, at least two hundred going out each month for charity, as well as the ninety francs for her board and lodging with us. It all goes so quickly... Would you care to bet that she'll ruin herself, Louise? Yes, you'll see, she'll be reduced to begging... And if she does ruin herself, who will look after her, what will she do for a living?'

At this Véronique could contain herself no longer:

'I do hope Madame wouldn't turn her out of the house.'

'What's that?' said her mistress angrily, 'whatever's the woman on about? Of course, there's no question of anyone being turned out of the house. I've never turned anyone out... I'm only saying that when someone has inherited a fortune, it seems to me the height of stupidity to go frittering it all away, only to become a burden on others... Now get along to your kitchen, my girl, and see if you can find me there!'

The maid went sullenly off, grumbling under her breath in protest. A silence fell while Louise poured the tea. The only sound was the slight rustling of the newspaper, which Chanteau always read in its entirety, down to the adverts. Now and then he exchanged a few words with the young girl.

'Go on, you can put me another lump of sugar in… Have you had a letter from your father yet?'

'Oh, no, not yet,' she answered with a laugh. 'But if I'm in the way, you know, I can always go. You have quite enough on your hands as it is, what with Pauline's illness… I intended to make my escape, but you insisted I stay.'

He tried to interrupt her.

'There's no question of it, it's very sweet of you to keep us company until the poor child is well enough to come down.'

'I can put myself up in Arromanches and wait for my father, if you've had enough of me,' she went on as if she had not heard him, teasingly. 'My aunt Léonie has taken a chalet there, and there are plenty of nice people, and a beach where you can at least bathe… Only, Aunt Léonie is such a bore!'

Chanteau always ended up laughing at the mischievous, ingratiating things she said. However, although he did not dare admit as much to his wife, his whole heart was reserved for Pauline, who nursed him with such a gentle touch. And he buried his head in the newspaper again as soon as Madame Chanteau emerged with a start from her cogitations, as if from a dream.

'And you see, there's one thing I can't forgive: she has taken my son away from me… He spends barely a quarter of an hour at table, and he's always rushing off when I want to speak to him.'

'That won't be happening for much longer,' Louise pointed out. 'But she does still need someone to sit with her.'

The mother nodded. She pursed her lips. The words she seemed to be trying to hold back burst forth, despite her efforts.

'Perhaps… but it just isn't normal for a young man to be always around a sick girl… There, I haven't minced my words, I've spoken my mind, and if it causes trouble, I can't help it.'

Then, noticing Louise's embarrassed look, she added:

'Besides, it really isn't healthy to breathe the air of that sickroom. She might very well pass on her sore throat to him… Girls like that who look so strong sometimes have all sorts of impurities in their blood. Shall I tell you something? Well, I don't believe she has a strong constitution at all.'

Louise went on gently defending her friend. She had always found her so nice!—which was her only argument against the accusations of a stony heart and poor health. Her need for a happy, pleasantly balanced environment led her to challenge Madame Chanteau's excessive resentment, although she listened with a smile as the recriminations grew daily more spiteful. She was moved to pride at by the which one of her words, but she also flushed with secret pleasure at feeling herself preferred, and now mistress of the household. Louise was like Minouche, enjoying rubbing up against other people and perfectly pleasant, as long as no one got in the way of her enjoyment.

Every evening the conversation, after going back over the same ground, would invariably culminate in an unfinished and pointedly spoken phrase:

'No, Louisette, the kind of wife my son needs...'

And from there, Madame Chanteau would launch into a speech about the qualities she required from her ideal daughter-in-law, her gaze remaining fixed upon Louise, trying to make her understand more than she was saying. The description was an exact portrait of her: a well-brought-up young person with some experience of society, able to entertain, who had grace rather than beauty, and above all, was truly feminine, for, as Madame Chanteau said, she detested tomboys who made blunt speaking an excuse for vulgarity. Then there was money, the only decisive issue, to which she made but the briefest allusion: of course, the dowry was immaterial, but her son had great plans for the future, and he could not contemplate a poor marriage.

'Let me tell you, my dear, if Pauline had arrived here penniless, without a shirt on her back, well, the marriage would have taken place years ago... But can you wonder that I'm nervous, when I see money slipping through her fingers like water? She'll get a long way now with her sixty thousand francs, won't she?... No! Lazare deserves better—I'll never give him up to a foolish woman who would scrimp on food, only to fritter her money away on charitable follies!'

'No, money doesn't mean anything,' replied Louise, lowering her eyes, 'but it is necessary.'

Although no explicit reference was made to Louise's dowry, her two hundred thousand francs seemed to be lying there on the table, glittering in the tranquil glow of the ceiling lamp. It was the vision and the feel of the money that sparked feverish excitement in Madame Chanteau, sweeping aside Pauline's paltry sixty thousand in her dream of conquering this newcomer with her fortune intact. She had noticed Lazare's flash of desire for Louise, before this tedious business that was now detaining him upstairs. If the girl loved him too, why not make a match of it? The father would give his consent, particularly in a case of mutual passion. So she worked to fan Louise's passion into life, spending the rest of the evening murmuring seductive nothings to her.

'My Lazare is such a good man! No one truly knows him. Even you, Louisette, can't imagine how affectionate he can be... I certainly won't pity his wife! She's sure to be well loved, whoever she is... And he's such a vigorous man! With soft, white skin. My grandfather, the Chevalier de la Vignière, had such white skin that in his day he'd go to masked balls as a woman, in a low-cut dress.'

Louise would blush and laugh in amusement at such details. She could have listened all night to the mother's sincere attempts at matchmaking on her son's behalf, poured out in whispered confidences which, between two women, might go a long way; but Chanteau always ended up nodding behind his newspaper.

'Isn't it about time we all went to bed?' he asked with a yawn.

Then, having long since lost the thread of the conversation, he added:

'Whatever you may say, she's not a bad sort... I shall be very glad when she is able to come downstairs again and sit by me at mealtimes.'

'We shall all be glad,' exclaimed his wife tartly. 'We may talk, and speak our mind, but that doesn't stop us being fond of someone.'

'The poor darling!' exclaimed Louise in her turn, 'I'd gladly take on half her pain, if such a thing were possible. She's so nice!'

Véronique, who was bringing in their candles, again put in a word of her own.

'You're quite right to be friends with her, Mademoiselle Louise, for you'd need a heart of stone to plot anything unkind against her.'

'That's quite enough!' said Madame Chanteau, 'nobody asked your opinion. You'd do better to keep your candlesticks clean... Just look what a mess this one is in!'

They all stood up. Chanteau, fleeing this peevish exchange, shut himself away in his ground-floor bedroom. But when the two women arrived upstairs, where their rooms faced each other, they did not go straight to bed. Madame Chanteau would almost invariably take Louise into her own room for a while, where she continued talking about Lazare, showing off portraits of him, and even getting out little childhood mementoes: a tooth which had been extracted when he was very young, a faded lock of baby hair, even some of his old clothes, the white lacy tie he had worn for his first Communion, his first pair of trousers.

'Look!' she said one night, 'you can have this lock of his hair. I can ꞏꞏꞏꞏꞏꞏ ꞏꞏ, I ꞏꞏꞏꞏ ꞏꞏꞏꞏ ꞏꞏꞏ of his at all the different ages.'

So when Louise got into bed at last, she could not sleep, obsessed by the thought of this young man whom his mother was thrusting into her arms. She tossed and turned with passionate insomnia, and his image, with his white skin, shone out through the darkness. Often, she would listen whether he was walking around on the floor above, and the thought that he was doubtless still keeping watch over the sleeping Pauline further stoked her ardour, until she threw back the sheets and slept with her bosom exposed to the air.

Upstairs, Pauline's convalescence was taking its slow course. Although the patient was out of danger, she remained very weak, drained by bouts of fever which took the doctor by surprise. As Lazare remarked, doctors were always being taken by surprise. He himself was growing more irritable by the hour. The sudden lassitude that he had felt once the crisis was over seemed to be increasing and turning into a kind of restless unease. Now that he was no longer battling death, he found he could not stand the stuffy bedroom, the spoonfuls of medicine that had to be given at set times, and all the other little servitudes of the sickroom which at first he had taken on so eagerly. Now that she could manage without him, he relapsed into the boredom of an empty existence: he would sit with his hands dangling idly by his side, shift from chair to chair, wander about the room gazing hopelessly at the four walls, or just stare vacantly out of the window. Whenever he opened a book to read by her side, he had to stifle a yawn between pages.

'Lazare,' Pauline said to him one day, 'you really should go out. Véronique can look after me.'

He refused with a violent gesture. Could she not stand his presence any longer, so that she wanted to send him away? It would be a fine thing, wouldn't it, to desert her like that before she was fully back on her feet? But he eventually calmed down as she gently explained what she meant:

'You wouldn't be deserting me by just going out for some fresh air... Go for a walk in the afternoon. It won't do either of us any good if you fall ill as well!'

But she added rather tactlessly:

'I see you yawning all day long.'

'Me, yawning?' he expostulated. 'You might as well call me heartless, and have done with it! Really, if that's all the thanks I get!'

Next morning Pauline's approach was subtler. She pretended she had a keen desire to see further work done on the groynes and revetments: the high winter tides would soon be upon them, and the trial works would be swept away if the defensive system wasn't completed. But Lazare's early enthusiasm had already cooled; he expressed dissatisfaction with the way crucial timbers were assembled, and further experiments were needed; but then they would overrun the estimate, and the Council had yet to grant them a single sou. For two days Pauline worked to rekindle his inventor's pride: was he going to let himself be beaten by the sea, in front of all the locals, who were already sniggering? As for the money, it would certainly be paid back if she advanced it as they had agreed. Gradually Lazare's old enthusiasm seemed to return. He made fresh designs and again sent for the carpenter from Arromanches, with whom he held discussions in his bedroom, leaving the door open so he could rush in to see Pauline if she called him.

'This time,' he declared one morning as he kissed her, 'the sea won't break so much as a matchstick, I am quite confident of that... As soon as you can walk again, we'll go down together and see how the construction is coming along.'

As it happened, Louise had just come upstairs to ask after the patient, and as she too was kissing her, Pauline whispered in her ear:

'Take him out!'

At first Lazare refused; he was waiting for the doctor. But Louise laughingly insisted he was too gentlemanly to let her go alone to the Gonins' house, where she wanted to choose for herself the lobsters she would send to Caen. On the way, he could have a look at the new groyne.

'Do go,' said Pauline, 'just to please me. Come on, Louise, take his arm... That's the way, now don't let go!'

She was in high spirits as the other two jostled each other playfully; but when they left she grew solemn again and leaned over the edge of her bed to listen, as their footsteps and laughter receded down the stairs.

A quarter of an hour later, Véronique appeared with the doctor. Then she installed herself at Pauline's bedside, without neglecting her cooking, for she was constantly up and down the stairs, spending an hour with her between one dish and the next. The change came about gradually. Lazare returned that evening, but went out again next morning; and becoming daily more absorbed in his life outdoors, he cut short his visits to Pauline, until he was there just long enough to ask how she was. In any case, it was Pauline who would send him away if he even mentioned sitting down. Whenever he and Louise came home together, she made them tell her all about their walk, pleased at their high spirits and the fresh air that clung to their wind-swept hair. They seemed such good friends that she no longer had any suspicions about them. And as soon as she saw Véronique bringing her medicine, she would call out cheerfully to them:

'Be off with you now, you're in the way.'

Sometimes she would call Louise back and remind her to take care of Lazare, like a child.

'Try not to let him get bored, he needs to be kept amused... And enjoy your walk, I don't want to see you back here for the rest of the day.'

Once she was alone, her gaze seemed to linger, following them into the distance. She spent the days reading and waiting for her strength to return, for she was still so weak that sitting up in an armchair for two or three hours at a time exhausted her. She would often let her book drop onto her knees, while her mind wandered dreamily off after her cousin and her friend. If they had gone along the beach, they would be reaching the caves, where it was so pleasant on the sand in the cool of the rising tide. In those persistent visions, she believed that her only regret was being unable to be there with them. In any case, she was bored of reading. The novels that lay about the house, love stories full of romantic betrayals, had always offended her natural honesty, her urge to give herself irrevocably. How was it possible to deceive your own heart, or, having once been in love, one day to cease loving? She pushed the book away. Now she could see in her mind's eye, far away beyond the walls, her cousin bringing her friend home, supporting her weary steps as they leaned against each other, whispering and laughing together.

'Your medicine, Mademoiselle.' Véronique's rough voice from behind her woke her up with a jolt.

By the end of the first week, Lazare no longer came in without knocking. One morning, as he opened the door he caught sight of Pauline, bare-armed, combing her hair as she sat up in bed.

'Oh, I'm sorry!' he cried, stepping hurriedly back.

'What's the matter?' she exclaimed, 'are you scared of me?'

Then he made up his mind to enter, but was afraid of embarrassing her, so he looked away while she finished doing her hair.

'Pass me a camisole, will you?' she asked calmly. 'There, in the top drawer... I must be getting better, I'm taking an interest in clothes again.'

He became flustered and could only find chemises. Finally, once he had thrown her a camisole, he stood by the window waiting until she had buttoned it up to her chin. A fortnight earlier, when he had thought she was at death's door, he had picked her up in his arms like a little girl without even noticing her nakedness. But now he was even offended by the untidiness of the room. And she too, noticing his embarrassment, soon stopped asking him to help with her personal needs, as he had done for a while.

'Véronique, do shut the door!' she cried one morning when she heard Lazare's footsteps on the landing. 'Hide all this stuff, and hand me that fichu.'*

Pauline's health, meanwhile, went from strength to strength. Her great pleasure, once she was able to stand up and lean against the window, was to watch the building of the sea defences in the distance. The noise of hammering could be heard quite clearly, and she could see the gang of seven or eight men, black dots bustling about like big ants on the yellow shingle of the beach. Between the tides they would beaver away energetically, but then they had to retreat before the advancing waves. But Pauline was especially interested in Lazare's white jacket and Louise's pink dress, which stood out brightly in the sun. Her gaze followed them constantly, and she could have said what they had been doing all day, down to the smallest details. Now that the work was being moved on so urgently, they could no longer wander off into the caves beneath the cliffs. She had them constantly in view, just a kilometre away, as amusingly fragile as miniature dolls beneath the sky's wide expanse. Although she did not realize it, the jealous pleasure she took in accompanying them in this way did much to cheer her convalescence and restore her strength.

'Well, it keeps you entertained all right, watching those men work,' Véronique would say every day as she swept the room. 'Certainly does you more good than reading. Me, books make my brain hurt. And when you're trying to build yourself back up, you'll see, you need to gobble up the sunshine like a turkey, by the beakful.'

Véronique was not normally a great talker, and was even considered taciturn. But with Pauline she would chatter away in a friendly manner, thinking it might do her good.

'It's all right Inside at the anyway, so long as it keeps Monsieur Lazare happy... I say happy, though he doesn't seem quite so keen on it any more. But he's a proud sort, and stubborn, even if he is bored stiff with it now... Anyhow, he'll need to keep a close eye on those boozy workers of his or they'll bang all the nails in crooked.'

After sweeping under the bed she added:

'And as for the duchess...'

Pauline, who was only listening with half an ear, jumped at the name.

'Duchess? Who do you mean?'

'Why, Mademoiselle Louise, of course! She seems to think she's the bee's knees, doesn't she?... Just look at all the little pots and creams and lotions she keeps in her room! Why, as soon as you open the door it gets you in the throat, what a pong... But she's not as pretty as you.'

'Oh, me, I'm just a country bumpkin,' said Pauline with a smile; 'Louise is so refined.'

'Perhaps, but she's all skin and bones with it. I can see that, when she's washing... For sure, if I was a man I wouldn't hesitate long between the two of you!'

Carried away by the force of her conviction, she came over to lean at the window beside Pauline.

'Just look at her down there on the beach, doesn't she look a real shrimp? Of course, it's a way off, you can't expect her to look as big as a house from up here. But she ought to have a bit more about her than that... Look! there's Monsieur Lazare lifting her up so she doesn't get her little booties wet. Not much of an armful, is she? I suppose there are some men as likes 'em bony...'

Véronique stopped short, for she felt Pauline quiver beside her. She was constantly harping on this subject, as if itching to say ever more about it. These days, everything that she saw and heard—the evening conversations when Pauline was ripped to shreds, Lazare and Louise laughing furtively together, the whole family's ingratitude, bordering on treachery—stuck in her throat and made her choke. Had she rushed upstairs the moment her good sense was offended by another great injustice, she would have told Pauline everything, but fear of making her ill again kept Véronique pacing up and down in her kitchen, clattering her pots and pans and swearing that things couldn't go on like that, one day she'd tell them proper what was what. However, as soon as she let slip a disturbing word in Pauline's room, she would try to take it back and explain it away with touching clumsiness.

'But thank goodness, Monsieur Lazare isn't the kind to like 'em bony! He's been in Paris, he's got more taste than that... Look! he's put her down again, just like dropping a matchstick!'

Then Véronique, fearing she might let slip other unfortunate remarks, brandished her feather duster and went on with the cleaning, while Pauline, deep in thought, followed Louise's blue dress* and Lazare's white jacket as they moved amongst the dark shapes of the workmen, until evening fell on the horizon.

Just as Pauline's convalescence was coming to an end at last, Chanteau was seized by another violent attack of gout, which induced her to come downstairs despite her feeble state. The very first time she emerged from her room, it was to go and sit by another sickbed; as Madame Chanteau remarked bitterly, the house had become a real hospital. For some time, her husband had been confined to his invalid chair. Following repeated seizures, his whole body was now affected by the disease, which had spread from his feet to his knees, then his elbows and hands. The small white bead on his ear had dropped off, but other larger ones had appeared. All his joints were swollen, and spots of chalky tophus showed white through the skin all over his body, like crayfish eyes. His gout was now chronic and incurable, the sort that stiffens joints and deforms limbs.

'Good God! it does hurt!' he kept repeating. 'My left leg is stiff as a board; I can't move my foot or my knee... and now my elbow is burning too. Just look at it!'

Pauline saw a badly inflamed swelling on his left elbow. That was the joint that was giving him the most trouble, and the pain in it soon became unbearable. He sighed, with his arm outstretched and his gaze fixed upon his hand, a pitiable sight, with the knuckles knotted and swollen and the thumb crooked as though it had been smashed by a hammer blow.

'I can't bear it like this, you must help me... I had found such a good position! Then it started again straight away, it feels like a saw scraping my bones... Try and lift me up a bit.'

Twenty times an hour he had to be helped to change his position; he was in a continuous state of anxious agitation, always searching for relief. But Pauline still felt too weak to try to shift him on her own. She murmured:

'Véronique, lift him gently with me.'

'No, not you Mademoiselle!' Clément would cry out, 'and if you me.'

Then Pauline would have to make an effort that almost put her back out. And, however gently she turned him, he would utter a howl that sent the maid fleeing from the room, swearing that it took a saint like Mademoiselle Pauline to tolerate such work, for Monsieur's bawling would put the Almighty himself to flight.

Although the attacks grew less acute, they persisted night and day, the maddening discomfort becoming a nameless torture when compounded by the anxiety of immobility. It was not just that his feet were being gnawed by animals' teeth, his whole body was being crushed as if by a relentless millstone. No relief was possible; Pauline could only stay with him, tending to his whims, always ready to move him into a different position, without ever gaining him an hour's respite. The worst thing was that the pain made him angry and unjust, and he spoke furiously to her as if she were some clumsy servant.

'Stop it! you're just as stupid as Véronique!... Must you dig your fingers into me like that? Are they gendarme's fingers you've got?... Get out and leave me alone! I don't want you touching me anymore!'

Never answering back, with unruffled resignation Pauline would try to be even gentler. When she felt he was getting too annoyed with her, she would hide for a while behind the curtains until, no longer seeing her, he calmed down. Often, she would weep silent tears in her hiding place, not for the poor man's brutality, but for the dreadful torment that made him so unkind. She would hear him muttering to himself between groans:

'She's gone and left me, the heartless creature... Ah! if I kick the bucket now, I'll only have Minouche to close my eyes. Surely to God it's not right to abandon a Christian soul this way... I bet she's down in the kitchen enjoying some broth!'

Then, after a moment's resistance, he would groan louder and finally bring himself to call her:

'Pauline, are you there?... Come and lift me up a bit, I can't stand it like this... Can't we try the left side, please?'

Then he would become emotional and beg her pardon for having been unkind. Sometimes he would ask her to bring in Mathieu to keep him company, imagining that the dog's presence would be beneficial to him. But it was above all Minouche who was his faithful companion, for she loved the stuffy sickroom atmosphere, and now spent her days lying on an armchair opposite the bed. However, she seemed startled whenever the patient let out an unusually loud cry, and would sit up on her tail to look at him suffering, her big round eyes gleaming with the indignant surprise of a righteous creature whose peace had been rudely disturbed. Why should he be making all that futile and unpleasant noise?

Every time Pauline went to the door with Doctor Cazenove, she implored him:

'Please, can't you give him an injection of morphine? It breaks my heart to hear him.'

But the doctor always refused. What was the use? The attack would only come back more violently. Since salicylate seemed just to have made the disease worse, he preferred not to try any new drugs. However, he did suggest a milk diet, once the worst of the attack was over. Until then, complete fasting, diuretic drinks, and nothing more.

'The fact is,' said Cazenove, 'he's a glutton and he's now paying the price for his greed. He has been eating game, I can tell, I saw the feathers. Well, that's his lookout! He's had enough warnings from me, let him suffer, since he prefers to stuff his face whatever the risks!... But what would be more unfair, my child, is if you were to make yourself ill again. Do be sensible, won't you? You still need to take care of your own health.'

But she was not particularly careful, instead devoting herself to her uncle at all hours, losing her sense of time, and even of life itself, in the long days that she spent at his side, her ears ringing from the wails that resounded through the room. This obsession became so powerful that she forgot all about Louise and Lazare, barely exchanging a few words as she hurried past them, only coinciding with them occasionally, when she walked through the dining room. By this time the work on the groynes was finished, and violent rainstorms had confined the young people to the house for the past week, so that, when the idea that they were together again came suddenly back to her, she felt happy to know they were close by.

Madame Chanteau had never seemed so busy. She was taking advantage, she said, of the confusion into which her husband's illness had thrown the household to go through her papers, do her accounts, and catch up with her correspondence. So in the afternoons she would shut herself away in her bedroom, deserting Louise, who immediately went upstairs to see Lazare, for she hated being alone. This became a habit, and they would stay together until dinner time in the big room on the second floor, which had for so long served as a school room and playroom to Pauline. Lazare's narrow iron bedstead was still there, hidden behind the screen, while the piano was gathering dust, and the huge table lay buried under untidy heaps of papers, books, and pamphlets. In the middle of it, between two lumps of dried seaweed, stood a toy-like model of a groyne, carved out of pine and reminiscent of the grandfather's masterpiece, the bridge in its glass case that adorned the dining room.

For some time, Lazare had been showing signs of nerves. His workmen had exasperated him, and the completed construction left him with a sense of relief at dispatching an oppressively difficult chore, without any particular pleasure at seeing his idea finally realized. He was preoccupied now with other plans, vague ideas for the future, positions he might obtain in Caen, works that would propel him into high places. Yet he never took any serious steps to achieve them, but relapsed into a state of idleness which embittered him and left him weaker and less courageous by the hour. This feeling of discontent was aggravated by the profound shock to his system of Pauline's illness, a perpetual need for the open air, and a peculiar physical agitation, as though he were obeying some imperious urge to avenge himself against pain. Louise's presence further excited his nervous fever: she seemed unable to speak to him without leaning on his shoulder, he felt the warm waft of her pretty laughter on his face and her feline graces, coquettish feminine scent, and friendly, disconcertingly free manner went straight to his head. He fell into the grip of an unhealthy desire, against which his conscience struggled. With a childhood friend, in his mother's house—that was quite impossible, and a sense of propriety robbed his arms of their strength whenever, in their games, he caught hold of Louise with a sudden, passionate rush of blood to the head. In this struggle with himself, it was never the thought of Pauline that held him back: she would have known nothing about it, much as a husband deceives his wife with a servant-girl. In the night, he would fantasize that Véronique had been dismissed for being unbearable and Louise was just a little maid, whom he tiptoed, barefoot, to visit. What a shame it hadn't all turned out differently! So he adopted an exaggerated pessimism against women and love, expressed in ferocious jibes from morning to night. Women were the origin of all evil, they were foolish and fickle, they perpetuated suffering by provoking desire, while love was nothing but delusion, the selfish urge of future generations to come into existence. He flung all of Schopenhauer into the mix, with vulgar details which made Louise at once blush and laugh. By degrees he fell more deeply in love with her, his disdainful fury gave way to a genuine passion, and he threw himself into this new affection with all his original enthusiasm, ever in quest of a happiness that seemed to elude him.

On Louise's side, for a long time there was nothing beyond a play of natural coquettishness. She loved delicate attentions, whispered compliments, and flirting with agreeable men, and immediately felt dejected and abandoned if they lost interest in her. Her senses remained virginal and dormant, she had not yet gone beyond the trivial chatter and acceptable familiarities of a constant, assiduous courtship. When Lazare neglected her for a moment to write a letter, or to plunge into one of his sudden, apparently motiveless fits of melancholy, she became so unhappy that she began to tease and provoke him, preferring risk to neglect. Later on, however, she was seized with fear one day when she felt the young man's burning breath playing like a flame on the nape of her delicate neck. She knew enough, from her long years of boarding school, to understand the threat she faced, and from that moment she had lived in delicious and frightened anticipation of a possible misfortune. Not that she had the least wish for it to happen, or was even thinking about it rationally, for she was confident of escaping the danger while, at the same time, continuing to toy with it, so crucial to her feminine happiness was this skin-deep conflict between her urge to give, and to refuse, herself.

Upstairs in the big room, Lazare and Louise felt an even stronger sense of belonging to each other, and the whole family seemed to be conspiring to push them towards disaster—he languishing in idleness and solitude, she unsettled by the intimate details and excited descriptions of her son with which Madame Chanteau had regaled her. They took refuge up there on the pretext of avoiding the bawling of Lazare's gout-ridden father below, and there they lived, without picking up a book or opening the piano, concerned only with themselves, in a stupor induced by interminable conversation.

On the day that Chanteau's attack reached its peak, the whole house shook with his screams: long, tortured lamentations like the howls of a beast having its throat slit. After lunch, which she had gulped down in a state of nervous exasperation, Madame Chanteau rushed from the room, saying:

'I can't stand it, it'll drive me to a winding too. If anyone wants me, I'll be up in my room, writing... And Lazare, do take Louise upstairs too, shut yourselves in your room and try to keep her amused; poor Louisette, she's not having much fun here!'

They heard her slam her door on the first floor, while her son and the girl continued up to the floor above.

Pauline had gone back in to see her uncle. She alone remained calm, full of pity for such suffering. Even if all she could do was sit with him, she wanted at least to give the poor man the comfort of not being left to suffer alone, sensing that he coped with his pain more stoically when she was watching him, even if she did not say a word. For hours, she would sit there beside the bed until she managed to calm him a little with her big compassionate eyes. But on this particular day, as he lay with his head tipped back on the bolster, his arm stretched out and his elbow racked with pain, he did not even recognize her, and screamed louder whenever she went near.

At around four o'clock Pauline, in desperation, went to the kitchen to look for Véronique, leaving the door open as she expected to be back immediately.

'We really must do something,' she murmured. 'I should like to try cold water compresses. The doctor says it's dangerous, but it sometimes works... I'll need some linen.'

Véronique was in a foul mood.

'Linen, huh!... I've just been up there to fetch some cloths, and a great welcome I got! Not to be disturbed, are they? Whatever next!'

'But you could ask Lazare,' continued Pauline, not yet catching Véronique's meaning.

Then the maid, in a fury, her arms akimbo, burst out without thinking what she was saying:

'Yes indeed, they're far too busy licking each other's faces up there!'

'What do you mean?' stammered Pauline, turning very pale.

Véronique, taken aback by the sound of her own voice and wanting to retrieve this secret that she had been bottling up for so long, tried to think up some explanation, some lie to tell, but nothing convincing came to mind. As a precaution, she had grasped Pauline by the wrists, but Pauline shook herself free with a jerk and rushed madly up the stairs, so choking and convulsed with rage that Véronique did not dare follow her, fearing the look on her face, an unrecognizable white mask. The house seemed to be asleep, the upper floors were wrapped in silence, and only Chanteau's howls rose up through the close, dead air. The girl rushed up to the first floor, only to run into her aunt, who was standing there blocking the landing like a sentry, and might have been on lookout for some time.

'Where are you going?' she asked.

Pauline, choking with anger and exasperated at the obstacle, was unable to reply.

'Let me past!' she finally stammered, with such an irate gesture that Madame Chanteau backed away.

Then she ran up to the second floor, while her aunt, petrified and speechless, simply threw up her arms. It was one of those fits of furious rebellion that could burst like a sudden storm upon the sunny gaiety of Pauline's nature, and which, from early childhood on, left her in a state of collapse. For years, she had believed herself cured of them. But this explosion of jealousy had taken such violent hold of her that she could not have contained it without doing herself violence.

When she reached Lazare's door on the top floor, she hurled herself against it. The door slammed back against the wall, bending the key. And what she then saw drove her completely wild. Lazare was holding Louise pinned against the wardrobe, devouring her chin and neck with kisses, while she, swooning in thrall to his male power, offered no resistance. They had doubtless started in fun, but the game was ending badly.

There was a moment of stunned silence. All three stared at each other. Then Pauline screamed:

'Oh! you slut! you slut!'

It was the woman's treachery that infuriated her the most. With a gesture of contempt, she pushed Lazare aside like a child whose weakness she knew only too well. But this woman, her friend, had stolen her husband from her while she was downstairs nursing an invalid! She grabbed her by the shoulders and shook her, gripped by a strong urge to slap her.

'Why have you done this? I want to know... It's disgusting, do you hear me?' Louise, wild-eyed and in a state of shock, faltered:

'It's him, he was holding me down, hurting me.'

'Him! Come off it, he'd have burst into tears if you'd just pushed him away!'

The sight of the room further fuelled her resentment, Lazare's room, where she and he had loved each other, where she, too, had felt her blood on fire at the touch of the young man's passionate breath. How could one take her revenge on this woman? Lazare, in a confusion of embarrassment, had just made up his mind to do something, when she flung Louise away from her so violently that her shoulder crashed into the wardrobe.

'See, I can't trust myself… Get out!'

And that was all she could find to shout, as she pursued Louise around the room, chasing her out onto the landing and down the staircase, screaming after her:

'Get out! Get out!… Get your things and go!'

Meanwhile, Madame Chanteau was still standing on the first-floor landing. The speed of events had left her no opportunity to intervene. But she now recovered the power of speech; she gestured to Lazare to shut himself up in his room, then she tried to calm Pauline, initially feigning surprise at what had happened. Pauline, having driven Louise into her bedroom, was still screaming:

'Get out! Get out!'

'What do you mean, get out? Have you lost your head?'

Then the young girl stammered out the whole story. She was overcome with disgust, for to her upright nature, this was the most shameful, inexcusable, unforgivable thing to do. The more she thought about it, the deeper her indignation became, for it offended her passionate honesty and her fidelity in love. Once you'd given your heart, you could never take it back.

'Get out! Pack your trunk and go… Now!'

Louise, overwhelmed and unable to find anything to say in her own defence, had already opened a drawer to get her underclothes together. But Madame Chanteau was now growing angry.

'Stay where you are, Louisette!… Am I mistress in my own house, or not? Who dares give orders here and presumes to send people away?… It's a disgrace! This is no place for petty bickering!'

'Don't you understand?' shouted Pauline, 'I caught her upstairs with Lazare… He was kissing her!'

Madame Chanteau shrugged her shoulders. All her pent-up resentment now came out in words of shameful suspicion:

'They were only playing around, where's the harm in that?... When he was nursing you in bed, did we ever poke our noses into what the two of you were up to?'

Pauline's rage suddenly subsided. She stood there motionless and white-faced, astounded that the accusation was thus being turned back against her. So now she had become the guilty party, and her aunt appeared to suspect appalling things.

'What do you mean?' she said quietly. 'If you had really believed that, you would surely not have tolerated it in your own house!'

'Well, you aren't children anymore! But I won't allow my son to be led into wicked ways... Leave those women in peace who can still make honest wives!'

For a moment Pauline stood speechless, with her great innocent eyes fixed upon Madame Chanteau, who averted her own. Then she climbed the stairs to her own room, saying abruptly:

'Very well, I'm the one who'll go.'

Silence fell again, a heavy silence, which seemed to submerge the whole house. Then, in that sudden quiet, Chanteau's howl rang out again like the cry of a dying, abandoned animal. It swelled remorselessly louder, dominating and drowning out all other sounds.

Now Madame Chanteau began to regret the words of suspicion she had let slip. She realized the irreparable damage she had done, and was alarmed at the idea that Pauline might carry out her threat and leave immediately. With such a stubborn creature, anything was possible, and what would people say about herself and Chanteau if their ward went around telling people about this quarrel? She might take refuge at Doctor Cazenove's, which would create a dreadful scandal in the locality. Underlying Madame Chanteau's predicament was a fear of the past, and all the wasted money, which could come back to haunt them.

'Don't cry, Louisette,' she repeated, with a new sense of anger. 'Here we are, in another fine mess, and all because of her. And such violence, it's impossible to live peacefully with her... But I'll do my best to sort it out.'

'Oh no, let me go away, I beg you,' Louise broke in. 'It would be too painful for me to stay... She's quite right, and I want to go.'

'Not tonight, at any rate. I must hand you back to your father... Wait a moment, I'll go up and see if she really is packing her bags.'

Madame Chanteau crept quietly up to listen at Pauline's door. She heard her walking rapidly around, opening and closing drawers. For a moment, she thought of going in and having the whole thing out, which would end in a flood of tears. But she was reluctant to do so, for fear of faltering and blushing in front of the child, which only increased her hatred. So instead of knocking at her door, she went down to the kitchen as quietly as she could. An idea had occurred to her.

'Did you hear Mademoiselle Pauline's latest scene just now?' she asked Véronique, who had started furiously polishing her brasses.

The maid, her head bent over the polishing powder, did not reply.

'She's becoming intolerable! I can't get through to her at all any more... Would you believe she's planning to leave us? Yes, she's packing her things this minute... Suppose you went upstairs and tried to make her see reason?'

Then, as she was still not getting any reply, she added:

'Are you deaf?'

'If I don't answer, it's because I don't choose to,' Véronique snapped back in a furious temper, rubbing a candlestick hard enough to skin her fingers. 'She's quite right to be going, in her shoes I'd have cleared out long ago.'

Madame Chanteau listened to her open-mouthed, astonished at this tirade.

'Madame knows I'm not one to blab, but don't you push me or I'll spill the beans... It's like this... I'd have chucked the girl straight in the sea, the day you first brought her here, only I can't abide anyone being unfairly done by, and you all treat her so bad, one of these days I'll thump the first one who touches her... Hah! I don't care, give me my notice if you want, but I've a few home truths to tell her, yes indeed, all the things you've done to her, you with all your airs and graces!'

'Hold your tongue, are you mad?' exclaimed Madame Chanteau, much disquieted by this fresh scene.

'No, I will not hold my tongue! It's a complete disgrace, d'you hear? I've been choked up about it for years! Wasn't it bad enough of you to take all her money? Did you have to break her heart as well? Oh yes, I know what I'm saying, I've watched you plotting the whole thing... And mark my words, Monsieur Lazare may not be so much of a schemer, but he's just as guilty in his own way, he'd give her the chop out of pure selfishness, just for a bit of excitement! Ah, me! Some people are born for others to prey on!'

She brandished her candlestick, then grabbed a pan, rubbing it so hard it resonated like a drum. Madame Chanteau was sorely tempted to throw her out, but she succeeded in restraining herself and said to her icily:

'So you won't go up and speak to her, then? It's for her own good, to avoid her making a fool of herself.'

Véronique again kept silent. Then she finally grumbled:

'All right then, I'll go up... Reason is reason, after all, and no good ever comes of acting in a temper.'

She took her time washing her hands, then removed her dirty apron. When she finally brought herself to open the door into the passage on her way to the stairs, a lamentable sound was heard: Chanteau's incessant, maddening wail. Madame Chanteau, following her, seemed suddenly to be struck by an idea, and whispered urgently:

'Tell her she can't leave Monsieur in the state he's in... Can you hear?'

'He's certainly bawling fit to burst, that's true enough,' admitted Véronique.

She went upstairs, while her mistress, who had turned her head towards her husband's room, deliberately left his door open. The plaintive groans resonated round the stairwell and up through the house. On the top floor, the maid found Mademoiselle on the point of leaving, having tied a few necessary items of linen into a bundle and intending to send old Malivoire to fetch the rest in the morning. She was calmer now but still very pale, heartbroken but coldly rational, and without a trace of anger.

'It's either her or me,' was her only answer to everything Véronique said, avoiding even mentioning Louise's name.

When Véronique came to report this reply to Madame Chanteau, she found her in Louise's bedroom. Louise had dressed and was also insisting on leaving immediately; she stood there trembling, and jumped every time a door creaked. Then Madame Chanteau had to admit defeat, and sent to Verchemont for the baker's cart, resolved to accompany Louise to her Aunt Léonie's in Arromanches; they would make up a story to tell her, using the violence of Chanteau's attack as a pretext and saying that his screams had become unbearable.

After the departure of the two women, whom Lazare had helped up into the cart, Véronique shouted from the hall at the top of her voice:

'You can come down now, Mademoiselle, they've gone.'

The house seemed empty and a gloomy silence had descended once again, broken only by Chanteau's regular groaning. As Pauline came down the last step, she found herself face to face with Lazare, coming back in from the yard. Her whole body shook with a nervous tremor. He paused for a moment as if he were about to admit his guilt and beg her forgiveness. But his voice was choked with tears and he stomped noisily up to his room, without being able to utter a word. She, dry-eyed and grave-faced, had gone into her uncle's room.

Chanteau was still sprawled across the bed with his arm outstretched and his head thrown back on the bolster. He no longer dared make a movement, and no doubt had not even noticed Pauline's absence, as he lay there with his eyes screwed shut, opening his mouth to bawl at will. None of the sounds of the house reached him, his only concern was to yell until he ran out of breath. Gradually his wails grew longer and more desperate, until they disturbed Minouche, who had had four more kittens destroyed that morning, but, having already forgotten them, was purring contentedly on the armchair.

When Pauline took her place again, her uncle was bawling so loudly that the cat stood up, anxiously pricking up her ears. She began to stare at him with the indignant look of a well-behaved creature whose peace and quiet is being disturbed. Things had come to a pretty pass, if you couldn't even purr in peace! And she withdrew, tail in the air.

CHAPTER 6

WHEN Madame Chanteau returned home again that evening, shortly before dinner time, no further mention was made of Louise. She simply called Véronique over to help her off with her boots. Her left foot was hurting.

'Gracious, it's no wonder!' the servant murmured, 'it's all swollen.'

And indeed, the leather stitching had left red weals on her soft white flesh. Lazare, on his way downstairs, took a look.

'You must've been doing too much walking,' he said.

But she had hardly walked from one side of Arromanches to the other. Besides, that day she was finding it hard to catch her breath, with a sensation of choking that had been getting worse for some months. So she blamed the boots.

'Cobblers never seem to make the instep high enough! As soon as I lace them up, it's torture.'

As the pain went away once she was in her slippers, no further notice was taken of it. Next day, the swelling had reached her ankle, but the following night it disappeared altogether.

A week went by. From dinner time on the evening of the disaster, when Pauline came face to face with Madame Chanteau and Lazare again for the first time, they all tried to behave normally. No allusions were made, nothing seemed to have changed between them. Family life went mechanically on, with habitual expressions of affection, customary good mornings and goodnights, and routine kisses at fixed times. However, it was a relief when they were able to wheel Chanteau up to the table. This time his knees had locked up and he was unable to stand. But he was still enjoying the relative peace of a respite from pain, so much so that, selfishly absorbed in his own comfort, he gave no thought to the joys or cares of anyone else in the household. When Madame Chanteau ventured to mention Louise's sudden departure to him, he begged her not to talk of such sad matters. Now that Pauline was no longer tied to her uncle's room, she tried to find herself things to do, but she could not hide her unhappiness. The evenings were particularly awkward, as their pretence of calm normality became painful. It was indeed the same existence as before, the same daily routine of trivial activities; but an occasional nervous gesture or a silence would remind them all of the inner rift, the wound of which they never spoke, but which deepened by the day.

At first, Lazare had been full of contempt for himself. The moral superiority of Pauline, so upright and so just, filled him with shame and vexation. Why did he not have the courage to make a frank confession to her and ask her forgiveness? He could have told her the whole story, how his senses had been caught unawares and the coquettish woman's scent had gone to his head, and Pauline was broadminded enough to understand. But insurmountable embarrassment stopped him, scared of diminishing himself still more in her eyes by an explanation in which he might well stammer like a child. Then again, behind his reluctance there lurked a fear of telling fresh lies, for Louise still haunted him and he kept imagining her, especially in the night, when he felt burning regret at not having possessed her while he had held her swooning in his embrace. In spite of himself, his long walks always seemed to lead him towards Arromanches. One evening he went as far as Aunt Léonie's little house and prowled round the walls, fleeing abruptly when he heard a shutter open, shocked at the indefensible act he had been on the point of committing. This sense of unworthiness greatly increased his distress: he accepted his guilt, but could not bury his desire; the struggle began again hourly in his mind, and never had irresoluteousness caused him such anguish. He retained just enough honesty and strength of character to stay away from Pauline, and thus avoid the ultimate dishonour of perjuring himself. Perhaps he still loved her, but the alluring image of the other woman was always present, erasing the past and barring off the future.

Pauline, for her part, was waiting for an apology. In her first outburst of indignation, she had vowed never to forgive him. Then she had begun to feel secretly pained at not being asked for forgiveness. Why did he keep silent yet look so agitated, why was he always out of doors, as though he were afraid of being alone with her? She was ready to listen to him and forget everything, if only he would show some remorse. As the hoped-for confrontation never came, she racked her brain to understand why, while her own pride kept her from speaking first; and, as the painful days dragged slowly by, she was able to master her feelings sufficiently to regain her previous active attitude to life. But this brave appearance of calm concealed an unremitting inner torture, and she would cry at night in her bedroom, stifling her sobbing in the pillow. Nothing was said about the wedding, though it was clearly on everyone's mind. Autumn was just around the corner; what was to be done? They all avoided expressing any opinion, apparently postponing a decision until a later date, when they might feel able to discuss it again.

This was the point in Madame Chanteau's life when the last shreds of her peace of mind deserted her. She had always had self-destructive tendencies, but the hidden processes undermining her better nature now seemed to reach a culmination, and never before had she appeared so unbalanced, so consumed by a nervous fever. The need for self-restraint only exacerbated her disorder. The cause was money, a raging obsession with it, which had been growing gradually more powerful, until it swept away all reason and all feeling. She was constantly blaming Pauline, whom she now accused of causing Louise's departure, an act of theft that she was convinced had despoiled her son. It was a bleeding wound that would not heal; the smallest details were magnified, she never forgot a single action, and she could still hear Pauline shouting 'Get out!', imagining that she too were being kicked into the street, along with all the family's wealth and happiness. As she tossed about at night in uneasy slumber, she even came to regret that death had not rid them of the accursed Pauline. Intricate schemes and complex calculations jostled in her brain, but she could find no practical means to dispose of the girl. At the same time, a reverse reaction redoubled her affection for her son, and she adored him now as perhaps she had never done as an infant, when she had had him to herself, cradled in her arms. From morning till night, she would gaze anxiously after him, and whenever they were alone she would embrace him and implore him not to upset himself. He wasn't hiding anything from her, was he? He wasn't weeping silly tears when he was by himself? And she would swear to him that everything would be all right, that she would willingly strangle anyone else, to ensure his happiness. After a fortnight of such continual inner conflict, her face had become waxy pale, though she had not lost weight. Twice the swelling in her feet had reappeared, only to go down again.

One morning, she rang for Véronique and showed her her legs, which had swollen during the night up to the thighs.

'Just look how big they've got! Isn't that annoying? I was intending to go out today!... Now I'll have to stay in bed! Don't say anything, so as not to alarm Lazare.'

She herself did not seem at all concerned. She simply spoke of feeling a little fatigued, and they all assumed it was just stiffness. As Lazare had gone out to ramble along the coast, and Pauline avoided going upstairs, sensing that her presence would be unwelcome, the sick woman regaled the maid with a torrent of strident accusations against the girl. She was now unable to contain herself. Her forced immobility, and the palpitations that made her gasp for breath at the slightest movement, seemed to drive her to ever-greater exasperation.

'What's she up to downstairs, eh? A lot of no good, I'll bet! She won't even bring me up a glass of water, you'll see!'

'But, Madame,' responded Véronique, 'it's you that's driving her away.'

'Nonsense! you don't know her! There's no bigger hypocrite! In front of people she acts ever so sweet, but she'll bad-mouth you behind your back... Oh yes, my girl, you were the only one to see through her, the day I first brought her here. If she had never entered this house, we shouldn't be in the state we are in… She'll be the end of us: Monsieur has suffered tortures since she's been looking after him, she's made me fret so much my blood has turned bad, and as for my son, he's completely losing his head…'

'Oh, Madame, how could you? She's so kind and good to you all!'

Still ranting, Madame Chanteau continued to get things off her chest. It all poured out, Louise's brutal eviction and, above all, the money. So when Véronique was able to go back downstairs after dinner and found Pauline in the kitchen, busy putting away the dishes, she gave vent to her own feelings; for a long time, she had been bottling up her indignation, but now the words spilled out of their own accord.

'Oh Mademoiselle, you're much too good, taking care of their plates like that. If it was me, I'd smash the lot!'

'Why on earth?' asked the girl in astonishment.

'Because you could never be half so bad as they make out!'

That was her starting point, and then she went back to the very beginning.

'Wouldn't the Almighty himself be furious to see such things? She's sucked the money out of you sou by sou, in a right disgusting way. Upon my word, anyone would think it was her paying for your upkeep… When she had your money in that secretaire of hers, she'd fuss about it like she was guarding a young girl's virginity, but that didn't stop her getting her greedy claws into it and helping herself… Good God, the act she put on to lumber you with the cost of that factory, then she used the rest of your money to keep it all going! Let me tell you: if it hadn't been for you, they'd all have starved! That's why she got so scared when the Paris lot looked like making trouble over the accounts! Lord, yes, she could have been had up in court for that… But she didn't learn her lesson, she's still robbing you now, and she'll end up stripping you of your last copper… Perhaps you think I'm not telling the truth, but I am, I swear it! I seen it with my own eyes and heard it with my own ears, and I'm not saying the worst of it, Mademoiselle, out of respect, like when you were ill and she was in a rage that she couldn't go rummaging in your chest of drawers.'

Pauline listened to her without finding a single word to interject. The thought that her family were living off her and cynically plundering her had often clouded her happiest days. But she had always refused to dwell on such things, preferring to turn a blind eye and accusing herself of meanness instead. Today, however, she could not avoid hearing the whole truth, and Véronique's outspoken tone seemed to make matters even worse. Every sentence awoke some memory in her, she went back over old incidents whose significance she had not realized at the time, and she could now retrace, day by day, Madame Chanteau's scheming to get her hands on her fortune. She slowly subsided onto a chair, as though suddenly overcome with great weariness, and her face wore a pained expression.

'You exaggerate,' she murmured.

'Me, exaggerate?' Véronique retorted violently. 'It's not just the question of the cash that makes me see red; no, what I can't ever forgive her for is taking Monsieur Lazare back, after she'd given him to you... Yes, and I mean it! You weren't rich enough any longer, and he had to have an heiress! What d'you say to that, eh? First they rob you, then they despise you because you've nothing left... No, Mademoiselle, I will not hold my tongue! It's not right to break someone's heart after you've already emptied their pockets. Since you loved your cousin, and he could only pay you back with kindness and affection, it's downright abominable to have stolen that from you as well! And that's what she's gone and done, I've seen her at it! Yes, every evening she got the girl all worked up and turned her on to Lazare with all sorts of filthy talk. As true as that lamp is shining, she's the one who pushed them at each other. Bah! she'd have pimped for him, if it would have forced them to marry. It wasn't her fault they didn't quite get that far... Defend her if you can, now she's trampled you underfoot, for it's on her account that you cry your eyes out every night. Yes, I can hear you from my room; it makes me sick, such misery and injustice!'

'Don't say any more, please!' stammered Pauline broken-heartedly, 'you're making me too unhappy.'

Great tears were rolling down her cheeks. She felt sure Véronique was telling the truth, and her torn heart bled within her. Every incident she mentioned seemed vivid and real: she saw Lazare pressing the swooning Louise to his chest while Madame Chanteau kept watch at the door. Oh God! what had she done, for them all to betray her like this when she had been so loyal?

'I beg you, don't say any more, I can't bear it!'

Then Véronique, seeing her so upset, finished by adding darkly:

'If I don't say no more, it's for your sake, not hers... Why, she's been up there spewing filth about you all morning. In the end my patience ran out, it made my blood boil, to hear her speak so ill of all your kindnesses to her... Honest to God, she claims you have ruined them and you're now killing her son! Go and listen at the door if you don't believe me!'

Then, as Pauline burst out sobbing, a deeply moved Véronique took her in and in her hands and stroked her hair, saying:

'There, there, Mademoiselle, I won't say no more... And yet, you have to know. It's just so silly, to let yourself be exploited like that... But there, I won't say no more, just you calm down now.'

There was silence. The maid raked out the embers that were still glowing in the stove. But she could not resist adding, in a low voice:

'I know why she's swelling up! All her wickedness has gone down into her knees!'

Pauline, who was staring hard at a single tile on the floor, her thoughts confused and burdened with grief, looked up. Why did Véronique say that, had the swelling come back? The maid was embarrassed at breaking her vow of silence; though she did not hesitate to judge Madame, she still obeyed her orders. Well, yes, both legs had been affected in the night, though she was not to say anything to Monsieur Lazare. While the maid was passing on these details, Pauline's expression changed from flat despondency to anxiety. Despite everything she had just learnt, she was alarmed at this symptom because she knew how serious it was.

'But we can't just leave her in that state,' she said, jumping up. 'She's in danger!'

'In danger, indeed!' exclaimed Véronique, unfeelingly. 'She doesn't look much like it, and she certainly doesn't think she is, she's far too busy slagging other people off and lording it over us from her bed... Besides, she's asleep just now, so we'll have to wait till the morning. It's the doctor's day for coming to Bonneville in any case.'

The next day it was impossible to conceal his mother's condition from Lazare any longer. All night long Pauline had been listening, waking every hour and constantly thinking she heard groans through the floor. Then at dawn she had fallen into such a deep sleep that the clock was already striking nine when she was jolted awake by the slamming of a door. As she was going downstairs for news, after flinging on her clothes, she ran into Lazare on the first-floor landing, emerging from his mother's room. The swelling had reached the abdomen, and Véronique had at last made up her mind to alert him.

'Well?' asked Pauline.

Lazare, looking distraught, at first made no reply. Out of habit, he gripped his chin between trembling fingers. And when he did speak, the first words he stammered out were:

'She's done for!'

He went upstairs to his own room, looking dazed. Pauline followed him. When they reached the big room on the top floor, where she had not set foot since she had caught him there with Louise, she closed the door and tried to reassure him.

'Come now, you don't even know what's the matter with her. At least wait for the doctor... She's very strong, there's always hope.'

But he insisted, pierced to the heart by a brutal certainty:

'She's done for, done for...'

This blow that now struck him down was completely unexpected. When he got up that morning he had looked out to sea as usual, yawning with boredom and complaining of life's emptiness and futility. Then, once his mother had uncovered her legs to the knee, the sight of those poor, oedema-swollen limbs, pallid and huge, like dead tree-trunks, had filled him with pity and horror. So that was it: disaster could befall you from one minute to the next! Even now, as he perched on the edge of his great table, shaking from head to toe, he did not dare name out loud the disease he had just identified. He had always been haunted by a dread of heart failure striking his loved ones or himself, and his two years of medical studies had failed to convince him of the equality of all diseases before death. To be stricken in the heart, the very source of life, still seemed to him the most appalling and merciless way to die. And this was the death that awaited his mother, and himself as well, in his turn!

'Why be so distraught?' Pauline asked him. 'Some dropsy* sufferers live a very long time. Remember Madame Simonnot? She went in the end with pneumonia.'

But Lazare shook his head: he was not a child, to be taken in so easily. His feet went on swinging to and fro, his shaking did not stop, while he kept his gaze fixed on the window. Then, for the first time since their break-up, she kissed him on the forehead, as in the old days. They were together again, side by side in that room where they had grown up, and all their ill feeling was subsumed in the great grief that hung over them. She wiped her eyes. Lazare, unable to weep, just repeated mechanically:

'She's done for! She's done for.'

Around eleven o'clock, when Doctor Cazenove called, as he generally did every week on his way up from Bonneville, he seemed astonished to find Madame Chanteau in bed. What could be the matter with the dear lady? He even made a joke of it, saying the whole household had gone soft and the place was starting to look like an infirmary. Then once he had examined the patient, felt her limbs and listened to her heart, his demeanour became serious, and indeed it took all his great experience not to betray a certain alarm.

In any event, Madame Chanteau herself had no idea of the gravity of her condition.

'I do hope you'll sort me out soon, Doctor,' she said with a chirpy laugh. 'The one thing that scares me is that this swelling might carry on upwards and choke me.'

'Have no fear,' he replied, with a laugh of his own; 'it won't go any higher, and if it did, we'd soon put a stop to it.'

Lazare, who had come back in after the examination, listened to his words with a shudder, longing to take him aside to question him and find out the truth.

'Now, my dear Madame,' Doctor Cazenove resumed, 'you mustn't worry about a thing, I'll come back tomorrow and have another chat with you... Goodbye, I'm going down now to write my prescription.'

Downstairs, Pauline prevented the doctor and Lazare from entering the dining room, for Chanteau was still being told it was just a case of stiffness. She had already set out ink and paper on the kitchen table. In the face of their urgent pleas, Doctor Cazenove admitted that it was serious, but he spoke in long, convoluted sentences and avoided committing himself.

'There's no hope for her, is there?' exclaimed Lazare with some irritation. 'It's her heart, isn't it?'

Pauline gave the doctor an imploring look, which he understood.

'Her heart?' he said, 'no, no, I doubt it... At any rate, even if we can't completely cure her, she may go on for a long time yet, if she looks after herself.'

The young man shrugged his shoulders in the angry manner of a child refusing to be taken in by the stories he is told. Then he went on:

'And you never warned me, Doctor, even though you attended her quite recently!... These horrible conditions never come on all at once. Didn't you notice anything?'

'Well, yes,' Cazenove murmured, 'indeed, I did notice a few little things.'

Then, as Lazare began to laugh contemptuously, he added:

'Listen to me, young man, I think I'm less of a fool than some, but this is not the first time an illness has caught me unawares and left me looking stupid... You're infuriating, you expect us to know everything, when it's already quite something, to understand even the basics of such a complicated machine as the human body.'

He was getting cross, and he scribbled the prescription with irritated strokes of the pen which dug into the thin paper. The naval surgeon in him was coming out again, in the brusque movements of his large frame. However, when he stood up, the expression on his old, wind-tanned face softened as he saw Pauline and Lazare hanging their heads hopelessly in front of him.

'My poor children,' he went on, 'we'll do everything we can to pull her through... You know I have no intention of playing the great man with you. So I'll tell you frankly, I can't promise anything. But she doesn't seem to me to be in any immediate danger.'

Then he left, after checking that Lazare had some tincture of digitalis.* The prescription was simply for the patient's legs to be massaged with this, and a few drops to be taken in a glass of sugared water. That would suffice for the moment, and he would bring some pills the next day. He might also decide to bleed her. Pauline, meanwhile, went with him to his cabriolet to ask him for the real truth; but the real truth was that he did not dare offer an opinion. When she returned to the kitchen she found Lazare reading the prescription again. The mere word *digitalis* had made him go pale.

'You mustn't upset yourselves so,' said Véronique, who had started peeling potatoes in order to stay and listen. 'Doctors, they're always killing folks. If that one can't think of anything to say, there won't be too much amiss.'

They stood arguing the question around the dish into which Véronique was chopping her potatoes. Pauline, too, seemed reassured. That morning she had gone in to kiss her aunt and had thought she looked well: with such good colour, you couldn't be at death's door. But Lazare kept turning the prescription over between feverish fingers. *Digitalis* glared back at him: his mother was doomed.

'I'm going up,' he said at last.

At the door, he hesitated and asked his cousin:

'Will you come in with me for a minute?'

She too had a slight hesitation.

'I'm afraid of upsetting her,' she murmured.

After a moment's awkward silence, he went upstairs by himself, without another word.

When Lazare put in an appearance at lunch, to avoid worrying his father, he was very white. From time to time the bell would ring to summon Véronique, who carried up bowls of soup that the sick woman barely touched. When she came back down again she would tell Pauline that the poor young man was losing his mind up there; he was a pitiable sight, shivering feverishly beside his mother, wringing his hands with a distraught expression on his face, as if he feared she might pass away at any moment in his arms. About three o'clock, the maid had just gone upstairs again when she leant over the banister and called for Pauline. Then, when the young girl arrived at the first-floor landing, she said:

'You ought to go in and give him a hand, Mademoiselle. Never mind if it upsets her! She wants him to turn her over, but if you could only see how he shudders and doesn't dare to even touch her!... What's more, she won't let me near her.'

Pauline went in. Firmly propped up on three pillows, Madame Chanteau might have been enjoying a lie-in out of sheer laziness, were it not for the short, gasping breaths that made her shoulders heave. Before her stood Lazare, stammering:

'So... you want me to turn you onto your right side?'

'Yes, yes, ease me round a bit... Ah! my poor boy, you are slow on the uptake!'

Already Pauline had taken gentle hold of her and was turning her over.

'Let me, I'm used to it with Uncle... There! Is that better?'

But Madame Chanteau complained irritably about them shoving her around. She was unable to make a single movement without immediately choking, and for a minute she would lie there panting and ashen-faced. Lazare had stepped behind the bed curtains to hide his despair. He stayed in the room, however, while Pauline rubbed her aunt's legs with tincture of digitalis. At first he looked away, but a need to see drew his gaze back to those monstrous legs, those inert masses of pallid flesh, the sight of which made him well up with anguish. When his cousin saw how distraught he was, she thought it wiser to send him out. She went up to him, and, as Madame Chanteau was dozing off, exhausted by the mere change of position, whispered softly to him:

'You'd do better to go out.'

For a moment he resisted, blinded by tears. Then he gave in and went downstairs, shamefaced and stuttering:

'Oh, God! I can't bear it! I can't!'

When the sick woman awoke, she did not notice her son's absence at first. She seemed stupefied, withdrawn inside herself, egotistically absorbed in the feeling of still being alive. Only Pauline's presence appeared to make her anxious, although the girl was deliberately sitting out of sight, keeping quiet and still. When her aunt looked round, however, she felt obliged to explain briefly.

'It's only me, no need to worry... Lazare has gone off to Verchemont, he has to see the carpenter.'

'All right,' Madame Chanteau murmured.

'You aren't so ill he needs to stop attending to his business, are you?'

'No, of course not.'

From that moment on, she rarely spoke about her son, despite the adoration for him that she had shown only the previous day. He was fading out of what was left of her life, after having been the cause and purpose of her entire existence. The decomposition that was now beginning to affect her brain left her preoccupied solely by her own physical health. She accepted care from her niece, seemingly unaware of the substitution, concerned simply to follow her with her eyes, as if distracted by the increasing mistrust that she felt as she saw Pauline coming and going around the bed.

Meanwhile, a distraught Lazare, his legs aching from standing, had gone down into the kitchen. The whole house scared him: he could not stay in his own room because of its oppressive emptiness, and he dared not walk through the dining room, where the sight of his father peacefully reading a newspaper made him choke with strangled sobs. So he kept going back into the kitchen, the one warm, cheerful spot in the house, where he was reassured by the sight of Véronique busying herself with her pots and pans, as in the peaceful days of old. As she saw him sit down again near the stove on his favourite straw-seated chair, she told him frankly what she thought of his lack of courage.

'Really, Monsieur Lazare, you're not a lot of use. It's that poor Mademoiselle Pauline that'll have to take charge all over again... To look at you, anyone'd think there hadn't ever been a sick person in the house before, but when your cousin nearly died of her sore throat, it was you that nursed her well enough, wasn't it?... Yes, you can't deny it, you spent a fortnight up there, turning her like a child.'

Lazare listened to her in great surprise. This inconsistency had not struck him before. Why should his feelings be so illogically different this time?

'That's true,' he said, 'quite true.'

'You wouldn't let anybody in,' the maid went on, 'and Mademoiselle was an even sorrier sight than Madame is, she was in such pain. I used to come downstairs in a right state, couldn't bring myself to swallow the least bit of bread... But now, seeing your mother ill in bed brings you over all queasy! You wouldn't even take up her cups of tisane...* Whatever she may be like, your mother's still your mother.'

Lazare had stopped listening and was staring into space. Finally, he murmured:

'I can't help it; I really can't... Perhaps because it's Maman, but I can't... When I see her with her legs like that, and tell myself she's dying, something seems to snap inside me and I'd howl like a wild animal if I didn't run out of the room.'

His whole body began to shake again. He had picked up a knife which had fallen off the table and was gazing unseeingly at it with tear-filled eyes. There was a silence. Véronique bent over her stock-pot to conceal the emotion that was choking her as well. At last she began again:

'Look here, Monsieur Lazare, why not go down to the beach for a bit? You're getting in my way, always hanging about here... And take Mathieu with you. He's a real nuisance, he's at a loose end as much as you are, and I'm forever having to stop him going up to Madame's room.'

Next morning, Doctor Cazenove was still non-committal. There could be a sudden collapse, or, if the dropsy abated, the patient might recover for a longer or shorter period of time. He gave up on bleeding her and confined himself to prescribing the pills that he brought with him, together with continued application of the tincture of digitalis. His air of vexation and suppressed irritation betrayed his lack of faith in these remedies in a case such as this, when the progressive failure of all the organs renders medical science helpless. In any event, he assured them that the patient was not suffering. Indeed, Madame

Chanteau did not complain of any acute pain: her legs felt as heavy as lead, her breathing was increasingly laboured whenever she moved, but as long as she lay still on her back, her voice remained strong and her eyes bright, so that she herself was deluded about her condition. Seeing her so cheery, none of those around her, with the exception of her son, could bring themselves to believe she was doomed. When the doctor climbed back into his carriage, he told them not to be too upset, for it was already a mercy, for both the patient and the family, not to see death approaching.

The first night had been hard for Pauline. Half-lying in an arm-chair, she had been unable to sleep, with the noisy breathing of the dying woman constantly in her ears. Whenever she started to nod off, the racket seemed to shake the house and rattle the rafters. Then, when she opened her eyes again, she was gripped by a feeling of suf-focation as she relived all the torments that had blighted her life in recent months. Even beside that deathbed, she could not make peace, she was unable to forgive. During her mournful, nightmarish vigil, Véronique's revelations caused her particular anguish. Old feelings of anger and bitter jealousy were rekindled as she brooded over the pain-ful details. No longer loved, oh God! Betrayed by those whom she had loved! All alone, boiling with scorn and rebellious feelings! The reopened wound in her heart bled; never had she felt such bitter pain at the wrong Lazare had done to her. Since they had killed her, let the rest of them die too! And she turned repeatedly over in her mind the theft of her money and her affections, obsessed by the laboured breathing of her aunt, which now weighed oppressively down on her own chest.

At daybreak Pauline was still in a state of conflict. She felt no returning affection; only a sense of duty kept her in her aunt's room. This completed her misery: was she too going to turn into someone spiteful? She spent the day in this troubled state of mind, and, dis-pleased with herself and repelled by her aunt's mistrust, she forced herself to be especially assiduous. Madame Chanteau received her ministrations with a grunt, and tracked her with a wary eye, suspi-cious of her every move. If she asked Pauline for a handkerchief, she would sniff it before using it, and when she saw her bringing in a flask of hot water she insisted on touching it first.

'What's the matter with her?' Pauline whispered to the maid. 'Does she believe I'm capable of harming her?'

When Véronique was giving her a spoonful of her medicine after the doctor's departure, Madame Chanteau, not noticing her niece, who was looking for some linen in the wardrobe, murmured:

'Was this prepared by the doctor?'

'No, Madame, by Mademoiselle Pauline.'

Then she tasted it with the tip of her tongue, and grimaced.

'It tastes of copper… I don't know what she's been making me take, but I've had the taste of copper in my stomach since yesterday.'

And suddenly she flung the contents of the spoon away behind the bed. Véronique was left gawping.

'For goodness' sake! Whatever's got into you?'

'I don't want to go before my time,' replied Madame Chanteau, as she laid her head back on the pillow. 'Listen—my lungs are still strong. And she could well go first, she's not the robust type.'

Pauline had heard. She turned round, mortified, and looked at Véronique. Instead of coming forward, she shrank back, ashamed for her aunt's sake of such an abominable suspicion. Suddenly she felt a sense of release, accompanied by deep pity for that unhappy woman, so consumed by fear and hatred. Far from feeling further resentment, she was overwhelmed by sorrowful compassion, when she bent down and saw all the medicine that her aunt had tipped away under the bed for fear of poisoning. Until the evening, she behaved with persevering gentleness, and did not even appear to notice her aunt's distrustful scrutiny of her hands. Her fervent desire was to overcome the dying woman's fear by kind attentions, so that she would not take such frightful thoughts with her to the grave. She forbade Véronique to distress Lazare any more by telling him what had happened.

Only once since the morning had Madame Chanteau asked for her son, and she had seemed to accept the first excuse that came to mind, expressing no surprise at not seeing him. And she spoke even less about her husband, completely unconcerned about how he might be getting on, alone in the dining room. The world was drawing in for her, it was as if the icy chill were spreading upwards from her legs, minute by minute, until it froze her heart. Every mealtime, Pauline had to go downstairs and tell her uncle some white lie. That evening she lied to Lazare as well, assuring him that the swelling was going down.

During the night, however, the disease progressed alarmingly. Next morning, when Pauline and the maid saw the sick woman in the full light of day, they were taken aback by the wild look in her eyes. Her face was unchanged and she still had no fever, but her mind appeared to be affected, her obsession was destroying her brain. This was the final phase; a single passion had gradually devoured her being, and driven her insane.

The morning, until Doctor Cazenove arrived, was a terrible ordeal. Madame Chanteau would no longer even let her niece come near her.

'Please, let me take care of you,' urged Pauline repeatedly. 'I'll just lift you up for a moment, you're lying so awkwardly.'

At this, the dying woman started struggling as if she were being smothered.

'No, no! You've got scissors, you're sticking them in me on purpose... I can feel them! I'm bleeding all over!'

Much distressed, Pauline had to keep her distance from her aunt; she felt weak with grief and fatigue, and her helpless urge to be kind. To get her aunt to accept the least attention from her, she had to put up with insults and accusations that reduced her to tears. Sometimes she would collapse, weeping and defeated, into a chair, despairing of ever winning back the former affection that had now turned to insane anger. Then her resigned acceptance would return and she made fresh efforts, with even greater gentleness. That day, however, her persistence sparked a crisis which left her shaking for a long time.

'Auntie,' she said, as she was preparing the spoon, 'it's time for your medicine. You know the doctor told you to take it at just the right time.'

Madame Chanteau insisted on seeing the bottle, then smelling it.

'Is it the same as yesterday?'

'Yes, Auntie.'

'I won't have it.'

However, after many affectionate entreaties, her niece persuaded her to swallow one more spoonful. The sick woman's face wore an expression of deep distrust, and as soon as she had the medicine in her mouth, she spat it violently out on the floor, shaken by a fit of coughing, and stammering between the spasms:

'It's vitriol,* it's burning me!'

Her fear and loathing of Pauline, which had been building up since the day when she had taken the first twenty-franc piece from her, now burst out in a mad flood of words, as her mania came to a climax, while the poor girl listened in shock, unable to utter a word in her own defence.

'If you think I can't tell! You put copper and vitriol into everything... That's what's choking me! There's nothing wrong with me, I could have got up this morning if you hadn't dissolved verdigris* in my broth last night... Yes, you have had enough of me, you want to see me in my grave. But I'm tough, and I'll bury you yet.'

̶H̶e̶r̶ ̶u̶t̶t̶e̶r̶a̶n̶c̶e̶ ̶w̶a̶s̶ ̶b̶e̶c̶o̶m̶i̶n̶g̶ ̶m̶o̶r̶e̶ ̶a̶n̶d̶ ̶m̶o̶r̶e̶ ̶c̶o̶n̶f̶u̶s̶e̶d̶,̶ ̶s̶h̶e̶ ̶w̶a̶s̶ ̶b̶r̶e̶a̶t̶h̶- ing with difficulty, and her lips were turning so black that a catastrophe seemed imminent.

'Oh Auntie, Auntie,' murmured Pauline in terror, 'if only you knew the harm you are doing yourself!'

'Well, that's what you want, isn't it? Oh yes, I know you! You've been planning this for a long time, you came into this house with the sole purpose of murdering us and taking our money. You want to get your hands on the house and I'm in your way... Oh you hussy, I should have slapped you down from day one... I hate you! I hate you!'

Pauline stood motionless, silently weeping. She could only repeat, as if in involuntary protest:

'Oh God!... Oh God!'

But Madame Chanteau was becoming exhausted, and her raving fit subsided into a childlike dread. She had sunk back into her pillows.

'Don't come near me, don't touch me... If you do, I'll scream for help! No, no! I won't drink it; it's poison!'

She clutched the bedclothes up around her and hid her face in the pillows, her head rolling from side to side, her lips clamped tight. When her niece, in great alarm, moved closer to try and calm her, she started yelling.

'Auntie, be reasonable... I won't make you drink any if you don't want to.'

'Yes, you will, you've got the bottle! Oh, I'm scared, I'm scared!'

The end was approaching; her head was flung right back in terror and covered in purple blotches. Pauline, convinced that her aunt was about to die in her arms, rang for the maid. It was as much as the two of them could do to lift her up and settle her properly on the pillows.

Then Pauline's personal sufferings and her unrequited love were completely swept aside by their shared grief. She had no thought for the wound that had made her heart bleed only the previous day; all her violent and jealous feelings evaporated in the face of such a great sorrow. Everything was subsumed in a boundless compassion; she wished she could have been more loving, devoted, self-sacrificing, putting up with injustice and insult, if that would help bring comfort to others. Hers was a courageous determination to shoulder the burden of life's dark side. From that moment on, she never once gave up, but displayed at her aunt's deathbed the same quiet resignation she had shown when she herself had been threatened with death. She was always ready, and nothing could discourage her. Even her former fondness for her aunt had returned: she forgave her all the outbursts during her crises, and pitied her slow decline into insanity, preferring to remember her as she had been in earlier years, and loving her again as she had done at the age of ten, on that stormy evening when they had arrived together in Bonneville.

That day, Doctor Cazenove did not call until after lunch. An accident, a farmer with a broken arm, which he had had to set, had detained him in Verchemont. After seeing Madame Chanteau, he came back down into the kitchen, and made no attempt to conceal his concern. Lazare was there, sitting by the stove, consumed by purposeless agitation.

'There's no hope, is there?' he asked. 'Last night, I reread Bouillaud's book on heart disease...'*

Pauline, who had come downstairs with the doctor, again threw him an imploring glance which made him interrupt the young man in his usual abrasive way, for whenever a patient took a turn for the worse, it made him irritable.

'Heart indeed! My dear fellow, that's all you ever go on about... How can we be sure of anything? In my opinion, the liver is in a worse state. Only, when the machine breaks down, everything goes to pot—lungs, stomach, even the heart... Instead of reading Bouillaud at night, which can only make you ill as well, you'd do better to get some sleep.'

By common agreement, everyone in the household told Lazare that his mother was dying of liver disease. He did not believe a word of it, and spent sleepless hours leafing through his old textbooks; then he would get the different symptoms mixed up, and the doctor's explanation that the organs succumbed to the disease one after the other only served to increase his alarm.

'Well then,' he said in a tone of distress, 'how long do you think she's got?'

Cazenove gestured vaguely.

'A fortnight, perhaps a month... Don't ask me to say, if I got it wrong you'd be justified in saying we doctors know nothing and can't do anything... It's frightening how the disease has progressed since yesterday.'

Véronique, who was busy wiping glasses, gazed at him open-mouthed. So it was true, then, that Madame was very ill, Madame was going to die? Until then, refusing to believe there was any danger, ◼◼◼ ◼◼◼◼ ◼◼◼◼◼◼◼◼◼ ◼◼◼◼◼◼◼◼◼ ◼◼ ◼◼◼◼◼◼ ◼◼◼◼ ◼◼ ◼◼◼ ◼◼◼ ◼◼◼◼◼ ◼◼ ◼◼◼◼ spitefulness, just to mess everyone about. She stood there in stupefaction, and when Pauline told her to go upstairs to Madame so that she would not be left on her own, she wiped her hands on her apron and left the kitchen, saying only:

'Well, I never! Well, I never!'

'Doctor,' continued Pauline, the only one with all her wits about her, 'we mustn't forget my uncle... Do you think we should prepare him for the worst? Please will you see him before you go?'

Just at that moment, however, Abbé Horteur appeared. He had heard only that morning of what he referred to as Madame Chanteau's indisposition. When he learned how gravely ill she really was, his suntanned face, so full of laughter in the open air, assumed an expression of genuine sorrow. The poor lady! How was it possible? She'd seemed so fit and strong only three days before! Then after a moment's silence he asked:

'May I see her?'

He had cast an anxious glance at Lazare, whom he knew to be irreligious, expecting a refusal. But the young man, lost in his grief, seemed not even to have understood the question. It was Pauline who replied firmly:

'No, not today, Monsieur le Curé. She doesn't know how ill she is, and your presence would come as a shock to her... We'll see tomorrow.'

'Very well,' the priest replied hastily, 'there's no urgency, I trust. But we must each do our duty, mustn't we?... For instance, the doctor here who doesn't believe in God...'

For some time, the doctor had been absorbed in staring at one leg of the table, plunged deep in doubt, as always when he sensed that nature was beyond his control. He had caught the abbé's meaning, however, and now interrupted him.

'Who says I don't believe in God?... He is not an impossibility, there are so many odd things!... After all, who knows?'

He shook his head and seemed to rouse himself.

'Look,' he went on, 'you come along with me and shake our good friend Monsieur Chanteau by the hand... He will soon be in need of great courage.'

'If you think it might cheer him up,' the priest replied obligingly, 'I should be glad to stay and play a few games of draughts with him.'

Then they both went into the dining room, while Pauline hastened back upstairs to be with her aunt. Lazare, left on his own, stood up and hesitated a moment about going up too, then went to listen to his father's voice, without finding the courage to go in; finally, he returned to the kitchen and slumped back in the same chair, in a lethargy of despair.

The priest and the doctor had found Chanteau rolling a paper ball around on the table, made from a prospectus that had come with his newspaper. Minouche, close by him, looked on with her green eyes. Disdainful of this trivial toy, she lay there with her paws tucked underneath her belly, declining to exert herself and bare her claws. The ball had come to rest in front of her nose.

'Hello you two!' said Chanteau. 'It's kind of you to call in, I do get rather bored on my own... So then, Doctor, is she better yet? Oh! it's not that I'm worried, she's the toughest one in the family, she'll see us all to our graves.'

The doctor took this as an opportunity to enlighten him.

'Well, although her condition doesn't seem to me particularly serious, I do find her very weak.'

'No, no, Doctor,' Chanteau exclaimed, 'you don't know her. She's incredibly strong... You'll see, she'll be back on her feet again before three days are out!'

And he refused to take the hint, such was his need to believe in his wife's vigorous constitution. The doctor, unwilling to tell him the harsh truth straight out, could say no more. In any case, it would be as well to wait and see. Fortunately, Chanteau's gout was leaving him in relative peace and he did not have too much pain, but it was affecting him increasingly in the legs, so that he now had to be carried from his bed to the invalid chair.

'If it weren't for these cursed legs of mine,' he kept saying, 'at least I could go up and see her.'

'Resign yourself, my friend,' said Abbé Horteur, mindful of his consoling ministry. 'We each have our own cross to bear... We're all in God's hands...'

But he noticed that these words, far from consoling Chanteau, were making him irritated and rather worried. So, considerately, he interrupted his stock exhortations and made a more entertaining proposal instead.

'How about a game? It'll clear your head.'

And he went himself to fetch the draughtboard from on top of the cupboard. A delighted Chanteau shook hands with the doctor as he was leaving. Just as the two were becoming engrossed in their game, oblivious to everything else, Minouche, no doubt annoyed that the paper ball had sat under her nose for so long, pounced and batted it away with her paw, then bounded after it in crazy antics all around the room.

'The wretched tease!' exclaimed Chanteau with annoyance. 'First she refuses to play with me, then she ruins our concentration by playing on her own!'

'Never mind,' said the priest benevolently; 'cats like to amuse themselves in their own way.'

Meanwhile, on his way out through the kitchen, Doctor Cazenove felt a sudden surge of emotion at the sight of Lazare still sitting and brooding miserably on the same chair, and, putting his long arms around the young man, wordlessly gave him a paternal kiss. At that very moment Véronique came downstairs, shooing Mathieu in front of her. The dog was forever prowling up and down the stairs, emitting little nasal whistles like the plaintive cry of a bird; and whenever he found the sickroom door open, he would go in and fill the place with his ear-piercing, high-pitched whine.

'Be off with you, off!' cried the maid. 'You won't make her any better by singing like that.'

Then, seeing Lazare, she added:

'Take him somewhere for a walk, it'll get him out from under our feet, and do you good too.'

This was an order of Pauline's. She had charged Véronique with getting him out of the house and forcing him to go on some long walks. But he refused; it was all he could do just to stand up. However, the dog had stationed itself in front of him and begun whining again.

'Poor old Mathieu, he's not as young as he used to be,' said the doctor, looking at him.

'True enough!' replied Véronique. 'He's fourteen, but that doesn't stop him chasing after mice like a mad thing... See, his nose is all scratched and he's got red eyes. He smelled one under the grate last night and he hasn't slept a wink, poking his muzzle in everywhere and turning my kitchen upside down, and he's still itching to find it. Such a huge dog after such a tiny creature, silly, isn't it?... And it's not just mice, anything small that runs about—chicks one day, Minouche's kittens the next—gets him so worked up he forgets to eat and drink. Sometimes he'll sniff around for hours under a cupboard where a cockroach has been... Just now, I'm sure he can smell something odd going on in the house...'

She broke off as she saw Lazare's eyes filling with tears.

'Go on my lad, take yourself off for a walk,' the doctor went on. 'You're doing no good here, you'll be much better out in the open air.'

The young man finally stood up with a painful effort.

'All right,' he said, 'come along, poor old Mathieu.'

After seeing the doctor to his cabriolet, he set off along the cliffs with the dog. From time to time he had to stop and wait for Mathieu, who had indeed aged considerably. His hindquarters were stiffening up, and his great paws padded and dragged along like slippers. He had given up digging holes in the kitchen garden, and when he chased his tail he quickly grew dizzy and fell over. Above all, he now tired rapidly, coughed whenever he plunged into the water, and would lie down and snore after a quarter of an hour's walk. On the beach, he got under his master's feet.

Lazare stood for a moment to watch a fishing-smack out of Port-en-Bessin, its grey sail skimming the sea like a seagull's wing. Then he set off again. His mother was going to die! The thought hammered away at the core of his being. If it receded from his mind for a moment, it would return more shatteringly than before, a horrible shock each time, an idea to which he could not reconcile himself, a renewed stupefaction which left no place for any other sensation. At times, even this idea became blurred and he felt only the vague oppression of a nightmare, the single definite quality of which was an anxious sense of impending calamity. For minutes at a time, everything around him would disappear, then, when he became aware again of the sands, the seaweed, the distant sea and far-reaching horizon, he felt a brief puzzlement, not recognizing the scene. Was this the place where he had walked so often? The meaning of things seemed to have altered for him, and never before had he perceived their shapes and colours so intensely. His mother was going to die! And he kept on walking, as if to escape from that refrain that buzzed deafeningly in his ears.

Suddenly he heard a panting sound behind him. He turned and saw the dog with his tongue lolling out, completely exhausted. Then he spoke out loud:

'Poor old Mathieu, you've had enough... Come on, let's go home! I can't shake off these thoughts, whatever I do!'

That evening they hurried through their meal. Lazare, whose tight stomach could only take a few mouthfuls of bread, rushed back upstairs to his own room, giving his father an excuse about some urgent work. When he reached the first floor, he went into his mother's room, where he forced himself to sit for five minutes before kissing her goodnight. In any case, she had completely forgotten about him, never expressing the least interest in what he might be up to during the day. When he bent over her, she offered him her cheek and seemed to consider his hasty goodnight normal, becoming hourly more self-absorbed, with the instinctive egotism that heralded her end. Pauline cut short his visit by inventing an excuse to send him out, and he escaped.

But up in his own room on the second floor, Lazare's mental torment was redoubled. It was above all the night, the long weary night, that weighed heaviest upon him. He took candles up so as not to be without a light, and lit them one after another until daylight, gripped by a horror of the dark. When he got into bed, he tried in vain to read; only his old medical textbooks were of any interest to him now, but he pushed them away, as he had come to fear them. Then he lay there on his back with his eyes wide open, conscious only that close to him, through the wall,* something terrible was happening which choked and oppressed him. His ears were full of the noise of his dying mother gasping for breath, which in the last two days had become so loud that he could hear it anywhere on the stairs as he hurried up or down. The whole house seemed to exhale the sound like a lament, it went right through him as he lay in bed, and when, occasionally, it fell worryingly silent, he would run barefoot out onto the landing and lean over the banisters to listen. Pauline and Véronique, keeping watch together downstairs, left the door of the room open to let the air in. Lazare could see the pale, still square of light cast by the night lamp on the tiled floor, then he heard the loud gasping again, amplified and prolonged in the darkness. When he went back to bed he, too, left his door open, for he needed to hear that death rattle, an obsession which pursued him until finally, at first light, he drifted off into an uneasy doze. As when his cousin had been ill, all dread of his own death had left him. His mother was going to die, everything was going to die, and he capitulated to this general disintegration of life with no feeling other than exasperation at his powerlessness to prevent it.

It was on the next morning that Madame Chanteau's death agony began, a voluble agony that lasted for twenty-four hours. She had become calmer and was no longer morbidly afraid of poison; she talked to herself constantly, in a clear, rapid voice, without raising her head from the pillow. It was no conversation, she was not speaking to anyone, it was rather as if, in the breakdown of her mechanism, the brain were whirring ever faster, like a clockwork running down, and this torrent of quick little words was like the final ticking of her mind as its spring unwound. Her whole past life flooded out, but never a word of the present, of her husband, her son, her niece, or the house in Bonneville, the scene of a decade's frustrated ambition. She became Mademoiselle de la Vignière once more, giving music lessons in the distinguished families of Caen; she alluded familiarly to names that neither Pauline nor Véronique had ever heard; she told rambling stories full of digressions, the details of which escaped even the maid, who had grown up in her service. She seemed to be emptying all the youthful memories from her head before she died, like someone clearing out a box of yellowed old letters from the past. For all her courage, Pauline shuddered at such revelations, involuntary confessions which were surfacing in the very labour of death. It was no longer her rasping breathing that filled the house, but this terrifying, rambling babble. Lazare caught snatches of it whenever he passed the door. He turned them over in his mind but could make no sense of them, and they scared him, strange stories his mother was telling from a place where he could not go, surrounded by people he could not see.

When Doctor Cazenove arrived, he found Chanteau and Abbé Horteur playing draughts in the dining room, as if they were still there, carrying on the previous day's game. Minouche sat near them, apparently engrossed in the draughtboard. The curé had arrived first thing in the morning to resume his consoling ministry. Pauline now had no objection to his going upstairs and so, when the doctor went to visit his patient, the curé left the game and accompanied him to the sick woman's bedside, introducing himself as a friend who had just come to enquire how she was. Madame Chanteau was still able to recognize them, and, having asked to be hoisted up on her pillows, received them with all the airs of a grand lady of Caen, smiling and lucid in her delusion. The dear doctor must be pleased with her progress, she would soon be up and about again; then she made polite ᴜɴQᴜɪʀɪᴜᴜ ᴏʄ ᴛɦᴜ ᴜᴜᴜᴜ ᴜᴜᴜᴜᴛ ɦɪᴜ ᴜᴡᴜ ɦᴜᴜᴛɦ. ɦᴜᴜᴛᴜᴜᴜ, who had come up with the intention of fulfilling his priestly duties, was taken aback by her deathbed ramblings and dared not open his mouth. In any case, Pauline was in the room and would have stopped him from mentioning certain subjects. She herself found the strength to put on a show of cheerful confidence. When the two men left the room, she went with them onto the landing, where the doctor lowered his voice to give her instructions for the final moments. The words 'rapid decomposition' and 'phenol' came up several times, while the indistinct murmur of the dying woman's ceaseless babble continued to come from the room.

'So, do you think she'll see the day out?' asked Pauline.

'Yes, she'll probably go on until tomorrow,' answered Cazenove. 'But don't lift her any more, or she might die in your arms... Anyway, I'll come back again this evening.'

It was agreed that Abbé Horteur should stay with Chanteau and prepare him for the worst. Véronique stood in the doorway and listened with a frightened expression while these arrangements were being made. Since she had accepted the possibility of Madame's death, she had scarcely uttered a word, but had fussed around her with the stolid devotion of a beast of burden. But they all fell silent, for Lazare was coming upstairs; he had been wandering about the house, unable to face being there during the doctor's consultation and learning the real gravity of the situation. The sudden silence that greeted him told him the truth in any case. He turned very pale.

'My dear boy,' said the doctor, 'you should come back with me. We could have lunch together and I'll bring you home this evening.'

The young man had turned even paler.

'No, thank you,' he murmured, 'I don't want to go anywhere.'

From that moment Lazare waited, feeling a terrible pressure in his chest, as if his ribs were being crushed by an iron band. The day seemed unending, and yet it did pass, without his being aware how the hours went by. He never remembered what he had done: wandering up and down the stairs, and gazing out at the distant sea, whose immense undulation lulled him gradually into insensibility. At certain moments, the irresistible march of time seemed to take on material form in his mind, becoming a granite bar that swept everything into the abyss. Then he grew frustrated and wished it could be over, so that he might finally be released from that terrible waiting. About four o'clock, as he was going up to his room one more time, he suddenly turned in through his mother's door: he wanted to see her, he felt the need to kiss her again. But as he bent over her, she carried on unwinding the tangled skein of her ramblings, and did not even offer him her cheek in the world-weary way in which she had greeted him since the beginning of her illness. Perhaps she didn't even see him. This grey face with its already blackened lips was not his mother any more.

'Go away,' Pauline said to him gently, 'go out for a while... I promise, it's not time yet.'

Then, instead of going up to his room, Lazare took to his heels. He ran out of the house, carrying with him the vision of that woeful face that he no longer recognized. Pauline was lying to him, the time was indeed close; but he felt choked, he needed space and air, and he strode on like a man possessed. That kiss was the last. The thought that he would never, ever see his mother again shook him to the core. Then he thought he heard someone coming along behind him, turned round and realized it was Mathieu, limping after him on his stiff old paws. For no reason, he flew into a rage, picked up some stones and threw them at the dog, swearing disjointedly at him, to drive him back home. Mathieu, bewildered by this reception, went back a little way, then turned and gazed at his master with gentle eyes that seemed to glisten with tears. Lazare was unable to chase away the animal, who followed him at a safe distance as though to keep watch over his despair. The immense sea was also getting on his nerves, so he fled across the fields, looking for out-of-the-way corners where he could feel alone and hide. He wandered until nightfall, tramping across ploughed land and clambering over hedges. At last, worn out, he was making his way home when he saw before him a sight which filled him with superstitious terror: by the side of a lonely track loomed a single poplar, tall and black, at the tip of which the rising moon lit a yellow flame: it looked like a huge candle burning in the dusk beside the corpse of some giant woman lying full length across the landscape.

'Come along, Mathieu!' he cried in a choking voice. 'Let's hurry home!'

He reached the house at a run, as he had left it. The dog had now dared to come up to him and was licking his hands.

Although night had fallen, there was no light in the kitchen. It lay empty and dark, with just the red glow from the embers in the stove playing on the ceiling. The gloom alarmed Lazare, and he could not find the courage to go further. He stood there with a feeling of desperation amidst the jumble of pots and cloths, listening to the noises filtering through the house. From the next room came his father's slight cough, and the continuous low drone of Abbé Horteur talking to him. But what scared him most was the sound of rapid steps and whispers on the stairs, then, on the floor above, an unaccountable scuffling noise, like the muffled sound of some task being carried out in haste. He did not dare to understand—could it all be over? He was still standing there motionless, without the energy to go up and find out, when he saw Véronique coming down: she ran in, lit a candle, and went out with it again in such a rush that she had neither a word, nor even a glance, for him. The kitchen, after being momentarily illuminated, fell back into darkness. Up above, the noise of scurrying feet subsided. The maid appeared again, this time coming down to fetch an earthenware bowl, and still with the same mute, desperate haste. Lazare no longer felt any doubt: it was over. Then, almost fainting, he perched on the edge of the table, waiting amidst the dark shadows for he knew not what, his ears ringing with the deep silence that had just fallen.

In the bedroom, the final, atrocious death agony, which filled Pauline and Véronique with horror, had been underway for the past two hours. At the last gasp, Madame Chanteau's dread of poison had returned, and now she was struggling to sit up, still chattering away in her quick voice, but gradually also becoming agitated with a furious delirium. She wanted to jump out of bed and flee from the house, where someone was going to murder her; and it was all that the young girl and the maid could do to restrain her.

'Leave me alone, you'll get me killed... I must get away at once, at once!'

Véronique tried to calm her.

'Look at us, Madame... You can't imagine we might do you any harm.'

The dying woman, exhausted, lay panting for a moment. She seemed to be searching the room with her clouded, now probably sightless, eyes. Then she began again:

'Shut the secretaire! It's in the drawer... Here she is, coming upstairs! Oh, I'm afraid, I tell you I can hear her! Don't give her the key, let me get away, at once, at once!'

Then she began to struggle again on her pillows, while Pauline tried to hold her down.

'Auntie, there's no one here but us.'

'No, no, listen, there she is... Oh God! I'm going to die, that hussy made me drink it all... I'm going to die! I'm going to die!'

Her teeth were chattering and she huddled in the arms of her niece, whom she did not recognize. Pauline pressed her mournfully to her heart, no longer trying to contest her aunt's horrible suspicion, and resigned to letting her carry it with her to the grave.

Fortunately, Véronique was watching closely and now flung out her arms, exclaiming:

'Look out, Mademoiselle!'

It was the final crisis. With a violent effort, Madame Chanteau had succeeded in swinging her swollen legs out of bed and, but for the maid's quick reaction, would have fallen on the floor. She was shaking dementedly, uttering nothing but inarticulate cries, with her fists clenched as if in unarmed combat against some phantom that was gripping her by the throat. In that final minute she must have realized she was about to die, for intelligence shone in her reopened eyes, dilated in horror. An appalling pain made her briefly clasp her hands to her chest. Then she fell back against her pillows and turned black. She was dead.

A great silence fell. Pauline, exhausted, forced herself to close her aunt's eyes, but she knew that she could do no more. She went out of the room, leaving Véronique to watch over the body, along with Prouane's wife, whom she had sent for after the doctor's visit; on the stairs, she felt faint and had to sit for a moment, unable to find the courage to go down and inform Lazare and Chanteau of the death. The walls were spinning around her. A few minutes went by; then she grasped the banister again, but hearing Abbé Horteur's voice in the dining room, she went into the kitchen instead. And there she found Lazare, silhouetted darkly against the red glow of the stove. Without a word she walked towards him, her arms open. He understood, and threw himself upon Pauline's shoulder, while she clasped him to her in a long embrace. Then they kissed each other's faces. She was weeping silently, but he was unable to shed a tear, so choked that he could hardly breathe. At last she unclasped her arms and uttered the first words that came into her head:

'Why are you here in the dark?'

He made a dismissive gesture, as if to say that he had no need of light in his great sorrow.

'We must light a candle,' she went on.

Lazare had collapsed onto a chair, unable to stand. Mathieu, very perturbed, was prowling around the yard and sniffing the damp night air. He came back in and stared at each of them in turn, then went and rested his great head on his master's knee, and there he stayed, gazing questioningly into the young man's eyes. Then Lazare began to tremble under the dog's scrutiny. Suddenly the tears welled up and he sobbed out loud, throwing his arms round the neck of the old household creature whom his mother had loved for fourteen years. He began to stammer brokenly:

'Oh, you poor old fellow! poor old fellow... We shall never see her again!'

Despite her emotion, Pauline had finally found and lit a candle. She made no attempt to console Lazare, relieved to see him shedding tears. A painful task still lay before her, that of breaking the news to her uncle. While she was screwing up her courage to go into the dining room, where Véronique had taken a lamp as soon as dusk fell, Abbé Horteur had managed to lead Chanteau round, by the use of long ecclesiastical phrases, to the knowledge that his wife was doomed and the end could only be a matter of hours away. So, when the old man saw his niece enter, red-eyed and emotional, he guessed at the catastrophe. His first exclamation was:

'Oh God, I would just have asked for one thing, to see her alive one last time... Oh, these cursed legs of mine! These cursed legs!'

He had hardly anything more to say. He shed a few tears which quickly dried, and sighed some faint invalid's sighs, then quickly returned to the subject of his legs, cursing them again and ultimately pitying himself. They briefly discussed the possibility of carrying him upstairs to kiss the dead woman; but, apart from the difficulty of the task, it was judged too risky to expose him to the emotion of such a final farewell, for which in any case he had stopped asking. So he stayed sitting in the dining room in front of the abandoned draught-board, not knowing what to do with his poor crippled hands, his head not even straight enough, as he put it, to read and understand his newspaper. When they carried him to bed, distant memories must have awoken within him, for he shed copious tears.

Then two long nights and one endless day went by, those terrible hours in a household where death has taken up residence. Cazenove had only returned to certify the decease, surprised again by the rapid-ity of the end. Lazare did not go to bed the first night, but stayed up until morning writing letters to distant relatives. The body was to be taken to the cemetery at Caen and interred in the family vault. The doctor had kindly offered to see to all the formalities, only one of which was really painful: as mayor of Bonneville, Chanteau was required to record the death. As Pauline had no suitable black dress, she quickly improvised one out of an old skirt and a merino shawl, from which she cut out a bodice. The first night passed, then the fol-lowing day, in dealing with these urgent tasks; but the second night stretched on for ever, made even longer by mournful expectations of the morrow. No one could sleep, all the doors were left open, and lighted candles stood on all the stairs and furniture, while the reek of phenol had spread even to the furthest rooms of the house. They had all succumbed to the stiffness and aches of grieving, with dry mouths and blurred eyes, feeling only an obscure need to regain some hold on life.

At last, about ten o'clock the next morning, the bell of the little church across the road began to toll. Out of regard for Abbé Horteur, who had behaved very considerately in such sad circumstances, it had been decided that the religious ceremony would be performed at Bonneville, before the body was taken to the cemetery in Caen. As soon as Chanteau heard the church bell, he began to fidget in his invalid chair.

'At least I want to see her off,' he kept saying. 'Oh! these wretched legs! What a curse to have such wretched legs!'

They tried in vain to spare him the dreadful sight. As the bell began to toll more quickly, he grew angry and exclaimed:

'Push me out into the passage. I can hear them bringing her down… Quickly, quickly! I must see her off!'

Pauline and Lazare, who were clad in full mourning, with gloves on, could only do as he said. One on his right, the other on his left, they pushed the chair to the foot of the stairs. The body was indeed being brought down by four men, who were struggling to carry it. When the coffin appeared, with its new wood, gleaming handles, and freshly engraved brass plaque, Chanteau made an instinctive effort to stand up, but his leaden legs held him down and he was forced to ʀ ᴍᴀᴛᴇ ᴛᴏ ʜɪs ᴄᴇᴀᴛ, sʜᴀᴋɪɴɢ ᴡɪᴛʜ sᴜᴄʜ ᴀ ᴄᴏɴᴠᴜʟsɪᴠᴇ ᴛʀᴇᴍᴏʀ ᴛʜᴀᴛ ʜɪs ᴊᴀᴡs chattered, as if he were talking to himself. The narrow staircase made the descent difficult; he watched the big yellow box coming slowly towards him, and, as it brushed past his feet, he bent down to read the inscription on the plaque. Now the passage was wider and the men advanced quickly towards the bier, which had been left standing in the courtyard at the bottom of the steps. Chanteau continued gazing at the coffin, gazing as forty years of his life were carried away, all those things from his past, good and bad, and he felt a wild longing to have them back, as we all long for our youth. Standing behind his chair, Pauline and Lazare wept.

'No, no! Leave me here!' he said as they prepared to wheel him back again to his place in the dining room. 'Off you go. I want to see.'

The coffin had been laid on the bier, which other attendants now lifted up. The cortège was forming in the yard, crowded with local people. Mathieu had been shut up in the carriage shed since early morning and his whining from under the door intruded into the solemn hush; while Minouche, sitting on the kitchen windowsill, scrutinized with surprise both the crowd of people and the box they were taking away. As they still did not set off, the cat lost interest and began to lick her belly.

'Aren't you going, then?' Chanteau asked Véronique, whom he had just noticed standing by him.

'No, Monsieur,' she replied in a choking voice. 'Mademoiselle told me to stay with you.'

The church bell was still tolling, and at last the body departed from the courtyard, followed by Pauline and Lazare, black-clad in the bright sunlight. And, from his invalid's chair in the open doorway of the hall, Chanteau watched it go.

CHAPTER 7

THE complexities of the burial arrangements and certain other matters that had to be attended to detained Lazare and Pauline in Caen for two days. When they set off home after a final visit to the cemetery, the weather had changed and a gale was blowing along the coast. They left Arromanches in a downpour, with the wind so strong it threatened to tear the hood off the cabriolet. Pauline thought back to that first journey, when Madame Chanteau had brought her from Paris: it had been in just such a storm as this, and her poor aunt had kept telling her not to lean out, refastening the scarf around her neck every other minute. Lazare, in his own corner, was also plunged in thought, seeing in his mind's eye his mother waiting impatiently on the road to embrace him each time he had come home; once, in December, she had walked two leagues to meet him, and he had found her sitting on that very kilometre-stone. The rain poured down unceasingly, and the girl and her cousin exchanged not a word between Arromanches and Bonneville.

Just as they were nearing home, the rain stopped, but the violence of the wind redoubled, and the coachman had to get down and lead the horse by its bridle. Finally, as the carriage was drawing up at the gate, Houtelard the fisherman came running towards them.

'Oh! Monsieur Lazare!' he cried, 'it's all over this time!... It's smashing up those contraptions of yours!'

The sea was not visible from that corner of the road; but the young man looked up and caught sight of Véronique standing on the terrace, gazing towards the beach. On the other side, sheltering behind his garden wall for fear the wind might rip his cassock, Abbé Horteur was looking in the same direction. He leaned forward and shouted:

'It's your groynes, it's washing them away!'

Then Lazare walked down the hill, followed by Pauline, despite the terrible weather. When they emerged at the foot of the cliff they stopped short, aghast at the sight that met their gaze. It was one of the September flood tides, rushing in with shattering force; no alert had been issued, but the gale, which had been blowing from the north since the previous day, had swollen the sea so monstrously that mountains of water were rearing up on the horizon and sweeping in, before crashing onto the rocks. In the distance, the sea was black beneath the shadow of the clouds as they galloped across the livid sky.

'You go up,' said the young man to his cousin. 'I'm going to take a look, I'll be back shortly.'

She made no reply, but followed him down to the beach. There, the groynes and a great breakwater which had been recently constructed were being subjected to a fearful assault. The waves, growing ever longer, marshalled their ranks into battering rams, a numberless army, its ranks constantly swelling. White horses reared up as far as the eye could see, great green-backed beasts with manes of foam, driven towards them with gigantic force until, crashing furiously down, they exploded in a torrent of spray; then they subsided into a seething white froth which the waters seemed to suck back and drain away. Each shattering wave made the timbers of the groynes crack and groan. The legs of one were already smashed, and a great central beam, still attached at one end, swayed hopelessly like a dead tree-trunk with its limbs shot away by a hail of bullets. Two others were putting up more resistance, but they were now also shaking in their foundations, straining and overwhelmed amid that surging flood which seemed intent on loosening their hold, before dashing them to pieces.

'Told you so!' repeated Prouane, leaning, very drunk, against the broken shell of an old boat, 'it's a different kettle of fish, with the wind blowing from out there... Sea doesn't give a toss for that lad and his matchsticks!'

Jeering laughter greeted these words. All Bonneville was there, men, women, and children, greatly amused to see the thunderous lashing the groynes were getting. The sea might smash up their hovels, they still loved it with awe-struck admiration, and would have taken the insult personally if that young bourgeois had managed to tame it with some beams and a few dozen bolts. And they felt excited and proud, as if it were a personal triumph, when they saw the sea rouse itself at last, fling off its muzzle, and bare its teeth.

'Look there!' shouted Houtelard, 'how was that for a hit, eh?... It's taken out two of the legs!'

They were yelling to each other. Cuche was counting the waves.

'It'll take three, you'll see... One, that's worked it loose! Two, oh! it's gone completely! Well now, the bitch did it in two! It's a real bitch of a sea tonight!'

And it was a term of endearment. Approving oaths were proffered on all sides. The children danced with joy whenever an even more terrifying mass of water smashed down onto one of the groynes and broke its back. Another one gone! and another! soon they would all be swept away, crushed like sea-lice beneath a child's clog. But the tide was still rising, and still the great breakwater stood firm. It was the moment they had been waiting for, it would be the decisive battle. At last the first waves swirled around the timbers. Now the real fun would begin.

'Pity he's not here, the young man,' shouted the jeering voice of rascally Tourmal, 'he could've leant up against them, to prop 'em up.'

A whistle silenced him, as some of the other fishermen had noticed Lazare and Pauline. They had heard Tourmal's sneer and they stood there, very pale, contemplating the disaster in silence. The smashing of the groynes was no catastrophe, but the tide was due to go on rising for two hours yet, and the village would certainly be in trouble if the breakwater did not hold out. Lazare had put his arm round his cousin's waist, and was holding her close to him to protect her from the vicious squalls that scythed into them. A funereal gloom descended from the black sky, the waves roared, and the pair stood there motion-less in their mourning attire, amidst flying spray and the ever-increasing clamour of the sea. Around them now the fishermen were waiting, with a last sneer on their lips, but increasingly anxious, beneath the surface.

'Won't be long now!' Houtelard murmured.

Yet the breakwater still resisted. Every time a breaking wave foamed over the top of it, the tarred timbers re-emerged black from the white waters. But once the first of the wooden sections snapped, the adjoining pieces began to give way, one by one. Not in fifty years had the oldest inhabitants seen such a mighty sea. Soon every-one was forced to retreat, as beams that had been ripped out battered against the rest and completed the demolition of the breakwater, the wreckage of which was hurled violently ashore. Only one support remained upright, like a marker-post on a reef. Bonneville was not laughing now, women were carrying away their crying children. The bitch had them in its clutches again, and they watched in resigned stupor as inevitable ruin bore down on them and their lives, lived so close to the great sea which both fed them and killed them. They stampeded back in a clatter of big boots, everyone taking shelter behind the shingle banks, the last line of defence for the houses. Some of the piles were already giving way, planks were being stove in, and enormous waves now swept over the revetment, which was not high enough.

There was nothing left to offer resistance, and a great mass of water came and smashed the windows of Houtelard's house, flooding his kitchen. Then the rout was complete and only the victorious sea remained, swamping all before it in one fell swoop.

'Don't go inside!' they shouted to Houtelard. 'The roof's going to cave in.'

Lazare and Pauline had gradually retreated before the deluge. There was nothing they could do to help. Halfway back up the hill, Pauline turned round to take a last look at the endangered village.

'Poor people!' she murmured.

But Lazare could not forgive their idiotic laughter. He was wounded to the core by the disaster, a personal defeat for him, and with an angry gesture he finally growled:

'The sea can lie in their beds, if they love it so much! I'm damned if I'll lift another finger to stop it!'

Véronique came down to meet them with an umbrella, for the rain had begun falling heavily again. Abbé Horteur, still sheltering behind his wall, shouted something to them that they could not catch. The appalling weather, the destruction of the groynes, the distress of the village that they were leaving to its fate, added to the sadness of their return home. When they entered the house, it seemed bare and chill; only the wind's ceaseless howling disturbed the silence of the dismal rooms. Chanteau, who was dozing before the coke fire, started weeping as soon as they appeared. Neither of them went up to change, in order to avoid the dreadful memories that the staircase held for them. The table was already laid and the lamp lit, so they had dinner straight away. It was a sinister evening, and the few words that they spoke were interrupted by the thunderous pounding of the waves, which made the walls tremble. When Véronique brought in the tea, she announced that the Houtelards' house and five others had been flattened already; this time, half the village would certainly go the same way. Chanteau, in despair that his pain was still preventing him from regaining his normal equanimity, silenced her by saying that he had enough troubles of his own and didn't want to hear about other people's. Once they had put him to bed, the others retired too, completely exhausted. Lazare kept a light burning till daylight, and a dozen times Pauline, concerned, opened her door quietly to listen; but from the now deserted first floor there came only a deathly silence.

The next day, the young man began to experience the slow, poignant hours that follow great bereavements. It felt like coming round again after passing out in a fall that had left his body stiff and aching: his mind was lucid and his memory clear, he had emerged from the nightmare he had just experienced, and the clouded vision of his fever. Each detail came back to him afresh, as he relived all the pain. The fact of death, which he had not previously encountered, was here in his own home, in the person of his poor mother, brutally snatched away after just a few days' illness. The horror of ceasing to exist was tangible: they had been four, then a hole had appeared, and three were left behind to shiver in their wretchedness, clinging desperately together in search of a little of the lost warmth. So, was this what dying meant—this sense of nevermore, these trembling arms vainly trying to embrace a shadow which left behind only shocked regrets?

Hourly he endured again the loss of his poor mother, whenever her presence came back into his mind. He had not suffered so intensely at first, not when his cousin had come downstairs and thrown herself into his arms, nor during the long cruelty of the funeral. It was only since his return to the empty house that he had truly felt his awful loss, and his grief was exacerbated by remorse at not having wept more bitterly, close to the end, while something of the dear departed still remained. The fear of not having loved his mother enough was a torture to him, at times making him choke and well up with tears. He thought about her all the time, haunted by her image. If he went upstairs he expected to see her emerge from her room and cross the landing with her quick, tripping step. Often, he would turn round, thinking he heard her, and he was so obsessed that he saw a hallucination of a fold of her dress slipping away behind a door. She was not angry, she did not even look at him, it was just a familiar apparition, a shadow from his past life. At night, he did not dare to put out the lamp, for in the darkness, furtive noises would approach his bed and he would feel a faint breath brushing across his forehead. And the wound, instead of healing, gaped ever wider, as the slightest recollection delivered the nervous shock of a vivid but fleeting illusion, which faded instantly to leave him with the anguish of what could never be.

Everything in the house reminded him of his mother. Her room had been left untouched; none of the furniture had been moved, a thimble still lay on the edge of a small table beside a piece of embroidery. The clock on the mantelpiece had been stopped at seven thirty-seven, the time of her death. He avoided going in. Then occasionally, as he was rushing upstairs, a sudden impulse would drive him to enter. As he stood there with wildly throbbing heart, it seemed to him that the old familiar furniture — its scrollative, the round table, the bed espe-cially—had acquired a transfiguring majesty. A pale light filtered through the permanently closed shutters, and its indistinctness added to his emotion as he went to kiss the pillow on which the dead woman's head had turned cold as ice. One morning when he went into the room, he stopped short in surprise: the shutters had been flung open to let in the light, a bright patch of sunshine lay across the bed up to the pillow, and the furniture was decked with flowers, filling every available vase. Then he remembered that it was an anniversary, the departed woman's birthday, a date they celebrated every year, which his cousin had not forgotten. They were only poor autumn flowers, asters, daisies, and the last lingering roses already nipped by frost, but they brought the sweet scent of life into the room, and their joyous colours framed the lifeless clock-face on which time itself seemed to have stopped. He was deeply moved by this pious feminine obser-vance, and he wept for a long time.

And the dining room, the kitchen, and even the terrace, were also full of his mother's presence. He found her in the everyday objects that he handled, or in old habits that he suddenly missed. It was becom-ing an obsession which he never mentioned, striving with a kind of anxious reticence to conceal the constant torture he was enduring, his continual dialogue with death. As he even avoided mentioning the name of the one who was haunting him, it might have been thought that he was starting to forget her already, whereas never a moment went by without his feeling in his heart the sharp stab of some recol-lection. Only his cousin saw through his concealment. Then he would risk lying to her, swearing he had put his light out at midnight, or had been absorbed in some imaginary work, and ready to fly into a rage if questioned further. His bedroom was a place of refuge where he would go to surrender to his feelings, secure in that space where he had grown up, free from the fear of betraying to others the secret of his distress.

From the beginning, he had certainly made efforts to go out and resume his long walks. At least he would have escaped Véronique's sulky silence and the painful sight of his father sitting listlessly in his chair, at a loss how to occupy his hands. But he now felt a distaste for walking which he could not overcome; he was bored outdoors, bored sick. The sea with its perpetual oscillation, that obstinate swell sweeping up to the cliffs twice a day, exasperated him: it was a senseless force, indifferent to his grief, wearing down the same rocks for centuries while never mourning the death of a single human being. It was too vast, too cold; and he would hurry home and shut himself indoors, to feel less insignificant, less crushed between the dual infinities of sea and sky. Only one place attracted him, the graveyard which surrounded the church; his mother was not there, but he could think about her fondly and peacefully, and, despite his terror of the void, he found it singularly calming. The graves lay sleeping in the grass, yew trees grew in the shelter of the nave, and the only sound to be heard was the calling of the curlews as they bobbed on the sea breeze. There he would lose himself for hours, unable even to read on the old gravestones the names of those long dead, erased by the driving westerly rains.

If only Lazare had had faith in another world, if he were able to believe he would one day see his loved ones again on the other side of the black wall—but this consolation was denied him. He was too deeply convinced of the finality of individual death, a dispersal back into the everlasting pool of life. And yet his ego secretly rebelled at the idea of such an end. What joy it would be to begin life again elsewhere, amongst the stars, along with all his friends and relations! Oh, how the thought of going to meet loved ones would sweeten death's bitter pill, how eager would be their embracing, what bliss to live together again in immortality! He suffered agonies at the thought of this charitable lie that religions peddled, solicitously concealing the terrible truth from those too weak to bear it. No, death was the end of everything, nothing we had loved could ever come back, our farewells were said for ever. Oh! those dreadful words 'for ever', which plunged his mind into the vertiginous spiral of nothingness.

One morning, as Lazare was brooding in the shade of the yew trees, he saw Abbé Horteur at the bottom of his vegetable garden, which was only separated from the graveyard by a low wall. Wearing an old grey smock and a pair of clogs, the priest was digging his cabbage patch; with his face tanned by the harsh sea air, and the back of his neck burnt by the sun, he looked like an old peasant toiling over the hard ground. With a meagre stipend and no income from fees in such a remote parish, he would have died of hunger if he had not grown a few vegetables. What little money he had went in alms, he lived alone, with just a small girl to help about the house, and was often obliged to cook his own meals. To make matters worse, the soil in that rocky spot was poor, the wind withered his lettuces, and it was scarcely worth battling the stony ground for the few measly onions it yielded. Still, he always donned his smock very discreetly, for fear people might make fun of religion. So Lazare was about to slip away when he saw the priest take a pipe out of his pocket, fill it with tobacco and light it, smacking his lips. But as he was enjoying the simple pleasure of his first puffs, the abbé in turn spotted the young man. He made a startled movement to hide the pipe, then broke into a laugh and called:

'You're out for some fresh air... Come on in, let me show you my garden.'

When Lazare came up to him, he added cheerily:

'So, you've caught me at my guilty pleasure then... It's my only one, my friend, and I'm sure God won't take offence.'

From then on, he puffed noisily away, only taking his pipe from his mouth to make the odd brief remark. For instance, he didn't understand the curé in Verchemont, a lucky man who had a magnificent garden with real soil which would grow anything—so wasn't it a shame that he never so much as raked it over? Next, he grumbled about his potatoes, which had rotted in the ground the last two years, though the soil should have suited them.

'Don't let me get in your way,' said Lazare. 'Please carry on with your work.'

The abbé picked up his spade at once.

'Yes, I'd better be getting on,' he said. 'Those young rascals will soon be turning up for catechism, and I want to get this patch done first.'

Lazare had sat down on a granite bench, some ancient tombstone propped up against the low wall of the churchyard. He watched Abbé Horteur tilling the stony earth and listened to him chattering on in his shrill voice, like an elderly child's, and he longed to be as poor and simple as him, with an empty head and a body at peace. That the bishop had left the good fellow to grow old in that wretched parish, said much for his simple-minded innocence. Anyhow, he was one of those who never complain, whose ambition is satisfied when they have bread to eat and water to drink.

'It can't be much fun living amongst all these crosses,' Lazare remarked, thinking out loud.

The priest stopped digging in surprise.

'What makes you say that?'

'Well, you have death constantly before your eyes, you must dream about it at night.'

The priest took his pipe out of his mouth and spat, at length.

'Well I don't know, I never think about it… We're all in God's hands.'

Then he took the spade again and drove it in with his heel. His faith preserved him from fear, and he never looked beyond the catechism: you died, you went to heaven, nothing could be simpler or more reassuring. He smiled stubbornly, for that constant idea of salvation had sufficed to fill the narrow confines of his skull.

From that day on, Lazare went into the curé's garden almost every morning. He would seat himself on the old stone bench and forget his troubles as he watched the abbé tending his vegetables, finding temporary consolation in the blind innocence that allowed the curé to live off death without feeling its dread. Why not become a child again, like this old man? Deep down, he had a secret hope of rekindling his lost faith through conversing with such a simpleton, whose tranquil ignorance he relished. He brought along a pipe of his own and the pair of them smoked, chatting about the slugs that were eating the lettuces, or the high price of manure; for seldom did the priest speak of God, having reserved Him, with the tolerance and long experience of an old confessor, for his own salvation. Other people looked after their business, he would look after his. After thirty years of issuing fruitless warnings, he now confined himself to the strict observance of his duty of ministry, with his peasant's logic that charity begins at home. It was very kind of the lad to come and see him every day, and since he did not want to annoy him or quarrel with his Parisian ideas, he preferred to discuss gardening, interminably; while Lazare, his head buzzing with the priest's empty gossip, occasionally felt himself almost relapsing into a happy state of ignorance, where fear has no abode.

But though the mornings slipped past, Lazare would find himself every night alone in his room with his mother's memory, unable to summon up the courage to put out the lamp. His faith was dead. One day, as he sat on the stone seat smoking with Abbé Horteur, the priest hastily concealed his pipe on hearing footsteps from behind the pear trees. It was Pauline, coming to fetch her cousin.

'The doctor's called round,' said she, 'and I have invited him to stay for lunch... You will come in soon, won't you?'

She was smiling, for she had noticed the pipe under the abbé's smock. He quickly took it out again, laughing cheerfully as he always did whenever he was caught smoking.

'Silly of me,' he said, 'you'd think it were a crime... Now then, I'll light up again in front of you!'

'I tell you what, Monsieur le Curé,' said Pauline gaily, 'come and join us and the doctor for lunch, and you can smoke your pipe over dessert.'

The priest was delighted, and immediately exclaimed:

'Well, that would be very nice... You go ahead, I'll just change into my cassock. And I'll bring my pipe too, I promise!'

It was the first lunch since Madame Chanteau's death at which laughter rang out again in the dining room. To everyone's amusement, the abbé smoked once the table was cleared, but he enjoyed his luxury with such good humour that it immediately seemed quite natural. Chanteau had eaten a lot and was relaxing, relieved that a lively new breeze was now blowing through the house. Doctor Cazenove told stories about savages, while Pauline beamed with pleasure at the happy commotion, which might perhaps distract Lazare and relieve his despondency.

After that, Pauline was keen to resume the Saturday dinners, which had been curtailed by her aunt's death. The abbé and the doctor came round regularly, and life reverted once more to its old pattern. There was much joking, and the widower Chanteau would slap his legs and say he still felt so full of beans he could get up and dance, were it not for that confounded gout. Only Lazare remained out of sorts, talking with exaggerated animation, then halting with a shudder in the middle of some verbal outburst.

One Saturday evening, they were on the roast course when Abbé Horteur was summoned to attend a dying man. He did not even empty his glass but set off at once, ignoring the doctor, who had visited the man on his way there and shouted after him that he would find the fellow already dead. That evening, the priest's conversation had been so dull that even Chanteau remarked, after he had left:

'Some days he doesn't seem so very bright.'

'I'd gladly change places with him,' Lazare snapped back. 'He's happier than we are.'

The doctor began to laugh.

'Maybe. But Mathieu and Minouche are also happier than us... Oh, you're just like the other young men of today, you've dabbled in science and it's made you sick because it didn't satisfy the old idea of the absolute that you all imbibed with your nursemaid's milk. You expect science to deliver all the answers straight away, but we're only just starting to understand the questions, and it will no doubt turn out to be an endless process of enquiry. And then you reject science and try to fall back instead on faith, but faith will have nothing more to do with you, so you relapse into pessimism... Yes! pessimism is the disease of our century's end—you're all just a lot of Young Werthers,* in negative.'

He grew quite animated, for this was his favourite hobby horse. In their discussions, Lazare always exaggerated his own denial of certainty, his belief in the finality and universality of evil.

'How can you go on living,' he asked, 'when at every step the ground gives way beneath your feet?'

This sparked an upsurge of youthful passion in the older man:

'Why can't you just live? Isn't it enough to be alive? Joy comes from action.' And Cazenove suddenly turned to Pauline, who was listening with a smile on her face.

'Come now!' he said, 'tell him how you always manage to stay so cheerful!'

'Me,' she replied, in a joking tone, 'Oh, I try to forget myself, for fear of feeling sad, and I think about others, which keeps me busy and helps put my own problems in perspective.'

This answer seemed to irritate Lazare, who asserted, in a spirit of bad-tempered contrariness, that women ought to be religious: he couldn't understand why Pauline had long since stopped going to church. She gave her reasons in her calm, quiet way.

'It's quite simple; I found confession painful, and I think a lot of women feel the same... And then, I can't bring myself to believe things that seem to me unreasonable. So what's the point of lying and pretending to accept them?... Anyhow, I'm not worried about the unknown, it's bound to be something logical, so it's best to wait for it as calmly as possible.'

'Hush! here comes the abbé!' interrupted Chanteau, who was getting bored with this conversation.

The man had died; the priest placidly finished his dinner, then they each drank a small glass of chartreuse.

Pauline had now taken charge of the household arrangements, with all the cheerful confidence of a good manageress. She dealt with the purchases and looked after every domestic detail, and the bunch of keys dangled from her waist. This came about as a matter of course, without any apparent objection from Véronique. However, since Madame Chanteau's death, the maid had been very crabby and still seemed in a state of shock. A new process seemed to be underway in her, a revival of her affection for the dead woman, whereupon she went back to treating Pauline with surly suspicion. However nicely the girl spoke to her, she would take offence at the slightest word, and she could often be heard grumbling to herself in the kitchen. When, after periods of stubborn silence, she began to think out loud in that way, her speech still conveyed stupefaction at the catastrophe. How could she have known that Madame was going to die? Of course she'd never have said the things she did! Justice came before everything, it was wrong to kill someone, even if they did have their faults. Anyhow, she could wash her own hands of the disaster, and too bad for the one who was the real cause of it. But this confident assertion brought her no peace of mind, and she continued to grumble, wrestling with her imagined sin.

'Why are you being so hard on yourself?' Pauline asked her one day. 'We all did our best, but there's nothing you can do against death.'

Véronique shook her head.

'No, but you don't just go for no reason... Whatever Madame's faults may have been, she took me in when I was little, and I'd cut my tongue out if I thought her death had anything to do with me... Let's not talk about it, it'll only make matters worse.'

No word of marriage had been spoken between Pauline and Lazare. Chanteau had risked one allusion to the subject when Pauline was sitting beside him with her sewing, to keep him company: he wanted the matter settled, now that the obstacle was no longer there. His main motivation was the need to keep her close by him, and his fear of falling back into the hands of Véronique, should he ever lose her. Pauline let it be known that no decision could be made until the end of the mourning period. It was not just respect for convention that prompted this prudent position: she was hoping that the passage of time would answer a question which she dared not ask herself. Such a sudden death, a terrible blow from which she and her cousin were still reeling, had brought about a kind of truce in their tormented affections. From this they were now gradually emerging into further suffering, rediscovering beneath their irreparable loss their own personal drama: Louise caught in the act and thrown out, their own love shattered, their existence perhaps changed for ever. What was to be done now? Were they still in love with each other? Was marriage still possible, and was it wise? Such questions floated in their minds, dizzied by the catastrophe, and neither seemed anxious to precipitate an answer.

In Pauline's case, however, the memory of Lazare's betrayal had softened. She had long ago forgiven him, and was ready to place both her hands in his as soon as he showed some remorse. This was not some jealous desire to triumph over him in his humiliation; her only thought was for him, to the point of being prepared to release him from his promise if he no longer loved her. Her whole anguish lay in that doubt: did he still hanker after Louise, or had he forgotten her and returned to his old childhood affections? However, whenever she imagined giving Lazare up rather than make him unhappy, her whole being was filled with grief: she trusted she would have the courage to do it, but hoped to die afterwards.

Following her aunt's death, the generous plan had occurred to her of bringing about a reconciliation between herself and Louise. Chanteau could write to her, and she herself would add a line to say that all was forgotten. Everyone was feeling so sad and lonely that Louise's childish and spontaneous presence would cheer them up. Moreover, after such a cruel shock, events of the recent past now seemed very distant, and she was also sorry for her own violent behaviour. But every time she was about to mention it to her uncle, a feeling of repugnance held her back. Would she not be risking the future, tempting Lazare and perhaps condemning him? She might still have found the confidence and the courage to put him to this test, had her sense of justice not rebelled: treachery was the one unforgivable crime. Besides, was she not capable of bringing joy back into the house by herself? Why call in an outside influence, when she felt herself brimming over with love and devotion? There was a touch of unconscious conceit in her self-sacrifice, and jealousy in her charitable feelings. Her heart was on fire with the hope of being the sole bringer of happiness to those whom she loved.

From now on, this became Pauline's great endeavour. She applied all her energy and ingenuity to making the household happy around her. Never before had she shown herself so resolutely kind and cheerful.

Each morning she awoke with a smile on her lips, determined to hide
her own troubles in order not to add to those of others. She defied
disasters by her gentle sociability, and disarmed ill-wishers with her
equable demeanour. Now she was fit and well again, strong and sound as
a young tree, and in her new-found health she radiated joy around her.
The routine of each new day delighted her, she took pleasure in doing
just what she had done the day before, with no further expectations,
and looked forward in tranquillity to the following day. Although
Véronique, who had become moody and capricious, carried on grumbling over her kitchen range, a new influx of vitality was driving melancholy from the house, as the laughter of bygone days brought the
rooms alive again and resounded up the staircase. But it was Chanteau
who seemed most delighted, for he had found sadness hard to bear,
and since being confined to his chair, he loved to sing bawdy songs.
For him life was becoming intolerable, yet he clung to it with the desperate grip of an invalid determined to hang on as long as possible,
whatever the pain. Every day that he survived was a victory, and he
felt his niece was warming the house like a burst of sunshine, in whose
radiance he could not die.

Pauline, however, still had one regret: she had failed to bring any
comfort to Lazare, and was concerned at seeing him fall back into his
dark moods. Underlying his grief for his mother was a resurgence of
his terror of death. Now that the passage of time had blunted his initial sorrow, this terror was coming to the fore, amplified by a fear
of hereditary disease. He too would die of a heart complaint, and he
went about convinced that his own tragic end was nigh. Every minute
he listened to his own living organism, in such a state of nervous
excitement that he could hear the mechanism working: painful stomach contractions, red secretions of the kidneys, the secret warmth of
the liver. But rising above the noises of the other organs was the deafening din of his heart, which rang peals of bells through all his limbs,
down to the very tips of his fingers. If he leant his elbow on the table,
his heart throbbed in the elbow; if he rested his neck against the back
of an armchair, it throbbed in the neck; if he sat down, or went to bed,
it throbbed in his thighs, his sides, his stomach; and on and on its bass
bell boomed, measuring out his life like the grating tick of a clock as
it ran down. Then, in the obsession of such ceaseless scrutiny of his
own body, he began to believe that it might break down at any moment:
his organs were wearing out and disintegrating, his monstrously

swollen heart would smash the machine to pieces with its great hammer blows. It was no life any more, listening to himself living in this way, trembling at the fragility of the mechanism and waiting for the grain of sand that would bring it grinding to a halt.

Thus, Lazare's anxieties had swelled. For years, whenever he lay down to sleep, the idea of death had brushed across his face and chilled his flesh. Now he dared not fall asleep, tormented by a fear of never waking again. He hated sleep, and loathed the feeling of losing himself as he plunged from alertness into the vertiginous void. Then he would be further jolted by sudden awakenings, which plucked him from the black depths as if a giant hand had grabbed him by the hair and dragged him back into life, still gibbering with horror at the unknown which had expelled him. Oh God, Oh God, he would have to die! Never before had he clasped his hands together in such a frenzy of despair. Every evening his torment was so great that he preferred not to go to bed. He had found that in the daytime he could lie down on a divan and fall asleep as gently and peacefully as a child. He could then enjoy deep, restorative rest, but unfortunately this ruined his nights. Gradually he fell into a state of regular nocturnal insomnia, preferring long afternoon siestas and only dozing off towards daybreak, once dawn had chased away his fear of the dark.

Yet he did have periods of respite: sometimes he could go for two or three nights at a time without being visited by death. One day, Pauline found an almanac in his room, dotted with red pencil marks. In surprise, she asked him to explain.

'What do these markings mean?... What a lot of dates you've ticked!'

He stammered:

'I've not been ticking anything... I don't know...'

She continued with merriment:

'I thought it was only girls who confided their private thoughts to their diaries... If you've ticked all the days when you were thinking about us, that's most kind of you... So, you have your secrets, do you?'

However, seeing him become more and more embarrassed, she was charitable enough to stop talking about it. She had noticed a shadow pass across his pale brow, the familiar shadow of that hidden malady for which she could find no cure.

For some time, she had also been astonished by a new mania of his. Convinced that his end was imminent, he could not leave a room, or close a book, or use an object without believing it was his final act, that he would never see the object, book, or room again; so he had developed a constant habit of bidding farewell to things, and a morbid need to touch and see them one more time. This was combined with ideas of symmetry: he must take three steps to the left, then three to the right, and touch the different items of furniture on either side of the fireplace or the door the same number of times, in the superstitious belief that a particular number of touches, five or seven for instance, in a certain order, would prevent the farewell from being final. Despite his keen intelligence and his denial of the supernatural, he observed these foolish rituals with animal-like docility, though he hid them like a shameful disease. This was the vengeance exacted by the deranged nervous system of a pessimist and positivist who claimed to believe only in facts and experiment. It was making him infuriating company.

'Why are you pacing around like that?' Pauline would exclaim. 'That's the third time you've gone up to that cupboard and touched the key... It's not going anywhere, you know!'

In the evening, he would take an eternity to leave the dining room, arranging the chairs in a special way, closing the door a certain number of times, then going back in again to lay his hands, first the left then the right, on his grandfather's masterpiece. Pauline, waiting for him at the foot of the stairs, ended up laughing about it.

'A fine maniac you'll be by the time you're eighty!... Honestly, what's the point of fiddling with things like that?'

But eventually she stopped joking about it, worried to see him so on edge. One morning, as she caught him giving seven kisses to the frame of the bed in which his mother had died, she was filled with alarm, guessing at the torments that were poisoning his existence. When he turned pale at finding some reference in a newspaper to a future date in the twentieth century, she gave him a compassionate look which made him avert his gaze. He felt sure she had read his thoughts, and ran to hide up in his room, with the embarrassed shame of a woman surprised in the nude. How often had he called himself a coward! How often had he vowed to fight his disease! He would reason with himself and manage to look death in the face, then in an act of defiance, instead of sitting up all night in an armchair, he would lie straight down on his bed; death could come when it wished, he would welcome the release. But at once the throbbing of his heart drove these vows from his mind, an icy breath chilled his flesh, and he stretched out his hands with the despairing cry: 'Oh God! Oh God!' These terrible relapses filled him with shame and despair, and his cousin's tender pity only made him feel worse. The days became so depressing that he began them without hope of seeing their end; as his existence crumbled, first he had lost his cheerfulness of mind, and now his bodily strength was deserting him too.

Pauline, however, in the pride of her self-sacrifice, was determined to win the day. She understood Lazare's illness, and tried to pass on some of her own courage to him by instilling in him a love of life. But in that, her kind intentions were constantly thwarted. First, she tried a direct attack, teasing him as she had previously done about his 'silly, horrid pessimism'. Just think! she was now the one singing the praises of Schopenhauer, the great saint, while he, like all those other pessimist jokers, was happy to blow up the world, just so long as it didn't include him! This mockery wrung a forced laugh from Lazare, but he seemed so pained by it that she desisted. Next, she tried to soothe him like a child that has hurt itself, surrounding him with a cheery atmosphere of peace and laughter. He always saw her happy and smiling, full of the joys of existence. The house was a place of sunshine. All he had to do was take pleasure in living, but that he could not do, as all this happiness only increased his horror of what awaited on the other side. Finally, Pauline changed tack again, trying to dream up some tremendous task that would take his mind off things. But his idleness was now a disease, he had no desire to do anything and even found reading too much, so he just spent his days in self-torment.

For one moment Pauline's hopes rose. They had gone for a short walk on the beach, when Lazare, standing before the remaining beams of the wrecked groynes and breakwater, started to explain a new system of sea defences which, he assured her, would definitely be strong enough. The problem had been the weakness of the supporting legs: the answer was to double their thickness and make the central beam slope more steeply. As his voice was vibrant and his eyes gleaming with all the old enthusiasm, she encouraged him to get back to work. The village was in a terrible state; with every high tide another chunk of it was washed away, and if he went to see the prefect, there was no doubt that he would get the grant. In any case, she offered to advance the money again, she'd be proud to help such a charitable cause. Her main aim was to spur him back into action, even if it took all the rest of her fortune. But already he was shrugging his shoulders. What was the point? And he turned pale, for it had occurred to him that, if he did embark on the work, he would be dead before it was finished. So, to conceal his confusion, he fell back on his grievance against the Bonneville fishermen.

'Stupid idiots who laughed in my face while that vicious tide was doing its worst!... No, no, it can finish them off for all I care! They won't get another chance to make fun of my matchsticks, as they called them.'

Gently, Pauline tried to calm him down. Those poor people were in such a desperate state. Since the tide that had swept away the Houtelards' house, the most solid in the village, along with the hovels of three poor families, their distress had only increased. Houtelard, who had been the rich man of the area, had found an old barn to move into, some twenty metres further back, but the other fishermen, who had no such refuge, were now camping in makeshift huts made from old boat hulls. Their destitution was pitiable as they squatted there in savage-like promiscuity, the women and children wallowing in vermin and vice. All the alms they received from people round about went on alcohol. The wretches even sold any donations in kind—clothes, kitchen utensils, items of furniture—to buy litres of the noxious Calvados, which laid them out in their own doorways like corpses. Only Pauline continued to plead their cause; the curé had given them up, and Chanteau talked of resigning, no longer willing to be mayor to such a herd of swine. Lazare too, whenever his cousin tried to stir his pity for that little community of boozers battered by the elements, would only repeat his father's mantra:

'Nobody's forcing them to stay. They can just go and build somewhere else... How can they be so stupid, trying to cling on there, right in the path of the sea?'

Everyone thought the same: people grew angry and called them stubborn fools. This made the villagers sullen and suspicious: after all, they'd been born there, so why should they leave now? Things had been that way for hundreds and hundreds of years, and they had no reason to go anywhere else. As Prouane always said when he was very drunk: 'Something'll always get you in the end, whatever.'

Pauline would smile and nod approvingly, for in her opinion, happiness did not depend on people or things, but on the reasonable way you adapted to people and things. She redoubled her caring efforts and gave even more generous donations. Finally, she had the joy of involving Lazare in her charitable works, in the hope that pity for others would distract him from his own troubles. Every Saturday he stayed there with her and together, from four o'clock till six, they received the little friends from the village, a queue of ragged urchins sent up by their parents to beg at Mademoiselle's house. They were a rabble of snotty lads and verminous girls.

One Saturday it was raining, so Pauline could not distribute her largesse on the terrace, as was her custom. Lazare had to carry a bench into the kitchen.

'Monsieur!' exclaimed Véronique, 'surely Mademoiselle isn't think-ing of bringing those lousy brats in here?... It's a fine idea, if you want creepy-crawlies in your soup.'

Pauline was just coming in, with her bag of silver and her medicine chest. She replied with a laugh:

'Oh, you can just give the place a quick sweep... Besides, it's rain-ing so hard they'll already have had a good wash, poor dears!'

And indeed, the first to enter were pink-cheeked and clean from the downpour. But they were so soaked that water trickled from their rags and pooled on the flagged floor; and the maid's temper did not improve, especially when Mademoiselle ordered her to light a fire to dry them a little. The bench was set up in front of the fireplace. Soon it was packed with a shivering row of impudent, leering ragamuffins, casting greedy looks at anything edible that had been left out, open bottles of wine, some leftover meat, or a bunch of carrots on the chop-ping block.

'The very idea!' Véronique went on grumbling, 'children that are growing up and should all be earning their keep... Hah! They'll have you treat them as kids till they're twenty-five, if you'll let them!'

Mademoiselle had to ask her to be quiet.

'That's quite enough! Just growing up doesn't fill their bellies.'

Pauline had sat down at the table, with her money and the gifts in kind in front of her, and she was about to start the roll-call when Lazare, who had remained standing, noticed the Houtelard boy in among them, and protested:

'I told you never to come here again, you great good-for-nothing oaf! Your parents have a real cheek, sending you here to beg, when they still have enough to eat and so many others are starving!'

The Houtelard lad, a skinny fifteen-year-old who had grown too quickly, with a sad and fearful expression, started crying.

'They beat me if I don't come,' he said. 'That woman took the rope to me, and Dad kicked me out.'

He rolled up his sleeve to show his purple bruise, from a knotted rope. The woman was the former servant his father had married, who flogged the boy within an inch of his life. Since they had been ruined, their avarice had become more callous and sordid; they now lived in complete squalor, and took their revenge on him.

'Put an arnica compress on his elbow,' Pauline said softly to Lazare. Then she held out a five-franc piece.

'Here you are, give them this to stop them beating you. And if they do, if there are any bruises on your body next Saturday, tell them you'll never get another sou from me.'

The other urchins along the bench, cheered by the blaze that was warming their backs, sniggered and dug each other in the ribs with their elbows. Their clothes were steaming, and big drops of water fell from their bare feet. One tiny lad had stolen a carrot and was munching it furtively.

'Stand up, Cuche,' Pauline continued. 'Did you tell your mother that I hope to get her admitted very soon to the Hospital for Incurables in Bayeux?'

Cuche's wife, that wretched creature abandoned by her husband, who would play the prostitute to any man in the coves along the coast for some small change or a scrap of bacon, had broken her leg in July; she had been left a cripple with a dreadful limp, though her repulsive ugliness, increased by this infirmity, did not put off her usual clientele.

'Yeah, I told her,' the lad replied in a hoarse voice; 'she don't want to.'

He was a sturdy fellow of almost seventeen. He stood there, arms dangling, shifting awkwardly from foot to foot.

'What do you mean, doesn't want to?' exclaimed Lazare. 'And you don't want to either, do you? I told you to come up here this week and lend a hand in the kitchen garden, but I'm still waiting.'

The lad was still fidgeting.

'I were busy, weren't I?'

Then Pauline, seeing her cousin about to lose his temper, intervened.

'Sit down, we'll talk about that later. Just give it some thought, or you'll make me cross as well.'

Next it was the little Gonin girl's turn. She was thirteen and still had her pretty, pink complexion beneath a mop of blonde hair. Without waiting to be asked, she launched into a flood of chatter, full of crude details about her father's paralysis and how it was going up to his arms, and even his tongue, so now he could only grunt like an animal. Cousin Cuche, the former sailor who had deserted his own wife and installed himself, bed and board, in their house, had jumped on the old man that very morning with a view to finishing him off.

'Ma beats him up too. She gets up in her nightshirt with the cousin, and she pours pots of cold water on our dad, because he groans so loud it disturbs them… If you could see the state they left him in! He's all bare, Mademoiselle, he needs some linen, his skin's rubbed raw…'

'All right, that's quite enough!' Lazare interrupted her, while Pauline, moved to pity, sent Véronique to fetch a pair of sheets.

Lazare found the girl far too knowing for her age. His view was that, though she might occasionally get in the way of a blow meant for her father, she had probably started mistreating him as well; added to which, everything they gave her, money, meat, or bed linen, rather than going to the old invalid, served the gratification of his wife and cousin Cuche. He began to question the child sternly:

'So what were you doing the day before yesterday in Houtelard's boat, with a man who ran away?'

She gave a sly smile.

'That weren't no man, that were 'im,' she replied with a jerk of her chin at young Cuche. 'He gave me a shove from behind…'

Again Lazare interrupted her.

'Oh yes, and I saw you, with your rags all up over your head. You're certainly making an early start, at thirteen!'

Pauline laid a hand on his arm, for all the other children, even the youngest, were looking on and laughing, with a glint of precocious vice in their eyes. How could the rottenness be stopped in that den where males, females, and their brood all depraved each other? When Pauline had given the girl the pair of sheets and a litre of wine, she spoke to her briefly in an undertone in an attempt to scare her about the consequences of such horrid things, which would make her sick and ugly before she even became a proper woman. It was the only way to keep her in check.

Lazare, to speed up the distribution, which after a while had started to disgust and annoy him, called Prouane's daughter forward.

'Your father and mother were drunk again last night… and I hear that you were worse than either of them.'

'Oh no, Monsieur! I had a headache.'

He placed before her a plate on which were arranged little balls of raw meat.

'Eat this!'

Once again, her skin was devoured by scrofula, and nervous disorders had reappeared at this critical moment of puberty. Her condition was aggravated by intoxication, for she had started drinking with her parents. After she had gulped down three meatballs, she refused the next with a grimace of disgust.

'I've 'ad enough, can't eat no more.'

But Pauline was holding up a bottle.

'Very well,' she said. 'If you don't eat your meat, you shan't have your little glass of quinine tonic.'

Then, with her gleaming eyes staring at the full glass, the child overcame her revulsion, before seizing the glass and downing its contents with a drunkard's practised flick of the wrist. But she showed no sign of leaving, and finally begged Mademoiselle to let her take the bottle with her, saying it was a nuisance having to come all that way every day, and promising to take the bottle to bed with her, and hide it so carefully in her skirts that her father and mother would not be able to find it and drink it. Mademoiselle refused point-blank.

'You'd guzzle it before you got down the hill,' said Lazare. 'It's you we can't trust now, you little boozer!'

The bench was thinning out as the children got up one by one, to be given money, bread, or meat. Some of them, after receiving their share, wanted to linger in front of the blazing fire, but Véronique, who had just noticed that half her bunch of carrots had been devoured, drove them mercilessly out into the rain: to think of it! carrots with all the dirt still on them! Soon there was no one left except the Cuche lad, looking sullen and downcast in the expectation of a lecture from Pauline. She called him over, spoke to him for a long time in a low voice, and finally handed him the usual Saturday loaf and five-franc piece; then he ambled off with the rolling gait of a stubborn, bad-tempered beast, having promised to work but determined to do no such thing.

Finally, Véronique was just heaving a sigh of relief when she suddenly exclaimed:

'They haven't all gone yet! There's another one over there in the corner!'

It was the Tourmal girl, the malformed little roadside beggar who, despite her ten years, was still the size of a dwarf. She grew only in impudence, more wheedling and persistent than ever, trained from the cradle for begging, like those precocious children made to practise gymnastics in order to become circus tumblers. She was crouching down between the dresser and the fireplace, as though she had squeezed herself into that corner for fear of being caught doing something naughty; she had a very shifty look.

'What are you doing there?' asked Pauline.

'I'm warming myself.'

Véronique glanced anxiously round her kitchen. Already on previous Saturdays, even when the children had been sitting out on the terrace, various small objects had disappeared. But everything seemed in its place, and the little girl, who had jumped to her feet, began to clamour in her shrill voice:

'Dad's in hospital, Grandad's injured himself at work, Mum's got no dress to go out in... Have pity on us, kind Mam'selle...'

'Will you stop pestering us, you little liar!' shouted Lazare in exasperation. 'Your father is in prison for smuggling, and when your grandfather sprained his wrist he was robbing the oyster-beds at Roqueboise; added to which, if your mother has no dress, she must go out thieving in her chemise, for she's been accused of strangling five chickens belonging to the inn at Verchemont... Do you think we're all fools, that you can lie to us about things we know more about than you do? Keep your tall stories for the people you con by the roadside.'

The child did not even seem to have heard him. She started again, with impudent confidence:

'Have pity, kind Mam'selle, the men are both sick and Ma doesn't dare leave them... The good Lord will bless you...'

'There! off you go now, and no more lies!' said Pauline, giving her a coin to end the conversation.

The child did not need to be told twice, but jumped up and ran out of the kitchen and across the yard as fast as her little legs could carry her. Just at that moment the maid let out a yell:

'Oh, good heavens, the beaker that was there on the dresser... She's run off with your beaker, Mademoiselle Pauline!'

Immediately she shot out in pursuit of the thief, and two minutes later dragged her back in, looking as fierce as a gendarme. It was a difficult business to search the child, for she struggled and bit, scratched and screamed as though she were being murdered. The beaker was not in her pocket, but they found it hidden in the rag that she wore as a chemise, next to her skin. Then she stopped crying and declared brazenly that she did not know how it could have got there, it must have fallen on her while she was sitting on the floor.

'Mademoiselle Pauline told you she'd rob you!' Véronique reiterated. 'If it was up to me, I'd send for the police.'

Lazare also talked of prison, annoyed at the defiant attitude of the girl, drawing herself up like a young viper whose tail had been trodden on. It made him want to smack her.

'Give the money back!' he shouted. 'Where is it?'

The child had already put the coin to her lips with the intention of swallowing it, when Pauline came to her rescue, saying:

'You can keep it this time, but tell them at home they won't be getting any more. From now on I shall come down myself to see what you need. Now be off with you!'

They could hear the girl's bare feet splashing through puddles, then silence fell. Véronique shoved the bench backwards and forwards, bending down to sponge up the pools of water that had trickled from the children's ragged clothes. Well, her kitchen was in a fine state, and it reeked so strongly of poverty that she opened the doors and the window to air it. With a serious expression, Pauline silently collected up her bag and medicines, while an indignant Lazare, yawning with disgust and boredom, went out to wash his hands at the pump.

It was a source of regret to Pauline that Lazare took so little interest in her young friends from the village. He was still prepared to help her on Saturday afternoons, but it was simply to oblige her, for his heart was not in it. While neither poverty nor vice could deter her, such hideous things angered and depressed Lazare. She could remain calm and cheerful in her love for others, whereas whenever he thought about anything beyond himself, he could find in the outside world only fresh reasons for gloom and despondency. Gradually the sight of that band of filthy brats, in whom all the sins of humanity were already fermenting, began to cause him real distress. This wretched brood cast the ultimate blight on his existence, and when they went away, they left him feeling worn out and despairing, full of hatred and contempt for the human herd. The two hours of good works made him malevolent, he would denounce the giving of alms and sneer at charity, exclaiming that it would be better to crush this nest of pernicious insects under his heel, rather than help them to grow up. Pauline listened to him, amazed at his vehemence and mortified to see how differently they felt.

On that particular Saturday, once they were alone, the young man vented all his spleen in a single remark:

'I feel as though I've just emerged from a sewer.'

Then he added:

'How can you care about those monsters?'

'It's simply that I love them for their own sake, not for mine,' she replied. 'You'd rescue a mangy dog at the side of the road, wouldn't you?'

He made a gesture of protest.

'A dog isn't the same.'

'Helping people because you can, isn't that something worth doing?' she continued. 'It's a shame they never mend their ways, for if they did, they might not be so wretched. But as long as they are warm and have something to eat, well, that's enough for me, and I'm happy; it's always one bit less suffering in the world... Why should we expect them to repay what we do for them?'

Then she concluded sadly:

'My poor friend, I can see you really don't enjoy this, you'd better not help me any more... I don't want to stir up your feelings and make you seem crosser than you really are.'

Lazare was slipping away from her, and she was grieved to see how powerless she was to lift him out of his crisis of boredom and fear. When she saw him so overwrought, she could not believe that it was all down to his secret torment, she imagined other reasons for his sadness, and the idea of Louise came back to her. Yes, he must still be thinking about her, and languishing from not seeing her. Then, with a sinking feeling, she attempted to recover her earlier pride in self-sacrifice, vowing once again to spread enough joy around her to ensure the happiness of all her loved ones.

One evening Lazare let slip a cruel remark.

'How lonely it is here!' he said, with a yawn.

She looked at him. Was this a hint? But she did not have the courage to question him directly. Her goodness of heart was being severely tested, and her life was again becoming a torture.

A final shock awaited Lazare: his old friend Mathieu was in a bad way. The poor creature, who had been fourteen that March, was getting stiffer and stiffer in the hindquarters. When the bouts of numbness came over him he could barely walk, and would stay in the yard, lying in the sun and watching people come and go with his melancholy gaze. It was the old dog's eyes, now dim and clouded by a bluish cast, and vacant like those of a blind man, that most upset Lazare. Yet he could still see, and would drag himself along to lay his great head on his master's knee, and gaze up at him fixedly, with a sad look of understanding. He was no longer his handsome self: his curly white coat had yellowed, and his nose, once so black, was turning grey; he was a woeful and shameful sight, dirty because they did not dare wash him on account of his great age. He had given up all his games, he no longer rolled on his back or chased his tail, and was not even moved to affection for Minouche's kittens, when the maid took them down to the sea. He now spent his days drowsing like an old man, and he had such trouble getting up onto his tired old legs that often someone in the house would help him out of pity, holding him for a minute until he could walk again.

He was also dripping blood, which made him more exhausted every day. They had sent for a vet, who laughed out loud when he saw Mathieu. Why were they calling him in for a dog in that state? They should just have him put down. It was one thing to keep a person alive as long as possible, but why let a dying animal linger on in pain? The vet was firmly shown the door, clutching his six-franc fee.

One Saturday, Mathieu lost so much blood that he had to be shut up in the carriage shed. He was leaving a trail of big red drops behind him. As Doctor Cazenove had arrived early, he offered Lazare to take a look at the dog, who was treated as a member of the family. They found him lying down, in a state of great weakness, but with his head held high and life still in his eyes. The doctor gave him a long examination, with the same thoughtful air that he displayed at the bedside of a human patient. At last he said:

'Such abundant haematuria* can only mean a cancerous degeneration of the kidneys... He's done for! But he may go on for a few more days, unless a sudden haemorrhage finishes him off.'

Mathieu's desperate condition cast a cloud over the meal. They recalled how fond Madame Chanteau had been of him, his fights with other dogs, the wild antics of his youth, the cutlets he had stolen off the grill, and the freshly laid eggs he had gobbled up. But over dessert, when Abbé Horteur brought out his pipe, their spirits rose again, and they listened to the priest talking about his pears, which promised to be superb that year. Chanteau, despite faint tingling sensations which announced an imminent attack, ended up singing one of the bawdy songs from his twenties. It was a charming evening. Even Lazare cheered up.

At about nine o'clock, just as tea had been served, Pauline suddenly exclaimed:

'Oh look! Here's poor old Mathieu!'

And indeed the old dog, gaunt and bleeding, was tottering into the dining room. Immediately, Véronique could be heard coming after him with a floor cloth. She entered, saying:

'I had to get something from the shed, and he escaped. Right to the end, he will insist on being where you are, and I can't take a step without him getting tangled in my skirts... Come along now, you can't stay here.'

The dog bowed his shaky old head with a gentle, humble expression.

'Oh! do let him stay!' begged Pauline.

But the maid was indignant.

'I should think not, indeed! I'm fed up of wiping up the blood after him. My kitchen's been full of it these past two days. It's disgusting! A fine state this room will be in if he goes wandering around... Come along, out you go, get a move on!'

'Let him stay,' repeated Lazare. 'And you can leave us.'

Then, as Véronique slammed the door behind her, Mathieu came and laid his head on his master's knee, as if he had understood. Everyone tried to be nice to him, breaking off lumps of sugar to get him excited. In days gone by, they had played a little game of placing a sugar lump on the far side of the table, then while Mathieu ran round to get it, quickly moving it to the other side, so that he would go rushing round and round the table, and the sugar kept moving, until at last he grew dizzy and bewildered at this perpetual conjuring trick, and started barking furiously. It was this game that Lazare tried to start up again, in the fraternal hope of bringing some amusement to the poor creature's final hours. The dog wagged his tail for a moment, went once round the table, then staggered against Pauline's chair. He could not see the sugar, his wasted body would not go in a straight line, and red drops of blood spattered the floor around the table. Chanteau had stopped humming, and everyone's heart was touched by the sight of the poor dying dog stumbling around, as they remembered the pranks of gluttonous Mathieu, in bygone days.

'Don't tire him,' the doctor said gently, 'or you'll kill him.'

Then the curé, who was smoking in silence, made a comment which was probably his way of understanding his own emotion:

'These big dogs, they're so like people.'

At ten o'clock, when the priest and the doctor had gone, Lazare, before going to his own room, went to shut Mathieu up in the carriage shed himself. He laid him carefully on fresh straw, made sure that he had his water bowl, embraced him, and was about to leave. But the dog clambered to his feet with a painful effort, and started coming after him. Lazare had to lie him down three more times before he at last submitted, but he raised his head to watch his master depart with such a sad expression that Lazare, heartbroken, came back to kiss him one more time.

Upstairs in his room, the young man tried to read until midnight. He finally went to bed but could not sleep, haunted by the image of Mathieu lying there on the straw, gazing unsteadily towards the door. By tomorrow, his dog would be dead. And despite himself, he kept sitting up in bed to listen, imagining he heard barking out in the yard. His straining ears caught all sorts of imagined sounds. Around two o'clock in the morning, there were moaning noises, which made him leap out of bed. Where could they be coming from? He went out on the landing; the house was dark and silent, and not a sound came from Pauline's room. Then he could no longer resist the urge to go downstairs. The hope of seeing his dog one last time suddenly made him rush. He barely gave himself time to slip into a pair of trousers, then ran downstairs with his candle.

When he reached the shed, Mathieu was no longer lying on the straw. He had preferred to drag himself a short distance away, onto the beaten earth. When he saw his master come in, he no longer even had the strength to lift his head. Lazare, after standing his candlestick on some old planks, bent down in astonishment at the black colour of the earth; then he fell, heartbroken, to his knees, realizing that the dog was in his death throes, lying there in a great bloody pool. It was his lifeblood ebbing away; he gave a feeble wag of his tail, and there was still a gleam in his deep eyes.

'Oh! my poor old dog!' murmured Lazare, 'my poor old dog!'

Then, in a loud voice, he said to Mathieu:

'Wait, I'll move you... No, does that hurt?... But you're completely soaked! And I haven't even got a sponge... Would you like something to drink?'

Mathieu's gaze was still fixed on him. Slowly, a rattle began to make his sides heave. Silently, as though flowing from some hidden spring, the pool of blood was spreading. Ladders and broken barrels cast great shadows, and the light from the candle was feeble. There was a rustling in the straw: it was Minouche the cat, who was lying on the bed made for Mathieu and had been disturbed by the light.

'D'you want a drink, you poor old dog?' Lazare repeated.

He had found a rag, which he dipped in the bowl of water and pressed to the dying animal's muzzle. This seemed to bring him some relief, and his fever-parched nose became a little cooler. Half an hour went by, Lazare kept rewetting the rag, his eyes filled with the lamentable spectacle and his chest aching with an immense sadness. As sometimes happens beside a sickbed, he was seized at times by wild hopes: perhaps this simple bathing action might restore the dog to life?

'What is it then?' he said suddenly. 'You want to get up, do you?'

Shuddering, Mathieu was making efforts to stand. He held his legs rigid, while his neck swelled with waves of spasms that rippled up from his sides. But it was the end, and he collapsed across the knees of his master, on whom his eyes remained fixed, straining from beneath heavy lids to see him one last time. Deeply moved by the intelligence in that dying look, Lazare held the dog to him; and the great body, as long and heavy as a man's, was wracked, in his sorrowing embrace, by a human death-agony. It lasted some minutes. Then Lazare saw great tears, real tears, roll down from the dog's clouded eyes, while the tongue came out from his convulsed mouth to give him one last lick.

'My poor old doggie!' cried Lazare, bursting into tears himself.

Mathieu was dead. A dribble of bloody foam trickled from his jaws. When he had been laid out on the ground, he seemed to be sleeping.

Then it seemed to Lazare as if everything had come to an end again. Now his dog had died, and this filled him with a grief out of all proportion, a despair sufficient to swallow up his whole life. This death revived the memory of others, and the hurt had not felt crueller when he had walked across the courtyard behind his mother's coffin. Some further part of her seemed to be torn from him, and now he had lost her completely. The months of concealed anguish came back to him, his nights disturbed by bad dreams, his walks in the little graveyard, his terror at the thought of eternal annihilation.

There was a sound, and when he turned, Lazare saw Minouche calmly grooming herself on the straw. But the door had creaked as Pauline came in, prompted by the same concern as her cousin. When he saw her, his tears redoubled, and the man who had hidden his grief at his mother's death out of a kind of fierce reticence, now exclaimed.

'Oh God! God! she loved him so much!… Do you remember? She first had him when he was tiny, she was always the one who fed him, and he'd follow her all around the house!'

Then he added:

'There is no one left now, we are utterly alone!'

Tears welled up in Pauline's eyes. She bent down to look at poor Mathieu in the dim light of the candle. Without attempting to comfort Lazare, she gave a gesture of discouragement, for she felt herself useless and impotent.

CHAPTER 8

THE root cause of Lazare's melancholy was boredom, an oppressive, unrelenting boredom that leached out from everything, like dirty water from a poisoned spring. He was bored with both work and rest, and with himself even more than with others. However, he took himself to task for his own idleness, and finally became ashamed of it. Wasn't it a disgrace for a man his age to waste the best years of his life in a hole like Bonneville? Until then, he had had some excuses, but now there was nothing to keep him there, and he despised himself for staying on uselessly, dependent on his family when they had barely enough to keep themselves. He should have been making a fortune for them, as he had once sworn he would, and this was a complete failure on his part. Admittedly, he still had no lack of plans for the future, grand enterprises, visions of wealth acquired by some brilliant stroke of genius; but when he emerged from these daydreams, he lacked the resolve to get down to action.

'It can't go on like this,' he would often say to Pauline, 'I must find work… I've a mind to set up a newspaper in Caen.'

And she always made the same reply:

'There's no hurry, wait till the end of your mourning. And think very carefully before you get involved in a business like that.'

The truth was that the newspaper idea alarmed her, despite her wish to see him occupied. Another failure might be the end of him, and she well remembered his previous abortive schemes: music, medicine, the seaweed factory—everything he had ever undertaken. And in any case, a couple of hours later he would refuse even to write a letter, as if overcome with exhaustion.

Further weeks went by, and another flood tide swept away three more of Bonneville's houses. Now, when the fishermen met Lazare, they would ask him if it was true he had given up the attempt. Of course, there was nothing to be done, but it was still infuriating to see so much good timber go to waste. And even in the way they expressed their grievances and begged him not to abandon the place to the waves, he sensed the fierce, mocking irony of sailors proud of their sea and its deadly power. Gradually Lazare grew so annoyed with this that he avoided passing through the village. The sight of the ruined breakwater and groynes in the distance became unbearable to him.

Prouane stopped him one day, as he was going in to see the curé.

'Monsieur Lazare,' he said obsequiously, with a malicious twinkle in his eye, 'you know them timbers rotting down there on the beach?'

'Well, what about them?'

'If you're not making anything of 'em, you could let us 'ave 'em... At least we'd use 'em for firewood.'

Repressed anger got the better of the young man and he snapped back, without thinking:

'That won't be possible, I'll be putting the carpenters back to work next week.'

That set tongues wagging across the district. They'd be seeing some more fun, since that young Chanteau seemed determined to try again. A fortnight went by, and the fishermen never bumped into Lazare without asking him if he was having trouble finding workmen. And he did end up getting back to work on the groynes, partly also to placate his cousin, who preferred to find him an occupation close by her. But he did so with no great enthusiasm, sustained only by his resentment against the sea, which he said he was quite certain of conquering this time: it would come up and lick the pebbles of Bonneville like a tame creature.

Once again Lazare drew up plans. He calculated fresh angles of resistance and doubled the strength of his supports. However, no major new expense was needed, as most of the old timbers could be reused. The carpenter presented an estimate of four thousand francs, and as the amount was so small, Lazare made no objection to Pauline advancing it: he was certain, he said, of securing a grant from the Departmental Council, and indeed this was the only way to recoup their previous outlay, for the Council would certainly not put up a penny so long as the groynes remained in ruins. This consideration instilled a little enthusiasm in him, and work began apace. He was also very busy, travelling to Caen every week to see the prefect and influential members of the Council. The construction of the timber frames was almost complete when he finally received assurances that an engineer would be sent to make a report, on the basis of which the Council would vote on the application. The engineer spent a whole day in Bonneville. He was a pleasant man, and gladly accepted an invitation from the Chanteaus to lunch after his walk on the beach. They refrained discreetly from asking his opinion, to avoid influencing him, but at table he showed such gallantry to Pauline that even she began to feel certain of success. And so, when Lazare returned from a trip to Caen a fortnight later, the whole household was astonished and appalled by the news that he brought. He was speechless with rage: would they believe it, that poseur of an engineer had put in a damning report! His language had remained polite, but he had made mock of every piece of timber, using an extraordinary number of technical terms. In any case, this was only to be expected, for these gentlemen wouldn't accept that even an official rabbit-hutch could be constructed without their say-so! And the worst of it was that the Council, after reading the report, had turned down the grant application.

This plunged the young man into a new crisis of discouragement. The groynes were complete, he could swear they would stand up to the biggest tides and that all the official engineers put together would burst with jealous rage at the sight, but that wouldn't put the money back into his cousin's pocket, and Lazare reproached himself bitterly for having dragged her into this disaster. However, Pauline, overcoming her economical instincts, insisted on taking responsibility for the whole thing, reminding him that she had made him accept the advance: it was an act of charity, she had no regrets, and would gladly have given more to save the unfortunate village. However, when the carpenter sent in his bill, she could not repress a gesture of pained surprise: the four thousand francs of the estimate had swollen to almost eight. All told, she had poured over twenty thousand francs into those few timbers, which might simply get swept away by the next storm.

By now Pauline's fortune had shrunk to around forty thousand francs. This meant a yearly income of two thousand, barely enough to live on, should she ever find herself alone and homeless. Her money had been gradually draining away on household bills, which she continued generously to fund. But she did begin to keep a close eye on this expenditure, with the energy of a prudent housekeeper. The Chanteaus no longer had even their three hundred francs a month, for, after the mother's death, it was found that a certain number of securities had been sold, with no trace of where the money had gone. When her own income was added to theirs, Pauline had little more than four hundred francs a month, and since the household expenses were substantial, she had to perform miracles of economy to safeguard the money she needed for her charitable works. Doctor Cazenove's trusteeship had come to an end the previous winter, and since Pauline was now of age, she had complete discretion over her money and her person. Admittedly, the doctor had never really got in her way, as he refused to be consulted, and his authority had legally ceased for some weeks before either of them realized as much. But she felt more mature and independent, like a complete woman, now that she was the mistress of the house, with no accounts to render to anybody, for her uncle begged her to deal with everything without bothering him. Lazare, too, hated anything to do with money. So Pauline held the common purse, stepping into her aunt's shoes with a practical common sense that sometimes made the two men marvel. Only Véronique found Mademoiselle dreadfully stingy: didn't they now have to make do with a single pound of butter every Saturday?

One day followed another with monotonous regularity. This order, this unvarying domestic routine, meant happiness for Pauline, but only made Lazare's boredom worse. Never had he gone about the house with such a feeling of disquiet, since she had cast her spell of cheerful calm over every room. The completion of the beach works came as a huge relief, for every occupation became an obsession with him; but no sooner had he slipped back into idleness than he was consumed again by shame and anxiety. Each morning he made fresh plans for the future. He had abandoned as unworthy of him the idea of launching a newspaper, and he raged against the poverty that prevented him from quietly devoting himself to some great literary or historical work. Finally, he toyed with the idea of becoming a teacher, taking exams if necessary, to provide the income to support his work as a man of letters. Between himself and Pauline there seemed to be nothing left except their old camaraderie, a habitual affection which again made them like brother and sister. Despite their intimate proximity, Lazare never spoke of the marriage, either because he had completely forgotten about it, or because it had been so much discussed that it was taken for granted. For her part, she also avoided mentioning it, convinced that Lazare would consent at the first word. And yet, a little of his desire for her had been slipping away every day; she sensed as much, but without realizing that her inability to relieve his boredom had no other cause.

One evening at dusk, when she went upstairs to tell him that dinner was ready, she caught him hastily concealing something she could not identify.

'What's that?' she asked, with a laugh. 'A poem for my birthday?'

'No, of course not!' he stammered in confusion. 'It's nothing.'

It was an old glove that Louise had left behind, which he had just discovered behind a pile of books. The glove had retained its peculiarly musky scent of Saxony leather, softened by the vanilla sweetness of Louise's favourite heliotrope perfume. Lazare, who was highly susceptible to smells, was violently disturbed by this blend of flower and flesh, and had been standing there in distraction with the glove pressed to his lips, drinking in voluptuous reflections.

From that day onwards, across the gaping void that his mother's death had left inside him, he began once more to desire Louise. He had doubtless never forgotten her, but the memory had remained dormant while he was grieving, and it had needed that token of her to bring it vividly back to life, with the very warmth of her breath. Once he was alone, he picked up the glove again, inhaled its scent, kissed it, and imagined that he was once more holding her tight in his arms, burying his lips in her neck. The nervous tension in which he lived, the mental fever brought on by his long idleness, made this sensual intoxication all the more thrilling: it was a luxurious debauchery, and it left him drained. He would emerge from such sessions angry with himself, then relapse once more, driven by a passion beyond his control. This increased his sombre mood, until he even came to behave rudely to his cousin, as if blaming her for his own weakness. She no longer had any physical appeal for him, and he would occasionally flee in the middle of a cheerful conversation they were having, to lock himself away and indulge his vice, wallowing in burning recollections of the other girl. Afterwards he would come back downstairs, feeling disgusted with life.

In the course of a month, he changed so completely that a despairing Pauline spent the nights in torment. During the day she could still put a brave face on it, keeping herself perpetually busy in the house which she now managed with gentle authority. But at night, once she had closed her door, she could allow herself to grieve, her courage evaporated, and she wept like a feeble child. No hope remained in her, and all her good intentions were rebuffed ever more harshly. Could it really be that charity was not enough, that you could love someone yet still not make them happy? For she saw that her cousin was indeed unhappy, perhaps through her own fault. And then, underlying such doubts, there lurked the growing fear of a rival influence. For a long time, she had reassured herself by attributing Lazare's black moods to their recent bereavement, but now there came back to her the idea of Louise, which had first struck her the day after Madame Chanteau's death; then, she had chased it away with proud confidence in the power of her own love, but now it revived every night in her defeated heart.

From then on Pauline was haunted. Once she had put down her candlestick, she would slump on the edge of her bed, without the will to take off her dress. The cheerfulness she had shown all day, her patient and ordered work, now weighed on her like over-heavy garments. The day, like those that had gone before and those that would follow, had been spent in the despondent atmosphere of the house contaminated by Lazare's boredom. What was the use of trying to be cheerful, since she was no longer able to warm that beloved place with her ray of sunshine? Lazare's cruel remark re-echoed in her mind: their life was too lonely; her jealousy was to blame for driving others away. She would not name Louise, she did not want to think about her, but she could not help seeing her passing by, amusing Lazare with her coquettish languor, cheering him up with a swirl of her skirts. The minutes would trickle by, and still Pauline could not get that picture of them out of her mind. It was clear Louise was the one Lazare was waiting for; nothing could be easier than to make him better by fetching her. And every evening when Pauline went upstairs and slumped wearily on the edge of her bed, she would see the same vision, tormented by the thought that the happiness of those dearest to her was perhaps in the other woman's hands.

She still experienced rebellious feelings, however, when she would jump up from her bed, rush to the window and fling it wide, gasping for breath. And she would lean there for hours, gazing out across the horizon and the beach, high above the sea whose lament rose in her ears, unable to sleep, while the breeze fanned her burning bosom. No, she could never be so lamentable as to tolerate the return of that girl! Had she not caught them in each other's arms? Was that not the lowest form of treachery, committed close to her, in a neighbouring bedroom, in the home that she regarded as her own? The callousness of it was unforgivable, and she would only be conniving if she brought them back together. The sights she then imagined rekindled her jealous resentment, she choked with sobbing as she hid her face in her bare arms, her lips pressed against her skin. The night wore on, the breeze blew around her neck and ruffled her hair, without calming the blood that pulsed angrily through her veins. But even in her most furious moments of revolt, a hidden, unstoppable battle was carrying on between her goodness and her passion. A gentle voice within her, which still felt quite foreign, whispered persistently of the joys of charity and the happiness of giving oneself to others. She tried to silence it: self-sacrifice carried to the point of cowardice was idiotic; but she listened to it nonetheless, for soon she could not help herself. She gradually recognized the voice as her own, and reasoned with herself: what did her suffering matter, so long as those she loved were happy? Her sobbing abated as she listened, exhausted and out of sorts, but not yet vanquished, to the sound of the tide rising through the darkness.

One night she had gone to bed after crying for a long time by the window. As soon as she had blown out her candle and found herself in darkness, her eyes wide open, she came to a sudden decision: first thing in the morning, she would make her uncle write to Louise and invite her to spend a month in Bonneville. Nothing seemed easier or more natural, and she immediately fell into a deep sleep, the most restful she had known for weeks. But when she came down to breakfast the next morning and found herself sitting once more between her uncle and her cousin, at the family table set with three bowls of milk, she suddenly felt a choking sensation, and saw her courage ebb away.

'You aren't eating,' said Chanteau. 'What's the matter?'

'Nothing,' she replied. 'On the contrary, I slept like a log.'

The mere sight of Lazare rekindled her inner struggle. He was eating in silence, already weary of the new day that was beginning, and she could not bring herself to give him up to another woman. The idea that Louise would take him from her and comfort him with her kisses was unbearable. Yet once he had left the room, she tried to carry out her resolution.

'Are your hands any worse today?' she asked her uncle.

He looked at his hands, which were again becoming pocked with tophus, and painfully flexed the joints.

'No,' he replied. 'The right even seems a little easier... If the curé comes round, we'll have a game.'

Then, after a pause:

'Why do you ask?'

She had no doubt been hoping he would be unable to write. She blushed and took the easy route of putting off the letter to the following day, with a faltering:

'Oh! I was just curious!'

From that day on, she had no peace of mind. In her room, after the weeping fits, she would overcome her feelings and vow to dictate the letter to her uncle in the morning. But as soon as she was back in the pattern of family life, surrounded by those she loved, her resolution failed her. It was the insignificant details that broke her heart: cutting her cousin a piece of bread, or telling Véronique to clean his shoes, all the ordinary, banal routine of family life. How happy they might have been, in these old familiar ways! What could be the use of bringing in an outsider? Why disturb the pleasant life they had been enjoying for so many years? The thought that one day it would no longer be her who would cut the bread and look after the clothes made her choke, and she saw all the hoped-for happiness of her existence crumbling to dust. This anguish, permeating every detail of her domestic work, now poisoned her busy days as mistress of the household.

'What's gone wrong?' she would sometimes ask herself aloud. 'We love each other, and yet we're not happy. Our affection only spreads misfortune around us.'

She was constantly trying to understand. Was it perhaps that her character and her cousin's were not well matched? She would willingly have given way and abdicated her own wishes, but she found this impossible because her common sense always prevailed, tempting her to impose the things that seemed reasonable to her. Often her patience failed her and led to petulant moments. She would have preferred to laugh off such irritations and drown them in gaiety, but she could no longer do this, for her nerves too were becoming frayed.

'A fine state of affairs!' Véronique repeated from morning till night. 'There are just three of you, but you'll end up tearing each other to pieces... Madame could be pretty unpleasant on her day, but at least while she was alive, you never got to throwing pots and pans at each other.'

Chanteau too was feeling the effects of this slow and inexplicable disaffection. When he had an attack, he bawled, as the maid put it, louder than ever. He became a capricious and violent invalid, constantly plaguing them all. The house was again becoming a hellish place to live.

Then Pauline, in the final throes of her jealousy, asked herself whether she had any right to impose her own happiness on Lazare. Of course, she wanted above all else for him to be happy, even at the cost of tears for herself. So why keep him secluded like this and make him endure a solitude which he seemed to find painful? No doubt he did still love her, and he would come back to her when he could judge her better, in comparison with the other girl. In any case, she ought to let him choose: it was only fair, and the idea of fairness was crucial to her.

Once a quarter, Pauline went to Caen to draw their dividends. She would set off in the morning and return the same evening, after working through an exhaustive list of small purchases and errands which she had drawn up during the preceding three months. That year, when it came to the June visit, the family waited in vain for her to come home, delaying dinner till nine o'clock. Chanteau was very concerned and sent Lazare off along the road, fearing an accident. On the other hand Véronique, quite unmoved, said they were wrong to be alarmed: Mademoiselle, finding herself running late and wanting to finish her errands, must have decided to stay overnight. They all slept badly in Bonneville, and at breakfast next morning their fears revived. About noon, as his father could barely sit still, Lazare had just decided to set off to Arromanches, when Véronique, who was keeping watch along the road, rushed in, exclaiming:

'Here comes Mademoiselle!'

Chanteau's chair had to be wheeled out onto the terrace, and father and son waited there while Véronique told them what she had seen.

'It's Malivoire's berline… I recognized Mademoiselle from way off by her crêpe ribbons. But it's a funny thing, it looks like there's someone with her… Whatever can be keeping that blasted nag?'

At last the carriage stopped by the door. Lazare had stepped forwards and was already opening his mouth to question Pauline, who had jumped nimbly down, when he stopped in amazement: another young woman in a pin-striped lilac silk dress was also jumping down after her. They were laughing together like good friends. His surprise was so great that he turned back towards his father, saying:

'She's brought Louise!'

'Louise! ah, that's a fine idea!' Chanteau exclaimed.

And when they stood side by side before him, one still in her deep mourning and the other in her pretty summer toilette, he continued, delighted at this fresh source of entertainment:

'So, you two have made up, have you?… You know, I never did understand what the matter was. Silly, wasn't it? And it was very naughty of you, my poor Louisette, to still be cross with us while we've been through such sad times!… Anyhow, that's all over and done with now, isn't it?'

The two girls stood there motionless and embarrassed. They blushed and avoided one another's gaze. Louise kissed Chanteau to hide her self-consciousness. But he wanted explanations.

'So, you bumped into each other, did you?'

At which Louise turned towards her friend, her eyes affectionately moist.

'Pauline was going up to see my father. I was just coming home. You mustn't be cross with her for staying the night, I insisted on it… As the telegraph doesn't go beyond Arromanches,* we thought we'd get here as quickly as any message could… Am I forgiven?'

She kissed Chanteau again in her former caressing manner. He wanted nothing more: when things were going in the direction of his pleasure, he was happy to give his approval.

'And what about Lazare,' he added, 'don't you have any words for him?'

The young man had been standing back, with an awkward smile on his face. His father's remark completed his confusion, especially as Louise blushed once more, without taking a step towards him. Why was she there? Why had his cousin brought home this rival, whom she had driven out with such violence? He could not get over his astonishment.

'Embrace her, Lazare!' said Pauline softly, 'since she doesn't dare.'

She seemed very white in her mourning attire, but her expression was tranquil and her eyes bright. She looked at them both with the maternal, serious expression that she assumed at important moments of household responsibility, and simply smiled when he finally brushed ⊺ ⊔⊔⊔⊔⊔ ⊔ ⊔⊔⊔⊔⊔⊔⊔⊔ ⊔⊔⊔⊔⊔⊔ ⊔⊔⊔⊔ ⊔⊔⊔ ⊔⊔⊔⊔.

When she saw this, Véronique, who was standing there with arms dangling, rushed back into her kitchen in stupefaction. She too was at a loss to understand. What a spineless way to behave, after everything that had happened! Mademoiselle was getting quite impossible, insisting on being so kind to everyone. Not content with dragging all those lousy brats into her kitchen, among her crockery, she was now bringing home mistresses for Monsieur Lazare! A fine state that would put the house in! Once she had let off steam by grumbling a bit more over her stove, she came back out and shouted:

'You do know lunch has been ready for the last hour... The potatoes are burnt to a crisp!'

They all tucked in with relish, but only Chanteau laughed freely, too cheerful to notice the continuing awkwardness between the other three. They behaved towards each other with affectionate consideration, beneath which, however, there lingered an uneasy sadness, as after a quarrel where all is forgiven, but the memory of some irreparable wrong still lingers. Then the afternoon was spent in settling the newcomer back in to her room on the first floor. That evening, if Madame Chanteau had come downstairs to dinner with her quick, light step, the past would have seemed to come completely back to life.

The awkwardness lasted for the best part of a week. Lazare, who did not dare question Pauline, was still unable to understand what he regarded as an extraordinary caprice, for the idea of a sacrifice, a choice deliberately made and generously offered, never crossed his mind. Even he, in the throes of the desire that ravaged his idle days, had never considered marrying Louise. So now that they were all three together again, they found themselves in an artificial position, which troubled them all. There were embarrassed silences, and sentences that remained unfinished for fear of an unintended meaning. Pauline, surprised at this unexpected outcome, felt compelled to exaggerate her laughter in the hope that they could rediscover the carefree atmosphere of the past. But her first emotion was one of deep joy, for she felt that Lazare was coming back to her. Louise's presence had calmed him and he almost ignored her, avoiding being alone with her, appalled at the thought that he might again betray his cousin's confidence. He turned instead to Pauline, tormented by a feverish affection for her and proclaiming her in emotional terms the very best of women, a true saint, of whom he was not worthy. She felt so happy, rejoicing ecstatically in her victory as she saw him treat Louise with such coolness. At the end of the week she even reproached him for it.

'Why do you always run away whenever she and I are together?... It makes me feel bad. She hasn't come here to be shunned by us.'

Lazare avoided answering with a vague gesture. Then she allowed herself the only allusion she would ever make:

'If I brought her home, it was to let you know that I forgave you long ago. I wanted to erase that horrid dream, and now it's all gone... You see, I'm not afraid any more, I can trust you both.'

He took her in his arms and squeezed her tight. Then he promised to be nice to Louise.

From that moment on, the days slipped by in charming intimacy. Lazare no longer seemed bored. Instead of going and shutting himself up in his room like a recluse made sick by isolation, he invented games and suggested walks from which they returned invigorated by the fresh air. And it was then that, imperceptibly, Louise began to take him back. He became used to her presence, dared to offer her his arm, then succumbed once more to the distracting perfume given off by her every lacy flounce. At first, he fought against it and tried to break away as soon as he felt the intoxication mounting. But in their clifftop walks, whenever there was a stream to be jumped, it was Pauline who called to him to help the girl; she herself would leap boldly across like a boy, whereas Louise, shrieking like an injured skylark, surrendered herself into the young man's arms. Then, on the way back home, she would lean on him, and their stifled laughs and whispered confidences began again. Nothing of this yet worried Pauline, who marched sturdily on, unaware that she was gambling with her happiness by not appearing weary or needing help; the healthy smell of her housekeeping arms was no distraction to anyone. With a kind of smiling bravado, she made them walk ahead of her arm in arm, as though to demonstrate her trust.

In any case, neither would have betrayed it. Even if Lazare was falling under Louise's spell again, he tried to steel himself, and afterwards made a point of being even more solicitous to Pauline. This was a surprise of his flesh to which he yielded with delight, while vowing that this time, the game would not go beyond harmless flirtation. Why should he deny himself this pleasure, since he was determined to behave like an honourable man? And Louise had even greater scruples: she did not imagine herself to be behaving like a coquette, for she was overly affectionate by nature, offering herself in a gesture or a breath, without realizing it, but she would never have done or said anything she thought might upset Pauline. She was moved to tears by her friend's forgiveness, and wanted to show herself worthy of it; she adored Pauline with the sort of exuberant feminine passion that finds expression in vows and kisses, and all sorts of passionate endearments. So she kept a constant eye on her, ready to run over if she thought she saw the slightest furrow cross her brow. Annoyed at her momentary lapse, she would suddenly drop Lazare's arm for Pauline's, clinging to her and trying to amuse her, even pretending to cold-shoulder the young man. Never had she appeared so charming as in this constant emotional vacillation between her urge to please and her consternation at doing so, as she filled the house with the swirl of her skirts and her caressing, kitten-like manners.

Little by little, Pauline's feeling of torment returned. Her brief hope and momentary triumph only made it crueller. She was not suffering those violent paroxysms and outbursts of jealousy that used to drive her wild for an hour at a stretch, but rather a slow, crushing sensation, as if a heavy weight had fallen onto her and was pressing down harder with each passing minute. Now there was no possible respite, no hope: she was surely plumbing the depths of her misfortune. True, she could not fault their behaviour, they smothered her with kindness, as they fought against the attraction which drew them to each other; but it was precisely this kindness that distressed her, for she was beginning to see clearly again, now that they seemed to be conspiring to avoid paining her with their love for each other. She found the two lovers' pity unbearable. The hurried whisperings whenever she left them on their own, the sudden silences when she reappeared, Louise's violent kisses, and Lazare's affectionate humility—were these not so many confessions of their love? She would rather they had been guilty and deceiving her secretly, whereas all this scrupulous honesty, these compensating caresses, which told her everything, left her quite disarmed, without either the will or the energy to defend her own position. The day when she had brought her rival home, she had intended to fight her if necessary; but what could she do against a couple of children who seemed so dismayed at being in love with each other? She had brought this on herself; she could simply have married Lazare, without bothering about whether she was forcing his hand. But even today, despite her torment, the idea of using him in that way and demanding the fulfilment of a promise that he doubtless regretted, was repugnant to her. Even if it killed her, she would have refused him if he had loved another woman.

Meanwhile, Pauline went on playing the mother's role to her little household, nursing Chanteau through another illness, lending a hand to Véronique, whose standards of cleanliness were slipping, as well as pretending to treat Lazare and Louise as boisterous children, so as to be able to smile at their escapades. She managed to laugh louder than they did, a clear, clarion laugh whose limpid notes rang out in testimony to her health and courageous vitality. The house was becoming a happy place again. She made herself busy from morning till night, refusing to go with the two of them on their walks on the pretext of spring cleaning, washing, or jam-making. Lazare, especially, was becoming quite noisy, whistling on the stairs, rapping on doors, and complaining that the days were so short and uneventful. Although he did nothing about it, the new enthusiasm that had taken him over seemed to demand more of his time and strength than he possessed. Yet again, he was going to conquer the world, and every dinner time he would propose extraordinary new schemes for the future. He had already lost interest in literature, and admitted he had given up preparing for the teaching qualification that he had been planning to take. For a long time, this had been his excuse for shutting himself up in his room, but such was his despondency, he had never so much as opened a book. Now he began to scoff at his own stupidity: wouldn't it have been idiotic to tie himself down like that, just in order to write novels and plays later on? No, politics was the thing, and he had a clear plan: he was slightly acquainted with the deputy for Caen, he would go with him to Paris as his secretary, and in a few months he would have made a name for himself. The Empire* was in great need of bright young men. When Pauline, concerned at this wild stream of ideas, tried to calm his enthusiasm by suggesting some smaller, steady position, he protested against her prudence and jokingly called her an old granny. And the clamour began again, and the house rang with an exaggerated merriment which betrayed the anxiety of an unspoken distress.

One day, when Lazare and Louise had gone to Verchemont on their own, Pauline needed a recipe for reviving velvet, and went upstairs to search for it in her cousin's great wardrobe, where she thought she had seen it on a scrap of paper between the pages of a book. And there, among some pamphlets, she discovered Louise's old glove, that forgotten memento which he had used secretly in his intimacy with his own to the point of hallucination. In a sudden flash of illumination, she recognized it as the object her cousin had hidden from her with such embarrassment that evening when she had burst in to tell him that dinner was ready. She collapsed into a chair, devastated by this revelation. Good God, he had already desired the girl even before she had come back, he had been living with her presence, wearing out the flimsy material with his lips because it retained a little of her scent! She was convulsed with sobbing and her eyes filled with tears as she stared at the glove, which she was still holding in shaking hands.

'Well, Mademoiselle, did you find it?' Véronique's loud voice called from the landing, as she came up behind her. 'I tell you, the best thing is to rub it with some bacon rind.'

She entered, and at first did not understand why Pauline was crying and clutching an old glove. But she sniffed the air in the room and finally guessed the cause of her despair.

'Well now!' she said, with the brutal frankness that was increasingly her way, 'this is something you really should have expected! I did warn you, ages ago. You bring them together again, they have fun... perhaps my mistress was right after all: he finds that kitten of a girl more of a turn-on than you.'

She shook her head and went on talking to herself, in sombre tones:

'Oh yes, Madame was clear-sighted, whatever her faults. I still can't get over the fact that she's dead.'

That evening, once Pauline had locked herself in her room and put her candle down on the chest of drawers, she slumped on the edge of her bed, telling herself that she must marry off Louise and Lazare. All day long, her head had been throbbing with a great buzzing sensation that had stopped her thinking clearly; and it was only at this hour of the night, when she could let herself go emotionally without anyone seeing, that she had come to this inescapable conclusion. They must be married, the idea resounded within her like an order, like a voice of reason and justice that she was powerless to silence. At one point, for all her courage, she jerked round in terror, thinking she heard her aunt shouting at her to obey. Then she flung herself on the bed, still fully dressed, and buried her head in the pillow to stifle her cries. Oh! to give him away to another! to know that he was in another woman's arms, for ever, with no hope of getting him back! No! she couldn't have that courage, she'd rather go on leading this wretched existence. Neither of them would have him, neither she nor that girl, and his face would grow wrinkled with waiting! For a long time, she lay struggling with herself, racked by a furious jealousy which conjured up deplorably carnal images before her eyes. As always, her reaction, which neither experience nor reason had been able to moderate, was violent and impetuous. Then, however, she collapsed in physical exhaustion.

Too weary to undress, Pauline lay for a long time on her back and debated with herself. She managed to prove to herself that Louise could do more for Lazare's happiness than she could. Had not that fragile child with her loving caresses already shaken him out of his boredom? He no doubt needed her continually clinging round his neck like that, driving away his gloomy thoughts, his terror of death, with her kisses. And Pauline belittled herself, thinking she was too cold and lacking in amorous, feminine graces, with nothing to offer but her goodness, which was far from enough for a young man. One further consideration finally convinced her. She was ruined, and her cousin's plans for the future, plans which so worried her, were going to take a great deal of money. Was it right to condemn him to the family's present penury, their mediocre lifestyle that he obviously found hard to bear? Theirs would be a terrible existence, poisoned by continual regrets and the bitter recriminations of failed ambition. She could only bring him the acrimony of poverty, whereas Louise, who was wealthy, would open the way to the great career of which he dreamed. People said the girl's father was keeping a job open for his future son-in-law, no doubt some position in the bank; and, though Lazare affected to despise financiers, satisfactory arrangements would certainly be made. She could hesitate no longer: it now seemed clear to her that she would be committing an unworthy act by not marrying them off. As she lay there unable to sleep, their union came to seem a natural and necessary outcome, which she must hasten, or lose her self-respect.

The whole night went by while Pauline wrestled with this dilemma. At daybreak, she at last undressed. She was very calm and lay in bed enjoying complete rest, though still unable to sleep. She had never before felt so blithe, so inspired, so detached. This was the end: she had cast off the shackles of her egotism, she had no further hopes in anyone or anything, and she felt deep down the subtle gratification of self-sacrifice. She had even lost her old desire to be the sole source of her family's happiness, for she now saw that authoritarian urge as the last retreat of her jealousy. Her pride in self-abnegation had left her, and she accepted that her loved ones could find happiness without her help. This was the pinnacle of love for others: to withdraw completely, to give everything and still feel it was not enough, to love so deeply as to rejoice in a felicity that one has not caused, and cannot share. The sun was rising when she fell into a deep sleep.

That morning Pauline came downstairs very late. When she awoke, she was delighted to feel the previous night's resolutions still clear and firm in her mind. Then she realized that she had forgotten about herself, and must think about her own future in the altered circumstances in which she would find herself. Though she might have the courage to unite Lazare and Louise, she would certainly never be brave enough to live with them and share in their private happiness; devotion has its limits, and she feared a return of her violent outbursts in some terrible scene which would be the end of her. Besides, was she not doing enough already, and could anyone be so cruel as to impose on her such a pointless torture? Her decision was thus immediate and irrevocable: she would go away and leave this house full of disturbing memories behind. Her whole life would be changed, but that did not deter her.

At breakfast, she behaved with the same calm cheerfulness as ever. The sight of Lazare and Louise sitting side by side, whispering and laughing, did not weaken her resolve, it simply left a great chill in her heart. Then, since it was Saturday, she encouraged them to go out for a long walk together so that she would be alone when Doctor Cazenove came. They went off, and Pauline took the additional precaution of walking down the road to meet the doctor. As soon as he saw her, he invited her to climb up into his cabriolet and drive to the house with him. But she begged him to get down, and they walked slowly back together, while Martin drove the empty vehicle a hundred metres ahead.

In a few simple words, Pauline poured out her heart. She told him everything, her plan of giving Lazare to Louise, and her determination to leave the house. She felt it necessary to make this confession to be sure she was not just acting on impulse, and the old doctor was the only one who could hear it.

Cazenove stopped abruptly in the middle of the road and put his long, lean arms around her. He was trembling with emotion, he planted a great kiss on her hair, and called her 'tu', with affection.

'You are right, my dear girl... And I'm delighted, you know, for things could have turned out even worse. I've been anxious about it for months, and coming to your house has been a trial, knowing how unhappy you were... Oh! they've robbed you good and proper, those nice people! First your money, then your heart...'

Pauline started to interrupt him.

'My dear friend, please... You're being unfair to them.'

'Perhaps, but that doesn't stop me from being pleased on your account. Go on, then, give your Lazare away to that woman, it's not as if you were making her much of a present! Oh, I dare say he has some charm, and the best of intentions, but I'd rather he made her unhappy, instead of you. Those young fellows who find life a bore are just too much of a burden, even for broad shoulders like yours. I'd rather you found yourself a hearty butcher-lad—yes, really—who'd be full of laughter all day and night.'

Then, seeing her eyes fill with tears, he added:

'All right, so you love him, let's say no more about it. Give me another hug, since you are brave enough to act so sensibly... He's such a fool not to understand!'

He took her by the arm and pressed her close to him. Then they talked earnestly together as they resumed their walk. It would certainly be a good idea for her to leave Bonneville, and he undertook to find her a situation. It so happened that he had a relative in Saint-Lô,* a rich elderly lady who was looking for a female companion. It would suit Pauline perfectly, particularly as the old lady, who had no children of her own, might well grow fond of her and, in due course, perhaps even adopt her. Everything was settled, he promised her a definite reply within three days, and they agreed not to tell anyone about her determination to leave. She was afraid that it might be seen as a threat, but her intention was to bring about the marriage and then leave quietly the following day, having become surplus to requirements.

On the third day Pauline received a letter from the doctor: she was expected at Saint-Lô as soon as she was available. It was that same day, while Lazare was out of the house, that she took Louise down to the bottom of the kitchen garden and sat her down on an old bench in the shelter of a tamarisk bush. Looking out over the low wall, they could see only the sea and the sky, a vast blue expanse bisected at the horizon by a long straight line.

'My dear girl,' said Pauline in her maternal voice, 'let's have a sisterly chat, shall we?... You love me a little?'

'You know I do!' interrupted Louise, putting an arm around her.

'Well then, if you do, it's wrong of you not to tell me everything... Why do you keep secrets from me?'

'But I haven't got any secrets.'

'Oh yes you have, just think harder... Come on, tell me all.'

For a moment, they looked so closely into each other's eyes that their warm breath mingled. Then the eyes of the one grew troubled under the clear, unruffled gaze of the other. The silence was becoming painful.

'Tell me all about it. Talking about something is the first step to making it right, but the things we hide can easily fester... It wouldn't be nice for us to quarrel, would it, and risk a repeat of what made us all so sorry?'

At this Louise burst into a violent sobbing fit. She clasped Pauline convulsively round the waist, and buried her face against her friend's shoulder, stammering through her tears:

'Oh! it's so unkind of you to bring that up! We weren't going to mention it again, ever! Send me away at once, rather than hurt me like that!'

Pauline tried to calm her, in vain.

'No, I know what you're getting at... You still suspect me. Why do you talk to me about secrets? I haven't got a secret, I do my utmost to make sure you have nothing to reproach me with. It's not my fault if there are things that worry you: I'm even careful how I laugh, though it may not show... But, if you don't believe me, I'll go away, go away at once.'

They were all alone in front of the vast, open expanse. The kitchen garden, scorched by the west wind, lay at their feet like a patch of waste ground, while beyond it the immobile sea extended into the infinite.

'But listen!' Pauline exclaimed, 'I'm not blaming you for anything, on the contrary, I want to reassure you.'

Then, taking Louise by the shoulders and forcing her to look up at her, she said gently, like a mother questioning her daughter:

'You are in love with Lazare, aren't you?... And he loves you too, I know.'

The blood rushed to Louise's cheeks. She was shaking more violently, and she tried to tear herself away and flee.

'Oh dear, I must have expressed myself clumsily for you not to grasp my meaning! Would I broach a subject like this just to torment you? You love each other, don't you? Well, I want to see the pair of you married! It's as simple as that!'

In bewilderment, Louise stopped struggling. Her tears ceased and she froze in astonishment, her hands dangling inertly.

'But what about you?'

'My dear, I've been thinking things over quite seriously for weeks now, especially at night, in those wakeful hours when you see things more clearly... And I have realized that my feelings for Lazare were just those of a good friend. Haven't you noticed it yourself? We are comrades, almost like two boys, there's no lovers' passion between us...'

She was casting around for the words to give plausibility to her lie. But her rival was still staring at her, as though seeing through to the hidden meaning behind what she had said.

'Why are you lying?' she murmured at last. 'Is it possible to stop loving, once you have been in love?'

Pauline grew troubled.

'Well, what does that matter? You two are in love, it's perfectly natural for him to marry you... I was brought up with him, and I'll still be a sister to him. When you've waited so long for each other, your ideas can change... And then, there are lots of other reasons...'

She was aware that she was floundering and losing the thread, but she ploughed on, carried away by her urge for sincerity:

'Oh! my dear, let me have my way! If I still love him enough to want him to be your husband, it's because I now believe you are necessary for his happiness. Can you object to that? Wouldn't you do the same in my place? Come on, let's talk it over as friends. Won't you join in my little plot? Can't we agree to work together to force him to find happiness? Even if he gets cross and feels he owes me a debt, you must help me persuade him, for you're the one he loves, and the one he needs... Be my accomplice, I beg you, and let's settle everything now, while we're alone.'

But Louise, seeing how trembling and broken-hearted she was while uttering those pleas, put in a last protest.

'No, no, I can't accept!... It would be an abominable thing to do. You still love him, I can tell, and you're just looking for ways to torment yourself even more... Instead of helping you, I'm going to tell him everything. Yes, as soon as he comes back...'

Then Pauline threw her charitable arms round her again and pressed her head to her own breast to prevent her from continuing.

'Hush, you naughty child... We must do it, we must think about him.'

Silence fell again, and they remained in their embrace. Her resistance overcome, Louise was giving in, yielding with her usual caressing languor, and new floods of tears welled up in her eyes, but happy ones now, trickling slowly down her cheeks. Without speaking, she squeezed her friend several times, as if this were the most discreet and heartfelt way she could find to express her gratitude. Pauline seemed so much above her, so elevated and self-denying, that she did not even dare look up for fear of meeting her gaze. After a few minutes, however, she risked tipping her head back, all smiling confusion, and reached up to give Pauline a silent kiss. In the distance, beneath an immaculate sky, the sea's blue immensity lay unruffled. It was a long moment of purity and simplicity, in which the thoughts floated, unspoken, between them.

When Lazare returned home, Pauline went up to see him in his room, that big, much-loved study where they had grown up together. She was eager to see her task through to the end, that very day. She did not beat about the bush with him, but spoke resolutely. The room was full of memories of days gone by: clumps of dried seaweed still lay about, the model of the groynes cluttered the piano, and the table was covered in scientific textbooks and sheet music.

'Lazare,' she began, 'can we have a talk? I've got something serious to say to you.'

He seemed surprised, and came over to stand in front of her.

'What is it?... Has father taken a turn for the worse?'

'No, listen... It's time we tackled the question, avoiding it will get us nowhere. As you remember, my aunt planned for us to be married; we talked about it a lot at the time, but nothing more has been said for months. Well, I think it would be sensible now for us to give up the idea.'

The young man had turned pale, but he did not allow her to finish, exclaiming angrily:

'Why? What are you on about?... Aren't you my wife? Tomorrow we'll go and see the abbé, if you like, and tell him to get on with it... Is that what you call something serious?'

She replied in a quiet voice:

'It must be serious, since it's making you angry... I say again, we need to talk about it. True, we're old friends and comrades, but I'm afraid we really aren't cut out to be lovers. What's the good of insisting on something that could well make neither of us happy?'

Then Lazare burst out in a flood of semi-coherent exclamations. Was she trying to pick a fight with him? But he really couldn't be clinging round her neck the whole time! If the wedding had been put off month after month, surely she realized it wasn't his fault? And it was quite unfair to suggest he didn't love her any more. He had been so much in love with her, and in that very room too, that he didn't dare let his fingers brush against her for fear of getting carried away and misbehaving. This reminder of the past brought a blush to Pauline's cheeks: he was right, she remembered his passionate fit, as his burning breath played upon her skin. But how distant were those deliciously thrilling hours, and what a cold brotherly friendship he displayed towards her now! So it was with an expression of sadness that she replied:

'My poor dear, if you really loved me, instead of arguing with me like this, you would already be sobbing in my arms and finding a different way of persuading me.'

He turned still paler and made a vague gesture of protest as he sank into a chair.

'No!' she continued, 'it's clear that you're no longer in love with me... It can't be helped, we were probably not made for one another. When we were shut up here together, you couldn't help thinking about me. But afterwards you changed your mind, it didn't last because I had nothing about me to hold your affection.'

He rocked in his chair as he stammered out, in a final burst of exasperation:

'So, what are you driving at? What's all this in aid of, I ask you? I get home, calm as you like, and come up here to put my slippers on, then you ambush me and launch into this harangue, without warning... I'm not in love with you any more, we aren't made for one another, we must break off the marriage... Once again, what does it all mean?'

Pauline, who had moved closer to him, said slowly:

'What it means is that you love another woman, and I advise you to marry her.'

For a moment, Lazare remained silent. Then he resorted to sarcasm: fine, so they were back to having one of their old scenes, her jealousy was about to mess everything up again! She couldn't bear to see him cheerful for a single day, without wanting to drive everyone away from him. Pauline listened to him with deep sadness; then she suddenly laid her shaking hands on his shoulders and uttered an involuntary cry from the depths of her heart:

'Oh, my friend, how can you believe that I am trying to torment you? Can't you see that all I want is to make you happy, that I would endure anything to win you a single hour's pleasure? You love Louise, don't you? Well, I'm telling you to marry her... Understand me: I no longer count, I'm giving her to you!'

He stared at her, alarmed. With his nervous, unbalanced nature his feelings would flip from one extreme to the other at the slightest jolt. His eyelids fluttered and he burst into tears.

'Don't say that, I'm a miserable wretch! Yes, I despise myself for everything that's been happening in this house for years... I'm your debtor, you can't deny it! We took your money, I squandered it like a fool, and now I've sunk so low that you are releasing me from my bond out of charity and sheer pity, as if I were a man without courage or honour!'

'Lazare! Lazare!' she murmured, in horror.

But he leapt angrily to his feet and began striding about the room, beating his breast with his fists.

'Leave me alone! I should kill myself straight away, it's all I deserve... Aren't you the one I should be in love with? Isn't it appalling for me to desire that other girl, probably because she was never meant for me and isn't nearly so good and healthy as you, how should I know? When a man sinks to such depths, there must be dirt in his soul! You can see I'm not hiding anything, trying to make excuses... Listen, rather than accept your sacrifice, I'd sooner turn Louise out of the house myself, then run away to America and never see either of you again!'

For a long time, Pauline endeavoured to calm him down and reason with him. Could he not, just for once, take life as he found it, without exaggerating all the time? Couldn't he see that she was talking sense, after thinking everything over very carefully? The marriage would be excellent for all concerned. If she was able to talk about this so calmly, it was because, far from it being painful to her, she now wanted it to happen. But, carried away by her desire to convince him, she made a tactless allusion to Louise's fortune and hinted that, immediately after the marriage, Thibaudier would find his son-in-law a position.

'That's right,' he shouted in a fresh outburst of violence, 'try and bribe me now! Why not say it straight out, I mustn't want you any-more because I ruined you, so all that's left for me is to stoop even lower and look for some other rich girl to marry... No, definitely not, the very idea's disgusting! Never! do you hear me? Never!'

Pauline, at the end of her tether, stopped pleading with him. There was silence. Lazare, his legs wobbling, had subsided back into the chair, while she in turn paced slowly up and down the big room, lin-gering before each piece of furniture: those old familiar things—the table on which she had leant her elbows, the wardrobe where her child-hood toys were still stored, all the scattered memorabilia—instilled in her heart a hope that she tried to ignore, but whose sweet message gradually took root and swelled within her. Suppose he really did love her enough to refuse to give himself to another woman! But she knew too well how the first flush of his fine sentiments was often followed, the next day, by a failure of will. Besides, it was cowardly of her to harbour hope, and she feared being taken in by her own weakness.

'Think it over,' she finished, pausing in front of him. 'I don't want to torment us both any further... Tomorrow, I'm sure you'll see reason.'

The next day, however, went by in a most awkward atmosphere. A mood of covert gloom and bitterness hung depressingly over the house. Louise was red-eyed, Lazare shunned her, and shut himself away in his room for hours on end. Then in the following days the awkwardness gradually dispersed, and the old laughter, hushed whis-pers, and affectionate touching returned. Pauline still waited, a prey to wild hopes, against her better judgement. Before that dreadful uncertainty, she felt she had never really known what suffering was. Finally, one evening at dusk, as she was going down to the kitchen to fetch a candle, she came upon Lazare and Louise kissing in the passage. Louise fled with a giggle, while Lazare, emboldened by the shadows, grabbed Pauline in her turn and planted two great brotherly kisses on her cheeks.

'I have thought it over,' he murmured. 'You are the best and wisest of women… and I still love you, I love you as I loved my mother.'

She found the strength to reply:

'So it's settled then, I'm so glad.'

She dared not go into the kitchen for fear of fainting, she could tell how white she must look from the chill looking in her face. Without the candle, she went back upstairs to her room, saying that she had forgotten something. And there in the darkness she thought she was dying as she fought for breath, unable even to cry. What had she done to him, Oh God! that he should be so cruel as to pour salt on the wound like that? Why couldn't he have accepted immediately, that day when she had been at her strongest, unweakened by vain hopes? Now the sacrifice was a double one, she was losing him for the second time, and all the more painfully since she had imagined she might win him back. Heavens, she would be brave and bear it, but it was wrong to make her task such a dreadful one.

Everything was rapidly settled. Véronique was aghast and could make no sense of it: the world seemed to have been turned on its head since the death of Madame. But the person most shocked by this outcome was Chanteau. Normally happy to let things drift by and nod his approval of whatever people wanted, wrapped up in selfish enjoyment of the moments of respite he could win from his pain, he burst into tears when Pauline herself told him of the new arrangement. He stared at her and blurted out a breathless, incoherent confession: it wasn't his fault, years ago he had wanted things done differently, both the money and the marriage, but she knew full well he had been too ill. Then she kissed him, assuring him that she was the one making Lazare marry Louise, for the best of reasons. At first, he dared not believe her, and blinking with lingering sadness, he asked repeatedly:

'Do you mean it? Really?'

Then, seeing her laughing, he quickly felt better, and even became quite jolly. He was relieved at last, for that old business had lain heavy on his heart, though he had never dared mention it. He kissed Louisette on both cheeks, and in the evening, over dessert, he came out with another ribald ditty. And yet, just as he was going to bed, a final worry occurred to him.

'You will be staying with us, won't you?' he asked Pauline.

She hesitated for a moment, then answered, blushing at her lie:

'Yes, probably.'

The formalities took just over a month. Thibaudier, Louise's father, immediately gave his consent to Lazare, who was his godson. The only disagreement between them occurred two days before the wedding, when Lazare refused outright to go to Paris and manage an insurance company in which Thibaudier was the principal shareholder. He intended to stay another year or two in Bonneville to write a novel, a masterpiece, before setting out to conquer Paris. At this, Thibaudier merely shrugged his shoulders and good-naturedly called him a young fool.

The wedding was to take place in Caen. The previous fortnight was occupied with continual comings and goings, an extraordinary flurry of journeys. Pauline numbed her feelings by accompanying Louise on these trips and returning home exhausted. As Chanteau could not leave Bonneville, she had to promise to attend the ceremony as the sole representative of her cousin's family. As the great day approached, her terror of it grew. The day before, she contrived not to spend the wedding night at Caen, for she thought she would find it less painful if she returned to sleep in her own room, lulled by her beloved sea. She made the excuse of concern for her uncle's health, saying she did not want to spend so long away from him. Chanteau himself pressed her in vain to stay on a few days in Caen: he wasn't ill, was he? On the contrary, he was overexcited at the idea of the wedding and the feast that he could not enjoy, and was secretly planning to have Véronique make him a forbidden dish such as partridge with truffles, which he could never eat without being certain of another attack. Despite everything, Pauline declared that she would come home that night, thinking as well that this would leave her freer to pack her trunk the next morning, and disappear.

It was drizzling, and midnight had just struck as Malivoire's berline brought Pauline home to Bonneville on the night of the wedding. Wearing a blue silk dress and barely protected by a little shawl, she was shivering and very pale, though her hands were hot. In the kitchen, she found Véronique waiting up for her, dozing at one corner of the table. The candle's tall flame made Pauline blink, her eyes deep black, as if still full of the darkness of the countryside into which they had been staring all the way from Arromanches. She could only drag a few incoherent words from the drowsy maid: Monsieur had not behaved himself, now he was asleep, nobody had come. Then she picked up a candle and went upstairs, chilled by the empty house, depressed to death at the gloom and silence that weighed upon her shoulders.

She reached the second floor in a hurry to take refuge in her own room, but then to her surprise an irresistible impulse made her open Lazare's door. She held the candle up high to peer in, as if she thought the room would be full of smoke. Nothing had changed, every piece of furniture was in its usual place, yet she felt a sense of disaster and annihilation, an aching fear, as in a bedroom where someone has died. Slowly she walked over to the table and looked at the inkstand, the pen, and a half-written page left lying there. Then she went away. It was all over, and the door closed on the room's echoing emptiness.

In her own room the same feeling of unfamiliarity awaited her. Was it really hers, with its blue roses on the wallpaper and its narrow iron bed draped in muslin curtains? And yet she had been living here for so many years! Without putting down the candle she anxiously inspected the room, pushed the curtains aside, looked under the bed and behind the furniture, with none of her usual bravery. She was so shaken and dazed that she could only stand and stare at things. She would never have believed that such anguish could descend on her from that ceiling, every mark of which was so familiar; she now regretted not staying in Caen, and felt scared in the house, so alive with memories and yet so empty, in the shivering gloom of the stormy night. She could not bear the thought of going to bed. She sat down without even taking off her hat and stayed without moving for several minutes, staring into the blinding candlelight. Suddenly, however, she gave a start of surprise: why was she sitting there, with her head in turmoil and throbbing so hard that she could not think? It was one o'clock, she'd better be going to bed. And she began to undress with feverish, fumbling hands.

Her orderly habits persisted even at this disastrous juncture in her life. She carefully put away her hat, and checked to see that her boots had come to no harm. Her dress was already folded and draped over the back of a chair, and she was wearing only a petticoat and chemise, when she glanced down at her own virginal bosom. Gradually a hot flush came over her cheeks. Into her troubled brain there sprang a vivid picture of the couple in their own room far away, a room she knew, for she herself had decked it that morning with flowers. The bride was in bed; he came in and went across to her with a loving laugh. In a violent movement, Pauline pushed her petticoat down, tore off her chemise and, naked now, gazed again at her body. So, would she never enjoy love's harvest? Her own wedding day would now never come. Her gaze moved down from her breasts, firm like buds bursting with sap, to her broad hips and her belly, where a powerful instinct for motherhood lay dormant. Yet she was ripe, life was coursing through her limbs and flowering in dark tufts in the secret recesses of her body, and she could smell her womanly scent, like a floral bouquet awaiting fertilization. Yet it was not her but that other woman, in the room that she could see so clearly, lying ecstatic in the arms of the husband for whom she herself had waited so many long years.

But she leaned further forward and was astonished to see the red trail of a drop of blood that had run down her thigh. Suddenly she understood: her chemise, lying on the ground, was spattered with blood, as if from a knife blow. So that was why she had felt faint all over since leaving Caen! She had not expected it so soon, the loss of her love had opened up this wound right at the very fount of life. And the sight of that life flowing uselessly away completed her despair. She remembered how she had screamed with terror, the morning when she had first found herself covered in blood. Later on, had she not been childish enough, before putting out her candle at night, to examine with a furtive glance the full flowering of her body, and her sex? She had been proud like a young fool, relishing the joy of being a woman. Alas, now the red rain of puberty was falling like the futile tears that her virginity wept within her. From now on, each month would bring its fresh flow, like grapes crushed at harvest-time, but never now would she be a woman, and she would grow old in sterility!

Then jealousy gnawed once more at her innards, as her fevered imagination conjured up further images. She wanted to live, live completely, and to create life, since she loved life so much! What was the use of being, if she could not give of her being? She could see the couple in her mind's eye, and an urge to scar her naked body made her look round for the scissors. Why not slash that bosom, cut those thighs, rip that belly right open and make the blood flow out to the last drop? She was more beautiful than that skinny blonde, stronger too, and yet it was not her he had chosen. She would never know him now, no part of her could expect him now, not her arms, nor her thighs, nor her lips. All her hopes could be tossed aside like an old rag. How was it possible that those two should be together while she was left alone, shivering with fever in that chill house?

Suddenly she flung herself face down on the bed. She seized the pillow convulsively in her arms and bit into it to stifle her sobs; and she tried to subjugate her rebellious flesh by pressing it down onto the .... head to toe. In vain did she screw up her eyelids to shut out the light, she still saw monstrous visions rising up out of the darkness. What should she do? Put out her own eyes but still go on seeing, perhaps for ever?

Minutes passed, and she was conscious only of the eternity of her torment. Suddenly she jumped to her feet in alarm. There must be someone there, for she had heard a laugh. But all she found was her candle which was burning so low it had shattered the drip tray. Yet what if somebody had seen her? That imagined laugh still made her skin creep, like a brutal caress. Was it really her, standing naked like this? Overcome by a sense of modesty, she crossed her arms despairingly over her bosom to avoid seeing herself any more. At last she hastily slipped a nightdress over her head and went to bury herself under the covers, which she pulled up to her chin; her shivering body lay huddled up small against the cold. When the candle went out, she lay quite still, annihilated with shame at this emotional crisis.

Pauline packed her trunk the next morning, but could not find the strength to tell Chanteau she was leaving. By that evening, however, she was forced to break it to him, for Doctor Cazenove was coming to fetch her the next day and take her himself to his relative's house. Once he had understood, Chanteau became distraught, and held up his poor invalid hands in a wild gesture, as if to hold her back, while pleading with her in a faltering voice. She could never do such a thing, she couldn't leave him, it would be murder, it would surely be the death of him. Then, seeing her quiet resolution and guessing at her reasons, he decided to confess his transgression of the previous day, eating partridge. He was already getting tingling pains in his joints. It was the same old story, he had given in to temptation: should he eat? would he be ill? and he always did eat, knowing it would make him ill, satisfied and terrified at the same time. Surely, though, she wouldn't have the nerve to abandon him in the middle of one of his attacks?

And indeed, around six in the morning Véronique came upstairs to inform Mademoiselle that she could hear Monsieur bawling in his room. She was in a foul mood, and went about the house grumbling that if Mademoiselle left, she would certainly be off as well, she was fed up of looking after such an unreasonable old man. Thus, Pauline was once again obliged to take up her post at her uncle's bedside. When the doctor arrived to take her away, she took him to see the patient, who was exultant, bellowing fit to burst and shouting to her to leave him now, if she had the heart to. Everything was put off.

Every day Pauline trembled at the prospect of Lazare and Louise coming home. Their new bedroom, the former guest room specially done up for them, had been waiting since the day after the wedding. They were lingering on in Caen, and Lazare wrote that he was making notes on the world of finance, before shutting himself away in Bonneville to start on a great novel, in which he would expose the truth about the speculators. Then one morning he turned up without his wife, and calmly announced that he and she were going to settle in Paris: his father-in-law had persuaded him to accept the insurance job, on the pretext that it would allow him to make his notes from observation, and he'd see about getting back into literature later on.

Once Lazare had filled two chests with the things he was taking with him, and Malivoire's berline had come to collect him and his luggage, Pauline went back indoors in a daze, drained of her former resolve. Chanteau, still in great pain, asked her:

'You'll be staying now, I hope? Do wait until you've buried me!'

She did not want to reply immediately. Upstairs, her trunk was still packed. She would stare at it for hours on end. Since the couple were going to Paris, it would be wrong for her to desert her uncle. She admittedly had little confidence in her cousin's decisions, but if they did come back, she would be free to leave. And when Cazenove angrily told her she was throwing up a splendid opportunity, only to ruin her life among people who had been sponging off her since she was a child, she suddenly made up her mind.

'Off you go!' Chanteau now kept telling her. 'If you're going to earn so much money and be so happy, I can't make you hang around here with an old cripple like me... Off you go!'

One morning she answered:

'No, Uncle, I'm staying.'

The doctor, who was there, went away raising his arms to the sky.

'Oh, that child is quite impossible! And what a hornets' nest she's got herself into! She'll never escape from it now.'

CHAPTER 9

THE days began to flow by once more in the house in Bonneville.
A very cold winter was followed by a wet spring, and the rain-lashed
sea looked like a muddy lake; then the delayed summer had extended
into mild autumn, with days of leaden sunshine, when the infinite
blue seemed to slumber in oppressive heat; then winter returned, and
another spring, and another summer, ticking on, minute by minute,
at a constant rate, as the hours pursued their measured march.

Pauline gradually regained her peace of mind, as if her heart were
governed by this clockwork of the seasons. The regular passage of the
days, devoted to the same unvarying occupations, dulled the keenness
of her grief. She would come down in the morning and kiss her uncle,
say the same things to the maid as she had the day before, sit down at
table twice a day, sew all afternoon, then go to bed early; and the next
day the same all over again, with nothing of note to break the monot-
ony. Chanteau, his limbs increasingly twisted by gout, with swollen
legs and crooked hands, sat there in silence whenever he was not
bawling, engrossed in the bliss of not being in pain. Véronique, who
seemed to have lost her tongue, had fallen into a mood of surly gloom.
Only the Saturday dinners broke this quiet routine. Cazenove and
Abbé Horteur came round with great punctuality, and conversation
could be heard until ten o'clock, when the priest's wooden clogs clattered away across the flagged yard and the doctor's cabriolet set off at
the best lumbering trot the old horse could manage. Even Pauline's
gaiety, which she had so valiantly sustained throughout her torments,
had become more subdued. The staircase and the rooms no longer
rang with her laughter, but she remained the generous, active spirit
of the household, bringing to it every morning fresh courage to
face the day. After a year had gone by, her heart seemed quiescent,
and it became possible for her to think that the days would now flow
on in the same gentle uniformity, with nothing to awaken her dormant pain.

For some time after Lazare's departure, every letter he sent had
upset Pauline. She lived for these letters, looking out for them impatiently, reading them several times and finding between the lines
things they did not explicitly say. For three months, they came regularly every fortnight, very long, full of details, and overflowing with
hope. Lazare had discovered yet another passion, he was throwing

himself into business and dreaming of making an instant and colossal fortune. According to him, the insurance company would yield enormous profits, and he would not stop there, he was getting into all kinds of other enterprises; he seemed enchanted with the world of finance and industry and the charming contacts he was making, and now reproached himself for dismissing them so crassly, like a poet. He seemed to have given up any idea of literature. He also went on about his domestic bliss, with lots of infatuated nonsense about his wife, their stolen kisses and nest-building, flaunting his happiness as a token of gratitude to his 'darling sister', as he called Pauline. It was these details, these intimate passages, that made Pauline's fingers prickle feverishly. The scent of love which clung to the paper, Louise's favourite heliotrope perfume, made her head reel. The paper had been kept close to their linen, and when she shut her eyes she could still see the writing in lines of fire, she could finish the sentences, and had the sense of sharing in the private intimacy of their honeymoon. But gradually the letters became shorter and less frequent, and Lazare no longer wrote about business matters, but confined himself to sending her his wife's love. He offered no explanation, he simply stopped telling her everything. Was he dissatisfied with his job and already fed up with finance? Was their domestic happiness starting to be undermined by misunderstandings? Pauline could only guess, and she was worried by the boredom and despair that she detected behind certain phrases that seemed to have been reluctantly written. Towards the end of April, after six weeks of silence, she received a four-line note telling her that Louise was three months' pregnant. Then silence fell once more, and she had no further word.

May and June went by. One of the groynes was smashed by the tide, an incident which made a considerable stir: the whole of Bonneville jeered derisively, and the fishermen made off with the broken timbers. Then came another sensation: at barely thirteen and a half, the Gonin girl gave birth to a daughter, and nobody was sure whether it was young Cuche's, for she had also been seen with an old man. Afterwards everything went quiet again and the village vegetated obstinately at the foot of the cliffs, like some marine growth. In July, repairs were needed to the terrace wall and the whole of one gable end of the house. After the first blows of the builders' pickaxes, the rest also threatened to collapse. The job took an entire month and the bill came to almost ten thousand francs.

It was always Pauline who paid. This made another dent in the hoard in her chest of drawers, reducing her fortune to about forty thousand francs.* She still kept the household running smoothly by eking out their income of three hundred francs a month, but she had to sell some more of her securities to avoid dipping into her uncle's investments. As his wife had done before, he kept telling her that it would all be reckoned up one day. Pauline would have given all she had, for as her inheritance had dwindled, so had her avarice, and now she only fought to keep the small change needed for her charitable works. The thought that she might have to stop her Saturday distributions distressed her deeply, for they gave her the greatest joy of the week. Since the previous winter she had been knitting stockings, and now all the urchins of the neighbourhood went about with warm feet.

One morning towards the end of July, as Véronique was sweeping up the rubble left by the builders, Pauline received a letter that greatly upset her. It had been sent from Caen, and contained few words. Without explanation, Lazare informed her that he would be arriving in Bonneville the next evening. She ran to tell her uncle the news. They looked at each other. Chanteau's eyes conveyed the fear that she would leave him, should the couple stay for any length of time. He dared not question her, for he could read in her expression that she was firmly resolved to go. In the afternoon, she even went up to check her linen. However, she did not want it to look as if she were running away.

It was around five o'clock on a lovely evening when Lazare stepped down from the carriage at the courtyard gate. Pauline had gone out to meet him. But, before even embracing him, she stopped in astonishment.

'What, have you come on your own?'

He simply answered 'Yes', and kissed her first, vigorously on both cheeks.

'But where's Louise?'

'In Clermont,* at her sister-in-law's. The doctor recommended mountain air for her... Her pregnancy is making her very tired.'

As he spoke, he walked towards the front steps, casting long glances around the yard. He also looked at his cousin, and his lips quivered with barely contained emotion. When a dog rushed from the kitchen and yapped around his legs, it was his turn to look surprised.

'What on earth is that?' he asked.

'That's Loulou,' Pauline replied. 'He doesn't know you… Down Loulou! You're not to bite master!'

The dog carried on growling.

'He's hideous! My dear girl, wherever did you pick up such a horrid creature?'

The dog was indeed a wretched mongrel, scrawny and full of mange. He also had a dreadful temper, was forever snarling, and had the melancholy look of an abandoned creature which might almost bring a tear to the eye.

'It's not my fault; when they gave him to me, they swore he would grow into a magnificent creature, but as you can see, he's stayed like this… He's the fifth we've tried to rear; all the others died, only this one seems determined to go on living.'

Loulou had sulkily made up his mind to lie down in the sun and turn his back on the people. Flies buzzed around him. Then Lazare thought of the old days, of all the things that were gone and the new, ugly ones that had come into his life. He looked around the yard once more.

'My poor Mathieu!' he murmured very softly.

On the steps Véronique greeted him with a nod of the head, and carried on peeling a carrot. But he walked straight on into the dining room, where his father was waiting, agitated at the sound of voices. Pauline called in from the doorway:

'You know, he's come on his own, Louise is in Clermont.'

The anxiety vanished from Chanteau's eyes and he began to question his son even before he had embraced him.

'Are you expecting her here? When will she come and join you?'

'No, no,' replied Lazare, 'I'll be meeting up with her at her sister-in-law's, before I take her back to Paris… I'll stay with you for a fortnight, and then I'll be off.'

Chanteau's gaze expressed deep, wordless joy, and when at last Lazare embraced him, he gave him two hearty kisses in return. Nevertheless, he felt duty-bound to express some regret.

'Such a pity your wife couldn't come, we would have been so pleased to see her!… You must bring her with you next time, without fail.'

Pauline kept silent, concealing her inner shock beneath a laughing, affectionate welcome. So, everything was changed again; she would not be leaving after all, and did not know whether to feel glad or sorry, so entirely had she now become a pawn in other people's hands. Moreover, behind her gaiety there was a feeling of sadness that Lazare looked older, with duller eyes and a bitter twist to his mouth. She knew well those wrinkles across his brow and cheeks, but they had now deepened into furrows, and she guessed that his boredom and anxiety had deepened as well. He, too, was astounded at her development, her increased strength and beauty, for he murmured with a smile:

'Well, you certainly don't seem any the worse for my absence. You all seem well fed… Father's looking younger, Pauline is magnificent… And it's a funny thing, but the house seems bigger.'

He glanced round the dining room, as he had done round the yard, with surprise and emotion. His gaze came to rest on Minouche, lying on the table with paws tucked snugly beneath her, in such a state of feline bliss that she had not budged.

'Even Minouche doesn't look a day older,' he continued. 'Look here, you ungrateful creature, you might at least show that you recognize me!'

He stroked her and she began to purr, still not moving.

'Oh, Minouche takes no notice of anyone but herself,' laughed Pauline. 'The day before yesterday we had to drown five more of her kittens, and, as you can see, she doesn't seem in the least bit bothered.'

Dinner was brought forward, as Lazare had lunched early. Despite Pauline's best efforts, the evening was a melancholy affair. Conversation was hindered by thoughts that remained unspoken, and there were awkward silences. Noticing Lazare's embarrassed replies, Pauline and Chanteau refrained from questioning him, making no attempt to find out how his business in Paris was going, or why he had only written from Caen to say he was coming. He brushed aside with a vague gesture any questions that were too direct, as if to put off answering until later. When the tea was served, he simply gave a great sigh of satisfaction. How cosy it was there, and what a lot of work he could have got through in such a quiet and peaceful place! He made mention of a verse drama he had been working on for the last six months. His cousin was astonished when he added that he intended finishing it in Bonneville; it shouldn't take him above a fortnight.

At ten, Véronique came in to say that Monsieur Lazare's room was ready. But when she tried to show him into the former guest room on the first floor which had been fitted out for the couple's use, he showed annoyance.

'If you think I'm going to sleep there, you can think again! I shall be upstairs in my own little iron bed.'

The maid grumbled. Why this whim? Since the bed was already made up, he surely didn't want to put her to the trouble of doing another one?

'Very well,' he replied, 'I'll sleep in an armchair.'

While Véronique angrily tore off the sheets and took them up to the top floor, Pauline felt an involuntary rush of joy, a sudden light-heartedness that made her fling her arms round her cousin's neck and wish him goodnight, in a spontaneous return to their old childhood camaraderie. So, he was occupying his big room once again, so close to her that for a long time she could hear him pacing about, as though agitated by the memories that were also keeping her awake.

It was only the next morning that Lazare started taking Pauline into his confidence, and he did not confess everything in one go: she only found things out from hints that he dropped into the conversation. Then she grew bolder and started to question him, full of affectionate concern. How was his life with Louise? Was their happiness still as complete as ever? He answered yes, but complained of little domestic disagreements and other trifling matters that had led to quarrels. Their relationship was not in crisis, but they were suffering from the perpetual friction that builds up between two highly strung temperaments incapable of experiencing joy or sorrow in a balanced way. There was between them a kind of covert bitterness, as if they were surprised and angry at having made a mistake, at finding their affections so shallow after the passion of the early days. For a moment, Pauline had the impression that they had become embittered by financial losses, but she was wrong, for their income of ten thousand francs a year remained practically intact. It was just that Lazare had become disillusioned by business, just as previously by music, medicine, and industry, and he had some very harsh things to say on the subject. Never had he encountered such stupid, decadent people as in the world of finance, and he would prefer anything, even the boredom of provincial life and the mediocrity of a small income, to that constant obsession with money, and the brain-addling whirl of figures. In any case, he had just resigned from the insurance company and was determined to try the theatre next winter, when he was back in Paris. His play would be his revenge, and in it he would portray money as a cancer eating away at modern society.

Pauline was not overly concerned by this latest failure, which she had already deduced from the self-conscious tone of Lazare's recent letters. She was most distressed at the misunderstanding that had slowly grown up between him and his wife. She tried to find out the cause; how had a young couple of ample means, with only their own happiness to consider, found themselves in this unfortunate state so quickly? She returned to the subject time and again, and only stopped questioning her cousin when she saw the embarrassment it was causing him: he stammered and turned pale, and would not look her in the eye. She well recognized that scared, ashamed expression, it came from the anguished anticipation of death that in the old days he had concealed like some secret vice; but could it be that the cold spectre of nothingness had come to lie down between the couple in the still-ardent heat of their marriage bed? For several days she remained in doubt, and then, without any further confession from him, she read the truth in his eyes one evening, when he rushed downstairs without a light, looking distraught, as if pursued by a ghost.

In Paris, in the first flush of love, Lazare had forgotten all about death. He had taken passionate refuge in Louise's embraces, and afterwards, completely spent, he would sleep like a child. She likewise loved him like a mistress, her voluptuous, feline graces seemingly made only for male adoration, and she became dejected and forlorn if he failed to pay attention to her, even for an hour. And the fevered satisfaction of their old desires, lost to the world in their passionate embraces, carried on for as long as they still believed such sensual delights to be never-ending. But then satiation set in; he was astonished at being unable to surpass the intoxication of their first days, while she, craving only his caresses and with nothing else to offer, could not provide him with the support or encouragement to face life's troubles. So, were these pleasures of the flesh so short-lived? Were there not always new depths to be plumbed, new sensations to be discovered, whose novelty would be powerful enough to create an illusion of happiness? One night, Lazare awoke with a start, chilled by an icy breath that prickled the hairs on the back of his neck, and he shivered, stammering out his anguished cry: 'Oh God, Oh God, we have to die!' Louise lay sleeping by his side. All their kissing had simply led him back to death.

More nights followed when he relapsed into his old anguish. It would afflict him unexpectedly as he lay sleepless in bed, powerless to

predict or prevent it. In moments of calm he would suddenly be convulsed by the shivers, whereas when he was irritable and having a bad
day, the fear would often leave him alone. And it was no longer just
a single jolt, as in the past, for his nervous lesion was growing worse,
and his whole being shuddered with each new shock. He could not
sleep without a night-light, for the darkness increased his anxiety,
despite his constant fear of his wife discovering his disorder. Indeed,
this fear only heightened his distress and made the attacks worse, for
previously, when he had slept on his own, he had no need to conceal
his cowardice, but now he was worried by the warm presence of this
living creature at his side. As soon as the terror jerked him bolt
upright from his pillow, his vision blurred with sleep, he would glance
towards her, fearful of seeing her eyes wide open and fixed upon his.
But she never stirred, and by the glimmer of the night light he could
make out her motionless face, her full lips and delicate blue-veined
eyelids. So he would start to feel a little easier, until one night his
long-standing fears were realized, and he found her staring back at
him. She said not a word as she looked at him, all pale and shivering.
Doubtless she too had felt the passing chill of death, for she seemed
to understand, and clung to him with the abandonment of a woman
imploring protection. Then, attempting to keep up their mutual
deception, they pretended to have heard footsteps and got up to
search under the furniture and behind the curtains.

From now on, they were both haunted. No admission escaped their
lips, it was a shameful secret not to be spoken of; but as they lay in
bed gazing up wide-eyed at the ceiling, they could clearly hear each
other's thoughts. She had become as neurotic as him, they must have
infected each other with the disease, like two lovers carried off by the
same fever. If he woke and found her asleep, he would grow alarmed:
was she still breathing? He could no longer even hear her breath,
perhaps she had died suddenly! For a moment, he would study her
face and touch her hands; then, even when reassured, he could not get
back to sleep. The thought that she would die someday plunged him
into a mournful reverie. Who would go first, him or her? He pursued
each alternative in turn, imagining their deathbed scenes in graphic
detail, with the final distressing throes of agony, the hideous laying-
out of the body, and the brutal, eternal separation. The thought made
his whole being rise up in revolt: never, ever to see each other again!
When they had lived together like that, flesh against flesh—he felt

himself going mad, his brain could not register such horror. With the bravado of fear, he hoped he might be the first to go. Then he would be filled with pity for her, imagining her a widow, carrying on with their daily routine and doing all the things that he would no longer be there to do. Sometimes, to drive away this obsession, he would gently take her in his arms without waking her; but he could not do it for long, since feeling her alive in his embrace made him all the more terrified. If he rested his head on her breast and listened to her heart, he could not follow its regular action without alarm, fearing it might suddenly miss a beat. Soon he could no longer bear the touch of those legs against which he had pressed his own, that waist that had yielded to his embrace, and her whole body, so lithe and so adored, gradually infused him with a fearful apprehension in his nightmare of oblivion. And even when she awoke, when desire entwined them more tightly together, lips crushed against lips as they rushed headlong towards climax in the hope of forgetting their misery, they emerged still trembling as before, lying on their backs and unable to sleep, revulsed by the joy of loving. In the darkness of the bedchamber, their wide-eyed stares were once again fixated on death.

This was about the time when Lazare grew tired of business. His laziness returned and he squandered whole days in idleness, giving himself the excuse that all financiers were contemptible. The truth was that his constant brooding on death was daily eroding his will, and his strength, to go on living. He was relapsing into his old apathy: what was the point? Since the final lurch into the void was coming, tomorrow, today, perhaps just an hour from now, what was the point of being busy and enthusiastic, committing himself to one thing rather than another? All his intentions were abortive. His existence was nothing but a slow, daily death, and when he listened to the clockwork ticking inside him, as in times gone by, he felt sure that the mechanism was winding down. His heart was no longer beating so quickly, the other organs were also becoming sluggish, and soon it would doubtless all stop working; and he observed with a shudder the diminution of vitality that age inevitably brought with it. He was losing parts of himself, in the continuous dilapidation of his body: his hair was falling out, he had several teeth missing, he could feel his muscles shrinking, as though they were already turning back to dust. The approach of his forties put him in a mood of black melancholy; now old age would soon be upon him, to finish him off. Already he felt ill all over, something was sure to snap, and his days went by in fevered anticipation of catastrophe. Then, he saw people dying around him, and every time he heard of the death of a friend, it came as a shock. Was it possible that so-and-so was gone already? But he had been three years younger, and built to last till a hundred! And then this other chap, whatever could have done him in? Such a careful man, who even weighed his food! For two days afterwards he could think of nothing else, stunned by the disaster, examining himself, observing his own symptoms, and ultimately resentful of those poor fellows who had died. Seeking reassurance, he would accuse them of responsibility for their own demise: the first had been guilty of inexcusable carelessness, while the second had succumbed to a complaint so rare that the doctors did not even have a name for it. But in vain did he try to banish the importunate spectre: he could hear inside himself the grating cogs of the machine about to malfunction, and he was sliding helplessly down the slippery slope of years, at the bottom of which loomed a black abyss that brought him out in a cold sweat and made his hair stand on end with horror.

When Lazare stopped going to the office, the couple began to argue. He went around with an irritability which flared up at the slightest contradiction. The increasing disorder that he was so careful to conceal, showed itself in irascibility, moodiness, and wild, obsessive behaviour. At one point, he was so ravaged by fear of fire that he moved out of a third-floor room to one on the first, in order to have an easier escape when the house caught alight. Constant anxiety about the future ruined the present for him. He lived in permanent expectation of disaster, jumping every time a door opened his heart going into palpitations whenever he received a letter. Then, he was suspicious of everyone, concealing small amounts of money in different places, and keeping his most basic plans and intentions a secret. He also felt embittered against the world, convinced that he was misunderstood and his successive failures were the result of a vast conspiracy against him, by people and things. But dominating and swamping everything else, his boredom was becoming without limit; it was the boredom of an unbalanced man, to whom the constantly present idea of death made all action distasteful, leading a listless and unproductive existence on the pretext that life was empty. Why bother with anything? Science was so limited, it could neither prevent nor predict. His was the sceptical boredom of a whole

generation, no longer the romantic ennui of a Werther or a René*
lamenting the passing of old beliefs, but the boredom of the new
doubting heroes, the young chemists who angrily proclaim the world
intolerable because they have not immediately found life at the bottom of their test tubes.

In Thomas's case, in a complete logical contradiction, a concealed
terror of annihilation went hand in hand with a constant display of
bravado towards the void. It was his neurotic dread, the instability of
his hypochondriac's temperament, that drove him towards pessimism
and a furious hatred of life. Since it could not go on for ever, he saw
life as nothing but a delusion. Did you not spend the first half of your
days dreaming of happiness, and the second in fear and regret? So,
he outdid in his pessimism even the theories of the 'old man', as he
called Schopenhauer, whose most violent passages he could recite by
heart. He talked of destroying the will to live, putting an end to the
barbarous and imbecilic spectacle of existence in which the power
that ruled the world found amusement, for some egotistical reason
known only to itself. He wanted to do away with life, and so do away
with fear. He always arrived at the same solution: wish nothing, for
fear of something worse, avoid all action, which leads to suffering,
then subside utterly into death. He brooded on the practicality of
universal suicide, the sudden and total disappearance of all living
beings by their own consent. He harped constantly on this theme, in
coarse and brutal outbursts which intruded into ordinary conversations. The slightest difficulty made him regret that he hadn't yet snuffed
it, and a mere headache would start him raging furiously against his
own carcase. Chatting with a friend, his talk would immediately
turn to the woes of existence and the damned good fortune of those
who were already pushing up daisies in the cemetery. Gloomy topics
obsessed him, and he was greatly impressed to read an article by some
eccentric astronomer announcing the arrival of a comet whose tail was
sure to sweep the earth away like a grain of sand: was this not indeed
the predicted cosmic catastrophe, the colossal explosive that would
blow the world out of the water like some rotten old vessel? And this
death wish, these cherished theories of annihilation, were just an
expression of his desperate struggle with his own terror, a vain babble
to mask the dreadful anticipation of his end.

His wife's pregnancy at just this moment gave him a further shock.
He felt an indefinable mixture of great joy and redoubled anxiety.

Contrary to the ideas of the 'old man', the thought of becoming a father, of having created life, filled him with pride. While affecting to believe that the same right was widely abused by idiots, his response was one of astonished vanity, as though he were the first to whom such a thing had ever happened. Then his joy turned sour as he tormented himself with forebodings that the birth would go badly: already he imagined that the mother would die and the child never see the light of day. And indeed, from the first months of her pregnancy, Louise suffered some painful episodes, and the household upheaval, the disruption of their habits, and their frequent quarrels soon made his misery complete. The child that should have brought the couple closer together only increased the misunderstandings and friction between them. Lazare was exasperated by her constant complaining of vague pains from morning to night. So, when the doctor suggested a stay in the mountain air, he was relieved to take her to her sister-in-law's and escape for a fortnight himself, on the pretext of visiting his father in Bonneville. He was rather ashamed of running away like that, but he argued with his conscience that a short separation would calm both their nerves, and it would really be enough for him to be there for the birth.

On that evening when Pauline at last heard the whole story of the past eighteen months, she was left momentarily speechless, stunned at the disaster. They were in the dining room; she had put Chanteau to bed, and Lazare had just finished his confession, while the teapot had gone cold in front of them and the lamp was starting to smoke.

After a silence, Pauline at last exclaimed:

'But, good heavens, you're not in love anymore!'

He had stood up to go to his room, and he protested, with a worried laugh:

'We love each other as much as anyone can, my dear child... Don't you know anything, cut off here in this hole? Why should love fare better than anything else?'

As soon as she had shut herself away in her own room, Pauline succumbed to one of those fits of despair that had so often kept her awake and in torment, in that same chair, while the whole house was asleep. Was their misery about to begin all over again? When she had believed it was all over, for others and for herself, when she had so completely torn out her heart as to give Lazare to Louise, she suddenly discovered the futility of her sacrifice: already they were no longer in love, and the blood and tears of her martyrdom had been shed in vain. This was the wretched outcome of all her efforts: fresh pain and impending conflict, the thought of which further added to her anguish. So, human suffering was without end!

And while she sat there with her arms dangling impotently, staring at her burning candle, the thought that she alone was guilty in this whole sorry business rose up from her conscience to oppress her. She struggled in vain against the facts: she alone had brought about the marriage, without understanding that Louise was not the right wife for her cousin; now she saw her for what she was, too nervously fickle to offer him stability, apt to lose her head at the merest trifle, with nothing to offer beyond her physical charms, of which he had now grown tired. Why had none of this occurred to her before? Were these not the same reasons that had decided her to let Louise take her place? Previously, she had found Louise more loving, and believed that her kisses might have the power to free Lazare from his dark moods. What a terrible mess! To have done harm while trying to do good, to have been so ignorant of life as to bring disaster on those she was trying to help! True, she had felt sure she was doing good, giving tangible expression to her charity, that day when she had bought their joy at the cost of such bitter tears of her own! Now she felt contempt for her kindness, since kindness did not always bring happiness.

The house was asleep, and in the silence of her room she could hear nothing but the throbbing of the blood in her temples. A surging wave of revolt swelled and broke within her. Why hadn't she married Lazare? He'd been hers, there was no need for her to give him away. Perhaps he might have felt despondent at first, but then she'd surely have managed to instil some of her courage in him and protect him from his ridiculous nightmares. She'd always had a foolish lack of trust in herself, which was the single cause of their misfortune. But an awareness of her own strength and health, and her boundless affection, eventually reasserted itself and protested. Wasn't she worth more than that other woman? Why had she been so stupid as to cut herself out? Now she even refused to acknowledge Louise's passion, for all her sensual, seductive posturing, for she found in her own heart a deeper passion, one capable of sacrificing itself for the man she loved. She loved her cousin enough to disappear, if the other had made him happy; but since that woman did not know how to sustain the great joy of having him, should she not act to break up their ill-starred union? And her anger kept on swelling, she felt herself more beautiful, more courageous, and she looked down at her virginal bosom and belly with a sudden flush of pride in the woman that she could have been. One shattering certainty struck her: she was the one who should have married Lazare.

Then she was overwhelmed by a flood of regret. The night hours crept past, one by one, but she had no thought of dragging herself to bed. She sat with eyes wide open, dazzled by the candle's tall flame at which she stared unseeing, absorbed in a dream. She was no longer in her room, she was imagining that she had married Lazare, and their life together unfolded before her eyes in a sequence of happy and loving scenes. They were in Bonneville, by the edge of the blue sea, or in Paris, in some bustling street; there was always the same peace and quiet in the little room, with books lying about and roses on the table, and the lamp giving out its golden glow in the evening, leaving the ceiling in deep shadow. Every minute, they reached for each other's hands; he had rediscovered the careless gaiety of his youth, and she loved him so much that he had ended up believing life would go on for ever. Now they were sitting down to eat; now they were going out together; tomorrow she would look over the week's accounts with him. She dwelt lovingly on these little domestic details and made them the foundation of their happiness, which was finally present and tangible, from their laughter as they got dressed in the morning, to their last kiss at night. In the summer, they travelled. Then one morning she realized she was pregnant. But a great shudder shattered the dream and she could not go on; she found herself back in her room in Bonneville, staring at the guttering candle. Pregnant, my God! That other woman was, and never would any of those things happen to her, never would she know such joys! The return to reality was so brutal that tears sprang to her eyes and she wept inconsolably, her chest convulsed with sobbing. The candle died and she had to go to bed in the dark.

That feverish night left Pauline in a deeply emotional state, with a great feeling of charitable pity for the estranged couple and for herself. Her grief was dissolving into a kind of tender hope. She could not have said what she was hoping for, she dared not analyse the confused feelings which so agitated her heart. Why torment herself so? Hadn't she at least ten days ahead of her? After that, it would be soon enough to take stock. What mattered was to calm Lazare again, so that his stay in Bonneville might do him good. She recovered her old cheerfulness, and together they threw themselves once more into their happy life of old.

They soon rediscovered their childhood camaraderie.

'Stop bothering about your play, you great silly! It'll get booed in any case... Come and help me see if Minouche has hidden my ball of wool on top of the wardrobe,' said Pauline.

He held the chair for her while she stood on tiptoes and had a look. It had been raining hard for the last two days and they were confined to the big room. Their laughter rang out as they rediscovered relics of the old days.

'Oh look, here's that doll you made from two of my old collars... And remember this? it's the drawing I did of you that day when you flew into a rage and made yourself look hideous with crying, because I wouldn't lend you my razor.'

She bet him she could still jump straight up onto the table. He jumped up too, glad of the distraction. His play already lay abandoned in a drawer. One morning when they came across the great Symphony of Suffering, she played portions of it to him, comically accentuating the rhythms, and he made fun of his own composition, singing along to bolster the feeble efforts of the piano, which could scarcely be heard. But one section, the famous March of Death, put them both in a serious mood; it was really not bad, they must hang on to it. They found everything amusing and touching: a collection of Floridiae that Pauline had once pressed, discovered under a pile of books; a forgotten flask containing a sample of bromide from the factory; a tiny half-broken model of a groyne, looking as though it had been smashed by a storm in a teacup. Then they would roam around the house, chasing each other like kids at play, hurtling up and down the stairs and in and out of rooms, slamming doors behind them. It was just like old times: she was ten again and he was nineteen, and she once more felt for him all the passionate friendship of her girlhood. Nothing had changed, the dining room still had its walnut veneer sideboard and ceiling lamp of lacquered brass, and the view of Vesuvius and the four lithographs of the Seasons were still there to amuse them. The grandfather's master-piece still slumbered in its glass case on the mantelpiece, having become so much a part of the furniture that the maid would put glasses and plates down on top of it. There was only one room that they entered with silent emotion, Madame Chanteau's old bedroom, which had not been disturbed since her death. The secretaire was never opened now, and the yellow cretonne hangings with their greenish foliage motif were fading in the bright sunlight which was occasionally allowed in. Another birthday came round, and they decked out the room with great bunches of flowers.

Soon, however, the wind blew away the rain, they rushed outdoors onto the terrace, into the kitchen garden and along the cliffs, and started reliving their youth.

'Are you coming shrimping?' she would call out to him through the partition wall, as soon as she was up in the morning. 'The tide's going down now.'

They would set off in bathing costumes and rediscover the old familiar rocks to which the sea, after so many weeks and months, had brought no visible change. It was as if they had discovered that part of the coast only the previous day. He remembered every detail.

'Careful, there's a hole there with big stones at the bottom.'

But she would reassure him quickly.

'Yes, I know, don't worry... Oh! come and see this huge crab I've caught!'

They were standing up to their waists in the cold swell, invigorated by the salty sea-breeze. And they resumed all their old excursions, wandering far afield and resting on the sands, sheltering from a sharp shower in some cave in the cliffs, and walking home along darkening paths as night was falling. Nothing seemed to have changed, either, beneath the sky; the infinite sea was still there, endlessly reproducing the same, constantly shifting horizons. Wasn't it only yesterday that they had seen this turquoise blue, with great shimmering patches of a lighter shade where currents ruffled the surface? And would they not see again tomorrow that same leaden water beneath a livid sky, that rainy squall sweeping in from the left with the high tide? Each day merged into the next. Little, forgotten incidents came back to them with all the vividness of present reality. He was twenty-six again and she just sixteen. Whenever he unthinkingly gave her a friendly little push, it took her breath away and filled her with delicious confusion. She made no effort to avoid him, however, for no thought of unseemly behaviour crossed her mind. They felt infused with new life, sharing whispered nothings and laughter for no reason, then long silences which left them quivering with emotion. The most ordinary things, asking for some bread, remarking on the weather, wishing each other goodnight as they went up to bed, took on extraordinary significance. A tide of memories came flooding back, with all the sweetness of long-dormant affections newly awakened. What was there in it to alarm them? They made no attempt to resist, languidly lulled by the sea and its endless, monotonous voice.

And so the days went calmly by. Already Lazare's visit was extending into its third week. Still he did not leave, despite several letters from Louise, who was very bored, but whom her sister-in-law was insisting on keeping there with her. He wrote back urging her to stay, passing on advice from Doctor Cazenove, whom he did indeed consult. Gradually he fell back into the quiet routine of the household, getting used once more to the old times for meals, for getting up and going to bed, which he had changed in Paris, as well as to Véronique's grumpy moods and the unremitting suffering of his father, who sat there motionless, his face racked constantly by the same pain, while the rest of life moved on rapidly around him. Lazare also rediscovered the Saturday dinners and the old familiar faces of the doctor and the abbé, with their endless conversations about the latest gales, or the bathers at Arromanches. Minouche still jumped up onto the table at dessert, as light as a feather, and came over to butt her head into his chin and rub herself against him, and the slight scratch of her cold teeth took him back many years. In this familiar routine from the old days, the only novelty was Loulou, a miserable and hideous creature who lay curled up in a ball under the table and growled whenever anyone came near. Lazare tried in vain to pacify him with sugar: having crunched it up, the dog only bared his teeth more belligerently than ever. They had been forced to give up on him, and he now lived on his own, a stranger in the house, like some unsociable being who asks no more of men and gods than to be left to his boredom.

On occasion, however, when Pauline and Lazare were out on one of their long walks, an adventure would befall them. One day, for instance, when they had left the clifftop path to avoid passing by the factory at Treasure Bay, they rounded a bend in the lane and came upon Boutigny. He was now grown portly, a man of substance, having made a fortune from manufacturing commercial soda; he had married the woman who had followed him, out of devotion, into that godforsaken hole, and she had just given birth to their third child. The whole family, accompanied by a manservant and a nurse, were driving along in a magnificent shooting brake harnessed to a pair of great white horses. The two walkers had to squeeze against the bank to avoid being caught by the wheels. Boutigny, who was driving, slowed the horses to a walk. There was a moment's awkwardness: they had not been on speaking terms for so many years, and the presence of his wife and children heightened the embarrassment. Finally, as their eyes met, they bowed slowly to one another, without a word.

When the carriage had gone, Lazare, who had turned pale, said with an effort:

'So, he's living like a prince now, is he?'

Pauline, who had been affected only by the sight of the children, answered gently:

'Yes, it seems he's made enormous profits of late... You know he's been redoing your old experiments.'

That was indeed what pained Lazare the most. The Bonneville fishermen, who took a sneering delight in being unpleasant to him, had put him in the picture. For some months now, with the assistance of a young chemist in his pay, Boutigny had again been applying the refrigeration technique to seaweed ash, and thanks to his cautious and practical perseverance, was obtaining extraordinary results.

'Damnation!' muttered Lazare in a dead voice, 'whenever science takes a step forward, it's because some fool has helped it along by sheer accident.'

Their walk was completely spoilt, and they continued in silence, gazing into the distance at the grey mists rising from the sea and draining the colour from the sky. When they arrived home at nightfall, they were shivering. The cheerful lamplight falling on the white tablecloth warmed them up again.

Another day, as they were following a path through a beet-field somewhere near Verchemont, they stopped in surprise to see smoke rising from a thatched roof. It was a fire, but the sun's vertical glare made it impossible to see the flames; the cottage, with its doors and windows closed, was ablaze by itself, while the peasants were doubtless at work nearby. At once they left the path and ran, calling out, towards the house, but only startled some magpies that were chattering in the apple trees. At last a woman with a handkerchief over her head emerged from a distant carrot patch, stared for a moment, then started frantically galloping across the ploughed field as fast as she could go. She was waving her arms and screaming something they could not catch, so choked was she with panic. She fell, got up, fell again, and set off once more, her hands bleeding. Her kerchief had blown off and her hair was flying loose in the sunshine.

'But what's she saying?' Pauline kept asking, gripped with fear.

As the woman rushed towards them they heard her scream hoarsely, like a howling animal:

'The child!... the child!... the child!'

Her husband and son had been working all morning about three miles away in a small field of oats that they had inherited. She had only been away for a short while to pick a basketful of carrots, leaving the child asleep and the house locked, something she never normally did. The fire had probably been smouldering for a long time, for the woman was astonished and swore she had put out every last ember in the hearth. Now the whole of the thatched roof was ablaze, with red flames shooting up into the quivering golden sunshine.

'Did you lock the door?' shouted Lazare.

The woman did not hear him. Panic-stricken, she rushed fruitlessly all around the house, as if trying to find some opening, some way in, which she knew was not there. Then she fell down again, for her legs had given way; her old grey face was contorted in terror and despair, while she kept on screaming:

'The child!... the child!'

Great tears welled up in Pauline's eyes. But Lazare was mainly irritated by the screams, which cut right through him. It was more than he could bear, and suddenly he exclaimed:

'I'm going in, to get her child out for her!'

His cousin looked at him in bewilderment. She tried to grab his hands and hold him back.

'You! I won't let you!... The roof's going to cave in!'

'We'll see,' was his only reply.

Then he shouted in his turn to the woman's face:

'Your key, where's the key?'

The woman just gaped at him. Lazare shook her and at last wrested the key from her. Then, while she lay screaming on the ground, he strode calmly over to the house. Pauline watched him go, without any further attempt to hold him back; she was rooted to the spot in fear and amazement, so naturally did he seem to go about his task. Sparks rained down around him, and he had to press close up to the door to open it, for handfuls of burning straw were falling from the roof, like water streaming off in a storm; then he encountered a problem, for the rusty key refused to turn in the lock. But he did not even swear, just took his time and at last succeeded in opening the door, waiting on the threshold a moment longer to let out the first billow of smoke, which blew in his face. Never before had he felt so self-possessed, moving as if in a dream, with assurance, skill, and caution born of the dangerous situation. He ducked under the door frame and disappeared.

'Oh God! Oh God!' stammered Pauline, choking with anxiety.

She had clasped her hands together involuntarily, moving them pleadingly up and down like a sick person in the grip of extreme pain. The roof was breaking up and already collapsing in places, her cousin would never have time to get out. She felt time standing still, it seemed he had been inside for an eternity. The woman on the ground was holding her breath, apparently shocked at seeing a gentleman rushing into the fire.

But then a great cry went up. It was uttered involuntarily by Pauline, from deep in her guts, as she saw the thatch fall in between the smoking walls.

'Lazare!'

He was on the doorstep, his hair barely singed and with slight burns to his hands; and when he had deposited the crying, struggling infant in the woman's arms, he almost scolded his cousin:

'What's the matter with you, getting all upset like that?'

She clung round his neck and burst out sobbing, with such nervous relief that, fearing she might faint, he made her sit down on an old moss-covered stone, against the side of the well. He himself was now beginning to feel faint. There was a water trough into which he plunged his hands with relief. The cold sensation brought him back to his senses, and now he too felt great surprise at what he had done. Had he really ventured into those flames? It was like seeing his double moving amid the smoke with incredible agility and presence of mind, like watching some wonderful feat performed by a stranger. A lingering exaltation uplifted his spirit with a subtle joy he had never before known.

Pauline had recovered a little and was now examining his hands, saying:

'No, it's nothing serious, the burns are just superficial. But we must go home and I'll dress them for you... Good heavens, you did give me a fright!'

She had dipped her handkerchief in the water to wrap around his right hand, which was in a worse state than the other. They stood up and attempted to comfort the woman, who, after frenziedly kissing the child, had laid it down beside her and then ignored it; now she was lamenting the fate of the house, screaming just as loudly and asking what the men would say when they found it in ruins. The walls were still standing, but black smoke was billowing up from the unseen inferno inside, amidst showers of crackling sparks.

'Come now, be brave, you poor woman,' Pauline said to her. 'Come and see me about it tomorrow.'

Some neighbours, alerted by the smoke, now ran across to them, and Pauline was able to lead Lazare away. Their return home was very sweet. Lazare was not in much pain, but she still insisted on giving him her arm to support him. They still felt too emotional to speak, they just looked at each other and smiled. Pauline, in particular, was filled with a kind of joyful pride. So, he really was brave after all, even though the thought of death made him blanch! As they followed the path home, she was absorbed in amazement at the contradictions of the only man she knew well: she had seen him stay up working night after night, then wallow in idleness for months at a time; speak with disconcerting honesty after impudently lying to her; and place a brotherly kiss on her brow, while her wrists were burning in the grip of his masculine hands, hot and feverish with passion. And now he was a hero! She had been right not to despair of life, nor to judge anyone wholly good or bad. When they arrived in Bonneville, their pent-up emotion burst forth in a flood of eager talk. They relived every little incident, relating the adventure a score of times and recalling forgotten details that came back to them both in a flash. There was much talk about it for a long time afterwards, and aid was given to the peasants whose house had burnt down.

Lazare had now been in Bonneville for almost a month. A letter arrived from Louise, complaining of desperate boredom. He replied that he would come to fetch her at the beginning of the following week. There had been more dreadful downpours, the kind of violent storms that so often deluged the coast with torrents of rain, as if a floodgate had been opened, wiping out earth, sea, and sky in a pall of grey mist. Lazare had mentioned making a serious effort to finish his play, and Pauline, whom he wished to have by his side to encourage him, went up with her knitting—little stockings that she distributed among the village girls. But he got very little done once she was sitting by the table. They kept up long conversations in hushed voices, endlessly repeating the same things without ever tiring of them, and gazing into each other's eyes. They no longer played games, avoiding touching each other with the instinctive caution of children who have been scolded, aware now of the risk of rubbing shoulders or catching each other's breath, about which they had laughed just the day before. In any case, nothing seemed to them more delightful than the languorous peace, the drowsiness that drifted over them while the rain rattled relentlessly down on the slates. A silence would make them blush, every word was an involuntary caress, in the impulse of feelings which had gradually rejuvenated, and made blossom inside them, a past life that they had believed gone for ever.

One evening, Pauline had sat up knitting in Lazare's room until midnight, while he, having let the pen slip from his fingers, explained in relaxed fashion his future works, great dramas peopled with colossal characters. The whole house was asleep, even Véronique had gone to bed early, and the deep, quivering stillness of the night, broken only by the familiar sighing of the high tide, had gradually imbued them with a sort of sensuous tenderness. Pouring out his heart, he confessed that his life was a fiasco, and if literature also failed him now, he was determined to run away to some isolated spot and live like a hermit.

'You know something?' he added with a smile, 'I often think we should have emigrated after my mother's death.'

'How do you mean, emigrated?'

'Gone away, a very long way—to one of those Pacific islands, for instance, where life is so pleasant.'

'What about your father, would we have taken him with us?'

'Oh, it's only a dream, you know! There's no harm in imagining nice things, when reality is so awful.'

He had got up from the table and come over to perch on the arm of Pauline's chair. She put down her knitting to laugh unhindered at his endless, childlike flights of fantasy, then tipped her head back against the chair to look up at him, while he was so close to her that he could feel the living warmth of her shoulder against his hip.

'You're crazy, my poor friend. Whatever would we have done out there?'

'Why, we should have lived out our lives!... Don't you remember that book of travel stories we used to read together, a dozen years ago?

It's a paradise for the people who live there. No winter, constant blue sky, life in the sunshine and under the stars... We'd have had a cabin and lived on delicious fruits, with nothing to do and nothing to worry about!'

'So, we'd have become a pair of savages straight away, wearing rings in our noses and feathers on our heads!'

'Well, why not?... We'd have loved each other from one end of the year to the other, never counting the days, and it wouldn't have been bad at all.'

She looked up at him with fluttering eyelids, and a slight shiver passed over her face, which turned pale. That thought of love went straight to her heart and filled her with a delicious languor. He had taken her hand without thinking, simply to be nearer her and hold a part of her, and he toyed with this warm hand, bending its slender fingers and laughing the whole while in a way that was becoming a little forced. She felt no anxiety, this was just another game from their youth; but then her powers of resistance weakened, and as her inner turmoil grew, she was already his. Her voice faltered as she said:

'Living off fruit the whole time wouldn't be very filling. We'd have to hunt and fish, and grow crops... If it's the women who do the work out there, as they say, would you have made me till the soil?'

'You, with those little hands of yours! What about monkeys? Can't they make excellent servants nowadays?'

She greeted this joke with a faint laugh, and he added:

'Besides, there'd have been nothing left of your little hands... I'd have devoured them—like this!'

He kissed her hands, then started nibbling them, while the blood rushed to his face in a sudden flash of blinding passion. Neither spoke another word, they were gripped by a shared, unthinking madness as they plunged headlong together into vertiginous rapture. She put up no resistance, sliding down in the armchair, her face flushed and swollen and her eyes closed, as if to avoid seeing what was coming. With one rough hand, he had already unbuttoned her bodice and was bursting the hooks on her petticoats, when his lips met hers. He gave her a kiss which she returned in a frenzy, clasping him round the neck with all the strength in her arms. But with this shock to her virginal body, she opened her eyes and saw herself sprawling on the tiled floor; she recognized the lamp, the wardrobe, the ceiling with all its familiar marks, and seemed to wake up, with the astonishment of someone emerging from a terrible dream, only to find themselves back home. She struggled violently to her feet. Her petticoats had slipped and her bare breasts had escaped from her open bodice. In the panting silence of the room, she let out a cry.

'Let go of me, this is unspeakable!'

Mad with desire, he no longer heard her. He grabbed hold of her again and tore off the rest of her clothes. With his lips, he sought out her naked skin, covering her all over with burning kisses, each of which made her quiver. Twice she almost fell again and succumbed to the irresistible urge to surrender to him, going through terrible agonies in this struggle against herself. They had chased round the table, both panting, their limbs intertwined, when he succeeded in pushing her down onto an old divan, making its springs creak. With arms rigid, she held him at bay, repeating increasingly hoarsely:

'Oh, please, leave me alone... It's unspeakable, what you want to do!'

Lazare, his teeth clenched, had not said a word. He thought he had got her at last, but she made one final bid to escape, giving him such a violent push that he staggered back against the table. Then, in her moment of freedom, she managed to flee across the landing and into her own room. Already he had followed her, and she had no time to slam the door. As he was pushing, she had to lean against it with all her weight to slide the bolt across and turn the key, and as she battled with him to close the narrow gap, she was sure she would be lost if he got even the tip of his slipper into it. The key turned with a loud squeak, then a great silence fell, when the sea could once more be heard, crashing against the terrace wall.

Meanwhile, Pauline stood there with her back against the door, without a candle, eyes staring widely into the darkness. She realized that on the other side, Lazare had not moved either. She could hear the noise of his breath, and she still imagined it hot on the nape of her neck. If she moved to one side, he might shove a door panel in with his shoulder. She felt safer where she was, and without thinking she carried on leaning all her weight against it, as if he were still pushing. Two interminable minutes went by, in which each was conscious of the other's stubborn determination through the thin wooden barrier that barely separated them, both on fire and shaking with unquenchable desire. Then Lazare spoke in a low whisper, stifled with emotion:

'Pauline, open up!... You're there, I know you are.'

A shiver ran up and down her body, his voice had aroused her from head to toe. But she did not reply. Head bowed, she was holding up her fallen skirts with one hand while the other clutched her undone bodice, to cover her bared bosom.

'You want to as much as I do, Pauline... Open the door, I'm begging you. Why deny ourselves this happiness?'

He was afraid of waking Véronique now, as her room was next door. His pleading became quieter, like the moans of a sick man.

'Come on, open the door... Open up, and we'll die afterwards if that's what you want... Haven't we been in love since we were children? You ought to be my wife, isn't it fated that you will be one day? I love you, I love you, Pauline!'

She was now shaking more violently, and his every word pierced her to the heart. The kisses that he had rained down on her shoulders like drops of fire made her skin tingle. She redoubled her resistance, fearful of opening up and yielding to the irresistible urging of her half-naked body. He was right, she did adore him, so why refuse themselves that joy which they would both conceal from the whole world? The house was asleep, the night was dark. Oh, to sleep in each other's arms in that darkness, to hold him as her own, if only for an hour! Oh, to live, to live at last!

'God, you're cruel, Pauline!... You won't even answer me, and I'm so miserable standing here... Open up, I'll take you and I'll keep you, we'll forget everything... Open the door, please, I beg you...'

He was sobbing and she too began to cry. Still she remained silent, despite the rebellious promptings of her blood. For an hour he continued, pleading with her, growing angry and using abominable language, then reverting to passionate endearments. Twice she thought he had gone away, and twice he came back from his room in an even more frantic state of amorous frustration. When at last she heard him slam his own door behind him, she felt an immense sadness. Now it was all over, she had prevailed, but her victory left her feeling such violent despair and humiliation that she undressed and got into bed without lighting a candle. The thought of seeing herself naked, with her clothes torn away, filled her with horrible shame. Yet the coolness of the sheets soothed a little the burning of the kisses which mottled her shoulders, and she lay motionless for a long time, as if crushed beneath a burden of despair and disgust.

Insomnia kept Pauline awake until morning. She was obsessed by the abominable events of the previous evening, a crime which made her shudder with horror. Now she could no longer excuse herself, and had to admit the duplicity of her own feelings. Her motherly affection for Lazare and her private reproaches against Louise were just a hypocritical resurgence of her former passion. She had slipped into such lies, and now she probed deeper into her heart's unavowed emotions, realizing her joy at the couple's estrangement and the hope of perhaps taking advantage of it. Wasn't she the one who had encouraged her cousin to resume their old intimacy? Shouldn't she have foreseen this disastrous outcome? Now they faced a terrible predicament, a barrier to their future: she had given him to another woman, but she adored him, and he desired her. This conundrum swirled round and round in her brain, clanging in her temples like a peal of bells. At first, she resolved to run away the next day. Then she felt that such an escape would be cowardly. Since he himself was leaving, why not wait? Her pride, too, reawoke within her and she resolved to overcome her feelings, to avoid taking with her the shame of doing wrong. Now she felt she could never again hold her head up high, if she stayed burdened with remorse for the events of that evening.

In the morning, she came down at her usual time. Only her puffy eyelids betrayed the night's torments. She was pale and quite calm. When Lazare came down in his turn, he explained his tired appearance by telling his father that he had stayed up working late. The day was spent in their usual activities. Neither made any reference to what had taken place between them, even when they were alone together, away from prying ears and eyes. They did not avoid each other, seemingly confident in their resolve. But that evening, when they said goodnight in the passage outside their rooms, they fell madly into each other's arms and their lips met in a passionate kiss. Then Pauline, full of alarm, went and locked herself in her room, while Lazare also fled, flinging himself down on his bed and bursting into tears.

This, then, was their life. The days slipped slowly by, and they existed alongside each other in anxious anticipation of possible misbehaviour. Though they never spoke of such a thing, and never referred again to that terrible night, they thought about it constantly and were afraid they might fling themselves to the ground together anywhere at all, as though struck by lightning. Would it happen in the morning, when they were getting up, or at night when they exchanged parting words? In his room or hers, or some hidden corner of the house? It remained unclear. Their reason was still intact, and each sudden lapse or moment of folly, each desperate embrace behind a door or burning kiss stolen in the shadows, left them harrowed by anger against themselves. The ground was shaking beneath their feet and they clung to the resolutions they had made in calmer moments, to avoid plunging into the abyss. But neither had strength enough to follow the only route to salvation: immediate separation. Pauline, on the pretext of being courageous, persisted obstinately in facing up to the danger; while Lazare, completely besotted and overwhelmed by the excitement of this new adventure, no longer even replied to the urgent letters from his wife. He had been in Bonneville for six weeks, and they had both begun to feel that this existence, with its cruel but delicious alarms, would now go on for ever.

One Sunday at dinner, Chanteau became quite merry after treating himself to a glass of burgundy, an indulgence for which he always paid dearly. That day, Pauline and Lazare had enjoyed some delightful hours on the seashore, beneath an expansive blue sky, exchanging tender glances in which flickered that haunting fear of themselves which gave such a passionate intensity to their present companionship.

They were all three laughing when Véronique, as she was about to bring in dessert, appeared in the kitchen doorway and exclaimed:

'Madame's here!'

'Madame who?' asked Pauline in astonishment.

'Madame Louise, of course!'

There were stifled exclamations. Chanteau, much alarmed, looked at Pauline and Lazare, who had turned pale; but Lazare stood up abruptly and stammered in an angry voice:

'What! Louise! But she never wrote to tell me! I would have forbidden her to come. Is she mad?'

Evening was falling, clear and very mild. Flinging down his napkin Lazare rushed out, followed by Pauline, struggling to regain her smiling serenity. It was indeed Louise, climbing down with difficulty from old Malivoire's berline.

'Are you mad?' her husband called out from the middle of the yard. 'You shouldn't do such a foolish thing without writing first!'

At this, she burst into tears. She had been so ill in Clermont, and so dreadfully bored! Since he hadn't replied to her last two letters, she'd felt an irresistible urge to come away, mixed with a strong desire to see Bonneville again. If she hadn't sent word, it was for fear he might tell her to stay put.

'And I was so looking forward to giving you all a surprise!'

'This is ridiculous! You will go back again tomorrow!'

Louise, dejected at such a reception, fell into Pauline's arms. She, noticing her awkward movements and swollen figure beneath the dress, had turned even paler. Now that she could feel the contact of this pregnant belly, she was filled with horror and pity. She finally managed to overcome her revulsion and jealousy, and silenced Lazare.

'Why do you speak to her so harshly? Give her a kiss... My dear, you are quite right to come, if you think you'll be more comfortable in Bonneville. You know how fond we all are of you, don't you?'

Loulou was howling, furious at the voices that were disturbing the usual peace of the yard. Minouche, having stuck her nose out onto the steps, had retreated again with a shake of her paws, as if she had barely avoided some unpleasant and compromising adventure. Everyone went indoors, Véronique laid another place and started serving dinner all over again.

'So, it's you, is it, Louisette?' Chanteau exclaimed, with an awkward laugh. 'You wanted to surprise us all, did you? Well, it almost made my wine go down the wrong way!'

In the end, the evening passed off well enough. Everyone regained their self-possession; they avoided making any plans for the following days. As they were about to go upstairs, there was another embarrassing moment, when the maid enquired whether Monsieur would sleep in Madame's room.

'Oh no, Louise will get a better night on her own,' murmured Lazare, who had instinctively caught a glance from Pauline.

'That's all right, you sleep upstairs,' said Louise. 'I'm dreadfully tired, and I'll have the whole bed to myself.'

Three days went by. Then Pauline at last came to a decision. She would leave the house on the following Monday. The couple were already talking of staying until the birth, which was not due for a good month, and it seemed clear to Pauline that her cousin had had enough of Paris, and would end up living off his savings in Bonneville, a man embittered by his perpetual failures. It would be best to make way for them at once, as she was unable to overcome her feelings and lacked the courage, even more than before, to live alongside them in their private existence as husband and wife. And wasn't this also the best way of escaping the perils of that revived passion which had been making herself and Lazare suffer so cruelly? Only Louise expressed surprise, on hearing of Pauline's decision. Pauline put forward her incontrovertible arguments: Doctor Cazenove was saying that the lady in Saint-Lô had make her an exceptional offer, which she couldn't put off any longer, and her family should be encouraging her to accept a position which would give her a secure future. Even Chanteau, with tears in his eyes, gave his assent.

On the Saturday, there was a last dinner with the abbé and the doctor. Louise, who was very unwell, could barely drag herself to the table. This completed the gloom hanging over the meal, despite Pauline's efforts to smile at everyone, even though she felt a sense of guilt at leaving sadness behind her in that house which for so many years she had filled with her cheerful laughter. Her heart was overflowing with grief, and Véronique served dinner with a tragic expression. Chanteau refused a drop of burgundy with the roast, having suddenly become excessively cautious, for he trembled at the thought that he would soon not have with him the nurse who, by her voice alone, could soothe his pain. Lazare quarrelled heatedly the whole time with the doctor about some new scientific discovery.

By eleven o'clock the house had subsided once more into deep silence. Louise and Chanteau were already asleep, while Véronique was tidying up in her kitchen. Then, upstairs, outside the door of the old bachelor room which he still occupied, Lazare stopped Pauline for a moment, as he did every night.

'Goodbye,' he murmured.

'No, not goodbye,' she said, trying to laugh. 'Just goodnight—I'm not going till Monday.'

They gazed at each other and, as their eyes clouded with emotion, they fell into each other's arms, their lips crushed together in a final kiss.

CHAPTER 10

THE next morning, as they sat down at breakfast to their bowls of milky coffee, they were surprised not to see Louise come down. The maid was about to go upstairs and knock on her bedroom door, when she finally appeared. She looked very pale and was walking with difficulty.

'What's the matter?' asked Lazare anxiously.

'I've not been feeling well since dawn,' she replied. 'I've barely slept a wink, and I must have heard every hour strike through the night.'

Pauline protested.

'But you should have called us, at least we could have looked after you.'

Having reached the table, Louise sat down with a sigh of relief.

'Oh!' she went on, 'there's nothing you can do about it. I know what it is, I've been having these pains almost continually for the last eight months.'

Her pregnancy had been very difficult, and she had grown used to constant nausea and abdominal cramps so severe that she sometimes spent whole days bent double. That morning, the nausea had gone but she felt as if she had a tight belt around her, cutting into her midriff.

'One gets used to pain,' said Chanteau sententiously.

'Yes, but I need to keep moving,' she continued. 'That's why I've come down... I can't bear sitting still upstairs.'

She swallowed just a few mouthfuls of coffee. All morning she dragged herself around the house, getting up from one chair to go and sit down on another. Nobody dared speak to her, for it irritated her, and whenever someone tried to help, it seemed to make the pain worse. It was unremitting. Shortly before noon, however, it did abate, and she was able to sit down at the table again and take some soup. But between two and three o'clock, terrible gripes set in, and she kept constantly moving between the dining room and the kitchen, then struggled up to her room, only to come straight back down again.

Upstairs, Pauline was packing her trunk. She was to leave the next day, and she had just enough time to empty her drawers and sort everything out. Nevertheless, every other minute she went to lean over the banister, distressed at the sound of Louise's heavy, painful tread that made the floorboards creak. About four o'clock, as she heard her agitation increasing, she made up her mind to knock on Lazare's door. He had locked himself away in a state of nervous exasperation at the misfortunes that he accused Fate of bringing down on his head.

'We can't leave her like this,' she said. 'We must speak to her. Do come with me.'

They found her halfway up the stairs to the first floor, bending over the banister, too weak to go either up or down.

'My dear child,' said Pauline gently, 'we're a little concerned about you... We'll send for the midwife.'

This annoyed Louise.

'For God's sake, why do you torment me like this when all I want is to be left in peace?... At just eight months, what use do you think the midwife can be?'

'It would still be more sensible to see her.'

'No, I won't, I know what the matter is... For pity's sake don't talk to me any more, stop tormenting me!'

And Louise was so obstinate and displayed such exaggerated anger that Lazare lost his temper in turn. Pauline had to promise categorically not to send for the midwife. This was a certain Madame Bouland, from Verchemont, who had an extraordinary reputation in those parts for her skill and determination. People swore that her equal was not to be found in Bayeux, or even Caen. That was why Louise, who was very delicate and had a presentiment that she would die in labour, had resolved to place herself in her hands. But she was nonetheless terrified of Madame Bouland, with the same irrational fear inspired by the dentist, who has the power to cure but whom we put off visiting as long as we can.

At six o'clock there was a sudden easing of her discomfort. Louise was triumphant: she'd told them so, these were just her usual pains, only stronger; much good it would have done to disturb anyone, for no purpose! However, as she was dead tired, she preferred to go straight to bed, after eating a cutlet for supper. Everything would be all right, she assured them, if she could only get some sleep. And she obstinately rejected offers to stay with her, insisting on being left alone while the family ate dinner, and even refusing to let them come up to see her, for fear of being woken up suddenly.

Dinner that evening was beef stew and a roast veal joint. The meal began in silence, for Louise's attack had added to the gloom caused by

Pauline's departure. They ate as quietly as they could, as if the sound of scraping cutlery might reach the first floor and further exasperate the suffering Louise. Chanteau, however, was just getting into his stride and relating stories of remarkable pregnancies, when Véronique, as she was bringing in the sliced veal, suddenly exclaimed:

'I'm not sure, but I think I heard her groaning upstairs.'

Lazare stood up and went to open the door into the corridor. They all stopped eating and strained their ears to listen. At first, they could hear nothing, but then the sound of prolonged, muffled groans reached them.

'It's started again,' murmured Pauline. 'I'm going up.'

She threw down her napkin without touching the slice of veal the maid was serving her. Luckily the key was in the door and she was able to go in. Louise was sitting on the edge of her bed, barefoot and wrapped in a dressing gown, swaying backwards and forwards with the regularity of a pendulum, in the grip of an unbearable pain which made her gasp periodically.

'Is it getting worse?' asked Pauline.

She did not answer.

'Shall we send for Madame Bouland now?'

Then Louise stammered, in frustrated resignation:

'All right, I don't care. Perhaps I'll get some peace afterwards… I can't stand it any longer, I can't!'

Lazare, who had followed Pauline upstairs and was listening at the door, dared to go in and suggest that it would be prudent to dispatch someone to Arromanches to fetch Doctor Cazenove, in case there were complications. But Louise began to cry. Hadn't they any pity at all for her condition? Why did they torture her like this? They knew full well that she had always loathed the idea of being delivered by a man. She had a coquette's unhealthy modesty, a squeamishness about allowing herself to be seen in the terrible state of lost control that pain brought about. Even in front of her husband and her cousin, this made her pull the dressing gown together around her poor contorted loins.

'If you bring the doctor,' she gasped, 'I'll get into bed, turn to face the wall, and not say another word to anyone.'

'At least go for the midwife,' said Pauline to Lazare. 'I don't believe it's time yet, either. It's just a matter of calming her down.'

They both went back downstairs. Abbé Horteur had just dropped round to wish them goodnight, and he was standing in silence before the alarmed Chanteau. They tried to persuade Lazare to eat at least a little veal before he started out, but he was so agitated, he declared that a single mouthful would choke him, and set off at a trot towards Verchemont.

'Did she just call for me?' said Pauline, rushing towards the stairs. 'If I need Véronique, I'll knock. Do finish your dinner without me, won't you, Uncle?'

The priest, embarrassed at turning up in the middle of a confinement, was unable to find his usual words of consolation. He eventually left, promising to come back after he had visited the Gonins' house, where the crippled old man was seriously ill. So Chanteau was left sitting alone at the table cluttered with the remains of the abandoned meal. The glasses were half full, the veal was going cold on the plates, and the greasy forks and lumps of half-eaten bread lay where they had been dropped in the sudden alarm that had overtaken the diners. As she put a kettle on the stove in case it might be needed, the maid grumbled at not knowing whether to clear away or leave the mess as it was.

Upstairs, Pauline had found Louise standing up, leaning against the back of a chair.

'It hurts too much when I sit down, help me to walk about a bit.'

She had been complaining of prickling sensations on her skin, as if she were being stung all over by insects. She was suffering internal cramps, as if her abdomen were being squeezed ever more tightly in a vice. As soon as she tried to lie down, it seemed as if a lead weight were crushing her innards, and she felt a need to keep walking, taking the arm of her cousin, who led her from the bed over to the window.

'You have a slight temperature,' said Pauline. 'Why not drink something?'

Louise was unable to reply. A violent contraction bent her up double and she clung to Pauline's shoulders with such a shudder that it rocked them both. She could not help crying out in mingled frustration and fear.

'I'm dying of thirst,' she murmured once she was finally able to speak. 'My tongue is dry and you can see how flushed I am... No, no, don't let go of me or I'll fall. Let's keep on walking, I'll drink something later.'

And she carried on, her feet dragging and her body swaying, leaning ever more heavily on the arm that supported her. For two hours, she walked without pause. It was nine o'clock. Why was that midwife still not here? Now she was desperate to see her, saying they must really want her to die, leaving her without help for so long. Verchemont was only twenty-five minutes away, an hour should have been plenty. Lazare must be fooling around, or perhaps there'd been an accident, and now no one would ever come. Then she was overcome with nausea, and vomited.

'Go away, I don't want you here!... Oh God, to be reduced to this, an object of disgust to everyone!'

In this dreadful torment, she remained solely concerned with her feminine charms and modesty. Despite her delicate limbs, she had great powers of nervous resistance, so she devoted her remaining strength to preserving her decency, frustrated at being unable to put on her stockings, and ashamed of any glimpse of bare flesh she was showing. But she was overcome with a still greater embarrassment, for she was endlessly tormented by imaginary needs for the chamber pot, and insisted her cousin turn her back while she went behind a corner of the curtain and tried to relieve herself. As the maid had come up to offer her assistance, when she felt the first urge she stammered in a frantic voice:

'Oh no, not in front of her... Please, take her out into the corridor for a moment.'

Pauline was becoming desperate. The clock struck ten, and she could not understand Lazare's prolonged absence. Probably he hadn't found Madame Bouland; but how was she going to cope, not knowing how to help this poor woman whose situation seemed to be getting worse? The books she had read years before came back to her, and she would have liked to examine Louise in the hope of reassuring her, and herself. But Louise was so excessively self-conscious that she hesitated to offer.

'Listen, my dear,' she said at last, 'why don't you let me take a look?'

'You? Oh no! never!... You're not a married woman.'

Pauline could not stop herself from laughing.

'Don't be silly, that doesn't matter... I'd be so glad if I could help make you feel better.'

'No, I'd die of shame and never dare look you in the eye again.'

The clock struck eleven, the waiting was becoming unbearable. So Véronique set off for Verchemont, taking a lantern with her, with orders to search all the ditches. Twice Louise had tried to get into bed, her legs were so aching with fatigue, but she had got straight back out again and was now standing with her elbows propped on the chest of drawers, her hips in constant agitation, gyrating on the spot. The waves of pain were now coming closer together and merging into one single agony so severe it took her breath away. She repeatedly took her fumbling hands off the chest of drawers for a moment and ran them down her sides, to grasp and support her buttocks, as if to relieve them of a crushing weight. And Pauline, standing behind her, could do nothing but watch her suffer, turning away and pretending to be busy whenever she saw her pull the wrap together with a mortified gesture, still worrying that her pretty blonde hair was dishevelled and her delicate features distorted by pain.

It was almost midnight when the noise of wheels brought Pauline rushing downstairs.

'What about Véronique?' she shouted from the steps, as she recognized Lazare and the midwife. 'Didn't you meet her?'

Lazare explained that they had come via Port-en-Bessin, after all sorts of problems: Madame Bouland had been nine miles away attending a woman in labour, and as he'd been unable to get either a carriage or a horse to fetch her, he'd been forced to run the whole distance, with endless other difficulties once he arrived. Fortunately, Madame Bouland had her own horse and trap.

'But the woman,' exclaimed Pauline, 'was everything finished, so Madame was able to leave her?'

Lazare's voice quivered as he replied hoarsely:

'The woman died.'

They went into the hall, which was lit by a candle placed on the stairs. There was silence while Madame Bouland hung up her coat. She was a short, dark-haired woman, thin and sallow as a lemon, with a large domineering nose. She had a loud voice and a despotic manner which earned her great respect from the peasants.

'If Madame will kindly follow me,' said Pauline. 'I didn't know what to do next, she has been moaning constantly since nightfall.'

In the bedroom, Louise was still standing in front of the chest of drawers, making treading motions with her legs. She burst into tears again at the sight of the midwife, who asked her a few short questions, about the dates, location, and character of her pains. Then she curtly concluded:

'We'll see... I can't say anything until I've determined the presentation.'

'So, is it going to come now?' murmured Louise tearfully. 'Oh, my God! at eight months! And I thought I had another month to go!'

Without replying, Madame Bouland started plumping up the pillows and stacking them in the middle of the bed. Lazare, who had come upstairs, had the awkward air of a man finding himself in the middle of a childbirth. Yet he had come over to his wife and placed a kiss on her sweating brow, though she seemed not to notice this encouraging touch.

'Come along, now,' said the midwife.

Terrified, Louise cast a silently pleading look towards Pauline, which she well understood. She led Lazare outside and they both remained on the landing, unable to go any further. The candle, still burning downstairs, cast a dim light, broken by strange shadows, up the staircase where they both stood, he leaning against the wall and she on the banisters, facing each other in motionless silence. They listened intently to the sounds coming from the room: constant dull moans, and two piercing screams. Then an eternity seemed to go by, until Madame Bouland at last opened the door. They were about to go in but she pushed them back, came out herself and shut the door behind her.

'Well, how is she?' murmured Pauline.

She made a sign for them to go downstairs, and it was only when they were in the passage at the bottom of the stairs that she spoke.

'This looks like a very serious case. It is my duty to warn the family.'

Lazare blanched. An icy chill passed across his face. He stammered:

'What's the matter?'

'The child is presenting left shoulder on, as far as I can tell, and I'm even afraid the arm may be out first.'

'What does that mean?' asked Pauline.

'In a case such as this the presence of a doctor is absolutely essential... I can't take responsibility for the delivery, especially at only eight months.'

There was silence. Then Lazare protested despairingly: where were they supposed to find a doctor at that time of night? His wife would have time to die twenty deaths before he'd be able to fetch the man in Arromanches.

'I don't believe there's any immediate danger,' said the midwife. 'Go at once... I can do nothing on my own.'

And as Pauline implored her, in the name of humanity, to try something at least to bring some relief to the unfortunate woman, whose loud moans continued to fill the house, she replied curtly:

'No, I'm not allowed... The last one died on me. I'm not taking responsibility for this one.'

At that moment, a whining appeal came up to them from Chanteau, in the dining room,

'Is anyone there? Do come in!... Nobody tells me anything. I've been waiting ages to hear what's going on.'

They went in. Since the abandoned dinner, Chanteau had been completely forgotten. He had remained seated at the uncleared table, twiddling his thumbs and waiting patiently, with the drowsy resignation of an invalid used to sitting for long periods on his own. He was saddened by this new catastrophe, which had turned the household upside down, and had not even had the heart to finish eating, but had just sat staring at his full plate.

'So, are things not going so well?' he enquired.

Lazare angrily shrugged his shoulders. Madame Bouland, who remained perfectly calm, advised him not to waste any more time.

'Take my trap!' she said. 'The horse isn't much good, but you should be able to get there and back in two, two and a half hours. Meanwhile, I'll keep an eye on her.'

Then with sudden determination Lazare dashed outside, certain that he would return to find his wife dead. They could hear him cursing and whipping the horse, as the trap clattered noisily away.

'What's going on?' called Chanteau again, since nobody had answered him.

The midwife went back upstairs, and Pauline followed her, after simply telling her uncle that poor Louise was going to have a difficult time of it. When she offered to put him to bed, he refused, insisting on staying up to know how things went. If he felt drowsy, he'd doze comfortably enough in his chair, as he often did for whole afternoons at a stretch. They had only just left him alone again when Véronique came back, her lantern extinguished. She was furious. Not for two years had she poured out such a torrent of words at once.

'Might've told me they'd be coming back the other way! And me peering into all the ditches and practically killing myself to get to Verchemont!... I hung around there, too, for a good half-hour, stood right in the middle of the road!'

Chanteau looked at her wide-eyed.

'Well, my girl, you were really quite unlikely to meet up.'

'Then on my way back, who should I see but Monsieur Lazare galloping along like a madman in some shabby old cart... I shout out to him that he's wanted back home, but he just whips the horse some more and almost runs me down!... No, I'm fed up of these errands where nobody tells me what's going on! To cap it all, my lantern blew out.'

And she started prodding her master to finish his food so that she could at least clear the table. He wasn't hungry, but he'd eat a little cold veal, really just for something to do. What was bothering him now was the abbé's failure to stick to his word. Why promise to keep a fellow company if you've already made up your mind to stay at home? Admittedly, a priest was rather a spare part about the place when a woman was in labour! This idea tickled him so much that he cheerfully set about dining on his own.

'Come along, Monsieur, do hurry up!' Véronique kept saying. 'It's nearly one o'clock, I can't have my dishes lying about like this till morning... What a house, there's always something to upset your routine!'

She was starting to clear the table when Pauline called urgently to her down the stairs. And Chanteau found himself once more alone and forgotten at the table, with nobody coming down to tell him what was happening.

Madame Bouland had taken command of the bedroom, rummaging in cupboards and giving orders. First, she had a fire lit, because she felt the room was damp. Then she declared the bed unsuitable, it was too low, too soft; and when Pauline told her that there was an old folding bed in the attic, she sent Véronique up to fetch it and set it up in front of the fire, laying a board across the base and covering it with a simple mattress. Then she required a quantity of linen, a sheet that she folded in four to protect the mattress, other sheets, towels, and cloths that she hung over chairs to warm in front of the fire. Soon the bedroom, with linen hanging everywhere and the extra bed, was looking like a field hospital hastily set up in anticipation of a battle.

Moreover, she was now talking continuously, exhorting Louise in military tones, as if she were issuing orders to pain itself. Pauline had asked her in a whisper not to mention the doctor.

'Everything will be just fine, dearie. I'd rather have you lying down, but since you find that uncomfortable, just keep walking around, you can lean on me... I've delivered some at eight months whose babies were the biggest of the lot... No, no, it doesn't hurt as much as you think. We'll soon have you relieved of it, in double-quick time.'

This did not make Louise any calmer. Her shrieks became dreadfully distressed. She clung to the furniture, at times uttering incoherent speech which even showed a touch of delirium. To reassure Pauline, the midwife explained in a low voice that the pain from the dilation of the cervix was sometimes more unbearable than that of the actual delivery itself. She had known this preparatory labour to go on for two days, with a first child. What she feared was that the waters might break before the doctor arrived, which would make the manipulation he was going to have to perform more dangerous.

'I can't bear it,' Louise kept panting, 'I can't bear it... I'm going to die...'

Madame Bouland made up her mind to give her twenty drops of laudanum in half a glass of water. Then she had tried friction on the loins. Poor Louise, her strength now failing, made less and less attempt to preserve her modesty: no longer insisting that her cousin and the maid leave the room, she simply hid her nakedness by clutching the dressing gown together around her. But the short respite brought about by the frictions did not last, and terrible contractions set in.

'We can only wait,' said Madame Bouland stoically. 'There's absolutely nothing I can do. We must let nature take its course.'

And she even started discussing chloroform, for which she expressed an old-school distaste. To listen to her, women in childbirth were dying like flies in the hands of doctors who used it. Pain was a necessary thing, and a woman asleep could never push as well as one who was awake.

Pauline had read the opposite. She did not answer, her heart flooding with compassion to see the ravages of pain systematically destroying Louise and turning her, with all her grace and delicate blonde charm, into a dreadful object of pity. She was filled with anger against pain and a desire to suppress it; she would have fought it like an enemy, if only she had known how.

However, the night was going by and it was almost two o'clock. Several times Louise had talked of Lazare. They lied and told her he was staying downstairs because he was feeling so shaken up himself, he was afraid he might discourage her. In any case, she had lost all sense of time: hours went by, but the minutes seemed to her to last for ever. The only idea that persisted through her agitation was that it would never stop, and everyone around her was deliberately making it worse. It was the rest of them who did not want her to be delivered, and she raged against the midwife, Pauline, and Véronique, accusing them of not knowing what needed to be done.

Madame Bouland said nothing. She kept glancing furtively at the clock, even though she was not expecting the doctor for another hour, for she knew how slow her worn-out horse would be. Dilation was almost complete now and the waters were on the point of breaking, so she persuaded Louise to lie down. Then she warned her what to expect.

'Don't be alarmed if you suddenly feel wet... And for heaven's sake stop moving around! This isn't the moment to be speeding things up.'

Louise remained motionless for several seconds. It took an extreme effort of will for her to resist the random jerks caused by the pain, and this only made it worse, so that soon, unable to struggle any more against the urge, she leapt up from the folding bed in a sudden exasperated reflex of her whole body. Just at the moment when her feet touched the rug, there came the plopping sound of a wineskin bursting, her legs were soaked and two big damp patches appeared on her dressing gown.

'There it goes!' said the midwife, cursing under her breath.

Despite the warning, Louise stood rooted to the spot and shaking, as she watched the liquid streaming out of her, terrified that she would see the dressing gown and rug turn red with her blood. But the patches stayed pale, the flow suddenly stopped, and she was relieved. Quickly they put her back to bed, and she felt a sudden calm, such an unexpected sense of well-being, that she started speaking in a cheerful and triumphant voice:

'That's what the trouble was. Now my pain's all gone, it's over... I knew I couldn't be having the baby at eight months. It'll be coming next month... You got it all wrong, the lot of you.'

Madame Bouland nodded, not wanting to spoil this momentary respite for her by replying that the real delivery pains were yet to come. She simply warned Pauline in an undertone and asked her to stand on the other side of the bed, to prevent Louise from falling out in case she started to struggle in her labour. But when the pains began again, Louise made no attempt to get up, unable to find either the strength or the will to try. With the first new pangs, her face had turned ashen

and taken on an expression of despair. She stopped speaking, with-
drawing into her endless torment, no longer counting on anyone's
help, feeling so abandoned and miserable now that she wanted to die
straight away. Besides, these were no longer the involuntary contractions which had been gnawing at her innards for the last twenty hours;
now they were excruciating exertions of her whole body which she
could do nothing to lessen, but was deliberately exaggerating, in her
irresistible urge to be delivered. The thrusting began just below her
ribs and travelled down through her loins to the groin, in a kind
of ever-widening split. Every muscle of her abdomen was labouring,
tensing across the hips, contracting and stretching like a spring; even
those in her buttocks and thighs were labouring, seeming at times to
lift her off the mattress. She was shuddering the whole time, wracked
by broad waves of pain sweeping down from her waist to her knees,
which could be seen rippling one at a time under her skin, as her body
went into ever more violent spasms.

'Won't it stop, good God, won't it ever stop?' murmured Pauline.

This sight was draining her of all her usual calm and courage. She
found herself making her own imaginary efforts to push, at every breathless groan wrung from the toiling woman in accompaniment to her
labour. Her cries, stifled at first, grew gradually louder and swelled
into wails of exhaustion and helplessness. It was like the desperate,
infuriated grunt of a woodcutter who has been attacking the same knot
with his axe for hours on end, barely even nicking the bark.

Between the spasms, in her short intervals of respite, Louise complained of a burning thirst. Her parched throat made painful choking
gulps.

'I'm dying, give me something to drink!'

She would take a few sips of the weak lime tea that Véronique was
keeping warm in front of the fire. But often, just as she was putting
the cup to her lips, Pauline had to take it back because the next spasm
was starting and her hands were shaking again, while her upturned
face became crimson and beads of sweat broke out on her neck, as her
muscles tensed against the new wave of pain.

She was also subject to stomach cramps, and talked constantly of
an urgent need to get up and go to the toilet, to which the midwife
objected energetically.

'Do keep still! It's an effect of your labour... If you do get up, you
won't be able to do anything, so what would be the good of that?'

At three o'clock Madame Bouland no longer concealed her anxiety from Pauline. Some alarming symptoms were developing, particularly a steady loss of strength. It almost seemed as if Louise were now in less pain, for the energy of her cries and her efforts was diminishing; but in truth, the labour was threatening to stop through excessive fatigue. She was succumbing to the endless pain, and each minute of delay added to the danger.

She grew delirious again, and even passed out briefly. Madame Bouland took this opportunity to feel her again and get a better idea of the position.

'It's just as I feared,' she murmured. 'Has that nag broken a leg, for them to be taking so long?'

And, as Pauline was telling her that she mustn't let the poor unfortunate woman die like this, she burst out angrily:

'Do you think I'm doing this for fun?... If I attempt to turn the child and it goes wrong, I shall be in all sorts of trouble... They're always so hard on us midwives!'

When Louise came round, she complained of a new discomfort.

'It's the little arm poking through,' Madame Bouland continued in a whisper. 'It's completely out... But the shoulder's stuck, it will never come free.'

However, at half past three, faced with an increasingly critical situation, she was on the verge of deciding to act when Véronique, coming up from the kitchen, called Pauline into the passage and told her that the doctor had arrived. Leaving the maid alone with the patient for a moment, she and the midwife went downstairs. In the middle of the courtyard Lazare stood cursing the horse in stammering tones; but once he heard that his wife was still alive, his relief was so great that he calmed down at once. Doctor Cazenove was already striding up the steps, putting hurried questions to Madame Bouland.

'Your sudden appearance would scare her,' said Pauline on the stairs. 'Now that you're here, she needs to be given warning.'

'Be quick!' was his brief reply.

Pauline went in alone, while the others stood back by the door.

'Dearest,' she explained, 'just think, after seeing you yesterday, the doctor guessed you might need him again, and he's just come... You really should see him, since this has been going on so long.'

Louise did not seem to hear her. She was desperately rolling her head about on the pillow. Finally, she stammered:

'Whatever you say; my God, what do I care now? I no longer exist.'

The doctor had come into the room. Then the midwife sent Pauline and Lazare downstairs: she would keep them informed and call them if any help was needed. They went out in silence. Downstairs in the dining room, Chanteau had just fallen asleep in front of the uncleared table. He must have dozed off in the middle of his little supper, having made it last as a distraction, because his fork was balanced on the edge of the plate, with a bit of veal on it. When she went in, Pauline had to turn up the lamp, which was smoking and about to go out.

'Let's not wake him,' she murmured. 'There's no need for him to know.'

She sat down quietly on a chair while Lazare remained standing, motionless. A terrible wait began, with neither of them saying a word; they could not even bear to see the apprehension in each other's eyes, but turned away whenever their gazes met. Not a sound came down from upstairs, the feeble moans could no longer be heard; they strained their ears but caught no sound except the frantic throbbing of their own pulse. As time went by, it was this shivering silence, the silence of death, that horrified them the most. What could be going on? Why had they been sent away? They would have preferred screams and struggling, the noise of a living being putting up a fight above their heads. As the minutes dragged by, the house sank ever deeper into this void. At last the door opened and Doctor Cazenove came in.

'Well?' asked Lazare, who had finally sat down opposite Pauline.

The doctor did not answer at once. In the smoky glimmer of the lamp, that dim glow that accompanies long vigils, they could not clearly distinguish his old tanned face, in which only the wrinkles were made paler by emotion. But when he spoke, the broken tone of his voice betrayed his inner torment.

'Well, I've not done anything yet,' he replied. 'I won't, before I have consulted you.'

Then he ran his fingers mechanically across his brow, as if to brush away some obstacle, a thorny problem he could not solve.

'But it is not for us to decide, Doctor,' said Pauline. 'We are placing her in your hands.'

He shook his head. He was haunted by memories that would not go away, of the few pregnant negresses he had attended in the colonies, and one in particular, a tall girl whose baby had presented shoulder-first like this and who had died while he was delivering her of a packet of flesh and bones. This was the only type of experience a naval surgeon could get, occasionally ripping women open during a tour of hospital duty out in the colonies. Since he had retired to Arromanches, he had certainly had more practice and become skilled by force of habit, but the dreadfully tricky case that confronted him in this house of friends had brought back all his former hesitancy. He was shaking like a novice, worried also about his old hands, which no longer had the strength of his younger days.

'I must tell you everything,' he continued. 'I can see no hope for either mother or child... There might still be time to save one or the other...'

Lazare and Pauline stood up, chilled by the same icy shudder. Chanteau, woken by the sound of voices, had opened his bleary eyes and was listening with horror to what was being discussed in front of him.

'Which am I to try and save?' repeated the doctor, shaking as badly as the poor people to whom he was putting the question. 'The child, or the mother?'

'Which?' exclaimed Lazare, 'Good God, how should I know? How could I?'

Tears choked him once more, whilst his cousin, white-faced, remained mute in the face of that dread alternative.

'If I attempt a version,'* continued the doctor, voicing his doubts out loud, 'the baby will probably be mangled on the way out. And I'm afraid of exhausting the mother, she's been in pain for too long already... On the other hand, a Caesarean would save the child's life, but the poor woman isn't in such a desperate state that I'd feel justified in sacrificing her like that...* It's a question of conscience and I beg you, tell me what I should do.'

Sobs prevented Lazare from answering. He had pulled out his handkerchief and was twisting it convulsively in an effort to collect his wits. Chanteau was still staring at them in stupefaction. And it was Pauline who managed to say:

'Why did you come down?... It's cruel to torment us, when only you know what to do, and how to do it.'

Just at that moment, Madame Bouland came in to tell them that the situation was getting worse.

'Have you made up your minds? She's getting weaker.'

Then, in one of his disconcertingly impulsive gestures, the doctor threw his arms around Lazare and spoke to him with the familiar 'tu':

'Listen, I'm going to try and save them both... And if they don't survive, well, I'll be even sadder than you, because I shall consider that it was my fault.'

Swiftly, with the energy of a man whose mind is made up, he discussed the use of chloroform. He had brought the necessary equipment, but certain symptoms made him fear a haemorrhage, which was an absolute counter-indication. He was very concerned about the fainting and the weakness of the pulse. So he resisted the pleas for chloroform from the family, greatly distressed by the suffering in which they had been sharing for almost the last twenty-four hours, and was encouraged in his refusal by the attitude of the midwife, who shrugged her shoulders in disgust and disdain.

'I deliver a good two hundred women a year,' she muttered. 'Do any of them need that stuff to get through it?... They have pain, but so does everybody!'

'Come along upstairs, you two,' said the doctor. 'I'll be needing you... And anyway, I'd rather you were up there with me.'

They were all leaving the dining room when Chanteau at last spoke up. He called his son over.

'Come and embrace me... Oh, poor little Louise! Isn't it terrible, things like this happening when you're not expecting them? If only it was light!... Come and tell me when it's all over.'

Once again, he was left alone in the room. The lamp was smoking and he blinked his eyelids against the flickering light, feeling drowsiness overtaking him again. He fought it for a few minutes, running his gaze over the crockery on the table and the chairs pushed back, with napkins still draped over their backs. But the air was too heavy and the silence too oppressive. He succumbed, his eyelids closed, and light, regular breaths came from his lips, surrounded by the tragic disorder of the previous evening's interrupted dinner.

Upstairs, Doctor Cazenove recommended that a large fire be lit in the room next door, Madame Chanteau's former bedroom: it might be needed after the delivery. Véronique, who had been looking after Louise while the midwife was out of the room, went straight off to see to it. Then everything was made ready: clean linen was put out in front of the fire, a second basin and a kettle of hot water were brought upstairs, along with a litre bottle of brandy and a lump of lard on a plate. The doctor felt it was his duty to inform the patient of what was happening.

'My dear child,' he said, 'don't be concerned, but I absolutely must intervene to help you... Your life is precious to us all, and if the poor baby is in danger, we can't leave you like this any longer... You will give me your permission to act, won't you?'

Louise no longer seemed to hear. Made rigid by involuntary straining, with her head lolling to the left on the pillow and her mouth hanging open, she was emitting a continuous low moan which sounded like a death rattle. When her eyelids opened, she looked up at the ceiling in confusion, as if she had woken up in a strange place.

'Your permission?' the doctor repeated.

Then she stammered:

'Kill me, kill me now.'

'Hurry up, I beg you,' Pauline whispered to the doctor. 'We're here to take full responsibility.'

Yet he went on talking, saying to Lazare:

'I'm confident about her, as long as there's no haemorrhage. But I don't think the child will survive. In this situation, we kill nine out of ten, there are always lesions and fractures, sometimes they get completely crushed.'

'Please, Doctor, please,' replied the father with a despairing gesture.

The folding bed was not judged sufficiently solid. The young woman was carried across to the big bed, once a plank had been placed under the mattress. She was lying with her head towards the wall and leaning against a pile of pillows, the small of her back on the very edge of the bed; they parted her thighs and propped her feet on the backs of two small armchairs.

'Excellent,' said the doctor as he considered these preparations. 'We're well set up, it's going to be very suitable... Only, it would be as well to hold on to her in case she struggles.'

Louise no longer existed. She had renounced her humanity and become like an object. Her feminine modesty, her resolve not to let herself be seen naked and in agony, had finally crumbled under the onslaught of pain. Without the strength to lift a finger, she had no awareness either of her naked skin, or of the people who were touching her. And she lay there, uncovered up to her breasts, belly open to the air and legs spread wide, without even a quiver, exposing the full spectacle of her bloody, gaping maternity.

'Madame Bouland will hold one thigh,' continued the doctor, 'and Pauline, you will be good enough to hold the other. Don't be afraid, hold her tight enough to stop any movement... Now if Lazare would be so kind as to give me some light...'

They followed his orders, for her nudity had become invisible to them too. They are only the pitiable misery of her condition, the high drama of a struggle to be born, which killed any idea of love. In the harsh lamplight, all sensual mystery had departed from that so delicate skin, with its secret places and its blonde triangle of tufted ringlets; there remained only suffering humanity, childbirth in blood and ordure, splitting open the mother's belly and horrifically stretching her red slit, like an axe wound in the trunk of a great tree, its life leaching away.

The doctor was still talking in an undertone as he took off his frock coat and rolled his left shirtsleeve up above the elbow.

'We've delayed too long, it will be difficult to introduce my hand... As you can see, the shoulder is already engaged in the cervix.'

Amidst the taut, swollen muscles, from between pinkish folds of flesh, the child was emerging. But it was stuck there, in the constriction of the organ, which it could not pass. Meanwhile, abdominal and lumbar contractions were still working to expel it, and even though unconscious, the mother was pushing violently, exhausting herself in that labour, in her mechanical urge to be delivered; waves of pain continued to sweep down her body, each accompanied by the yelp of her obstinacy, as she battled against the impossible. The baby's hand was dangling from the vulva. It was a little black hand, its fingers opening and closing intermittently, as though clutching at life.

'Let the leg relax a little,' Madame Bouland told Pauline. 'There's no need to tire her out.'

Doctor Cazenove had positioned himself between the knees, held by the two women. He turned in surprise at the way the light was dancing around. Behind him, Lazare was shaking so much that the candle flame flickered in his hand, as if in a gust of wind.

'My dear fellow,' he said, 'do put the candlestick down on the bedside table. I shall see much better.'

Unable to keep watching, the husband retreated to the far end of the room and collapsed onto a chair. But he could still see the little creature's pathetic hand, striving for life, seemingly groping for help in this world where it was arriving first.

Then the doctor knelt down. He had smeared his left hand in lard and began to introduce it slowly, placing the right hand on the belly. He needed to push the little arm right back inside to make room for his own fingers, and that was the dangerous part of the operation. Then, forming a wedge with his fingers, he was gradually able to work his hand in up to the wrist, with a slight rotating motion. It went in deeper and deeper, feeling for the baby's knees, then its feet, while the other applied increasing pressure on the lower abdomen to assist the internal operation. But there was nothing to be seen of this, beyond an arm that had disappeared inside a body.

'Madame is being very good,' remarked Madame Bouland. 'Sometimes it takes strong men to hold them down.'

Pauline could feel the wretched thigh shivering with fear, and she clutched it maternally to her body.

'Be brave, darling,' she murmured in turn.

There was silence. Louise could not have said what was being done to her, she just felt a growing anxiety, a sensation of having something ripped from her. Pauline could no longer recognize the slim girl with her fine features and delicate charm, in this creature lying twisted across the bed, her face ravaged by pain. Globs of mucus had squeezed out between the doctor's fingers and stuck to the golden tufts that graced her white skin. A few drops of black blood trickled down a fold of flesh and fell one by one onto the cloth that had been put down to cover the mattress.

Louise passed out again, seeming as if dead, and the muscular labour came to an almost complete stop.

'I prefer it like that,' said the doctor when Madame Bouland drew his attention to it. 'She was crushing my hand, the pain was getting so unbearable I was going to have to pull it out... I'm not as young as I was, or else it would be over by now!'

His left hand had already been holding the feet for a while, bringing them gently round in order to turn the baby. Things stopped momentarily and he had to compress the lower abdomen with his right hand. The other was coming smoothly out, first the wrist, then the fingers. And the baby's feet at last appeared. They all felt relieved. Cazenove heaved a sigh; his brow was bathed in sweat and he was panting as if after violent exercise.

'We're getting there, I think all's well, the tiny heart is still going... But we haven't quite got the little mite out yet!'

He stood up again with a forced laugh. Urgently, he asked Véronique for hot towels. Then, while he was washing his hand, bloodied and dirty like a butcher's, he tried to encourage the husband, who was slumped on his chair.

'Won't be long now, my lad. Look on the bright side, for heaven's nalue!'

Lazare did not move. Madame Bouland, who had just roused Louise from her faint by holding a flask of ether under her nose, was particularly concerned to see that the labour had stopped. She mentioned this in an undertone to the doctor, who replied out loud:

'I was expecting as much. I shall have to help her.'

And, turning to the patient:

'Don't hold back, use your pain as much as you can. If you can help me a little, we'll soon have you right.'

But she gestured feebly that she had no strength left. They could barely hear her mumbling:

'I can't feel a single part of my body any more.'

'Poor darling,' said Pauline, giving her a kiss. 'Come on, your troubles are almost over now!'

The doctor was already kneeling down again. Once more the two women held on to the thighs, while Véronique passed him warm towels. He had wrapped them around the little feet and was pulling slowly, in one gentle and continuous movement; his fingers moved up as the baby came out, holding it round the ankles, the calves, then the knees, grasping each new part as it emerged. When the hips appeared, he avoided putting pressure on the belly, but moved his hands around the loins and pressed with both on the groin. The baby was still sliding out, distending the folds of pink flesh which were becoming ever tighter. But the mother, who had been docile up to this point, suddenly jerked in resistance to the pain that came flooding in once again. These were no longer just contractions, her whole body was writhing, she felt as if she were being split in two by a heavy cleaver, like the beef carcases she had seen being chopped up in a butcher's shop. She fought so violently that her leg escaped her cousin's grasp and the baby slipped out of the doctor's hands.

'Careful!' he cried. 'You must stop her moving!... We'll be lucky if the cord hasn't been compressed.'

He had caught the tiny body and was hurriedly freeing the shoulders, bringing the arms down one at a time to avoid adding to the volume of the head. But the mother's convulsions were making his task difficult and he had to keep stopping, for fear of causing a fracture. Although the two women struggled with all their might to hold her down, she threw them off and arched her body up from her bed of pain with a single uncontrollable jerk of her neck. In her struggle, she grabbed hold of the wooden bed frame and refused to let go, levering herself against it and kicking out violently with her legs in the obsessive idea of shaking off these people who were torturing her. She was in a complete frenzy, uttering horrible screams, with the sensation that she was being murdered, ripped apart from groin to belly.

'Only the head to go now,' said the doctor, his voice trembling. 'I don't dare touch it if she keeps jerking about like this... Since the pains have come back, she'll probably deliver herself now. Let's just wait a little.'

He needed to sit down. Madame Bouland, without letting go of the mother, was keeping an eye on the child, which was lying between the bloody thighs, still held in by its neck as if it were being strangled. Its little limbs twitched feebly, then the movements stopped. They became concerned once more and the doctor decided to stimulate the contractions, to speed up the process. He stood up and applied sudden, repeated pressure to the mother's abdomen. And there were several dreadful minutes, with the unfortunate woman screaming louder than ever, as the head emerged, pushing back the flesh into a broad whiteish ring. Down below, between the two distended, gaping cavities the delicate skin bulged horribly, stretched so thin that it threatened to split. There was a spurt of excrement, and with a final spasm the child slid out, in a shower of blood and foul waters.

'At last!' said Cazenove. 'Well, this one can certainly boast that it didn't have an easy passage into the world.'

So great was the tension that nobody had noticed the sex of the child.

'It's a boy, Monsieur,' Madame Bouland announced to the husband.

Lazare, his head turned to face the wall, burst into tears. He felt immense despair at the thought that it would have been better for them all to die, rather than to go on living after such terrible suffering. The birth of this new being filled him with a deathly sadness.

Pauline bent over Louise and kissed her once more on the forehead.

'Come and kiss her!' she said to her cousin.

He came across and leaned down in his turn. But a fresh shudder came over him when his lips touched her face, covered in cold sweat.

His wife was lying there with closed eyes, scarcely breathing. Resting his head against the wall at the foot of the bed, Lazare tried to control a fresh bout of sobbing.

'I think it's dead,' said the doctor quietly. 'Quick, tie the cord.'

The newborn had not given the usual high-pitched mewing cry, accompanied by the low gurgling sound of air entering the lungs. It was blackish-blue in colour, with livid blotches, small for its eight months, with an exaggeratedly large head.

Madame Bouland deftly cut the cord and tied it off, after letting out a small quantity of blood. The child was still not breathing and had no detectable heartbeat.

'That's it,' declared Cazenove. 'We might perhaps try friction and mouth-to-mouth resuscitation, but I think we'd be wasting our time... And besides, there's the mother, who is in great need of my attention.'

Pauline was listening.

'Give him to me!' she exclaimed. 'I'll see... If he doesn't start breathing, it will be because I have no breath left myself.'

Then she carried the child into the room opposite, along with the bottle of brandy and some towels.

Fresh pangs, now very much weaker, were bringing Louise round from her prostrate state. These were the final birth pains. Once the doctor had assisted the expulsion of the afterbirth by pulling on the umbilical cord, the midwife raised her up to remove the towels, red from the thick flow of blood. Then the two of them stretched her out, having washed her thighs and put a cloth between them, and wrapped a broad linen band tightly round her midriff. The doctor was still deeply concerned about the risk of haemorrhage, even though he was satisfied there was no blood left inside and that the amount she had lost was more or less normal. The afterbirth also seemed complete; but the patient's weakness, and particularly the cold sweat that covered her, remained very alarming. She was not moving and looked pale as wax, lying with the sheet pulled up to her chin, weighed down by blankets which were not warming her up.

'Stay with her,' said the doctor to the midwife while he continued to feel Louise's pulse. 'I won't be leaving her until I'm completely sure she's out of danger.'

Across the passage, in Madame Chanteau's old room, Pauline was battling against the increasing asphyxia of the pathetic little creature she had carried in there. She laid him in an armchair before the blazing fire, then knelt down and massaged him continuously with a flannel that she had dipped in a saucer of brandy, stubborn in her faith and oblivious to the cramp that was gradually numbing her arm. The baby was so scrawny and pitiably fragile that her great fear was of finishing him off by rubbing too hard. And so the to-and-fro motion that she used was gentle and caressing, like the repeated brush of a bird's wing. She carefully turned the child round and tried to coax the life back into each of his tiny limbs. But still he did not stir. Though the friction seemed to warm him up a little, his chest remained hollow, with no breath to inflate it. On the contrary, he seemed to be turning even bluer.

Then, with no feeling of repugnance for that flaccid, barely washed face, Pauline pressed her own lips to the inert little mouth. She exhaled long, slow breaths, adjusting the flow to the capacity of the compressed little lungs which the air had been unable to enter. When she felt herself starting to run out of air, she had to stop for a few seconds; then she began again. The blood rushed to her head, her ears began to buzz, and she felt dizzy. Yet she did not give up, but kept on offering her breath for more than half an hour, without the slightest result to encourage her. Whenever she inhaled, all she could taste was the sickly savour of death. She had tried in vain to make the ribs move by pressing them very gently with the tips of her fingers. But nothing was working, and any other woman would have renounced such an impossible resurrection. Pauline, however, brought to her task the despairing obstinacy of a mother striving to bring into the world the puny fruit of her loins. She was determined the child was going to live, and at last she felt a stirring of life in that poor body, as the tiny mouth twitched slightly beneath her own.

For nearly an hour she had been alone in that room, absorbed in the frantic anxiety of the battle against death, oblivious of everything else. That faint sign of life, that brief tremor against her lips, gave her fresh hope. She started the friction again, alternating every other minute with breathing into the lungs, giving her all, in an upwelling of charitable emotion. She felt a compelling need to win, to produce life. For a moment, she feared she had been mistaken, for the lips against which her own were pressed remained unresponsive. Then she became aware of another rapid contraction. Little by little the air was going in, taken from her and then returned. Beneath her bosom, she seemed to hear the little heart picking up a regular beat. Her mouth never left the tiny lips; she shared her life with the little being, they had but one breath between them in that miraculous resurrection, a long, slow exchange of air flowing from one to the other like a common soul. Pauline had slime and mucus on her lips, but her joy at saving the child took away any sense of revulsion. now she was inhaling the warm pungency of life, which made her light-headed. When the baby at last gave a feeble, plaintive cry, she sat back on the floor in front of the armchair, moved to the very depths of her womb.

The great fire was blazing away, filling the room with cheerful light. Pauline stayed sitting on the floor in front of the child, which she had still not looked at properly. How puny he was! What a pathetic, half-formed creature! In a last stirring of inner revolt, her own robust health protested against this wretched son Louise had given Lazare. She looked down in despair at her own hips, at her virginal belly which had just felt such a sympathetic thrill. Her broad flanks might have held a strong, sturdy son. She felt immense regret at her own frustrated life, her womanly sex destined to remain for ever sterile. The crisis that had so tormented her on the night of the wedding was beginning again in reaction to this new birth. That very morning, she had woken to find herself bloodstained from the discharge of her barren fertility, and just now, after the emotions of that terrible night, she could feel it running away beneath her, like waste water. Never would she be a mother, she wished all the blood in her body could run out in the same way, since she could never make new life with it. What use was that vigorous puberty she had experienced, her organs and muscles swelling with vitality, the powerful scent of her firm flesh, its energy flowering in dusky down? She would remain for ever like a field unploughed, desiccated and ignored. In the place of that pitiful abortion lying in the armchair like a naked insect, she saw the bouncing boy that her own marriage might have given her, and she mourned the child that she would never have.

But the poor creature was still wailing. She was afraid he might fall on the floor. Then the sight of such ugliness and weakness reawoke her charitable instinct. She would at least comfort him and help him to go on living, as she had had the joy of helping in his birth. So, forgetting herself, but still shedding tears of mingled sorrow for her own unfulfilled maternity, and pity for the misery of all living creatures, she took the child on her knees to complete the first steps in his care.

Once Madame Bouland had been told, she came in to help wash the baby. First, they wrapped him in a warm sheet, then they dressed him and laid him in the big bed to wait until the cradle was ready. The midwife, astonished to find the child alive, had given him a careful examination and announced that he seemed physically well formed, but was so weakly he would be difficult to bring up. Then she hurried back to be with Louise, who remained in a critical state.

As Pauline was settling down next to the baby, Lazare, who had been informed of the miracle, entered the room in his turn.

'Come and see him!' she said, with great emotion.

But as he drew near, he began to tremble and could not help exclaiming:

'My God, you've put him in that bed!'

The moment he had come through the door, a shiver had run down his spine. He discovered that deserted room, so rarely entered and still in the shadow of mourning, now warm and bright, enlivened by the crackling of the fire. Yet all the furniture was still in its accustomed position, the clock still said seven thirty-seven, and nobody had lived there since his mother's death. And it was in that very bed where she had breathed her last, that sacred, awful bed, that he now saw his own child reborn, so tiny amid the expanse of bedclothes.

'Do you object?' Pauline asked in surprise.

He shook his head, speechless with emotion. At last he stammered:

'I'm just thinking about Maman... She's gone, and now here's another one who will go in just the same way. Why has he come?'

His words were strangled by sobbing. Since Louise's terrible delivery, his fear and loathing of life had burst out again, despite his efforts to keep silent. When he touched his baby's wrinkled brow to kiss it, he recoiled, imagining he could feel his lips denting the soft skull. Looking at this frail creature that he had cast into the world, he was filled with desperate remorse.

'It's all right,' Pauline went on, to reassure him. 'We'll make a strapping lad out of him... It makes no difference that he's so small now.'

He looked at her, so overwhelmed that a complete confession burst from his heart:

'Yet again, we owe his life to you… So, am I destined to be forever in your debt?'

'Me?' she exclaimed, 'I only did what the midwife would have done if I hadn't been here.'

He silenced her with a wave of the hand.

'Do you think I'm so contemptible as not to realize I owe you everything?… Since the day you came into this house, you have never stopped sacrificing yourself. I won't mention your money, but I know now that you were still in love with me yourself when you gave me to Louise… If you could only guess how ashamed I feel when I look at you, and remember! You would have given your own lifeblood, you were always generous and cheerful, even when I was breaking your heart. Yes, you were right, cheerfulness and generosity are all that counts, everything else is just a nightmare.'

She tried to interrupt him, but he continued, his voice growing stronger:

'What a fool I have been, with all that arrogance and negativity, wallowing in pessimism out of fear and vanity! I'm the one who has made our lives a misery, yours and mine, and the whole family's. Yes, you've been the only sensible one! When everyone's feeling positive and living for each other, life is so easy!… If the world is to die in misery, let it at least go out with a song on its lips, and pity for itself!'

The violence of his language made her smile, and she seized his hands.

'Come now, just calm down… Now that you admit I'm right, you've learnt your lesson and all will be well.'

'Learnt my lesson, perhaps! I'm saying these things now because there are times when the truth will out, come what may. But tomorrow I shall slide back into all my old torments. Do we ever really change?… No, all won't be well, on the contrary, it'll get worse and worse. You know that as much as I do… It's my own stupidity that infuriates me!'

Then she pulled him gently towards her and said, in her serious voice:

'You are neither contemptible nor stupid, you're just unhappy… Kiss me, Lazare.'

They exchanged a kiss, in front of the poor little creature, who seemed to have nodded off; and it was a brotherly and sisterly kiss, completely devoid of the desire that had raged within them only the previous day.

Dawn was breaking, a grey dawn of supreme gentleness. Cazenove came to see the baby and was astonished to find him doing so well. He advised taking him back into the other room, for he was satisfied that Louise was now out of danger. When the infant was presented to his mother, she smiled wanly. Then she closed her eyes and fell into the deep, restorative slumber which a woman who has given birth needs for her convalescence. The window had been opened a little to air the smell of blood away, and a delicious coolness, like the breath of life, was drifting up on the high tide. They all stood for a moment motionless, exhausted and happy, by the bed in which she was sleeping. Finally, they tiptoed out of the room, leaving only Madame Bouland to watch over her.

The doctor, however, did not leave until around eight o'clock. He was very hungry, and Lazare and Pauline themselves were famished, so Véronique made them some milky coffee and an omelette. Downstairs they found Chanteau, whom they had all forgotten, sound asleep in his chair. Nothing had been touched, but the room reeked of acrid fumes from the lamp, which was still burning with a long flame. Pauline remarked with a laugh that the table, from which the dishes had still not been removed, was already set. She swept up the crumbs and tidied up a little. Then, since the coffee was taking its time, they set about the cold veal, joking about how the dinner had been interrupted by the terrible confinement. Now that the danger had passed, they were as light-hearted as children.

'Believe it or not,' a delighted Chanteau kept repeating, 'I wasn't really asleep at all... I was furious nobody came down to tell me what was happening, but I wasn't the least bit worried because I dreamt that all was well.'

His delight was increased by the appearance of Abbé Horteur, who had rushed round after saying Mass. Chanteau made boisterous fun of him.

'And where on earth did you get to, then? A fine way to keep me company! Are you scared of babies, or what?'

To save face, the priest told how one night he had delivered a woman at the roadside, and christened the child as well. Then he accepted a small glass of curaçao.

By the time Doctor Cazenove finally took his leave, the yard was filled with bright sunlight. As Lazare and Pauline were walking with him to the gate, he whispered to the girl:

'Weren't you leaving today?'

She stood silently for a moment. She raised her wide, pensive eyes and ｓｔａｒｅｄ ｉｎ ｇａｙ ｔｏｗａｒｄｓ ｔｈｅ ｄｉｓｔａｎｃｅ, ａｎｄ ｔｏｗａｒｄｓ ｔｈｅ ｆｕｔｕｒｅ.

'No,' she replied. 'I must wait.'

CHAPTER 11

AFTER dreadful weather throughout May, the first days of June were very warm. Westerly gales had been blowing for the past three weeks and storms had devastated the coast, eroding the cliffs, swallowing up boats, and claiming lives; but now the broad blue sky, the satin sea, and hot, bright days seemed infinitely pleasant.

On this glorious afternoon, Pauline had decided to wheel Chanteau's chair onto the terrace and put the baby down close by him, in the middle of a red woollen blanket. Little Paul was already eighteen months old; she was his godmother, and she spoilt the child as badly as the old man.

'You won't mind the sun, Uncle?'

'Certainly not! I haven't seen it for ages!... Are you going to leave Paul here to have his sleep?'

'Yes, the fresh air will do him good.'

She had knelt down on the edge of the blanket and was gazing at the child in his white robe, with his bare legs and arms poking out. His eyes were closed and his still, pink little face was turned towards the sky.

'Look, he's gone straight off,' she said softly. 'He was tired out from rolling around... Do make sure Minouche and Loulou leave him in peace.'

She wagged a warning finger at the cat, who was sitting on the dining-room windowsill, licking herself all over. Some distance away, the dog lay stretched out on the gravel, opening a wary eye from time to time, ever ready to snap and snarl.

As Pauline was getting to her feet again, Chanteau gave a low moan.

'Is it coming back again?'

'Coming back! It never really goes away... I must have groaned, did I? Isn't that odd. It's come to the point where I'm not even aware I'm doing it.'

He had become an appalling and pitiful sight. His chronic gout had gradually led to an accumulation of chalk in all his joints, and enormous tophi had formed, their off-white growths breaking through the skin. His feet, concealed by his slippers, had curled up on themselves like the claws of a sick bird. But the horrible deformity of his hands was there for all to see, swollen as they were at every joint with shiny red nodules, the fingers distorted by growths which splayed them apart, the left hand made especially hideous by a tophus the size of a small egg. On the left elbow, a larger deposit had brought on an ulcer. And his ankylosis was now complete, he could no longer use either hands or feet, and the few joints which could still flex a little made a cracking noise, like a bag of marbles being rattled. As time went by, his whole body seemed to have become petrified in the position he had adopted to cope with the pain as best he could, leaning forward, with a marked twist to the right; and he had so completely shaped himself to his invalid chair that even when he was put to bed, he remained in that same bent and twisted posture. His pain never left him now, and the slightest change in the weather, or a drop of wine, or a mouthful of meat in excess of his strict diet, would bring on an inflammatory episode.

'Would you like a glass of milk?' Pauline asked him. 'It might refresh you.'

'Hah! milk indeed!' he replied, between two groans. 'That was another of their fine inventions, milk therapy! I think they finished me off with that one... No, no, nothing for me, that's what suits me best.'

However, he did ask her to change the position of his left leg, for he could not move it by himself.

'The swine's really stinging me today. Push it further over, go on, give it a shove! That's better, thank you... What a lovely day! Oh Lord! Oh Lord!'

With his eyes fixed on the limitless horizon, he continued to moan without even realizing it. His cries of pain had now become as automatic as breathing. He was wearing a big blue fleece, baggy enough to conceal his limbs, gnarled like tree roots, and his poor deformed hands, looking pitiable in the full sun, lay helplessly on his knees.

He was absorbed by the sea and the white sails criss-crossing its blue infinity, a boundless highway stretching out before him, while he himself was no longer able to put one foot in front of the other.

Pauline, concerned about little Paul's bare legs, knelt down again to cover him up with a corner of the blanket. Every week for the lᴀᴏᴛ ᴛʜʀᴇᴇ ᴍᴏɴᴛʜꜱ ꜱʜᴇ ʜᴀᴅ ʙᴇᴇɴ ꜰɪɴᴇ ᴄᴀʟʟɪɴɢ ᴏɴ ʜᴇʀ ᴀɴᴅ ᴛʜᴇ ꜰᴏʟʟᴏᴡɪɴɢ Monday. But the child's feeble hands held her back with an invisible strength. In the first month, they had feared each morning that he would not live to see the day out. She alone had constantly renewed the miracle of saving him, for his mother was still confined to bed and the wet nurse they had been forced to employ merely gave him the breast, with the docile stupidity of a heifer. It took continuous care to compensate for the month's gestation that he had missed, and Pauline monitored his temperature and kept him alive hour by hour, with the obstinacy of a broody hen. By the end of the first month he had fortunately gained the strength of a full-term baby, and was now slowly developing. But he was still rather puny, and Pauline never left him for a minute, especially since his weaning, which had been diffi-cult for him.

'Like this,' she said, 'he won't catch cold... See, Uncle, how pretty he is on the red rug! It makes him look quite rosy.'

Chanteau painfully turned his head, the only part of his body that he could still move. 'If you kiss him,' he said quietly, 'you'll wake him up. Don't disturb the little angel... You see that steamer over there? It's out of Le Havre.* Making good speed, isn't it?'

Pauline had to look at the steamer, to please him. It was a black speck on the immense expanse of water, its thin trail of smoke leaving a smudge on the horizon. She stood still for a moment, gazing out at the sea so serene beneath the limpid blue of the sky, rejoicing in the beauty of the day.

'What am I thinking of, my stew will be burning!' she exclaimed, hurrying off towards the kitchen.

But just as she was about to go indoors, a voice called from the first floor:

'Pauline!'

It was Louise, who was leaning out of the window of Madame Chanteau's old bedroom, which she and Lazare had now taken over. With her hair half done and wearing only a camisole, she carried on in shrill tones:

'If Lazare's there with you, tell him to come up.'

'No, he isn't back yet.'

At this, Louise lost her temper:

'I knew full well we wouldn't see him again till this evening, if he deigns to come home at all!... He's already stayed out last night, despite promising faithfully... Oh! he's a nice one. When he goes to Caen, there's no getting him away again.'

'He has so little to entertain him,' Pauline replied gently. 'Besides, this fertilizer business will have taken him some time... He'll probably get a lift home in the doctor's cabriolet.'

Since Lazare and Louise had been living in Bonneville, they had bickered constantly with one another. They did not quarrel openly but were forever bad-tempered with each other, their lives made miserable by the lack of understanding between them. Her convalescence after the birth had been long and painful, and she was now leading an empty existence, for she had a great distaste for housework and would kill time by reading and spending the whole day until dinner getting dressed and doing her make-up. He had again lapsed into complete boredom, never even opening a book, but spending hours gazing abstractedly out to sea; he would attempt an escape to Caen every now and again, only to return home wearier than ever. Pauline, who had been obliged to carry on in charge of the house, had become indispensable to them, for she patched up their squabbles several times a day.

'Hurry up and get dressed!' she added. 'The curé will be here any time now, you can keep him and my uncle company. I'm much too busy!'

But Louise could not let her annoyance drop.

'How can he stay away all this time? I had a letter from my father about it yesterday, he says the rest of our money is being squandered.'

Lazare had, indeed, already let himself be swindled in two unfortunate business ventures, to the point of making Pauline so concerned about the child's future that, as his godmother, she had gifted him two-thirds of what she still possessed, taking out a life insurance policy for him which would bring him a hundred thousand francs the day he came of age. Her own income was now only five hundred francs, but her sole regret was the limit that this put on her usual charitable activities.

'A fine speculation, that business with the fertilizer!' Louise continued. 'My father is sure to have talked him out of it, so if he still hasn't come back, he must be out having a good time… Well, what do I care? He can swan around as much as he likes!'

'Then why are you so cross?' retorted Pauline. 'Come on, the poor man doesn't mean any harm… Do hurry on down, won't you? Whatever can have possessed that Véronique to disappear like this on a Saturday, and leave me all the cooking to do!'

This was a complete mystery that had been puzzling everyone for the last two hours. Véronique had peeled the vegetables, plucked and trussed a duck, and even got a plate of meat ready for the stew; then she had vanished as if into thin air, and had not been seen since. Pauline, astonished at her disappearance, had in the end resolved to cook the stew herself.

'Hasn't she reappeared then?' asked Louise, diverted from her complaining.

'Well, no!' replied Pauline. 'You know what I am beginning to think? She bought this duck for forty sous from a woman who was passing by, and I remember telling her that I had seen better ones for thirty at Verchemont. Her expression changed straight away and she gave me one of her dirty looks… Well, I'll bet she has gone off to Verchemont to check if I was telling the truth.'

She laughed, but with a touch of sadness, for she was finding Véronique's renewed and unmotivated hostility towards her hard to bear. The reversal of feeling that had been going on in the maid's heart since Madame Chanteau's death had gradually led her back to her former dislike of Pauline.

'Nobody's been able to get a word out of her for over a week,' said Louise. 'You never know what stupid things someone with a character like that will get up to.'

'Well,' said Pauline with a tolerant gesture, 'let's leave her to satisfy her curiosity. She'll be back before long, and we shan't die of hunger in the meantime.'

But now the baby was stirring on the rug; she hurried across and bent over him.

'What is it, my sweet?'

The mother, still at the window, glanced out for a moment before disappearing back into the room. Deep in his own thoughts, Chanteau only turned his head when Loulou began to growl, and it was he who alerted his niece:

'Pauline, here come your crew from the village!'

Two ragged urchins were arriving, the first of the gang that she received every Saturday. As little Paul had gone straight back to sleep, she got up, saying:

'This is a fine time for them to turn up! I haven't a moment to spare... Oh well, you might as well stay, go and sit down over there on the bench. And Uncle, if any more come along, tell them to sit next to these two... I simply must go and check on my stew.'

When she came back after a quarter of an hour, there were already two boys and two girls on the bench, some of her poor little friends from earlier days, grown taller now but still habitual beggars.

Never before had such terrible misfortune befallen Bonneville. During the May storms the three remaining houses had been dashed to pieces against the cliff. It was the end: the spring tides had swept the rest of the village away, after centuries of attack and constant encroachment by the sea, which every year had swallowed up a fresh chunk of land. Now the shingle belonged entirely to the conquering waves, and every last trace of the ruins had gone. The fishermen, driven from the precarious perch where for generations they had battled obstinately against the eternal threat, had been forced to move up the ravine to higher ground, where they were encamped on top of one another. Those who were better off were building, the rest took shelter behind rocks, all of them founding another Bonneville, which would last until their descendants were driven out in their turn after further centuries of struggle. Before it could complete its work of destruction, the sea had needed to demolish the groynes and revetments. That day the wind had been blowing from the north, and huge mountains of water had crashed down so thunderously as to make the church shake. Lazare was alerted but would not go down. He had remained on the terrace, watching the sea sweep in, while the fishermen rushed out to look, excited by the furious attack. They were gripped by a mixture of pride and terror: ah! how the hussy was shrieking! Now she was going to clear all that junk away! And indeed, in less than twenty minutes it was gone, the revetments ripped apart, the groynes smashed to matchwood. And the fishermen roared along with the sea, gesticulating and dancing like savages, intoxicated by wind and water, wallowing in this orgy of destruction. Then, with Lazare shaking his fist at them, they ran for dear life, at their heels the furious, galloping waves with no more obstacles in their path to hold them back. Now they were destitute, moaning with hunger in the new Bonneville, accusing the hussy of ruining them, and commending themselves to the charity of the kind young lady.

'What are you doing here?' cried Pauline, when she noticed Houtelard's son. 'I told you never to set foot here again!'

He had now turned into a great strapping lad of almost twenty. His earlier sad and frightened expression, the look of a beaten child, had become a sly leer. He looked down as he replied:

'You gotta take pity on us, Mam'selle. We're so hard up, now our dad's dead!'

Houtelard had put out to sea one stormy night and not come back; they never found his body, nor his mate's, and not even a single plank of the boat. But Pauline, who had to watch how she dispensed her charity, had sworn never to give a single sou to either son or widow as long as they lived together openly as a couple. After the father's death, the stepmother, the former maidservant who used to beat the boy, had taken him for a husband out of avarice and malice, now that he was too old for a hiding. This new arrangement made them the laughing stock of Bonneville.

'You know why I won't have you in my house,' Pauline replied. 'Once you've changed your ways, we'll see.'

Then in wheedling tones he began to plead his case.

'It was 'er as put me up to it. She'd 've thrashed me again. Anyhow, she's not me mum, so it makes no difference if she goes with me or some other bloke... Come on, Mam'selle, give us a little something. We ain't got nothing left. I'd be alright, I would, it's for her that's sick, sick she is, honest to God!'

Moved to pity, Pauline finally sent him away with a loaf of bread and some beef stew. She even promised to call on the sick woman and take her some medicine.

'Medicine, indeed!' muttered Chanteau. 'Just you try getting her to take it! All that one wants is good meat.'

But Pauline had already turned her attention to the Prouane girl, whose cheek had a deep gash in it.

'However did you do that?'

'I fell against a tree, Mam'selle.'

'A tree?... It looks more as if you did it on the corner of a table.'

She was a big girl now, with prominent cheekbones and still the same wild, staring eyes, and she was trying in vain to stand up in a polite manner. Her legs were wobbling and she struggled to get her tongue around the words she was speaking.

'But you've been drinking, wretched girl!' exclaimed Pauline, scrutinizing her.

'Oh, Mam'selle, p'raps I 'ave, just a bit.'

'You're drunk and you fell over at home, didn't you? I don't know what possesses you all... Sit down, I'll fetch some arnica and linen.'

She bandaged her up, trying at the same time to make her feel ashamed of herself. Wasn't it disgraceful for a girl her age to drink like that with her father and mother, a pair of drunkards who'd be found dead one of these days, ruined by Calvados? The girl listened, her eyes clouding over as if she were nodding off. When the bandage was on, she stammered:

'Dad's always complaining of his aches and pains, I could rub them better if you'd let me have a little spirits of camphor.'*

Pauline and Chanteau could not help laughing.

'No, I know where that would end up! I'll let you have a loaf, though I know they'll probably sell it to buy drink... Stay on the bench, and Cuche will take you home.'

Young Cuche stood up in his turn. He had nothing on his feet, and was wearing only some old breeches and a ripped and ragged shirt through which showed his skin, burnt black by the sun and scratched by brambles. Now that his mother had sunk into appalling decrepitude and the local men wanted nothing to do with her, he went out scouring the countryside for customers. He could be seen running along the roads, jumping hedges with the agility of a wolf, living like an animal starved enough to pounce on any kind of prey. He had sunk to the lowest depths of abjection and misery, such an abyss of human degradation that Pauline looked on him with remorse, as if she herself were guilty of leaving a fellow creature in such a sewer. But whenever she attempted to drag him out of it, he would always run away, hating the idea of work, or being tied down.

'Since you have come back again,' she said gently, 'I assume you have thought over what I said to you last Saturday. I'm prepared to take your continuing visits as a sign that you still have some decent feelings left... You can't go on leading such a disgraceful existence, and I haven't got enough money left to support you in idleness... Have you made up your mind to accept my proposal?'

Since losing her fortune, she had tried to compensate for her own lack of money by involving other charitable people with her poor children. Doctor Cazenove had finally succeeded in getting Cuche's mother admitted to the Home for Incurables in Bayeux, and Pauline was keeping a hundred francs in reserve to kit out the son, for whom she had found a crew berth on a steamer out of Cherbourg. He hung his head while she was speaking, and listened with a mistrustful air.

'So that's settled, then?' she continued. 'You'll take your mother, then you'll go and join your ship.'

But as she moved towards him, he leapt backwards. He still scowled up at her, thinking that she intended to grab him by his wrists.

'What is the matter?' she asked in surprise.

Then, with the furtive caution of a startled animal, he mumbled:

'You're going to take me and shut me away. I won't have it.'

From that point on, nothing she could say had any effect. He let her go on talking, and seemed persuaded by her arguments; but as soon as she moved nearer, he made a dash for the gate, and with an obstinate shake of the head rejected her help for both his mother and himself, preferring to starve and be free.

'Get out of here, you idle rascal!' shouted Chanteau at last, full of indignation. 'Pauline, you're far too kind, trying to help such a wastrel!'

Pauline's hands shook at the thought of her rejected charity, her love of others that had foundered on the rock of this self-imposed destitution. She gestured with despairing tolerance:

'Come on, Uncle, they're in a bad way and they need to eat, after all.'

She called Cuche over again to give him a loaf and a forty-sou piece, as she did every Saturday. But he shrank further away, finally saying:

'Put it down on the ground and go away... I'll come and pick it up.'

She had to do as he said. He cautiously stepped forward, keeping a watchful eye on her. Then, once he had picked up the money and the loaf, he scarpered as fast as his bare feet could carry him.

'The young savage!' exclaimed Chanteau. 'He'll strangle us all in our beds, one of these nights... Just like that convict's brat over there; I'd swear she's the one who stole my scarf the other day.'

He was referring to the Tourmal girl, whose grandfather had been sent to join her father in prison. She was the last one left on the bench alongside little Prouane, still stupefied with drink. She jumped up without seeming to notice the accusation of theft, and starting whining:

'Have pity on us, kind Mam'selle... There's just Ma and me in the house now, the gendarmes come in to beat us every night, I'm black and blue all over and Ma's dying... Oh! kind Mam'selle, give us some money, and some meat soup and some good wine...'

Chanteau was squirming in his chair, exasperated by such lies. But Pauline would have given the shirt off her back.

'Hush,' she murmured. 'You'd get more if you didn't talk so much... Stay there and I'll make up a basket for you.'

When she came back with an old fish-hamper into which she had put a loaf, two litre-bottles of wine, and some meat, she found another of her clients on the terrace, the Gonin girl, who had brought along her daughter, already twenty months old. The young mother, just sixteen,* looked so fragile and slight of figure that she seemed more like the elder sister taking the child out for a walk. She could scarcely carry the infant, but she always dragged her along with her because she knew Mademoiselle adored children and could refuse them nothing.

'Goodness, what a weight she is!' exclaimed Pauline as she took the little girl in her arms. 'And to think she's not six months older than our Paul!'

Involuntarily, she gave a sad glance at the little boy, who was still lying asleep on the rug. This child-mother, who had given birth so young, was fortunate to have such a strapping infant. Yet she began to complain:

'If you knew what a lot she eats, Mam'selle! And I've got no linen, I don't know what to dress her in... And since Dad died, my mum and her fella are always pestering me. They treat me like dirt, and tell me that going with men is supposed to bring money in, not cost us.'

The old invalid had indeed been found dead one morning in his coal chest, so covered in bruises that at one point it had seemed the police might become involved. Now the wife and her lover kept talking of strangling the useless brat that was eating up a share of their food.

'Poor darling!' said Pauline softly. 'I've put some things to one side for her, and I'm knitting her some socks... You should bring her to see me more often, we've always got milk and she could eat a bit of gruel... I'll drop round to see your mother and give her a good talking-to for threatening you.'

The young Gonin girl picked up her daughter again, while Mademoiselle prepared a parcel for her too. She sat holding the child on her lap, with the clumsiness of a little girl playing with her doll. Her bright eyes betrayed unending surprise at having produced the baby, and although she had suckled it, she often almost dropped it while rocking it against her flat chest. Mademoiselle had scolded her severely one day for putting the child down on a pile of gravel by the roadside while she had a stone fight with the Prouane girl.

Then Abbé Horteur appeared on the terrace.

'Here come Monsieur Lazare and the doctor,' he announced.

At that moment they heard the cabriolet drawing up, and while Martin, the ex-sailor with the wooden leg, was leading the horse to the stable, Cazenove came round from the yard, calling out:

'I've brought you back a fellow who seems to have been playing truant. You won't be chopping off his head, I hope!'

Lazare now appeared, with a wan smile. He was ageing rapidly, his shoulders were hunched and his face ashen, as though he were being eaten up by an inner anguish that was destroying him. He was doubtless about to explain the reason for his delay, when the first-floor window, which had been ajar, was slammed furiously shut.

'Louise isn't quite ready yet,' Pauline explained. 'She'll be down in a minute.'

They looked at one another in embarrassment: that angry slam heralded a quarrel. Lazare made a move towards the stairs, then changed his mind and decided to wait. He kissed his father and little Paul; then, to conceal his anxiety, he turned on his cousin, muttering irritably:

'Hurry up and get these vermin out of here! You know I can't stand having them under my feet.'

He was referring to the three girls still sitting on the bench. Pauline quickly tied up the Gonin girl's parcel.

'There! off you go now,' she said. 'The two of you can take your friend home, and make sure she doesn't fall over again… And you, be sensible with the baby, do try not to leave her anywhere on the way.'

As the girls were finally about to go, Lazare insisted on searching the Tourmal girl's hamper. She had managed to hide in it an old coffee pot which she had found lying in a corner, and decided to steal. All three of them were sent packing, the drunk girl tottering along between the other two.

'What a rabble!' exclaimed the priest, sitting down next to Chanteau. 'God has assuredly turned his back on them. Those little hussies have hardly made their first Communion before they start making babies, and they drink and thieve like Mum and Dad... Ha! didn't I warn them about the misfortunes that would befall them?'

'By the way, dear chap,' the doctor asked Lazare in an ironical tone, 'are you proposing to rebuild those famous groynes of yours?'

Lazare made a gesture of annoyance; any allusion to his defeat by the sea exasperated him. He exclaimed:

'I'd sooner let the tide flood into our house, without sticking so much as a broom in its way to stop it... No, definitely not! I was a fool to attempt it, and it's not the kind of mistake you make twice! To think, I saw those miserable wretches dancing on the day of the disaster!... And you know what I suspect? They must have sawn through the beams the day before the spring tide, they couldn't possibly have snapped on their own.'

This was his way of salvaging his engineer's pride. Then, pointing an outstretched arm towards Bonneville, he added:

'Let them rot, then it will be my turn to dance!'

'You mustn't say such spiteful things!' said Pauline in her quiet manner. 'Only the poor have any right to be cruel... You would still reconstruct those groynes, for all that.'

He had calmed down already, as though exhausted by this last passionate outburst.

'Oh, no!' he muttered, 'it would be just too boring... But you're right, it's not worth getting angry about. Whether they drown or whether they don't, why should I care?'

A new silence fell. After raising his head to receive his son's kiss, Chanteau had relapsed into his posture of painful immobility. The priest was twiddling his thumbs and the doctor pacing up and down with his hands behind his back. Now they were all looking at sleeping little Paul, whom Pauline guarded even from his father's caresses, to prevent him being woken up. Since they had arrived, she had begged them to speak more quietly and not tread so heavily around the rug, and she even shook a threatening whip at Loulou, who was still growling at the noise of the horse being led off to the stable.

'If you think that'll shut him up!' continued Lazare. 'He'll go on making his racket for an hour yet... I've never known such a horrible creature. You only have to move to upset him, and you don't even know whether he's your dog at all, he's so self-centred. A nasty piece of work, all he's good for is to remind us how much we miss poor old Mathieu.'

'How old is Minouche now?' asked Cazenove. 'I've always known her about the place.'

'She's over sixteen,' Pauline answered, 'and looking quite well on it.'

Minouche, who was still licking herself on the dining-room windowsill, had looked up as the doctor spoke her name. For a moment, she paused with one paw in the air, sunning her belly, then went back to licking her fur, daintily.

'Oh, she's not deaf!' Pauline continued; 'but I don't think her eyesight is as good as it was, which doesn't stop her playing the hussy... Can you believe it, barely a week ago we had to drown seven more kittens. She keeps on having them, so many it's really quite shocking. If they'd all been allowed to live, over the last sixteen years, they'd have eaten up everything for miles around... And you know, she took off again on Tuesday, and you can see she's cleaning herself now, she only came back this morning, after three wild nights and days away.'

Cheerfully and without any embarrassment or blushing, she recounted the cat's amorous behaviour. Such a fastidious creature, delicate to the point of not setting foot outside in damp weather, yet four times a year she would wallow in all the filth of the gutters! The previous day she had seen her on top of a wall with a big tom, the two of them swishing and bristling their tails, then, after exchanging blows, they had rolled into the middle of a puddle, emitting blood-curdling yowls. This time, Minouche had come back from her nights on the tiles with a slit ear and the fur on her back all caked in mud. But she was still the worst possible mother. Every time they destroyed another of her litters, she would just lick herself as she had in her youth, seemingly unaware of her boundless fertility, and go straight back out to get another bellyful. 'Well, at least she keeps herself clean,' concluded Abbé Horteur, watching Minouche wearing her tongue down with licking herself. 'Many's the slattern that doesn't wash at all!'

Chanteau, whose gaze was also turned towards the cat, sighed out loud, a constant and involuntary reflex which he no longer even noticed.

'Is the pain worse?' the doctor asked him.

'Eh, what's that? Why do you ask?' he said, as if waking with a start. 'Ah, because I'm breathing heavily... Yes, the pain is rather bad this evening. I thought the sun would do me good, but I'm suffocating in the heat, and I've got a burning sensation in all my joints.'

Cazenove examined his hands. Everyone shuddered at the sight of those poor deformed stumps. The priest parted with another shrewd observation:

'Fingers like that aren't much good for playing draughts... That's another amusement you'll have to give up now.'

'Be careful what you eat,' the doctor urged. 'The elbow is badly inflamed, and that ulceration is spreading.'

'How much more careful can I be?' Chanteau wailed in despair. 'They measure out my wine and weigh my meat, must I stop eating altogether? It really isn't a life at all... If I could only eat by myself, but how can I, with useless lumps like these on the ends of my arms? But Pauline, who feeds me, makes quite sure I don't get too much of anything.'

The girl smiled.

'Yes, but you did overeat yesterday... It's my fault; when I see how unhappy your craving makes you, I don't have the heart to refuse.'

Then they all pretended to laugh, and teased him about his continuing self-indulgence. But there was a catch in their voices as they looked in pity at that inert remnant of a man, with life enough only to carry on suffering. He had reverted to his usual position, his body twisted to the right, his hands on his knees.

'For instance, this evening,' Pauline continued, 'we're having roast duck...'

But she checked herself and asked:

'By the way, I don't suppose you bumped into Véronique on your way through Verchemont?'

And she told them about the maid's disappearance. Neither Lazare nor the doctor had seen her. They discussed her strange behaviour with surprise, which gave way to amusement: when she came home to find them already eating, her face would be a picture!

'I must leave you, I'm on kitchen duty,' said Pauline cheerfully. 'If I let the stew burn, or serve the duck underdone, Uncle will give me my notice!'

Abbé Horteur gave a hearty laugh, and even Doctor Cazenove seemed tickled at the idea, when the first-floor window was suddenly flung wide with a tremendous rattle of the catch. Louise did not show herself, but merely called down in a sharp voice through the half-open window:

'Get up here, Lazare!'

He made an annoyed gesture, refusing to obey a summons delivered in such a tone. But Pauline, anxious to avoid a scene in front of the guests, threw him a pleading glance, and he went off inside, while she stayed a while longer on the terrace to smooth over the unfortunate impression that had been made. Silence fell and everyone stared in embarrassment at the sea. It glittered like a sheet of gold in the slanting sunlight, which lit flickering flames atop the little blue waves. The distant horizon was turning a soft lilac colour. The lovely day was drawing to a serene close, with the infinite expanses of sea and sky unbroken by a single cloud or sail.

'Oh well,' Pauline ventured with a smile, 'since he's been absent without leave, a bit of a telling-off is only to be expected.'

The doctor looked at her with an ironic smile of his own, in which she recognized his far-sighted prediction, that she would not be making them much of a present by giving them to each other. At which she turned to go towards the kitchen.

'Well, I must be getting along, try and keep yourselves amused... And do call me, Uncle, if Paul wakes up.'

In the kitchen, once she had stirred the stew and got the spit ready, she clattered the pans together in frustration. The increasingly raised voices of Louise and Lazare came down through the ceiling, and she despaired at the thought that they must also be audible from the terrace. Really, it was unreasonable of them to shout as though they were both deaf, and broadcast their private discord like that. And yet she was reluctant to go up, partly because she had the dinner to cook, but also because she felt awkward about intervening between them in their own bedroom. Usually, it was downstairs, in the everyday flow of family life, that she played her role as peacemaker. She went through to the dining room for a moment and laid the table noisily. But the shouting continued, and she could no longer bear the thought of them making each other miserable; so she did go upstairs, guided by that spirit of active charity which made her own existence dependent on the happiness of others.

'My dears,' she said as she went straight into the bedroom, 'you'll tell me it's none of my business, but you really are shouting much too loudly... There's no need to get so worked up and disturb the whole house.'

She hastily crossed the room to close the window, which Louise had left ajar. Fortunately, neither the priest nor the doctor had stayed on the terrace. With one quick glance she saw that there was nobody left outside except the brooding Chanteau and little Paul, asleep by his side.

'We could hear you downstairs as plainly as if you'd been in the room,' she went on. 'Now, what is it this time?'

But with the bit firmly between their teeth, they went on arguing without even seeming to notice her presence. She now stood motionless, feeling ill at ease again in that room where the couple slept. The yellow cretonne with its green leaf-pattern, the red carpet and old mahogany furniture, had been replaced by heavy woollen hangings and furniture in delicate feminine taste, erasing all trace of the dead mother. A heliotrope scent hung in the air near the dressing table, strewn with damp towels; Pauline found it rather cloying, and cast an involuntary glance round the room, where every object was eloquent of the couple's private routine. While she had finally agreed to go on living in the house with them, after her resistance had been worn down day by day, and while she could now sleep at night despite knowing that they were close by, perhaps in each other's arms, she had never yet gone into their room, the scene of their conjugal intimacy, where clothes lay untidily scattered around and the bed was already turned back for the night. A shiver ran through her again, the shiver of her old jealousy.

'How can you hurt each other like that?' she murmured, after a silence. 'Why can't you be reasonable?'

'No,' shouted Louise, 'I'm utterly fed up of it, by now! Do you think he'll ever admit he's wrong? Not him! I was simply pointing out how worried we were about him not coming home last night, and he went for me like a savage and accused me of ruining his life, and threatened to run away and live in America!'*

Lazare interrupted her in a voice of thunder:

'That's a lie!... If you'd criticized me for being late as mildly as that, I'd just have kissed you and that would have been the end of it. But it was you who accused me of making your life a misery. Yes, you threatened to go and drown yourself in the sea, if I went on making your life unbearable.'

Then they started on each other again, giving free rein to all the bitterness built up by the constant friction between their characters. The slightest pretext would set them bickering, until they gradually worked themselves into a state of acute antipathy which shrouded the rest of the day in gloom. Despite her placid expression, Louise would turn spiteful as soon as he interfered with her pleasures, like a cat that rubs up against people to be stroked, only to lash out with its claws afterwards. Lazare, for all his indifference, found that these arguments spurred him out of his mind-numbing apathy, and would pursue them for the distraction and excitement they brought him.

Pauline, meanwhile, had to listen to them. It pained her more than it did them, for she could not understand this way of being in love. Why not spare each other, out of pity? Why not make allowances, since they had to live together? To her it seemed so easy to find happiness in shared habits and compassion. And she was mortified because she still regarded the marriage as her doing, and she would have wanted it to be happy and enduring, so that the knowledge she had acted wisely might be some compensation for her sacrifice.

'I'm not reproaching you with squandering my fortune,' Louise continued.

'That would be the last straw!' shouted Lazare. 'It's not my fault I was swindled.'

'Huh! only a gullible fool would let himself be conned like that... In any case, we're reduced to a wretched income of four or five thousand francs, barely enough to live on in this hole. If it wasn't for Pauline, our boy would be going naked soon enough, for I fully expect you to squander the rest as well, with your ridiculous ideas and crazy schemes that collapse one after the other.'

'Ha! do go on, your father paid me the same pretty compliments yesterday. I guessed you had written to him. That's why I dropped the fertilizer business, even though it was a dead cert to return a hundred per cent. But I'm just like you, I've had my fill and I'll be damned if I lift another finger!... We'll just settle down here.'

'And a fine life that will be, for a young woman like me! A real prison, without even the chance of going out and seeing anyone; and that stupid sea wherever you look, which seems to make the place even more boring... Oh! If only I'd known, if only!'

'And how much fun do you think it is for me, eh?... If I hadn't married you, I could have taken off to distant parts, gone in search of adventure. I've wanted to a score of times. But that's all impossible now, I'm stuck for good in this godforsaken hole where there's nothing to do but sleep... You've finished me off, I'm only too aware of that.'

'Me, finish you off!... Did I force you to marry me? You were the one who should've seen we weren't suited to each other. It's your fault our life is a disaster.'

'A disaster, yes, it certainly is that, and you're doing your damnedest to make it more unbearable every day.'

At that moment, although she had vowed to keep out of it, Pauline intervened in a quivering voice:

'Be quiet, you wretched pair!... It's true that you're both doing your best to ruin what could be such a good life together. Why do you goad each other into saying such unpardonable things that you'll regret later?... Quiet now, the pair of you! I won't hear any more of this!'

Louise had collapsed on a chair in tears, while Lazare was pacing up and down the room in a state of wild agitation.

'Crying's no use, my dear,' Pauline continued. 'You aren't exactly tolerant, and you have plenty of faults of your own... And you, my poor friend, how can you treat her so thoughtlessly? It's horrible of you, and I thought that you at least had a kind heart... Yes, the pair of you are just overgrown children, both equally to blame, and doing everything you can think of to torment each other. But I won't have it, do you hear? I won't have miserable people around me... Come along, kiss and make up, and be quick about it!'

She tried to laugh, and she no longer felt any hint of that jealous shudder that had so disturbed her. There remained in her heart only an ardent, charitable longing to see them fling their arms around each other in front of her, to ensure that their quarrel was really over.

'Kiss and make up?' exclaimed Louise, 'I should think not! He's said too many hurtful things.'

'Never!' cried Lazare.

Then Pauline burst out laughing.

'Now, now, don't sulk! You know how stubborn I am about having my own way... My dinner will be burning, our guests are waiting... If you don't do as I tell you, Lazare, I shall make you. Kneel in front of her and clasp her lovingly to your heart... Come on, you can do better than that!'

And she pushed them into a lovers' embrace, and watched them kiss each other's faces, with an air of joyful triumph, without the least sign of envy in her shining eyes. She felt a warm glow of joy, like a subtle inner fire, which lifted her up high above them. Meanwhile, her cousin clutched his wife to him with frantic remorse, while she, still in her camisole and with bare neck and arms, returned his caresses in new floods of tears.

'There! you see! that's much better than fighting, isn't it?' said Pauline. 'I must run along now, you don't need me to make your peace any longer.'

She was already at the door as she spoke, and quickly she closed it on that chamber of love, with its inviting bed and scattered clothes, and the heliotrope perfume, which now touched her heart, as her accomplice in completing the task of reconciliation.

Downstairs in the kitchen, Pauline began to sing as she gave her stew another stir. Then she lit a faggot of sticks, set up the turnspit for the duck, and kept an expert eye on it as it roasted. Wearing a big white apron, she enjoyed doing this menial work, and was delighted to be able to serve them all and take on these most humble duties, so as to tell herself that today they would all owe their good humour and their well-being to her. Now that she had got them into a laughing mood, her dream was to serve them up a delicious feast, of which they would eat their fill while relaxing round the table.

Suddenly remembering her uncle and the little boy, she rushed out onto the terrace, where she was astonished to see her cousin sitting beside the child.

'What!' she exclaimed, 'so you're down already?'

In reply he merely nodded, once more in the grip of his weary apathy, sitting there with hunched shoulders, his hands lying idle. So she asked him anxiously:

'I hope you didn't start again behind my back?'

'No, no!' he finally managed to reply. 'She'll be down too, once she has put on her dress... We've forgiven each other. But how long will it last? Tomorrow there'll be something else, then every day, and every hour! People don't really change, and you can't stop things from happening!'

Pauline had become solemn and was looking sadly down at the ground. He was right, she could see clearly a long sequence of such days ahead of them, with the same incessant quarrels that she would have to smooth over. And she herself no longer felt so sure that she was cured, and might not succumb again to violent fits of jealousy. Oh! were these daily miseries to carry on repeating themselves for ever? But already she was looking up again: she had mastered her own feelings so often! And then, she would see if the two of them didn't tire of quarrelling before she did of reconciling them. This idea cheered her up, and she laughingly told it to Lazare. What would there be left for her to do, if the household became too happy? She'd be bored, they had to leave her a few little disputes to clear up.

'Where have the abbé and the doctor gone?' she asked, surprised not to see them there.

'They must be in the kitchen garden,' replied Chanteau. 'The abbé wanted to show the doctor our pears.'

Pauline was walking over to the corner of the terrace to take a look, when she stopped short in front of little Paul.

'Look, he's woken up!' she cried. 'He's already trying to go gallivanting about!'

Indeed, in the middle of the red rug, Paul had just pulled himself up onto his little knees and was about to crawl off on all fours. But before he got as far as the gravel, he must have tripped over a fold in the rug, for he rolled on his back with his frock rucked up and his legs and arms waving in the air. He lay there kicking and wriggling, pink and naked on the peony-red rug.

'Well now! he's showing us everything he's got,' cried Pauline merrily. 'Wait, you'll see how well he can walk, since yesterday.'

She had knelt down beside him and was trying to stand him up. He had grown so fitfully that he was very backward for his age, and for a while they had feared he would always be weak in the legs. So it had been a great joy to the family to see him take his first steps, clutching at the air with both hands, and sitting abruptly down on his bottom when he encountered the first bit of gravel.

'Do stop messing around now!' Pauline said to him. 'This is a serious matter, show us that you are a man... There now, stand up steady and go and kiss Daddy; then you can go over to kiss Grandfather.'

Chanteau, his features drawn by twinges of pain, turned his head to watch the scene. Despite his despondency, Lazare consented to play along.

'Come on then!' he said to the child.

'Oh! you have to hold your arms out to him,' Pauline explained. 'He won't risk it otherwise, he wants a safe place to fall... Come on, my treasure, be brave!'

He had three steps to take. There were fond exclamations and great enthusiasm when Paul made up his mind to go that little distance, ▨▨▨▨▨▨ ▨▨▨ ▨ ▨▨▨▨▨▨▨▨ ▨▨▨▨▨▨ ▨▨▨▨▨▨ ▨▨ ▨▨▨ ▨▨▨▨▨▨▨. ▨▨▨ ▨▨▨▨▨▨▨ ▨▨▨▨ the arms of his father, who kissed the still downy hair on his head, then he laughed with that vague, delighted laugh that all tiny children have, opening wide his moist and rosy little mouth. Then his god-mother even tried to make him talk, but his tongue was more back-ward than his legs and he just uttered gurgling cries, in which only the parents could recognize the words 'dada' and 'mama'.

'That's not all,' said Pauline, 'he's promised to go and give Grand-father a kiss too... Haven't you? a real journey for you this time!'

From where Lazare was sitting to Chanteau's invalid chair was at least eight steps. Paul had never ventured so far across the world before, and it was no small matter. Pauline stationed herself along the way to prevent accidents, and it took a good two minutes to nerve the child up to it. At last he set off, tottering along and waving his arms in the air. For a moment, she felt sure she would have to catch him in her arms, but he pushed courageously on and finally subsided against Chanteau's knees. There was a burst of applause.

'Did you see how he launched himself?... Ah, he's not the least bit afraid, he'll be a plucky little chap, that's for sure.'

After which they made him repeat the journey a dozen times. He no longer showed any fear, starting off at the first call, going from his grandfather to his father and back again, laughing loudly and greatly enjoying the game, though he always seemed about to tumble over, as if the ground were unsteady beneath his feet.

'Over to Daddy one more time!' Pauline cried.

Lazare was starting to weary of all this; children, even his own, quickly bored him. As he looked at the boy, so merry now and com-pletely out of danger, the idea that this little creature would outlive him, and doubtless close his eyes for the last time, sent a shiver down his spine and choked him with panic. Since he had made up his mind to go into retirement in Bonneville, he had been obsessed by a single concern, the idea of dying in the same room as his mother; and he never climbed the stairs without telling himself that one day his coffin would inevitably be carried down the same way. The entrance to the passage was very tight, there was an awkward bend, and he worried all the time about how the bearers would manage to get him out without jolting him. As advancing age took away another piece of his life every day, this constant dwelling on death hastened the disintegration of his being, until it annihilated the last vestiges of his manhood. He was finished, he told himself, completely useless now; what was the point of staying active, when he was growing daily emptier, and sliding deeper into the slough of his bored existence?

'Once more to Grandfather!' cried Pauline.

Chanteau could not even stretch out his arms to catch and hold little Paul; and although he parted his knees, the feeble fingers clutching at his trousers drew long sighs of pain from him. From living around the old man, the infant was already used to his ceaseless moaning, and probably imagined, in his barely awakened mind, that all grandfathers suffered in the same way. That day, however, in the bright sunshine, as he came up and fell against him, Paul raised his little face and stopped laughing, looking up at the old man with his wavering gaze. The two deformed hands seemed like hideous lumps of flesh and chalk; the face, riven with red wrinkles, disfigured by pain, seemed to be violently twisted against the right shoulder; while the whole body was broken and knobbly, like the fragments of some old stone saint inexpertly stuck back together. Paul seemed surprised to see him there in the sunshine, so ill and so old.

'Again! Again!' cried Pauline.

Vibrant with good cheer and health, she kept propelling the little lad between them, from the grandfather, slumped morosely sideways in his pain, to the father, consumed already by a dread of the morrow.

'Perhaps his will be a less foolish generation,' she said all of a sudden. 'He won't blame chemistry for ruining his life, and he'll believe that it's possible to go on living, even in the knowledge that you'll die one day.'

Lazare gave an embarrassed laugh.

'Huh!' he muttered, 'he'll get gout like his grandfather, and his nerves will be worse than mine... Look how weedy he is! It's the degenerative law.'

'Will you be quiet!' exclaimed Pauline. 'I shall bring him up, and you'll see if I don't make a man of him!'

There was silence as she picked up the child in a motherly embrace.

'Why don't you get married, if you're so fond of children?' asked Lazare.

She stared at him in astonishment.

'But I already have a child! Haven't you given me one?... Me get married! Never! The very idea!'

She cradled little Paul in her arms and laughed more freely, as she joked that Lazare had converted her to the doctrines of his great saint, Schopenhauer, so she wanted to stay single and work for universal deliverance; and she was, indeed, the incarnation of renunciation, love for others, and a goodness extending to the whole of errant humanity. The sun was setting in the vastness of the sea, perfect serenity descending in the fading light; the infinity of air and water alike lay suffused in the mellow gentleness of the ending of a beautiful day. One tiny white sail, far away across the deep, gleamed like a last spark, which was extinguished as the sun sank beneath the long, unbroken line of the horizon. Then there remained only the slow descent of dusk over the motionless sea. And Pauline was still rocking the child, laughing bravely as she stood in the middle of the terrace, now blue with shadows, between her despairing cousin and her groaning uncle. She had given away all she had, but happiness rang out in her clear laugh.

'Aren't we dining this evening?' asked Louise, appearing in an elegant grey silk dress.

'Well, I'm ready,' Pauline replied. 'I can't imagine what they're up to in the garden.'

Just at that moment, Abbé Horteur appeared, looking shattered. In reply to their anxious questioning, after hunting in vain for some words that would soften the blow, he finally announced bluntly:

'Poor Véronique, we've just found her hanging from one of your pear trees.'

They all cried out in shock and horror, and their faces paled as they felt the chill wind of death passing.

'But why?' exclaimed Pauline. 'She had no reason, she'd even started making dinner... Good heavens, surely it couldn't be because I said she'd paid ten sous too much for the duck?'

Doctor Cazenove now came to join them. For a quarter of an hour he had tried in vain to revive her, in the coach house where they had carried her with Martin's help. How could anyone know what went on in the head of an obsessive old servant like her? She had never really got over her mistress's death.

'It will have been quick,' he said. 'She just strung herself up with her own apron strings.'

Lazare and Louise, chilled with dread, said nothing. Chanteau, after listening in silence, was suddenly annoyed at the thought of the spoilt dinner. And that wretched creature without hands or feet, who needed to be put to bed and fed like a child, that pitiable relic of humanity whose shrinking life was just one long howl of pain, exclaimed in furious indignation:

'Only a damn fool would kill themselves!'

EXPLANATORY NOTES

3   *Caen*: capital of the modern region of Basse-Normandie in north-western France, and préfecture of the département of Calvados. The Paris–Cherbourg railway, built by the Compagnie des chemins de fer de l'Ouest, arrived at Caen in 1857 and Bayeux, some 30 km further west, in the following year. Zola's house in Médan was close to the main Paris Saint-Lazare–Le Havre line, the setting of *La Bête Humaine* (1890), from which the line to Caen diverged at Mantes-la-Jolie.

  Bayeux: *sous-préfecture* of the Calvados *département*; a medieval town famous for its tapestry representing the Norman conquest of Britain in 1066.

  berline: type of covered four-wheeled travelling carriage with two interior seats, first used in the late seventeenth entury.

  Arromanches: small seaside resort and fishing port, 10 km north of Bayeux.

  Bonneville: fictitious, ironically named village ('Goodtown') on the Normandy coast.

4   *his cousin Quenu*: Pauline's parents, Quenu and his wife Lisa Macquart, are central characters in *The Belly of Paris* (1873). Pauline was born in 1852.

  the Nord: *département* in north-eastern France, on the Belgian border, with Lille as its capital.

  charcuterie: pork butcher's, as opposed to the *boucherie* which sells beef and lamb, or *boucherie chevaline* which specializes in horsemeat.

  Les Halles: central wholesale food markets in the first *arrondissement* of Paris where *The Belly of Paris* is set. Constructed between 1851 and 1936, the market was demolished in the 1970s to make way for a shopping complex, and moved out to Rungis, to the north of the city.

6   *Angelus*: bell rung in the morning, at noon, and at sunset to announce a Roman Catholic devotion commemorating the Incarnation (from the Latin opening words *Angelus domini*, 'the angel of the Lord').

  Verchemont: a nearby village of Zola's invention.

7   *cabriolet*: two-wheeled, lightweight, one-horse carriage with a hood but no doors, first used in eighteenth-century France, and the origin of the modern 'cab'.

11   *tu*: familiar form of the second-person pronoun, normally used to children and between family members in preference to the more formal *vous*.

12   *light the lamp*: the ceiling-mounted oil lamp would be lowered on a cord or chain to allow it to be lit, then pulled part way back up until its pool of light illuminated just the table and people seated round it.

12 *silver beaker*: no doubt a christening present.

13 *the cheese . . . a Pont-l'Évêque*: local, square-shaped soft cheese with a white crust and pungent aroma, originally made near the town of the same name in the Calvados *département*.

16 *the Cotentin*: peninsula in the west of Normandy, extending north into the English Channel.

francs: depending on the method of calculation, 1 franc in 1863 may have been worth between 2 and 5 euros today.

18 *prefect*: the senior representative of the central government, as well as the chief administrator, in a *département*; the office was created in 1800 by Napoléon Bonaparte (later Napoleon I) after his successful *coup d'état* of 9 November 1799. Each *arrondissement* within a *département* had its sub-prefect.

19 *placed under seal*: legal procedure to safeguard items of value by preventing access to them. A metal strip secured at both ends by wax imprinted with an official seal was placed across the openings of doors, furniture, etc., until after the completion of the legal process.

Octave Mouret: central character of *Pot Luck* (*Pot-Bouille*, 1882) and department-store proprietor in *The Ladies' Paradise* (1883), Octave Mouret also appears briefly in *The Fortune of the Rougons* (1871) and plays a larger role in *The Conquest of Plassans* (1874).

Claude Lantier: (b. 1842), an aspiring young painter who appears in *The Fortune of the Rougons* and *The Belly of Paris* (1873), before becoming the lead character of *The Masterpiece* (*L'Œuvre*, 1886).

Monsieur Saccard: a pseudonym of the character Aristide Rougon, a ruthless and greedy financier, who is the central figure in *The Kill* (1872) and *Money* (1891).

22 *beadle*: minor parish officer who acted as usher, kept order during services, and had various other subordinate functions.

24 *invalid chair*: often, in the nineteenth century, an actual armchair with a metal frame screwed to the legs, carrying two large wheels and a footrest at the front, and a small wheel for manoeuvring at the rear.

cretonne . . . secretaire: cretonne is a heavy cotton or linen fabric generally printed with a floral pattern, used for (often matching) upholstery, curtains, and wall hangings; a secretaire is, typically, a substantial piece of furniture with a lockable drop-down lid to serve as a writing surface, sometimes with bookshelves above, and a range of drawers and storage compartments inside.

25 *sugar*: probably a bowl of sugar lumps broken off a crystallized sugarloaf with a hammer, not the modern granulated kind.

28 *autumn crocus and lithium hydroxide*: colchicine, a toxic natural product still used today to treat gout, was originally extracted from plants of the genus *Colchicum*, typified by autumn crocus. Lithium salts, now used primarily

for psychiatric medication, were prescribed in the nineteenth century for gout, epilepsy, and cancer.

blistering: also known as vesiculation, blistering consisted in applying caustic agents, such as a mustard plaster, to create blisters on the skin which were thought to draw out toxins and infection. The blisters were then drained.

Wiesbaden ... Carlsbad ... Vichy: well-known spa towns with curative waters, situated, at the time when Zola was writing, in Prussia (Germany), Bohemia (part of the Habsburg Empire), and France respectively. (Carlsbad is now usually known as Karlovy Vary, and is part of the Czech Republic.)

30 *tophic matter*: *tophus* (Latin: 'stone'), a typical symptom of gout, is a deposit of crystalline uric acid which forms at the surface of joints, or in skin or cartilage. Tophi sometimes break through the skin and appear as white chalky nodules.

topical treatment: one applied to the body externally.

31 *Norman wardrobe*: typically, a tall piece of furniture with carved wooden doors, containing three or four evenly spaced deep storage shelves, in addition to drawers and hanging space.

32 *Pulcinella*: character from seventeenth-century Italian *commedia dell'arte*, who became Mr Punch in the traditional British Punch and Judy puppet show.

Érard instrument: Sébastien Érard (1752–1831), an innovative French instrument maker of German origin, whose factories in Paris and (after the French Revolution) London produced world-renowned pianos and harps. Pianos by the firm of S & P Érard were favoured by many pianist-composers of the nineteenth century, including Liszt and Mendelssohn; one was built in 1856 for Queen Victoria as a showpiece for the State Rooms at Buckingham Palace.

still-unrecognized works of Berlioz and Wagner: the music of Hector Berlioz (1803–69), French Romantic composer best known for his *Symphonie fantastique* (1830), and Richard Wagner (1813–83), German late Romantic opera composer (*The Ring of the Nibelung* cycle, 1869–76), was still regarded as highly avant-garde.

33 *Conservatoire*: the Conservatoire de musique et de déclamation (now Conservatoire de Paris), a college of music and dance founded in 1795.

34 *tamarisk*: shrub of the genus *Tamarix*, with long slender branches and pink or white flowers, that thrives by the sea.

35 *Port-en-Bessin*: small harbour some 14 km west of Arromanches. Bonneville would be about 4 km to the east of Port-en-Bessin, though its model, Vierville, is actually 10 km to the west.

36 *Hippocrates*: Hippocrates of Kos (460–370 BCE), Greek physician, regarded as the father of Western medicine, originator of the Hippocratic Oath which is still sworn by doctors today.

36 *Ambroise Paré*: (1510–90), barber-surgeon who served French kings Henri II, François II, Charles IX, and Henri III.

39 *some maternal ancestor*: Adelaïde Fouque (b. 1768), also known as Aunt Dide, the common ancestor of the Rougon and Macquart families, is introduced in the first novel of the cycle, *The Fortune of the Rougons* (1871). She suffers from mild insanity, is subject to nervous fits and convulsions, and behaves capriciously.

40 *Saint-Eustache*: built between 1532 and 1632, the spectacular Église Saint-Eustache stands adjacent to Les Halles in Paris.

41 *centime*: coin of small value. There were 100 centimes to the franc and 5 centimes to the sou.

Latin Quarter: the University and student quarter in the fifth and sixth *arrondissements* of Paris, on the Left Bank of the Seine, historically ill-famed for its drinking dens and brothels.

42 *Rouen*: historic capital of Normandy, situated on the river Seine about 130 km from both Paris and Caen.

47 *Longuet . . . Cruveilhier*: François-Achille Longet [*sic*], *Traité de physiologie*, 2 vols. (Paris: Victor Masson et fils, 1850–61); Jean Cruveilhier, *Anatomie descriptive*, 4 vols. (Paris: Béchet jeune, 1834–6; 3rd revised and aug-mented edn., Paris: Labé, 1851–2). Details of these and other textbooks that a medical student would need to buy were supplied by Zola's friend and fellow Naturalist author, Henry Céard: Zola himself may well not have seen them, as perhaps indicated by his misspelling of the first author's surname.

Manual of Pathology and Clinical Medicine: perhaps Zola has in mind Ambroise Tardieu's *Manuel de pathologie et de clinique médicale* (Paris: Librairie Germer-Baillière, 1873), but the date of publication would make this an anachronistic reference.

50 *Herbelin*: a character of Zola's invention.

51 *Departmental Council*: the department (*département*) is an administrative territorial division of France, about the size of an average British county. It was and is led by a prefect, the central State's representative, and is governed by a locally elected General Council (*Conseil général*).

deputy: local member of the French parliament, in Paris.

53 *oedema*: excess accumulation of watery fluid in body cavities or tissues, often leading to swelling.

54 *zostera*: also known as eelgrass.

ulva: also known as sea lettuce.

laminaria: commonly called kelp.

56 *liquor*: the liquid remaining after a substance has crystallized out.

bromide diet: bromides, abundant in seaweed, were commonly used as sedatives in the nineteenth and early twentieth centuries.

neurosis: a complex affection of the nerves typified by hysteria, neurosis was regarded in Second Empire France as a widespread, frightening, and obsessive pathology. Thought to result from the era's excesses, it was often seen as punishment for a decadent society incapable of repressing its desires.

69 *sous*: the sou was a small coin to the value of 5 centimes, making 20 sous to ꓥꓥꓥꓥ ꓥ ꓥꓥꓥꓥ

71 *one hundred and eighty thousand francs*: Pauline's original fortune of 150,000 francs, increased by subsequent dividend payments.

73 *Civil Code*: the Code Civil des Français ('Civil Code of the French People', also known as the Code Napoléon), established under Napoleon I in 1804, is the foundation of modern French law.

74 *Schopenhauer*: Arthur Schopenhauer (1788–1860), German philosopher best known for his 1818 work *The World as Will and Representation*, in which he presents the world as the product of a blind and insatiable will. His atheistic metaphysical and ethical system was regarded as an exemplary manifestation of philosophical pessimism.

75 *vile slanders about women . . . fondness for animals*: Schopenhauer's 1851 essay 'On Women' asserted that women were childish, frivolous, and short-sighted, and lacked artistic sensibility or sense of justice: 'woman is by nature meant to obey'. He regarded animals, like humans, as manifestations of the one underlying Will, and therefore as fellow sufferers in the world who should be treated sympathetically.

78 *Sorbonne*: La Sorbonne in Paris, the second oldest university in Europe, founded around 1150.

83 *salicylate*: any salt or ester of salicylic acid. The salicylates, used as drugs for their analgesic, antipyretic, and anti-inflammatory properties, include aspirin.

84 *approving the acounts by private deed*: a deed contracted between private parties without the involvement of public officials, and validated simply by signature.

stamped sheet of paper: the deed would have to carry a *timbre fiscal* ('tax stamp') proving that the appropriate administrative fee had been paid.

87 *groynes and revetments*: a groyne is a sturdy timber barrier built down a beach and into the sea, to control erosion and drifting; a revetment is a slatted, backward-sloping wooden barrier running across a beach, designed to retain shingle behind it and form a breakwater.

88 *arnica*: genus of perennial, herbaceous plants of the sunflower family, the oil of which was used to treat bruising, muscular strains, wounds, and swelling.

Saint Teresa: presumably Teresa of Ávila (1515–82), a Spanish mystic and reforming Carmelite nun who was made a Roman Catholic saint in 1622.

91 *Roqueboise*: a fictional location.

94 *Complete Carpenter's Handbook*: a title seemingly invented by Zola.

102 *two leagues*: around 10 kilometres.

103 *pseudomembranes*: layer of coagulated fibrin, leukocytes, and bacteria overlying a badly damaged mucous membrane and giving the appearance of being a viable tissue; also called false membrane.

105 *quinsy*: peritonsillar abscess, also known as quinsy, is a serious complication of tonsillitis.

116 *marshmallow*: tall, pink-flowered plant growing in marshes, whose roots were formerly used to make the confectionery of the same name and which was cultivated for medicinal use.

124 *fichu*: small triangular shawl, worn round a woman's shoulders and neck.

126 *blue dress*: previously, it was pink.

144 *dropsy*: an older term for oedema.

146 *digitalis*: drug extracted from dried leaves of the foxglove plant (genus *Digitalis*), containing substances that stimulate the heart, here dissolved in alcohol.

149 *tisane*: herbal tea.

152 *vitriol*: sulphuric acid.

153 *verdigris*: green crystals formed on copper by the action of acetic acid, sometimes used as a medicine.

154 *Bouillaud's book on heart disease*: Jean Bouillaud, *Traité clinique des maladies du cœur* (*Clinical Treatise on Heart Disease*) (Paris: Librairie J.-B. Baillière, 1835).

159 *close to him, through the wall*: Madame Chanteau's room is actually downstairs.

178 *Young Werthers*: Werther, the hero of Johann Wolfgang von Goethe's 1774 novel *The Sorrows of Young Werther*, is a young and idealistic Romantic artist of sensitive and passionate temperament, who is caught up in a love triangle and finally commits suicide to resolve it.

193 *haematuria*: blood in the urine.

206 *the telegraph doesn't go beyond Arromanches*: in Chapter 1, the telegram received by Chanteau from his wife in Paris may therefore have been delivered by the postal service from Arromanches.

210 *The Empire*: the Second French Empire, the imperial Bonapartist regime of Napoleon III (1852–70).

214 *Saint-Lô*: capital of the *département* of Manche, around 50 km south-west of Arromanches.

229 *reducing her fortune to about forty thousand francs*: her fortune had already fallen to this level in the previous chapter.

Clermont: Clermont-Ferrand, a town in the volcanic Puy de Dôme area of the Massif Central mountains, in the Auvergne region of south-central France, almost 600 km from Caen.

237 *René*: *René* (1802), a novella by François-René de Chateaubriand (1768–1848), influenced early Romanticism as much as Goethe's *The Sorrows of Young Werther*. It too deals with a sensitive and passionate young man at odds with contemporary society.

270 *a version*: manual turning of the foetus in the womb, to improve presentation. Cazenove is perhaps using technical vocabulary to compensate for his insecurity about what to do.

sacrificing her like that: with the introduction of antiseptics and anaesthetics, both mothers and babies commonly survived caesarean delivery at this period, but Cazenove is no expert and the operating conditions would be primitive.

285 *Le Havre*: major Channel port on the right bank of the Seine estuary, about 60 km by sea to the east of Arromanches.

290 *spirits of camphor*: an alcohol based solution of camphor, a white substance extracted from the evergreen camphor tree, used topically to relieve pain and itching.

291 *Cherbourg*: major port about 100 km west of Arromanches, at the northern end of the Cotentin peninsula.

292 *just sixteen*: Zola's chronology seems to have slipped a little here: if the mother was 13½ when the child was born (p. 228), she would now be 15.

298 *threatened to run away and live in America*: in *Doctor Pascal*, the final novel in the Rougon-Macquart cycle, we learn that Lazare does indeed finally emigrate.

The Oxford World's Classics Website

www.worldsclassics.co.uk

- Browse the full range of Oxford World's Classics online

- Sign up for our monthly e-alert to receive information on new titles

- Read extracts from the Introductions

- Listen to our editors and translators talk about the world's greatest literature with our Oxford World's Classics audio guides

- Join the conversation, follow us on Twitter at OWC_Oxford

- Teachers and lecturers can order inspection copies quickly and simply via our website

www.worldsclassics.co.uk

American Literature

British and Irish Literature

Children's Literature

Classics and Ancient Literature

Colonial Literature

Eastern Literature

European Literature

Gothic Literature

History

Medieval Literature

Oxford English Drama

Philosophy

Poetry

Politics

Religion

The Oxford Shakespeare

A complete list of Oxford World's Classics, including Authors in Context, Oxford English Drama, and the Oxford Shakespeare, is available in the UK from the Marketing Services Department, Oxford University Press, Great Clarendon Street, Oxford OX2 6DP, or visit the website at www.oup.com/uk/worldsclassics.

In the USA, visit www.oup.com/us/owc for a complete title list.

Oxford World's Classics are available from all good bookshops. In case of difficulty, customers in the UK should contact Oxford University Press Bookshop, 116 High Street, Oxford OX1 4BR.

LUDOVICO ARIOSTO	Orlando Furioso
GIOVANNI BOCCACCIO	The Decameron
LUÍS VAZ DE CAMÕES	The Lusíads
MIGUEL DE CERVANTES	Don Quixote de la Mancha Exemplary Stories
CARLO COLLODI	The Adventures of Pinocchio
DANTE ALIGHIERI	The Divine Comedy Vita Nuova
GALILEO	Selected Writings
J. W. VON GOETHE	Faust: Part One and Part Two
FRANZ KAFKA	The Metamorphosis and Other Stories The Trial
LEONARDO DA VINCI	Selections from the Notebooks
LOPE DE VEGA	Three Major Plays
FEDERICO GARCIA LORCA	Four Major Plays Selected Poems
NICCOLÒ MACHIAVELLI	Discourses on Livy The Prince
MICHELANGELO	Life, Letters, and Poetry
PETRARCH	Selections from the Canzoniere and Other Works
LUIGI PIRANDELLO	Three Plays
RAINER MARIA RILKE	Selected Poems
GIORGIO VASARI	The Lives of the Artists